THE FACELESS WOMAN

EMMA HAMM

Write the story. Leap into the pages and allow others to follow you.

For all those who dream of being writers, I hope someday I get to read your tale.

GLOSSARY OF TERMINOLOGY

Tuatha dé Danann - Considered to be the "High Fae", they are the original and most powerful faerie creatures.

Seelie Fae - Otherwise known as the the "Light Fae", these creatures live their lives according to rules of Honor, Goodness, and Adherence to the Law.

Unseelie Fae - Considered the "Dark Fae", these creatures follow no law and do not appreciate beauty.

Badb - An embodiment of the Morrigan, considered the Crone and war crow. She is a very dangerous faerie, who enjoys making deals with humans.

Will-o'-the-wisps - Small balls of light that guide travelers into bogs, usually with the intention for the humans to become lost.

Brownies - Friendly, mouse-like creatures who clean and cook for those who are kind to them.

Pixie - A winged faerie whose face resembles that of a leaf.

Changeling - Old or weak faeries swapped with human children, usually identified as a sickly child. Very rarely, these are ugly children whose parents are ashamed of them.

Gnome - Generally considered ugly, these small, squat faeries take care of gardens and have an impressive green thumb.

Dullahan - A terrifying and often evil faerie who carry their heads in their laps.

Bean Sidhe - Also known as a banshee, their screams are echoing calls that herald the death of whomever hears them.

Hy-brasil - A legendary isle which can only be seen once every seven years.

Boggart - A brownie who grows angry or loses their way turns into a boggart. They are usually invisible, and have a habit of placing cold hands on people's faces as they sleep.

Pooka - A faerie which imitates animals, mostly dogs and horses.

Kelpie - A horse like creature who lives at the edge of a bog. It will try to convince you to ride it, at which point it will run underneath the water and drown the person on its back.

Selkie - A faerie which can turn into a seal, as long as it still has its seal skin.

FOREWORD

As always, I like to lead off my books by saying I am not a historian. All the books in the Otherworld Series are set in a fictional Ireland with no set time period other than "medieval". I apologize to any reader who wishes a historical retelling or finds fault in this lack of exact dates.

There are a lot of incredible historical novels out there. I ask you to remember, this is a fantasy. Some things will be stretched, others might be historically inaccurate, but it's never my intent to insult anyone.

Happy reading!

PROLOGUE

Once upon a time in a faraway land, there lived a pair of swan sisters. They were beautiful creatures and were coveted throughout the kingdom for their magic feathers.

Stories claimed a single feather, freely given, could grant one wish with no limitations. Kings, knights, and lords from far-off lands gathered at the swans' pond. For the promise of a wish was too powerful a temptation for them to disregard.

One proud king set his crown at their feet and said with pleasure, "I am the most powerful king in this land. I request a single feather from your side."

"What shall you do with it?" the eldest sister asked.

"I will wish for wealth, so that my kingdom can prosper."

But the swans saw there was only pride in his heart, not compassion. They turned him away and told him to focus his attention on enriching his people rather than his pockets.

A knight knelt before them, setting his helm on the ground near their feet. "Lady swans, I have protected many kings, I have fought in many wars, and I have saved many maidens. I beseech from you a single feather."

"What shall you do with it?" the youngest sister asked.

"I will wish for unmeasured strength so I might better protect my charges."

But they saw he had no wish to protect, only to harm. They turned him away and requested he learn from his mistakes rather than beg for brute strength.

The strongest and richest men and women of the kingdom gathered at the water's edge, each begging for a feather, but each were turned away. After many years of disappointment, the sisters swam close together in the center of the pond. They feared what the future might bring, for they saw greed devouring the hearts of man.

Then a day came when a raven croaked above them, perched on a branch of the ancient oak that shaded their waters.

The youngest swan lifted her head and stared up at him. "Will you request a wish as well?"

"I have no need of wishes. I am happy in my nest." He cocked his head to the side. "But if you will freely give me a feather, I would make use of it."

"What shall you do?"

"I shall wish you human, so I might provide for you a life of wealth and happiness."

It was a strange request, and the sisters stared at each other in surprise. No one had ever wished for *them* before. They conferred and finally agreed to gift the raven a single feather.

The youngest sister swam to shore, plucked a white plume from her side, and set it in front of the raven. "Make your wish," she said.

"I wish for you to be human and to never leave my side."

Magic shimmered, and the swan became a beautiful woman with hair the color of midnight. She held out an arm for the raven, but gasped when he, too, became a man.

"I am a prince of the Fae," he said, "and I have come to take you as my wife."

CHAPTER 1

THE WITCH AND THE RAVEN

Children clustered around the cauldron, their eyes round and chests still as they held their breath in anticipation of magic. They were curious little things. Some faces Aisling recognized, others she did not. They always ended up at her door as the sun set, and she always filled their empty bellies.

She pulled out a radish with a flourish and held it in front of her. "What is this?"

"A radish," a girl with pumpkin-colored hair observed.

"*No*." She held it against her chest as if the child had insulted the root vegetable. "It is *not* something so mundane as a radish. Who else has a guess?"

The children paused, looked at each other, and a little girl whispered, "Is it a giant's eye?"

Aisling snapped her fingers and pointed at the girl. "Precisely. It's a giant's eye, and I hunted the thing myself."

"You did not!" one of the boys shouted, wiping a dirt-smudged hand under his runny nose.

"I did. I followed it back to its cave by smell." She touched her nose. "Giants never take baths, so they're easy to find."

The boy scowled. "But what about his footprints?"

"Well, those are exceedingly large, but he knew I was following him. He walked through the rivers so I would lose track of his steps. The waters flowed over the deep grooves he left in the earth and made them disappear."

He scratched his cheek, narrowed his eyes, and tried to find a flaw in her story. "What do you need his eye for?"

"Why, my potion of course!" She gestured at the cauldron and let the radish plop into the heated water. "It's an elixir of immortality."

Ten sets of eyes blinked at her.

The words were too large. She berated herself. "A potion that will make us live forever."

Cheers lifted to the ceiling and smothered Aisling in excitement. The children had no families to provide for them, or if they did, they weren't families who had regular food or a safe place to spend the night.

It took a witch to feed the poor, and she certainly didn't mind.

Aisling adjusted the many layers of clothing that obscured her body from view. She'd learned early in life that a lovely woman alone was bound to attract trouble. And though she had wished for ugliness, she was not an ugly woman.

Once the long sleeves covered her hands, she cleared her throat. "Now, the elixir will need to set until the moon has risen. Shall we gather around the fire?"

The shyest girl of the bunch bit her lip and quietly asked, "For a story?"

"If that is what you wish."

15

Tiny bodies fell over each other as the children rushed toward the hearth. Aisling held her breath, hoping none of them tripped or hurt themselves.

The hut she lived in was hardly a home. The rotted thatch roof revealed glimpses of the moon peeking through as it listened to her tales. Dirt smeared the floor from wall to wall, the sturdy planks long since ripped up for firewood, and the hearth itself was cracked from floor to ceiling. But it was home, and no one in town remembered it existed.

That was enough.

She settled onto a small stool as the children gathered around her. Once they were in a dirty pile, they stared at her expectantly.

"What do you want to hear tonight?"

"Everything!" the most freckled little girl shouted.

"Not everything," Aisling chuckled. "We won't be able to eat our elixir."

"Fine" — she sighed — "then tell us a love story."

One boy lifted his head, outraged. "Not a love story!"

Aisling shook her head as the children argued. It was the same every night. The girls wanted to hear a romance, the boys wanted to listen to an adventure, and no matter how much she tried to accommodate them both, someone always ended up disappointed.

She glanced toward the sky in exasperation and watched a dark shadow cross over the moon. Wings spread wide, the raven hovered above them for only a moment then disappeared. It was unusual for a raven to fly at night, and it inspired an old tale.

"I'll tell you a story from my childhood," she began. "Back

when I lived on the streets, just like you."

"You lived on the streets?" a boy asked, a drop of something gooey stuck to his forehead. "But you're a witch!"

"Even witches have simple beginnings. Perhaps someday I shall teach you how to be a witch as well."

He wiggled in excitement.

Aisling grinned and tugged her sleeves over her hands again. "There was a legend, long ago, of a faerie who looked after children like us. We called him Fiach Dubh Ri, the Raven King.

"He was a monstrous being and King of the Underfolk, those whose names we never utter for fear they will take our souls in the night." She held a hand to her mouth and whispered the Underfolk's true name, "*Sluagh.*"

The children gasped, their eyes widened, and they flinched back in fear of the word.

Playing into her tale, she leaned forward while shaking her head. "And I would not risk your journey home, children, so I would never say the word." Aisling winked, then continued her story "He rules their ranks with an iron fist, but let them play whenever they wish.

"Such creatures will suck the soul from your chest before you are given last rites. They listen for those who have lost all hope so they might coerce them into the shadows. They'll steal you back to Underhill with them, deep inside the earth, beneath the faerie mounds."

A hand touched her foot. "Is the king a bad man?"

"No, though many may argue with me. He lets his subjects run wild, but Fiach Dubh Ri looks after children like us. All we have to do is call his name, and he will come to our rescue."

"Have you ever seen him?" asked the boy who always questioned her.

"I have. When I was young, a boy like you called out for Fiach Dubh Ri. His father beat him every night until his ribs were black and blue. One night was worse than the others. He lay on the floor, holding his sides and wondering when death would take him. Then he cried out for the Raven King to come and save him." She curled her hands into fists. "I've seen nothing like it before. The king arrived in a flock of ravens. They were swift and cold, their beaks flashing like swords in the night, until his father's last breath rattled in the air. They freed him from years of cruelty, leaving nothing behind but a single black feather."

She left out most of the details. None of the children would sleep if she told them the ravens pecked out the father's eyes and then vanished as if they never existed. The son had wondered if it really happened until he awoke and saw the body still cold on the floor.

"You must be careful invoking his name," she advised. "He is a powerful faerie who will extract a high price."

"I thought making deals with faeries was bad?"

"It is." She nudged a few of her fingers into view, their tips tattooed black. "And if you intend to make deals, then you need to take precautions."

A little girl reached out and took her hand. She pulled it out of the folds of fabric, turning it upside down to reveal the tattooed eyes on Aisling's palms. "What are these?"

"Protection against the Fae."

"Why do you need to be protected?"

Aisling bit her tongue to prevent the words from coming out.

Because she knew what cruelty the faeries were capable of and so that they could never find her. Because she was a bad woman and not a single one of these children should be inside her house.

But she didn't want to scare them away. She collected poor souls, and these were the rarest of all. The children glowed with innocence like fireflies in the night. If she could, Aisling would have bottled them up and kept them on her shelf. They reminded her that life could be good if she only remembered the possibilities.

She curled her fingers to her palm and drew her hand away from the little girl. "That's a story for another time."

A scrabbling sound came from the window. Graceless and clumsy, an overly large black cat clambered up onto the windowsill and let out a dramatic sigh.

"Hello there, Lorcan. Did you catch anything for supper?" Aisling asked.

He stared at her with a severe expression then glared at the children. They knew better than to pet him. A few had battle scars from the ferocious creature's claws.

"Aisling," a little girl asked, "does he want us to go?"

She met the cat's gaze, and he slowly nodded.

Narrowing her eyes, she replied, "Yes, I think he does. Which way, Lorcan?"

He nodded toward the back exit. It was the secret way to leave her home, only used when absolutely necessary. By telling her to send the children that way, he also warned her danger was near.

Aisling burst to her feet. "Come along, children. I apologize we won't have any elixir tonight, but I'll keep it warm for tomorrow. If there is no light in the hut, you know not to come."

A small flap of leather covered the hole in the back wall. She lifted it so each child could slip through the crack, their bodies small enough to flee.

The last little girl, an angelic thing with a dandelion puff of blond hair but who was much too thin, hesitated and glanced up. "Is everything all right, Aisling?"

She saw the worry in the little girl's eyes and didn't know how to make it better. "Go on now. And if you run into trouble, call for Fiach Dubh Ri to help, yes?"

"Will you call for him tonight?"

Aisling was considering it, but didn't want to frighten the child. "Off with you!"

The little girl darted out of the house and chased after her friends. Their feet were silent as they raced through the woods. Aisling couldn't hear them, even when they were right next to her home.

She whirled and glared at the cat sidhe sitting on her windowsill. "Do you want to tell me what that was about?"

"How can you like those things? They're disgusting." Lorcan jumped off the ledge, hit the ground with an audible thump, and waltzed through the hut like he owned the place. A bright white starburst on his chest caught the light, glimmering when he passed through a shadow.

"They're cold and hungry. Do you expect them to wash in the stream just in case they might see you here?"

"It would be appreciated."

"They aren't here to see *you*."

He sat and licked a paw. "Well they aren't here for *you* either. They're here for your 'elixir,' and that is the most ridiculous story I've ever heard."

"It's just a bit of fun."

"And a lie."

"It's not a lie!" She tossed her hands in the air. "It's just a tall tale to make them enjoy being here. There's no harm in that."

"Lying always comes back to bite you."

"So you have told me for my entire life." Lorcan had been with her through hardships unnumbered. Big yellow eyes with black slit pupils were her first memory when she woke up alone in the forest, not knowing her own name. She blew out a breath. "You said there was trouble?"

"The villagers cometh," he said sarcastically. "They're walking down the road right now. We should slip out the back."

"I'd rather pretend to curse them. They'll leave me alone for a little longer."

"It's not...that kind of trouble." Lorcan set his paw down. "It's the pitchfork and torches kind of crowd."

She cursed. "So it's come to that."

"It was bound to happen, eventually. We should go."

There were so many things to pack. She would need all her spell books. How was she going to travel with those? Aisling could pick her favorites, but that meant the villagers could find the others. And the damage the townsfolk could do with a faerie book was something she didn't want to think about.

She raced through the hut, her heart beating faster with

21

every passing moment. "How much time do we have?"

"Enough."

"Enough time to get away or enough time to hold our breath and hurl curses as we run?"

Her door banged opening, slamming against the wall so hard dirt rained from the ceiling. A man raised a pitchfork and stalked inside, his eyes wild with fear and anger. "I knew you'd be too wily and have something up your sleeve, witch."

Aisling didn't recognize him. She knew everyone in this town, although few knew her. Why didn't she know him?

His beard was nicely trimmed with specks of gray, suggesting he was of a mature age. His clothing was neatly pressed, almost too nice for their rural village. A white collar rose up his throat, and a gold pendant swung from his neck.

She bared her teeth in recognition. "They hired a witch hunter?"

"No one is prepared to deal with the devil's spawn but those who have the training."

"The training?" She chuckled and gestured at the pitchfork in his hands. "I see you've had all the necessary training required to catch one such as me."

He pulled the cross from his neck and swung it wildly. "Put your back against the wall. Now!"

The man was mad. He wouldn't know how to catch a witch if he tried. She flicked her gaze at Lorcan who loped to the corner.

"Stop!" the witch hunter shouted. "Tell your familiar to leave."

"I don't know what you've heard about witches, but I can't control animals."

"I know your ways. Tell it to leave."

Aisling shook her head, holding up her hands, waiting for Lorcan to knock over the pot that would fill the entire hut with smoke. They had plans for every situation. Pitchforks and torches were at the top of the list. Witch hunter was a little lower.

She hadn't expected the townsfolk to *pay* to get rid of her. She helped them! Love potions, spells for their cattle, charms to ward off nightmares.

Lorcan jumped onto the counter, heaved his body onto the shelves above, and touched his paw to the clay pot. Just a few moments now. She'd have to run out the front door, not the back like the children, but hopefully there was time before the mob reached them.

"You don't give me enough credit witch," the man growled.

She'd been staring at Lorcan or she would have noticed the witch hunter's grip changing. He swung the pitchfork and caught her across the cheek.

Crying out, Aisling fell against the wall. She slapped her palm to the stone and blinked through the stars. Warm blood dripped down her cheek. She couldn't focus. Her vision skewed to the side just as her body listed. He'd hit her so hard she couldn't tell up from down.

A loud yowl slapped her in the ear.

"Now, Lorcan." She might have screamed the words or whispered them. Either way, her faithful feline tipped the jar over, which exploded into dust so thick it made her cough. The room was spinning, but she knew where the door was. She knew this room like the back of her own hand. She could do this.

Lorcan jumped from the counter. At least she thought it was him. The heavy thud against the floor sounded familiar.

She swiped at her cheek and coughed out the smoke. Only a few more steps and the door would be…*there.*

As she reached the door frame, a cold metal chain slid over her head and around her throat. She pulled at it with her fingers, clawing so frantically a few nails split. But the chain was too thin, too strong, and he had wrapped it around her neck so tightly she couldn't breathe.

She choked, wheezing as his hot breath played across her neck.

"I know your tricks, witch. You won't get away that easily."

"Lorcan, can—"

Something struck the witch hunter's back, slamming them both forward onto the grass in front of her hut. The chain loosened for a brief second, enough for her to desperately inhale and roll onto her knees. Her lungs were on fire, and no manner of coughing seemed to help.

Crawling, she freed herself from the witch hunter as Lorcan screamed. Black fur surged over the man's writhing body, claws gleaming in the moonlight. He'd claw the man to pieces if the witch hunter gave him a chance.

"Quickly," she murmured, "get it over with and let's go."

"I don't think that's very likely," a deep voice interrupted. She recognized the village leader, Master O'Connell, without turning to look.

Aisling ground her teeth so hard her gum's bled. She turned on her hands and knees, leaving Lorcan and the witch hunter behind. The entire town was piled on the road that snaked up from the village. Pitchforks and torches were an understatement. This was a veritable army with hatred burning in their eyes.

They were led by a tall, thin man with a mustache that twitched whenever he was exceedingly emotional. She could gauge by its current movement that the man was bound to either lose his facial hair or wouldn't calm down any time soon.

"Master O'Connell," she said and coughed again. "How is your wife? I hope my potion cleared up that cough in her throat."

"A little too well, witch."

"And Mistress Hayes? I hope your cow is producing milk as requested."

"Aye, she is. But she won't stop crying in the middle of the night, as if the devil is pulling her tail."

She met the gaze of every person who she'd helped over the many years she'd lived here and realized not a single one would pity her. They feared her.

"Now," Master O'Connell said as he stepped forward and tugged his ancient suit lapels, "call off your familiar. We've work to do."

"Work," she repeated. "That's what you're calling it? After all I've done for you and your kin."

"What have you done but curse us with your black magic?"

"I've helped you survive!" She pressed her fists into the ground.

"No, you haven't," he growled. "Witches aren't capable of doing anything but harm. Now tell that wee beastie of yours to get off our witch hunter."

She spat at his feet.

"Or we could kill him. Your choice."

Icy tendrils ran down her spine. Lorcan meant too much to her. He looked after her, and it was far pastime for her to do the same for him.

"Lorcan," she croaked. The curses and weak cries from the witch hunter paused. "Let him go."

Harsh thumps suggested the cat sidhe stomped on the human as he removed himself, and the witch hunter moaned.

Aisling glanced over her shoulder and wiped away the blood dripping into her eyes. "Run."

He gave her an offended look.

"Run now and don't stop until you can't hear me anymore."

"That's enough, witch." Master O'Connell grabbed the rags at the back of her neck and hoisted her up. He twisted her arms sharply behind her and tied a rope around her wrists that bit into her skin.

His chuckle made her grind her teeth together.

"She's marked!" he shouted. "Eyes in the center of her palms, like the devil himself!"

"You wouldn't know the devil if you met him on the street, you goat-brained idiot!" She struggled against his hold, pulling and twisting as he shoved her forward. "Those marks aren't from the devil."

He ignored her and pushed her into the waiting arms of the crowd. They pulled at her clothing, crowing when they yanked bits of fabric off of her form.

She stared up at the night sky, floating scraps of fabric obscuring her vision of the stars. Hands tugged at her flesh, stroking the long lengths of her arms, palming her breasts, trailing along the delicate lines of her collarbone. Not the first time, and it wouldn't be the last.

"Lookee here!" Rosamund shouted. Since Aisling regularly delivered a cure for her spots, the woman now had claim to porcelain skin. "Not an old woman after all, are you witch? And here I thought you covered your face because of pox scars!"

The first nail hammered into her coffin, sending gooseflesh down her arms.

"A young woman?" The voice of old Hamish was easy to recognize. She'd helped his goose lay more eggs just last summer. "But she's been here so long. It's not possible she's this young."

"How long has she been here? She showed up out of the blue years ago. Maybe she's always been young." The man was one she didn't recognize, and he twisted her arms painfully behind her, voice deepening to a growl. "Or maybe she was just a child when she arrived."

"Or she's a bride of the devil!" a woman shouted, her nails digging into Aisling's arms. "He's kept her young all this time!"

If she knew the devil that well, she wouldn't be in this situation.

Aisling was thrust through the crowd and fell onto her knees in little more than a raggedy shift she'd had since she was a little girl. It hit the middle of her shins and no longer had sleeves. They'd left her dressed in next to nothing for the men to jeer and call at.

She curled her fingers into the dirt. A spell, any spell, something with the earth and blood... There had to be something she could do.

A hand twisted in her hair. "Oh no, we're not taking any chances. It's too late for that, witch."

He brought her head up, and she saw what had taken them so long to reach her hut. They had piled bundles of kindling around an ancient dead tree. It waited for her with ominously raised limbs sticking straight up into the air and rattling in the wind.

"A bonfire?" she asked. "I thought it was customary to hang witches."

The witch hunter stumbled in front of her, blood staining his white collar, and his perfectly pressed clothing was shredded. "I've found when it comes to witches, the old ways are best."

Her heart stuttered and her palms slicked with sweat as they pushed her toward the tree. She didn't want to burn alive. Lorcan screamed but kept his distance. She could hear him in the woods, cracking through broken twigs and hissing his frustration. There were too many people between them. It was too risky for him to try to help. Instead, he was forced to watch.

They were going to tie her to the tree and burn her.

Aisling couldn't breathe, as if the smoke had already filled her lungs. "Don't do this. Don't make me prove you right."

"We already know you're a witch!" someone shouted from the crowd.

"I've *helped* you. I've given you everything you ask for, everything you desire. What more can I do?"

She didn't listen to their screams of rage and justification for what they were about to do. Spells boiled at the tips of her fingers, curses that would turn them inside out, set boils to ravaging their skin, or vomit spewing from their nose. So many missed opportunities she regretted as they tied her to the tree.

She couldn't remember a single spell. They leaked out of her ears in the wake of terror and fear so raw her knees quaked.

Bark bit into her arms, drawing blood that smeared her skin with violent streaks. The rope tore at her sensitive flesh, and the twigs pulled at her shift as they piled the wood higher and higher around her. It must have looked as if she were some strange faerie growing out of the tree. Locks of her dark hair tangled on the trunk, pulling at her scalp in pinpricks of pain.

Aisling tilted her head back and rested it against the bark as the witch hunter preached his nonsense.

"Witches must return to the hell from whence they came! She will say things that will make you feel pity, but know we are *saving* her. This is the only way to purify her soul."

She chuckled, her laughter dancing on the wind that tousled his hair and fluttered the shredded fabric of his clothing. "Witch hunter, I think you enjoy this. I think you find a perverse pleasure in burning women at the stake."

"Witch!" he screamed and whirled to glare at her with fire in his eyes. "You are no woman. Remember that while you burn and your master refuses to help you."

"I have no master."

"Renouncing your deeds will not save your soul now! You're too late."

After he turned away from her, Aisling closed her eyes. She didn't want to see the hatred in theirs. She needed to focus.

A spell, a spell, any spell would do. She'd spent years memorizing every page of every book and yet nothing would bubble to the surface.

Bark. She could use the bark. The trees listened to everything, and the tree was going to burn as well.

She twisted her hands in her rope bindings. The witch hunter continued with his drivel, foolish man. He wouldn't guess she had other tricks up her sleeves because he had never dealt with a witch who learned from the Fae.

Palms pressed flat against the bark, she whispered, "Roots will pull and branches bend, flee these folk, it's not our end."

No magic tingled on her tattooed fingertips. The tree was long dead; its soul dashed to the wind.

"No," she muttered. "Wake up. Wake up, old friend, and run."

Cold silence met her quiet cries for help.

And she had run out of time.

"Witch"—the man turned and cast a cold gaze over her form—"you have been tried and found guilty of lying with the devil. Although it's not my belief, your townsfolk have requested to allow you one last moment with God. Beg for forgiveness."

She spat at him. "I'm not consorting with the devil, and I've no need to beg. I've done *nothing* wrong. It's the townsfolk who will wear this mark on their soul."

"Do you curse us?"

Aisling noted the feverish excitement in his eyes. He wanted her to curse them. He wanted something else to demonstrate he was right, that his foolish need to prove himself to the world as a "good" man had steered him true.

If he wanted that satisfaction, then she would give it to him and hoped his sleep was plagued with nightmares of the real witch he'd found. The townsfolk had never seen the true extent of what she could do, and they never would.

She'd learned a long time ago the most effective curse was a fake one.

"I curse you," she started quietly, building up her voice into a wail. "I curse your souls to wander the earth and question whether you made the right decision. Forever more you shall wonder if I was an innocent woman, if your own wives are next, and never shall your souls rest!"

The witch hunter rolled his eyes. "Enough. Burn her."

There was no hesitation at his order. Three men dropped their torches to the bundles of dried sticks that burst into terrible flames.

The townsfolk flinched back, raising their arms to their faces, as if that might keep them safe from the burst of bright light and the wave of heat. She smelled the sting of pitch and whale oil. They hadn't wanted to wait long for her screams.

Fire licked at her ankles. The scent of burning flesh filled the air and stung her nostrils. She wouldn't wail. She wouldn't give them the satisfaction of knowing they had broken her.

Aisling lifted her head and stared defiantly into the crowd of people. She met their gaze even as flames made her eyes water with their brightness. Smoke clogged her lungs, but she did not cough. She wanted to sear their faces into her memory forever.

Shadows moved behind the crowd. No, she realized, not shadows at all. Ravens, a great unkindness of ravens seated throughout the trees. They lifted their wings as one and flew to the ground, merging into one dark being who stared at her with soulless eyes. A single raven sat next to him on a branch.

"Fiach Dubh Ri," she whispered. He had come for her

31

without a single utterance of his name.

The flames reached the rope on her hands and loosened her restraints. She twisted her wrist free and stretched a hand out for him. Legs still bound, she felt the aching pain of her flesh burning. "Help me," she cried out. "Lord Fae, *please*."

He was more beautiful than she remembered, but she had only looked at him through the eyes of a child. He was incredibly tall, at least two heads higher than the largest man she'd ever seen. His skin was porcelain smooth, dark hair framing a chiseled face. His head was shaved on one side, giving him a wild look. A silver earring glinted in his left ear, blinking in the moonlight.

He grinned at her, canine teeth too pointed to be comforting.

"Please," she begged again.

Neither he nor his raven moved. He stared at her as if she were some strange bug he'd just discovered. A creature who made little sense but existed no matter that he didn't think she should.

"Will you not help me?" She bared her teeth. "After all you and your people have done to me? You will leave me to burn?"

"You see?" The witch hunter spread his arms and turned toward the crowd. "She calls out to her master for help! Hold your families close, townsfolk. We shall not allow her to open a rift in our world for the devil to step through."

"Useless man," she ground through her teeth. The pain was unbearable now. The fire had climbed up her shift and burned her thighs. Her feet were red hot coals burning through the very fiber of her being, and the blasted faerie wouldn't help.

Damn them all. Damn each and every one of them.

She flattened her hand, no longer reaching for him but baring her palm to his sight. There were energies she could use in this world, but only one would make a lasting curse. Aisling poured her life into a single pinprick in her palm. The eye tattoo shifted, pulling at her skin in a blink she could feel. "Flesh will tear, bones will break, and you shall feel every ache. I bind you raven, here and now. I bind you, Fae, from feet to brow."

The spell sizzled through the dark ink on her hands. It burst from her fingertips and struck him in the chest so hard he stumbled back. He pressed a hand against his sternum, then stared at her in disbelief.

It was a dangerous spell, one she'd never cast on a person before. Binding spells should never be used unless in the direst of circumstances. They harmed more than they helped, but they could protect the spellcaster in strange ways.

Blood trickled down her cheek, cool compared to the flames licking her hips. Her abused body ached, pain sparking behind her eyes even as tears fogged her vision.

"Now we're in this together, faerie," she slurred. Her tongue felt heavy in her mouth, her lips numb from pain and shock. "If I die, so do you."

The world tilted to the side, or perhaps that was her head. She tried to stay awake, wanting to remain cognizant as long as possible. It was her last view of the earth. And if that vision was of people who hated her, then so be it.

Cool wind brushed her cheeks. The tree branches rattled like bones, the corpse of a once green thing cradling her against its side. They would go together even though it was only a shell giving her comfort.

The moon burst from behind clouds and flooded the clearing in silver light. Her lips twisted in a sardonic smile as her eyes drifted shut.

It was a good night to die.

Bran wasn't supposed to be here. He should return to the Unseelie court where he was greatly missed, rather than meddling in the Seelie kingdom and now here in the human realm. There were more important things to do than watch humans in their daily toils.

And yet, he flew through the night sky surveying mortal lands. Again.

He always found himself wandering the human world when his thoughts grew too chaotic. Humans were a simple folk. Easily convinced of superstitions and arcane wickedness when they should remember who first brought magic into this world.

A raven croaked in his ear, tilting its head and staring down at a gathering in the wood. It was unusual for humans to be out this late. They feared the dark almost more than they feared the unknown.

Furrowing his brow, Bran landed in the thicket and crouched to watch the screaming men and women.

They'd tied a woman to a tree while brandishing pitchforks at her. A man stood in the center, feeding the frenzy with callous words and a tone filled with fervor.

Witch hunter.

Humans always wanted to grasp just a little more power before their souls fled the shells of their flesh.

Snorting, he glanced at one of his ravens. "Why are we stopping?"

Again, it croaked.

"It's the same story as last time. A woman burns, a crowd finds peace, and then they return to their sordid lives to find another witch to blame."

The corvid shuffled his feet and clacked his beak. Something was bothering the beast, although Bran couldn't figure out what.

He smoothed a hand against the shaved side of his skull. "We aren't here to save a witch. We're here to forget meddling women."

It wasn't his job to help those in need. They could save themselves, or rot for all he cared. He'd meddled enough in the Seelie court to last a lifetime, and to give himself an honorary Unseelie title for the rest of his days.

Bran shifted, placing a knee against the ground and resting his arm on the other. "What is it you see? Show me."

The corvid spread his wings and took to the sky. They shared a special bond because these birds weren't real; they were a part of him. Bran was an Unseelie with two natures, that of a Tuatha de Danann and that of a predatory bird.

It unfortunately warped his form into half man and half beast. His face was twisted on the left side, and glossy black feathers encircled a raven eye that moved on its own. His left leg was thinner than the other and had a taloned foot that clicked as he walked. Feathers sprouted from the side of his head that he plucked every week to make it look as though it was shaved.

He exhaled, covered his human eye, and let his raven take control of his sight.

They soared through the skies for a moment before the beast landed on a branch near the crowd. It tilted its head to the side and stared at the woman strapped to the tree.

Flames crawled up the pale fabric of her shift. She wore little for a human woman, and his gaze halted at the outline of her legs. Pretty, long legs, shapely waist, strong muscles that were unusual for a human. Usually they were soft. And if they weren't soft, then they were crude and base creatures made for working in fields.

But she wasn't muscled like a farm woman. There was a grace to her beauty.

Who was this witch? What a shame she wouldn't live to see the sunrise.

Her dark hair stuck to the rough bark like a spiderweb. The dark tangles seemed to absorb the light, falling in front of her face in ragged curls.

Bran drew in a harsh breath, and the raven spread its wings in surprise.

Her face.

The witch tied to the tree didn't have a face. Magic blurred what he was certain to be a vision. Why didn't she have a face?

"Corvin, return to me."

Bran shut his raven eye, refusing to see her anymore. He didn't want to know what kind of creature she was. The temptation of a challenge, of a story left untold, burned through his veins.

"No," he muttered.

He was still curious. He stepped out of the brush and held himself still at the edge of the clearing. She was looking at him, he was certain of that. She reached out a hand in his direction, and a few heads turned.

Humans couldn't see him. Bran's glamour was a powerful thing, and he'd learned the spell at an early age. But *she* could see him.

What was she? A changeling? He would have known if she was. Faeries knew faeries, and she didn't smell like magic.

Although, so much smoke filled the air he might not have been able to smell her magic at all. And it would explain the beauty of her body, the grace of her fingers, even stiff with pain.

He didn't know of any changelings in these parts. He kept track of the poor creatures and tried to give them advice whenever he could. Their luck was horrible. The least he could do was tell them how to prank the humans so they could free themselves from their adopted family's grasp. Changelings were notoriously mistreated by humans, but did remarkably well if they took their life in their own hands.

His skull prickled, sharp feather nubs standing on end just before the most powerful curse he'd ever felt struck him hard in the chest.

Bran stumbled back, lifting a hand and pressing it against the bruised, singed skin of his chest. It had gone clear through his shirt, leaving a starburst scorched over his heart. "What—?"

Pain, raw and agonizing, seared his flesh. His feet were on fire, his legs, his arms, everything in so much pain he clenched his teeth. Bran locked his knees and breathed through the initial shock.

The witch had cursed him.

No.

Bound him.

He growled and shoved through the crowd. Humans scattered, shouting that the invisible devil had arrived, come to take their souls. Footsteps thundered through the forest, back to their safe village and warm beds. They couldn't see him, but if they had, they would have had even more reason to scream.

The witch hunter swung his cross back and forth in front of the flames. "Begone demon! I will not allow you to take back your whore."

Bran palmed the man's face and shoved him to the ground.

He stepped through the fire, pushed aside the brambles in his way until he could stand in front of her. The ravens rose behind him and beat back the flames with rushing wings and squawking cries.

"Who are you?" he growled.

She spat at him. Sticky and overheated, her saliva slid down his cheek in a wet, sluggish crawl.

Angered, he grasped her chin and turned her head. Nothing. No face, not even a hint of a face, nothing but faint fog the color of her ivory skin.

"You cursed me," he accused. "Remove it, witch."

"If you want it gone so bad, remove it yourself."

"I won't ask again."

"You won't have to." Her chin slid from his grasp as she fainted.

He'd touched her face, felt her delicately pointed chin

pressing into his palm. He just couldn't see it, and what a strange curse to put on a person.

Almost as bad as binding a strange faerie's life with her own.

A raven cried out and landed on his shoulder. Talons dug through his shirt and pricked his skin.

"What do you think she is?" Bran asked.

The croaking reply was simple. Could she be a changeling? There was no other human creature who could perform a binding spell like that, yet they would know about her. They *should* know about her.

Footsteps, soft and animalistic, quietly sounded in the forest beyond. A Fae beast didn't want Bran to know it was there. He narrowed his gaze at the shadows then looked back at the woman slumped against the smoking, charred tree.

He didn't want to take her with him. It was a useless endeavor, only satisfying his curiosity and likely to cause more trouble than it was worth.

He tucked his finger under her chin and tilted her face up to the moonlight. "Strange," he muttered. "Who wanted to hide your face? And why?"

Questions he intended to answer as soon as possible. Bran was already behind on his plans, but what were a few more nights? Besides, he needed to remove the binding spell this ridiculous curiosity had placed on him.

Didn't she know binding spells were dangerous? She was lucky he knew magic. Most Unseelie had no idea how to cast complicated curses, and they were more likely to kill her rather than attempt to break the curse.

"Did you cast it because you thought you would die?" he

asked her as he circled the tree. "It's a strange punishment for a person you've never met."

He reached forward and hooked a claw on the rope that gave way beneath his fingers and dropped to the ground. He winced as an echo of pain rocked through his chest, stealing his breath and reminding him they were bound. Her pain was his, her life was his, and he'd have to take care.

"Can't have you dying prematurely, now can we?" He stooped and hefted her over his shoulder. "Now, why don't we find a quiet little place to chat. Hm?"

CHAPTER 2

THE WOMAN WITHOUT A FACE

Dreams plagued Aisling, memories from her childhood that she had desperately tried to repress.

"Aisling." The voice shook with age but remained direct and firm. "It's for the best."

She twisted her hands in her lap, staring at the offending fingers as if it were their fault she was in trouble. "I did nothing wrong. All I wanted was to say hello, and they — they — "

Hands covered her own. They were beautiful hands, long-fingered with smooth skin. The spotted flesh was uneven and strange but more familiar than her own in ways.

Badb always said she was two people trapped in the same body. One light-skinned, one dark, and both battled across her body in hopes they would dominate the other. She was beautiful and made all the more otherworldly by her speckled skin.

She was one of the most feared Tuatha de Danann to ever live. A mirrored reflection and sister of Morrighan, goddess of battle and war, Badb was known to soar over battlefields, inciting fear and panic in warrior's hearts. Most only saw her as a hooded crow, speckled like her skin. They feasted on the carrion of war and answered only to her call.

And yet, she had been a staple in Aisling's life. Badb was her silent protector and the quiet figure who healed her scraped knees.

"Child, you did nothing wrong. They are small-minded creatures and incapable of understanding what you offer."

"I offer nothing but friendship," she whispered, "but they threw rocks at me."

She was only seven years old, and already she'd lost so much. Her family had abandoned her a year ago. No human wanted to take her in but a scruffy young witch who made her work more than cared for her. Faeries wouldn't even look at her because she was a changeling and, therefore, unworthy. She was nothing to every person who looked at her.

Badb sighed and tucked a strand of Aisling's hair behind her ear. The slow swipe of dark locks was gentle but still scraped against bruises and tiny cuts caused by pelted stones. It wasn't the first time the villagers had attacked Aisling, although it was the first time she'd called the Tuatha de Danann to her side.

"They do not understand outward beauty like yours."

"I'm not beautiful." Aisling shook her head, causing the hair to fall forward in front of her face again. "Not like you."

"You're sweet, but there are many who think I am ugly. Beauty changes in the hearts of every living creature. Remember that. Now, I cannot protect you from man. That is your curse to bear. But I can protect you from faeries."

"I'm not worried about the Fae. They've always been kind to me."

42

Badb's expression hardened. She narrowed her eyes, and something dark passed through her gaze that made Aisling shiver. "The Fae are not your friends, child. We do not know how to be friends with people like you."

"Like me?"

"You are a marvelous creature made for great things, Aisling. But you are not to consort with the Fae. Do you hear me?"

"Yes, my lady."

She didn't like it. Faeries were oddly addicting creatures. She'd seen them in the woods her entire life. Their wings fluttered in the moonlight, laughter dancing on the wind and magic pulsing in the air until she could taste citrus on her tongue. Aisling loved to play in the faerie circles and dance with them in the evenings.

Perhaps that was why the humans didn't like her. She knew things she shouldn't.

Aisling ducked her head and blew out a breath. "But do I have to give up my face?"

"The only way to hide you from the faeries is to make sure they don't know who you are."

"*I* don't know who I am."

Badb leaned forward and pressed her lips to Aisling's forehead. "I'm sorry we have to keep it that way, my little warrior. Someday, you will find out who you are. Until then, we must hide you in whatever way possible."

She didn't want to hide. She wanted to run away from the humans who hated her and live with the faeries. But she'd begged Badb for that future so many times it made her throat raw.

43

Aisling was not meant to live with the faeries. It wasn't safe, Badb had told her.

She sighed and held out her hands. "Will it hurt?"

"A little. Some pain is worth enduring."

Badb traced her fingertips over Aisling's palm, drawing lines that felt white hot. Her nails left dark streaks like fine calligraphy. Over and over she traced until Aisling stared down at an eye in the center of her hand.

"Why an eye?" she asked.

"To keep your energy open. I want you to protect yourself regardless of your chains. Give me the other."

Magic slithered up Aisling's fingers and arms. It wasn't pain, not really, but it wasn't comfortable either. She hissed out a breath and focused on steadying her heartbeat as the second eye was drawn. It was worse this time now that she knew what to expect.

Electricity sparked in the air, lifting strands of hair from her head and stinging her body wherever it touched. Badb worked diligently until twin eyes stared up at her.

Aisling lifted her hands and met the strange gaze. They blinked, the tattoos shifting against her skin.

"Whose are they?" she asked.

"Yours from another time. Who better to look after you than the woman you will become?"

She nodded. It was a good decision. Even in her young age, Aisling had learned long ago she could trust no one other than herself. "And now?"

"Now is when you will feel pain."

Badb reached for her hands again and pinched the tips of her fingers. Fire burned the sensitive pads, so painful she couldn't breathe.

"It hurts," she whimpered. "Badb, please."

Sweat trickled between her shoulder blades, but there were still seven fingers to go. Her jaw ached from clenching, and she held her breath. Had her hands been severed? It felt like Badb was slowly sawing through the joints, but they were still attached. Why wouldn't they fall off if she was cutting through the bone?

"Done," Badb said with a sigh. She pinched the tip of Aisling's last finger and all the pain disappeared.

Slumping to the side, Aisling wiped at her sweaty brow. "You're finished?"

Badb reached out and cupped her cheek. "I can no longer see your pretty face. You're safe."

Aisling lurched upright, gasping at the painful memory. She pressed a hand to her chest and tried to force herself to breathe.

That hated dream again. The moment when she lost all sense of self and became the witch. It would plague her for the rest of her life.

The curse lingered at the edges of her existence, always lifting its ugly head at the worst moments. She wasn't human; she wasn't Fae. She wasn't anything other than a marked creature who hovered between both worlds.

45

What had brought about the dream?

Sensations returned as sleep loosened its hold. She winced, agony digging claws into her hips and raking down her legs.

"Right," she muttered. "They burned me at the stake."

"They *tried* to burn you."

She stiffened.

The voice was not one she recognized, although she knew the tones. It was too smooth, too pretty, too lovely to slip off the tongue of a human.

"Faerie," she grumbled.

"I see my reputation precedes me."

Aisling glanced around the wooded area but couldn't find any markers that were familiar. She was seated on the ground amid fallen red leaves in nothing more than her white linen shift. A black cloak covered her legs, the sensitive, burned flesh turning white hot when she shifted the abrasive fabric.

A fire crackled nearby, small enough to shed light and warmth but not large enough to give her flashbacks. Still, she glared at it before reaching for the cloak.

"I wouldn't do that if I were you," the disembodied voice called out. "You're still healing."

"I wouldn't do that if I were you," she mocked.

Hissing through her teeth, she pulled the cloak off her legs and stared down at the mangled mess. Blisters covered the long length of her legs, raw and filled with pus. She'd have to be careful moving, let alone trying to get back to her hut.

But she needed her spell books. There was a spell to heal burned flesh since enough witches had gone through the same thing. All she needed to do was *find* it....

"As you can tell, you aren't going anywhere."

"That's what you think." She flattened her hands to the ground and then searched through the dark for a stick. She'd need something to help her stand, but once she had a crutch, she could hobble back to her home and —

"What are you doing?"

"Leaving."

"I think it's quite obvious you aren't in any state to be getting up."

"You're entitled to your opinion, faerie." She'd stand up if she wanted to, and he couldn't stop her.

"You called me by another name before," he said. She heard a hint of desperation in the words. A distraction, perhaps? "You may call me that if you wish."

"No."

"No?"

"I prefer 'faerie.'" It had a flavor of insult she appreciated. "I have my doubts you are Fiach Dubh Ri."

"Why?"

Leaves rustled in the thicket behind her. Was he there? Or was it some creature sneaking up on her?

Aisling tried to find the outline of a faerie body in the forest, but all she could see were trees. She couldn't understand why he was hiding. She couldn't even remember much other than a shadowy figure and a kind touch on her cheek. Faeries *liked* people to see them. They were the most beautiful creatures to ever exist. Or perhaps the Unseelie were not.

She didn't know much about their kind. The Seelie were open with their laws, the way they lived, how they looked. The

Unseelie stayed away from humans other than to trick them, and in those situations, they always hid themselves with glamours. She'd never met an Unseelie before.

She heaved a sigh. "I don't think the true Fiach Dubh Ri would ever have waited so long to pull a dying woman from a bonfire."

"Witch fire."

"Excuse me?"

He cleared his throat. "I believe it's called a witch fire if they're trying to kill a witch."

"Well aren't you a ray of sunshine?" She shifted her legs and winced. How the hell was she going to stand up? If Lorcan were here… Her fists clenched. "Where is my familiar?"

"Your what?"

"My familiar."

A chuckle drifted through the air like rain falling from the sky. "Are you still pretending you're a witch?"

"I am a witch. Now where is—"

"Yes," he interrupted sarcastically, "your familiar. How should I know where the cat sidhe disappeared? They are notoriously unfaithful companions."

The leaves rustled again, this time mingling with a faint hissing sound. She tensed until a warm, soft body rubbed against her back.

Aisling sighed. "There you are, Lorcan."

He purred and bumped his head on her elbow. "Unfaithful? I think I could say the same about you, Fae."

"Me?" The unnamed man snorted. "You don't even know who I am."

"Do I not?" Lorcan butted Aisling's elbow with his head, a

suggestion to stand up so they could leave. "When did Unseelie learn how to read minds?"

She frowned down at her cat. "Unseelie?"

"No Seelie Fae would lurk in the shadows while a lady needed help." Lorcan sneered at the darkness. "Not unless they had something to hide."

A sizzle of pain traveled from the bottom of her feet all the way up to the top of her head. She arched her back with a hiss. "That's it," she growled, "I don't have time to watch this pissing contest. You two can stay here, but I'm going home."

She rolled onto her knees, sucked in a lungful of air, and shoved herself to her feet. Her mind blanked as agonizing pain streaked through her body and stole her sight. She hadn't realized there were blisters on her feet that would pop as soon as she put weight on them.

She cried out and would have fallen to the ground, but she was caught against a strong chest. He held his arm around her waist and lifted her up onto her toes.

The deep voice was in her ear now, husky and deep. "I don't think it's appropriate for you to walk just yet."

"I'm not staying here."

"Yes, you are."

"I don't even know where *here* is." She anchored her hands on his forearm, pressing down to take any lingering weight off her mangled feet. "I need to heal, and I can only do that with my spell books."

"Have a little faith in me, witch."

"Lorcan?"

The cat sidhe sat down next to the fire, rolled onto his

side, and bared his belly to the warmth. "Here's as good as anywhere else."

"I need to heal myself."

The faerie behind her snorted. "You need to trust someone else to take care of you."

"Oh, and who would that be? You? The man I have yet to see."

"You saw me at the edge of the forest."

She shook her head. "No, not really. I saw a form through the flames and thought it was a childhood story come to save me. Not a flesh and blood man."

He didn't respond. Instead, he leaned away and laid her back to the ground.

She hadn't noticed there had been another cloak beneath her. Surly and uncomfortable, she admitted he had at least been kind. Faeries weren't usually so considerate of anyone's comfort.

"I would like to treat your legs if you will allow it."

Aisling bit her lips, considering the options. She could let him heal her legs and then deal with the consequences of taking a faerie's help. Or she could insist he let her go and stumble through the woods until she happened upon her hut.

There wasn't a choice.

She sighed and kept her eyes on the ground. "Yes, fine. What do you want in return?"

"Do I need to ask for something?"

"Faeries always want to make a deal."

"Ah." She could hear him shifting, walking around her and then kneeling beside her legs. "How about you remove the binding curse?"

"Funny. I'll do that the moment you heal my legs."

"I'm not joking. And why aren't you looking at me?"

Because a part of her was still holding onto hope he might be Fiach Dubh Ri. She licked her lips, "Faeries prefer privacy. I don't want to insult you, Master Fae."

"Master? Been a long time since anyone called me that." His voice was laced with humor. "You may look upon me if you so wish, witch."

She ground her teeth together, took another breath, and looked up.

At first, her eyes couldn't understand what she was seeing. The man kneeling in front of her was handsome. His jaw was chiseled, his lips full and wide. When he grinned at her, a dimple appeared.

And then she realized he wasn't handsome at all.

What looked like a shadow covering the left side of his face was actually dark feathers flattened against his skull. His head wasn't shaved at all. Instead thick points poked through the skin that looked like quills. His eyes didn't match—one was green, and the other was swallowed entirely by a yellow iris that wildly rotated as it looked her up and down while the other eye remained still. The foot planted on the ground next to her knee had four taloned toes, black skin, and rigid scales.

Her jaw dropped open, and she stared at him with burning cheeks. "What are you?" she whispered.

"Unseelie." His lips quirked to the side, and his eyes twinkled. "Or did you expect some handsome Fae to have saved you?"

She could barely breathe when he was looking at her like

51

that. He didn't look like a raven at all, but a hungry wolf. "I've yet to find any Fae handsome."

"No? Then why are you blushing?" He pressed his hands flush against her legs, the movement too quick for her eyes to track.

"Lucky guess." She bared her teeth in a grimace, releasing a growl at the pain. "You did that on purpose," she accused.

"Did what?"

"Distracted me so I wouldn't know when you were going to touch me. You can't see my face. *Ouch*. Who taught you how to heal? You have the least delicate touch I've ever had the displeasure of feeling."

"Delicate? What about me makes you think I would be delicate?" He smoothed his hand down her shin to her feet. The blisters deflated and flattened against her skin in the wake of his touch. She was still red but no longer raw.

"Healing means making the person feel better, not hurting them more."

"Do you feel better?" He arched a dark brow and flicked an amused glance her way. "Or worse?"

She pursed her lips. "I don't intend to answer that question."

"Ah. Your silence speaks louder than words."

Aisling crossed her arms and watched him work. She couldn't argue that he was quite talented. The blisters faded, the ache was nearly tolerable, and she was certain he was doing it with very little concentration.

He stared at the surrounding forest with an intensity that made her heart hammer in her chest. If there was danger in the forest, she doubted he would try to keep them safe. He could leave her easily if trouble arose, and he likely wouldn't feel guilty about it. She might have thought he was lost in his own thoughts if the raven eye of his wasn't whirling in its socket.

"So what is it?" she blurted, cutting through the silence.

"What is what?"

"Your eye. It's unusual to see a faerie marked like that."

She realized how rude the question was the exact moment his hands clenched around her ankles. A soft whine escaped her lips, and he gentled his grip. "It *is* uncommon."

"Care to explain?"

He shook his head and slid warm hands up her calves. She held her breath as he reached her knees. A heated stare somehow met hers, and Aisling lost herself in his eyes.

Leaves unfurled in a bright ray of sunshine. Emeralds glistened in a crown made for a king. A sea of verdant grass rolled in a breeze she could not feel. All of nature was trapped in the well of his gaze.

When his fingers shifted to the back of her knee, warmth bloomed in their wake. His touch gentled. Was the Unseelie trying to be considerate of her wounds? Yet another oddity about him that she couldn't understand.

Her thoughts skipped a beat when he stroked her legs again. When was the last time someone had touched her like this? She couldn't remember. The children were polite and touched her hands when she allowed it, but they never touched her like this.

The light touch captivated her attention until she could focus on nothing other than the gentle fingers soothing the pain in her legs. He wanted to *help* her even if he wanted something in return.

"Breathe," he said with a chuckle.

Aisling snapped her gaze away from his hands on her legs to see laughter in his eyes. She tried to untangle herself from his warm grasp, but he tightened his hold.

"I'm not done yet, witch. Don't let my charms overwhelm you."

"Charms?" She rolled her eyes. "You seem to think I'm affected by you. I am not."

"My mistake then. Usually when I have my hands on a woman's bare legs and she stops breathing, I assume she's waiting for more."

"Perhaps you know some women, faerie, but you do not know *me*."

He made a noncommittal hum and slid his hands up the rest of her legs. When his nails scraped against the top of her thighs, she bit the inside of her lip to keep herself silent. She would not give him the satisfaction of knowing he was right. He did affect her.

Aisling didn't like it.

He made quick work of her healing, pulled down her skirt until it rested against her shins once more, and leaned back. "All done."

"We'll see about that." She already intended to make as many comments about his lack of healing skills as possible. But when she leaned down, pulled up her skirt, and looked at his work, she found little to disagree with. The blisters were gone. Her skin was still red, but more like a sunburn than an attempt at her life.

Begrudgingly, she sniffed. "It's a fine job."

"Would you go so far as to say I 'healed' you?"

She already hated his teasing. Frowning, she gave him a look that should have shriveled him up. "Don't push it, Fae."

He held up his hands and laughed. "What do you have against the Fae anyway?"

"I have nothing against them. I have him, don't I?" She pointed at Lorcan.

"Cat sidhes are a different breed because they aren't always born faeries." He arched a brow. "You have no inclination to trust me at all. You're a surly little thing whose hackles rise the moment I step near you. Why's that?"

"It's not as if you're easy on the eyes."

It was a low blow, and she knew it. Aisling cast her eyes to the side even though he couldn't see her. Speaking with faeries could be difficult when they couldn't see her expressions. Luckily, he wouldn't know she was embarrassed by her own rudeness.

"No, I don't think that's it," he replied. "You're not afraid. You're throwing out barbs so I won't get too close."

He saw too much. Far more than she was comfortable with.

"Thank you for healing me," she ground between clenched teeth, "but I really must be on my way."

She pushed to her feet, holding her breath for the blinding pain that had stolen her breath. She released a sigh when the pain didn't come. He really had done a fine job healing her.

Damned faeries. They were always good at everything.

"Lorcan, let's go."

"But it's warm here." He let out a rumbling purr. "The fire feels nice."

"We're not staying."

"My legs aren't working."

"They work fine." She rolled her eyes and snapped her fingers at the lazy cat. "Get up! We're going home."

He opened one eye and narrowed it on her. "Did you just snap your fingers at me like I was a common household pet?"

Aisling clenched her fists. The damned cat might be a witch, but that didn't mean he wasn't required to listen. If he wanted to live with her, then they needed to compromise.

She opened her mouth to blurt out a scathing retort, only to be interrupted by the Unseelie.

"I must also request you remain where you are."

"We've already heard your arguments, faerie. I need not hear them again."

"And yet you made a deal with me."

She let out a slow breath. The words shouldn't have been sensual, but they slid along her senses like the finest of velvet. A deal. She'd been the fool who had made a deal with an Unseelie faerie just to spite him.

"Of course," she mumbled, "the binding curse."

"Remove it." He smoothed a hand down his chest, rearranging his tunic and vest as if he were about to do something important. He tapped a finger against the faint scorch mark over his heart. "Right here, in case you need a reminder."

"I don't."

"Good. Then cast your spell, and we can both be on our merry ways."

She looked him up and down. The faerie was a strange man and immediately grated on her nerves, but she wanted to remember him.

The feathers on his face flattened and his brow furrowed. His fingers twitched, and his taloned toes tapped against the ground as he waited to see what she would do next. It was a shame she couldn't get to know him better. Of the few faeries she'd met, he was the most interesting.

Aisling lifted a hand and opened her palm. The eye shifted against her skin, twitching as it surveyed the landscape. "Hex break, curse release, all magic from my lips cease. So mote it be."

The power building on her fingertips sizzled and popped in her hand. A flare of static made her hair stand on end while searing pain bounced between her fingertips in bolts of tiny lightning. Crying out, she grabbed her wrist and forced her hand down. The magic gathered and cracked in the air like thunder.

The clearing fell silent other than the rasp of her breath. She held her hand palm down, pointed at the ground, so the eyes could not see anything else.

"What was that?" the faerie growled.

"I don't know."

"What do you mean you don't know? It's *your* magic!"

"*I don't know.*" This had never happened before. The eyes on her palms helped channel her magic, while the bindings at the tips of her fingers concealed her face. They had never rebelled against her before.

She swung her hand up to try again, only to get hit in the chest by a ball of magic so strong it knocked her back a few steps. She heard the crackle of power gathering in her palm again and swung her hand back toward the ground.

"I release this spell back to the earth," she frantically said.

Electricity slammed into the ground with an audible bang. Aisling winced. She'd left a hole in the earth in the exact shape of her hand, and she hadn't even touched the ground.

At some point during the scene, Lorcan had fled the fire. He now sat next to the Unseelie, nearly on his foot, staring at her with wide eyes. He sneezed. "What's going on with the eyes?"

"I'm not sure."

"They've never done that before."

She hesitantly turned her hand over and examined the eye closely. "No, they have not."

The Unseelie rubbed the side of his head, a scraping sound that echoed in the silence. "Is someone going to explain what's going on here?"

Lorcan looked up at him. "No."

The other faerie glanced at the sky. "I forgot how much I hate cat sidhes."

She recognized Lorcan's quivering whiskers as a warning sign. She didn't know what the tiny witch could do to such a massive faerie but didn't want to tempt fate.

"About that binding curse…" She bit her lip. "Just how bad did I curse you?"

"Enough to knock me back a few steps." He stuck out the taloned foot, motioning to peeling skin with a grimace. "And enough to share the pain."

"Bollocks."

"Mine are fine, thank you for asking." He arched a brow. "How are yours?"

She hated him. She hated him with a burning passion that festered worse than the blisters. Huffing out a breath, she opened her arms wide. "What do you want me to do, faerie? I can't remove the binding curse."

"You must. I am not giving up immortality for a mistake made by a pathetic little human witch," he ground out.

"This pathetic little human witch managed a curse so powerful a faerie can't break it, so I'll ask you to watch your tone."

"I can use whatever tone I want. You stole my *life*, and now you aren't willing to give it back?"

She wanted to tear her hair in frustration. "I'd give it back if I could."

"Try harder."

"Did you not see the giant lightning bolt that just came out of my hands? That's where my magic comes from. I can hit you with it — believe me, I'd love to — but I don't think it would end well for either of us."

The raven eye stopped spinning and focused on her with such intensity that she took a step back. His lip curled. "I've been kind thus far. I haven't asked much about the curse or tried to figure out who you are. Don't make me be unkind."

"Are you threatening me?"

"Only if you refuse to undo the binding curse again."

"I'm not refusing."

He visibly relaxed.

Before he could speak, she licked her lips and continued. "I *can't* undo the binding curse. There's a reason spell books warn against casting them. They don't want to let go. It's like trying to unravel a tapestry tied in knots and then felted."

"I will not tell you again—"

"And I will not keep repeating myself," she interrupted. "You can threaten me all you'd like, but the binding curse is not something I know how to break."

"Then you shouldn't have cast it!"

Aisling tossed her hands in the air. "Finally, something we can both agree on."

A blast of air blew the hair back from her face, and downy feathers touched her cheek. He had leaned down to intimidate her, crowding her with his body and great height. His breath fanned across her face as he whispered, "Remove the curse."

"Remove it yourself," she hissed.

"I will not be bested by a grubby little girl—"

"Who are you calling grubby?"

" —with subpar magical powers who is incapable of—"

"Subpar? I cursed *you*, didn't I?"

" —controlling her own curses because she does not understand how to work magic."

"How dare you?" Aisling gasped.

"Oh, I very much dare." He was so close she could smell his unique scent of oak and moss. "You have no idea who I am, witch. You have no idea what I can do."

"Likewise."

Lorcan's voice cut through their argument. "Why don't we all take a few steps away from each other?"

She curled her fingers into a fist and shook it at him, daring him to step away first. She wouldn't take the hit to her pride when he was the one in the wrong.

Other than the binding curse. That was likely her fault.

Lorcan hissed. "At the same time if it makes it easier. Three, two—"

They both stepped back. The Unseelie's chest heaved in anger, and Aisling had to pinch herself so she wouldn't send yet another curse hurtling through the air. He'd look pretty with a hole in his chest. Or his head.

Lorcan glanced back and forth between them. "It looks like the binding curse will stay, at least for a little while. Which means you two need to stick together and figure out a way to break the curse."

"I'm not working with him," Aisling vehemently spat.

"I'm not working with her," the Unseelie growled.

"Well, that's too bad, because your lives are bound together now. You either have to live with sharing a life force or figure out a way to break it."

The Unseelie's raven eye rolled in its socket. He turned away from them and stalked toward the forest. "I need to think."

Aisling plopped back onto the ground. "I wish you the best of luck! I'm certain it's impossible for you to have a thought in your head."

When they could no longer hear the Unseelie's footsteps, Lorcan turned toward her and blinked. "Was that really necessary?"

"Absolutely."

"You don't have to be so rude." Lorcan stretched, his paws flexing in front of the fire before he turned and flicked his tail. "Why do you push everyone away? Hm?"

She rubbed her hands over her arms and stared into the

flames. She remembered all too well what happened when people got close to her. Aisling preferred to never have them than lose them.

Bran stalked through the forest, slapping branches out of his way and snapping them in his anger. How dare she? What human had any right to refuse him anything?

Him? An Unseelie prince?

But then again, she couldn't be entirely human. No mortal witch could cast a curse this strong, and no mortal witch had a face hidden by magic. There was more to her, and if he wasn't so infuriated, he might have been able to figure out her secret. He didn't have time to deal with a binding curse. He had his own mess to deal with.

The forest opened into a hidden glen. Trees gave way to emerald green hills and water trickling from multiple streams, gathering in the middle to create a still silver pool.

Bran blew out a breath. He only meant to stop in the human realm for a short time, a passing dalliance, before he continued on his journey. After all these years, he had finally found a way to break the chains that bound him.

He lifted his hands, almost expecting to see silver glinting in the moonlight. But his burden was not entirely physical. It was the weight of being an Unseelie prince and the cursed future that title came with.

He was so close he could taste it. Freedom beckoned with the dying of the light.

Paws pattered on the ground, and the cat sidhe scampered up a stone to sit next to him. "She's not all bad."

"I wasn't thinking about her at all."

"Sure you weren't."

Bran cleared his throat. "I thought a lady would be more pleased with the man who saved her life."

"She wouldn't be pleased with anyone who saved her life. She's independent to a fault."

"Not all that intelligent then."

"Easy there, prince" — the cat gave him a sidelong glance — "you're both too young to be throwing insults around that hurt. You've yet to learn how to curb your tongue."

Bran didn't want to agree with the creature, but he had a point. As the youngest of his family, Bran had always gotten what he wanted. He wandered away from them when he wished, but always had a home waiting in the Unseelie palace. "Spoiled" was an accurate word to describe him.

He crossed his arms over his chest. The feathers coming in on the side of his head itched, only adding to his ornery disposition.

"What is her story?" he asked. "She can't be human."

"Why not?"

"Look at her. She's too graceful, her temper runs too hot. And anyone with any magical knowledge can see that curse on her face is faerie made."

"Would you like me to tell her *your* story?"

Bran felt the cat's eyes sweep him from head to toe. "What do you know of my story?"

"The field mice speak of the Unseelie prince searching for a way to free himself from his family's responsibilities. Considering you are the only Unseelie prince who has left the dark castle in centuries, a cat can draw conclusions."

"You see too much, sidhe."

"You may call me Lorcan." The beast hopped from the stone onto the ground. "Follow me."

"Why?"

"You'll see." Lorcan shook his head, padding to the edge of the pool. "You're more like the girl than you know. She's just as stubborn."

"And far more prickly."

"Is that such a bad thing?"

Not in most situations, Bran mused. He liked his women with a little more fight than most. He'd always chased the "wrong" kinds of faeries because it was just a bit more interesting.

This woman was an entirely different situation. She was stubborn, senseless, foolish… He rubbed a hand over the burn mark on his chest. She couldn't think past a few minutes before doing whatever she wanted.

"Stop rubbing at it," Lorcan grumbled. "It's not coming off any time soon."

"I wasn't touching the mark."

The cat gave him a disbelieving look.

"Fine, I might have been. But you would be, too, if you were bound to a witch."

"Come here, Unseelie prince. Let me show you something." The cat reached forward and drew a rune on the ground with his paw.

Bran stepped beside the cat sidhe, staring down at him in curiosity. "What is it?"

"Look."

He glanced down at the pool and frowned. Two men stared back at him, both warped by the magic streaming from the glowing runes that created waves rolling with power and truth.

The cat sidhe's reflection was a man with wiry arms and legs. He wasn't as tall as a Tuatha de Danann, but perhaps tall for a human. His hair was long but his face neatly shaven. Dark hair and eyes matched his other form.

Bran's gaze locked upon his own reflection. A pang struck him over the binding mark as he saw himself as a man, entirely whole and without Unseelie disfigurements. His eyes matched, his leg was sturdy and strong, and he had a full head of hair. It was the dream he had always desired but had never seen come to life.

"This is what we both desire," Lorcan said. "But that end cannot be reached without her."

"How's that?"

"Oh, because we'll love and hate an Irish lass, but neither of us will get her out of our hearts."

The words sank like a stone deep into Bran's belly. They pulled him toward a future he didn't like the look of. "My end can be reached without help from a witch."

"Is that so, prince? The lake never lies."

Bran rolled his eyes. "That's all well and good if you want to sound mysterious, but this is a temporary pool caused by an overabundance of rain. A rune etched in the ground doesn't change my plans, and how do you know any of them?"

"Cat sidhes aren't always faeries."

65

The pieces fell together in Bran's mind. "You're a witch," he accused. "A real, honest-to-god witch who's used up one of his lives to become...what? Another witch's familiar?"

"She's not a witch. But you already knew that."

He had an inclination, and it wasn't sitting right with him. Bran cleared his throat. "Is she Fae then?"

"Did you ever think she was human? You already know the answer." Lorcan twitched his tail. "How many humans could survive this long with a faerie curse placed on them?"

The cat sidhe had a point. Bran stared down at their reflections and wondered how he had gotten here. Had some ancient Tuatha de Danann sent him down this path for a reason?

"I cannot afford to be distracted," he replied.

"I think, if you asked, she's more likely to help than hinder."

"With all that arguing? I'm uncertain you're right." He crouched and placed a hand on the cat's soft fur. "But I appreciate the help."

"You must take her with you, wherever you plan on going. The villagers will try to burn her again."

"And our lives are tied together," he said with a sigh. "A binding curse neither of us can seemingly break."

"Despite what you may think, she is gifted in the magical arts. If the curse could be easily broken, she would have managed just fine."

"That's what I was afraid of." He didn't want to bring the girl. She would distract him as much as he was loath to admit it. She was a puzzle he didn't know how to solve.

That was the only reason he was interested, Bran told

himself. It was nothing to do with the milky pale skin of her legs, softer than velvet, and the way her muscles had tensed under the stroke of his fingers as he healed her.

His own thighs burned in response. It was their binding, an answering ache he felt because she was feeling it. That was the only reason he was thinking of touching her again.

Bran refused to believe it was anything else.

"If we must travel as companions, then we shall." He met Lorcan's gaze and ground his teeth together. "Now, the question is if she will agree."

"If I will agree to what?" Her voice cut through the darkness and shattered his mood.

Frowning, he straightened his shoulders in anticipation of yet another argument. "I know of another way to break the binding curse, but you will need to help me first."

"A smart man would try the other way around. Break the curse so my death won't affect you, and then ask for payment afterwards."

"Does everything have to be an argument with you?"

She lifted a shoulder. "Not everything, but you make it so easy."

Traveling with this wench would be harder than he thought. Bran recognized wickedness when he saw it, along with mirth dancing just under the surface as she widened her stance and crossed her arms over her chest. He heard her quiet huff of breath, and though it likely she was holding in laughter.

She wanted to make this a challenge for him. She enjoyed the annoyances she caused and wanted it to be difficult.

The girl expected him to give in.

He narrowed his eyes like a bird of prey homing in on a

mouse. "Do you want the binding curse to remain intact?"

"I'd rather break all ties with you now."

"Good. I know the way to do it, but you have to help me first. Which means we both have to keep each other alive. Think you can do that?"

She recognized the challenge in his voice. Her shoulders squared, and she did her best to look down her nose at him. "As long as you stay out of trouble, I'm sure it will be an easy enough task."

"Oh, I'm not worried about myself. What we're going to do is not for the faint of heart."

"Out with it then. What are we doing that is so dangerous?"

Bran sent her a wicked grin. "First, we need the blood of a dead god."

CHAPTER 3

A JOURNEY BEGINS

"The blood of a dead god?" Aisling asked for the tenth time. "What the hell do you mean by that?"

She hadn't wanted to go with the Unseelie, but Lorcan could be convincing when he wanted to be. The cat sidhe had yowled directly in her ear for an entire night in the forest before she gave in and agreed she would entertain the idea.

They had traveled for a few days across dale and glen. They passed by clusters of sheep so white they blinded her eyes and others so dirty they blended into the countryside.

She hefted the small pack the faerie had given her with their provisions. The Unseelie did not carry a single thing. Instead, he sauntered ahead of her with his hands in his pockets, whistling and pretending he didn't hear her asking questions.

"Unseelie," she growled, "I won't stop until you explain."

"I think it explains itself."

"It most certainly does not. How are we supposed to get this blood? How is there blood left in a dead body? Are we killing the god first and then gathering its blood? There's a thousand and one questions, and you aren't answering any of them."

"We'll figure it out when we get there."

She jerked to a halt and stared incredulously at his back. "That's your plan?"

"I haven't had any issues with it yet."

"Because we haven't gotten there!"

"At which point, I'll figure it out. There, you see? The plan hasn't changed even after we argued about it."

Blasted man. Had he no interest in keeping himself alive? She stared at his silhouette and wondered if he would burst into hundreds of ravens and disappear at any moment. The man obviously had a death wish or was sent by the Tuatha de Danann to plague her.

Any moment she would wake up attached to that tree again with the flames burning her knees. The villagers would yell at her, she would realize she wasn't on an adventure with a mysterious faerie, and this was just a fever dream.

Aisling pinched her arm hard.

When the green rolling pastures didn't fade away, she huffed out a disappointed breath. She wasn't certain whether she preferred certain death by fire or uncertain death with an Unseelie who hated plans.

The grass parted in a wave rushing toward her at full speed. Just before the rustling line reached them, Lorcan bounded up into the air. His ears flopped against his skull as he bounced. "I think I might have found a portal," he called out.

The Unseelie grinned. "Good! Lead the way then, sidhe."

That smile was as dark as midnight and just as mysterious. Aisling pressed a hand against her chest, suddenly uncomfortable. He was almost too pretty when he did that.

Shaking her head to clear it of the ridiculous thoughts, she hurried to catch up with the two faeries. "Wait a minute, portal?"

"We need to get into the home of my people, to the Otherworld," the Unseelie replied. "I thought that was rather painfully obvious. No?"

"You omitted going to the Otherworld. I can't go there." Her heart raced at the mere thought of that cursed faerie land. She rubbed her grumbling stomach that threatened to toss her meager breakfast onto the ground.

"That's where I'm going, witch. And if I remember right, binding curses require the pair to be in the same realm, do they not?"

"You are correct, so it would behoove you to—"

He spun on his heel and leveled her with a glare so filled with rage it stopped her in her tracks. "I'm going to the Otherworld with or without you. I suggest you think good and hard about just how much you want to keep that head on your shoulders. I care very little if I live or die. Do you?"

Aisling gulped, feeling like a mouse being watched by a large cat. He stared at her a few moments longer, nodded, and then turned around as if he hadn't just threatened to kill them both.

Faeries.

She glared at Lorcan. "Did you have to find a portal to the Otherworld? Of all places?"

He flicked his tail. "I'm on his side with this one. You're bound to him, and I don't like it. The sooner we break the curse, the sooner we can return to our normal lives."

71

Normal? Since when had their lives ever been normal?

Aisling watched the cat sidhe disappear into the grass again. The only way she could track him was by the moving line that parted the rolling pastures. Lorcan liked telling people what to do, and now she'd have to deal with the fat head he'd get from ordering an Unseelie around like he was one of the cat's subjects.

Lorcan guided them to a stream falling from a cliff high above them. White foam frothed on the ground where it struck, the water swirling with movement and life. The stones at the base were smoothed by years of runoff.

She tilted her head back and stared at the wild beauty. Sometimes it startled her how lovely the land was. Emerald green moss clung to the rugged stones, and speckles of color showed through where granite peeked through the dirt and earth. Ui Neill was a land untouched, pristine and pure.

"What is this?" the Unseelie exclaimed. "Some kind of jest?"

Lorcan sauntered to the stream's edge and stuck his paw in the cold water. He flicked droplets in their direction and then licked his pads. "This is it."

"Running water negates faerie magic. This isn't a portal."

"But it can be."

"What are you blathering on about?"

Lorcan flicked his gaze towards Aisling. "She'll be more useful in this situation than I am. Ask her."

"Ask the witch?" The Unseelie planted his hands on his hips and turned toward her with a severe look. "What do you have to do with this?"

"Aren't you glad we're bound now?" She tossed her loose

hair over her shoulder.

"You'd have to come up with a miracle for that to happen. Now, explain yourself."

"I can open a portal to the Otherworld." Aisling shrugged her shoulder. "Magic is wonderful like that, isn't it?"

"*You* can open a portal to the Otherworld?"

"Yes."

"A witch."

"Yes."

"I don't believe it." He rubbed the side of his head, scraping over budding feathers. "It's not possible."

"Correction, it's very possible. I've done it before."

Aisling thoroughly enjoyed watching him struggle for words. If he asked, she didn't plan on telling him she'd opened a portal only once for a faerie-blooded lass. The woman had been kind enough, and all Aisling had done was let her slip through the portal and then sealed it behind her. She didn't even know if the woman survived.

The Unseelie's eyes sparked in anger, as if he could read her thoughts.

"Would you like me to show you?" she asked, fluttering her hand in the air with a pretend fan.

"How?" He dropped his hands to his sides, in all appearances giving up. "How did you learn to do that?"

"My grandmother. She had lots of books she shouldn't have had and gave them to me to memorize. I'll admit, I'm bad at memorizing spells, but I did steal away a few them to keep for myself. She took whichever ones I finished back to where they came from."

"Which is?"

"I never asked."

"Why wouldn't you ask? Some old woman gives you spell books that contain faerie secrets, and you don't think to ask *where she was stealing them from?*"

Aisling pursed her lips. "I highly doubt she was stealing them."

"Then how was she getting them?"

"Borrowing."

He let out a growl so loud it made Lorcan jump. "What are you, a brownie? No one borrows spell books from the Fae!"

"Do you want me to open this portal or not?"

"Yes!" he shouted. Frustration laced his tones with a breathy quality that sounded far too sensual for her liking. She felt her cheeks burn and was glad he couldn't see her reaction.

Why were faeries always so appealing? Why couldn't they be ugly, malformed creatures who limped in the shadows? Well, she supposed this one was close to that. And he was still appealing!

She took a deep breath and sighed. "Fine. We're in agreement that I'll open a portal, and then we'll go to the Otherworld. Where I don't want to go."

"Care to explain that?"

"Not really."

"Secrets, secrets, and more secrets," he muttered. "You're an infuriating woman, you know that?"

"You aren't the first to say so."

"I bet." When his hands opened and then closed, she heard the audible crack of his knuckles. "I need to clear my head. Just open the portal. I'll be back soon."

"It takes a while to open a portal. It probably won't be done

74

by the time you get back."

"Don't bet on it, witch."

"You intend to be gone for a full day then?"

He glared at her. "Just get it done."

Aisling stared at his back after he turned from her. Strong and lithe, the lines of his muscles should have been on a dancer, a soldier, even a prince. Not some unruly Unseelie who —

She gasped when he dissolved into ravens. They all took flight in the same cluster she'd seen in the trees when the flames had licked at her knees. It hadn't been an unkindness of ravens. It had been one faerie staring at her through pieces of himself.

"Dramatic," Lorcan grumbled. He flattened himself on a large rock, the sun dancing across his glossy black fur. "Faeries always like to put on a show."

"Ridiculous creatures. Think he'll be back soon?"

"If he went through the effort to shape-shift, it's unlikely."

"Good."

She stretched out on her belly next to the cat and let the sun warm her tired bones. The pack weighed down on her ribs, but she didn't care anymore. Her entire body pulsed with relief at being able to pause for a few moments.

Walking hadn't always been this hard. Or maybe she'd never walked this far in her life. Either way, her feet felt like they were going to fall off and her thighs quivered just standing still.

How did the faerie do it? He wandered through the fields without a care, whistling sometimes or plucking grass from the ground to weave in his hands. It was like he didn't feel the same fatigue she did.

"They're impressive, aren't they?" Lorcan asked. He rolled

onto his back, the white starburst on his chest glowing.

"Who?"

"Faeries."

"I've yet to see him do anything impressive."

"Bursting into a flock of ravens doesn't do it for you?"

"An unkindness," she whispered.

"What?"

"It's not a flock of ravens. It's an unkindness of ravens, like a murder of crows."

Lorcan snuffled, almost as if he were mimicking laughter. "I don't know which one I prefer."

"I do." Aisling rolled over onto her side and scrubbed his belly. "I'll take neither of them and live a much happier life."

"Don't," he grumbled, wiggling under her hand. "Stop it, Aisling, it tickles!"

"Oh, I'm sorry, I can't hear you. What did you say?"

His claws shone brilliantly as he unsheathed them and placed them dangerously close to the back of her hand. "I will scratch you."

"You have to get up and get me a bird anyway."

"The sacrifice? Again?"

She nudged his side, poking at his soft underbelly until he rolled to his feet grumbling. "Yes, the sacrifice. I can't cast a spell without one."

"I'm not sure other witches would agree with you."

"And I'm certain *every* witch would agree with me. Faeries might do things differently, but witches have to get the job done in creative ways. So go find a grouse or something similar in the bushes and bring it back. I'll work on the rune frame."

"I don't like the mess you make when you do this."

"Lorcan, you eat these birds raw all the time."

"Well, it all seems like a terrible waste."

She snorted. "I've told you before. I am not giving you the remains of the bird. It absorbs a lot of magic, and I have no idea what might happen if you eat it."

"Like turning into a human?"

Poor Lorcan. He wanted to turn back into a human desperately, but magic wasn't that easy. Witches could use one of their lives as a cat and usually had no issue turning back into their previous form, but Lorcan was stuck. He didn't know why or how. Aisling had a feeling it was because he didn't really want to turn back. Life was significantly harder as a human.

He raced off into the undergrowth, grumbling the entire way. She shook her head at his antics. Lorcan liked to help, no matter how much he complained. And catching a grouse would distract him from the black magic she was about to perform. He hated black magic.

Aisling slowly tugged the pack from her shoulders and groaned. Her back felt like it was on fire, tingles racing down the long lengths of muscle and embedding in her back.

The Unseelie's bag clanked when it hit the stone beside her.

"I wonder," she murmured.

Curiosity had always plagued her. It whispered in her ear to investigate, to look at things she shouldn't, touch that which was not hers.

She searched the shadows for any hint of the Unseelie. He wasn't so stupid that he trusted her with his pack, was he? He didn't know her at all, and leaving a witch with access to everything he carried…

She did not hesitate as she ripped at the ties. What kind of man was this Unseelie? If he wasn't going to expand on his history, then she would find out herself.

Some food, spare clothes, a belt, along with other odds and ends filled the pack to the brim. Most of the weight came from the food, although heavy gems encrusted the belt.

She pulled it from the folds of fabric. It was pretty, not functional. So many gems all carefully placed in a pattern that resembled the night sky. She'd never seen such crystal-clear stones.

Aisling ran a finger over the pattern. He had grown up in a wealthy family, and though it shouldn't have surprised her, it did. She had thought perhaps he was like her—a cast off, a forgotten son, a boy sent away because his family didn't want him.

The belt suggested otherwise.

She let it slide back into the pack and dug through the pack farther. Just when she was about to give up, a glint at the bottom caught her eye.

A cord became tangled in her fingers. A silver key with a gray moonstone embedded at the top hung from the end. Aisling lifted it to the light and gasped.

She'd never seen a stone so smooth. It was a good omen, albeit a dangerous one. Gray moonstones were stones for perceiving beyond the veil. They saw through glamour, lies, even the future itself if decisions were hazy.

"So," she murmured, "you know more magic than healing, Unseelie."

She dropped the key back into the pack, fearful of the sudden desire to continue touching it. Moonstones always vibrated with magic, yearning to be used even though they showed things the user didn't want to see. They were vindictive when they wished to be.

Her arm shook as she forced herself to release the necklace cord. She didn't need to use magic, she wasn't addicted to its power, and she refused to allow it to rule her.

It was a battle she had fought every day.

Something in her wanted to use magic all the time. It wanted sparks flying from her fingertips and the world at her feet. Which likely was the reason she ended up burning in the first place.

The memory brought with it the lingering sting along her feet and legs. She winced and pulled up her shift. Her white flesh was still red and angry.

The faerie had done a remarkable job healing her, but he hadn't finished it. Aisling frowned and pressed her thumb to the redness. A white mark remained when she removed her hand and then disappeared as blood returned to the aching area.

If they were going to keep walking like this, she'd need to do something about it. Her shoes had barely held on through the fire and the soles were falling off.

Aisling glanced back at the Unseelie's pack.

"If you don't want me wearing your extra clothes, shout now, Unseelie," she called out, and then waited for a response. "No complaints? Perfect."

She dragged the pack to the edge of the water and laid the clothes out in the sun. They would heat up on the rocks while she washed away the grime of travel. Cold water would cool the slight burn of her legs and hopefully bring down the swelling around her ankles.

Stretching her arms over her head, she let the sun dancing on top of the water blind her. The sparkles were mesmerizing.

"Lorcan, don't you be spying on me or you're going to get an eyeful!"

When no one responded, and no leaves rustled, she figured she was safe enough to duck into the water.

Yanking her shift over her head, she left it in a heap near the Unseelie's clothes. It was strange feeling to be unclothed where anyone could come upon her. Not that it mattered. If it was a human, she could curse them into a toad. If it was a faerie, they would not know who she was.

She hissed as the cold water touched her toes. "Spring water." Icy and clear, it rushed directly from the earth in frigid temperatures that nearly burned.

But it would help her wounds better than anything else. Aisling gritted her teeth and waded through the eddies frigid enough to create ice until she was up to her chest in the water.

Her jaw ached from keeping the chattering still. She would freeze to death in this water. Forcing herself to remain until the bitter cold became more tolerable, she finally released the breath she was holding with a sigh.

Small currents butted against her sides, tugging and pulling her this way and that. A burble of laughter escaped her lips. How long had it been since she swam?

She couldn't even remember the last time she was *clean*. She made do with rags and a few buckets of water once a week while she was in the hut. There wasn't streams or rivers nearby safe enough for her to bathe in, not while the villagers thought she was an old woman.

It couldn't hurt to indulge herself a bit. Aisling tucked her toes between algae-covered stones, and let her arms float at her side.

Waves lapped at the top of her head with soothing strokes. Birds chirped in the air, singing songs that soothed her battered soul. The water chilled her flesh and pressed a balm to her wounds.

The spell could wait a few moments more. First, she would heal her body and heart.

Bran spread his wings wide and let the wind calm his anger. It whistled through his feathers, stirring something feral in his heart.

He had no reason to be angry at the girl. She couldn't know the implications of such a curse, and it was unlike him to be so cruel in blaming an innocent. Albeit a powerful innocent. He was the nice brother, the one the Unseelie court thought might eventually defect and go to the Seelie court for his dislike of harming others.

Why did this little witch get under his skin?

He wanted to throttle her every time she opened that mouth of hers. She thought she was so intelligent, so learned, but she was a mere second in the great tapestry of time.

And she knew how to open a portal to the Otherworld.

He didn't know how to do that.

Bran refused to entertain the idea she might know more

81

about magic than he did. He'd spent his entire life learning and honing his skills. She was merely lucky to have gotten a few spell books that were rare.

And who was her grandmother, anyway? What kind of woman had access to books like that?

The question burned in his mind until it was the only thing he could think of. There was something off about that tidbit of information, and he wouldn't put it past the witch to lie. Had she been stealing from the Fae?

It was an interesting theory that made him tilt his wings and head back toward the waterfall. He clacked his beak in anticipation of what she would do.

He'd already seen her holding her fists at her side as if she wanted to strike him. What would happen if she did? A fire burned in his chest at the thought. She could try to harm him, but it wouldn't do anything. He was larger than her, trained in the art of war, and had survived countless battles.

He soared through the skies, knocking clouds out of his way as he returned. The witch might be done with the portal by now, although he doubted it. She had made it seem as though it was a laborious creature, and he hadn't been gone very long.

Magic coiled around his body, expanding his form in a quiet pop. He rolled as he hit the ground, ending in a crouch with one hand pressed against the solid earth. The nubs of feathers on the side of his head stood up with a sudden chill.

Where was she?

He stayed low, surveying the landscape for some hint of where she'd gone. If she thought she could run from him, she was horribly wrong. He'd twist the binding curse around and track her to the ends of the earth if she made him.

The sound of splashing water burst his angry thoughts like a bubble.

Was she…?

He carefully crept across the small stream, stepping over rocks so he wouldn't alert her that he had returned. Bran didn't understand why he was being so careful. It made little sense when he had no reason to sneak. If she had worried about him seeing her, then she would never have bathed without knowing where he was.

Blackthorn bushes hid him from her view. He reached through the sharp points and parted them ever so slightly.

He thanked the gods he was kneeling, or he might have fallen over. She rose out of the water like a nymph, all slick skin and trickling water. Her dark hair swirled over her pale flesh in a waterfall of dark color and movement. She was turned away from him, giving him the perfect view of an hourglass figure and tiny dimples in the small of her back.

Gods, she was beautiful. For all that she might have buck teeth, warts, and a third eye, her body was enough to make a man crazed.

She slicked her hands over her head, smoothing her hair until it resembled a well-oiled seal skin. Her head tilted to the side, and he wondered what she was thinking of. Him? Their predicament?

Bran would prefer it if she was thinking of him, for she had plagued his thoughts from the moment he met her. He couldn't get the little witch out of his head, and it was driving him mad.

She shifted, and every muscle in his body tensed. A little more to the left, and he would see a lot more than just her back.

He could make the right decision here. He could look

away, let the brambles fall back in place, stop being the man lurking in the bushes while a woman bathed. And yet, he couldn't.

The curve of her hip crested the water. She stepped a few feet forward, just enough that the ends of her hair covered the swell of her bottom. She really was lily white all over, so pale she almost looked like a being carved out of marble rather than flesh and blood.

He felt a light touch on his foot. Glancing down, he saw the cat sitting on his foot with a paw resting on the other shoe.

Alarmed, Bran breathed, "How long have you been there?"

"Long enough to know you've been staring for quite some time."

"It means nothing."

"Right. In the meantime, I'll observe that you look like a man who's either walking to the gallows or has just realized he's in over his head with a beautiful woman. Which one are you?"

Bran swallowed. He would admit to nothing, especially not to a cat sidhe masquerading as a familiar. "I'm staring at the witch who bound me to a mortal life. Gallows, obviously."

The cat flexed his paw and dug sharp nails into the supple leather of his boot. "Keep telling yourself that. Someday you might believe it. But do try to close your mouth. You'll catch flies that way, and they don't taste as good as they look."

Bran furrowed his brows. He glared at Lorcan as the cat wiggled through the brush and made his way down to the streambed. The witch glanced toward her familiar, frowning with glittering, mirth-filled eyes.

Now, he was stuck. If he walked out of the bushes, then the

84

witch would know he had been staring at her. If he didn't, then the cat would likely point him out. Damned cat sidhe. They always leaned toward the Unseelie side of the Fae and liked to cause trouble a little too much.

Thinking quick, he shifted back into a raven had hopped all the way back to the stream. It was easier to stay hidden in a small form, but it hurt his pride. When was the last time he had to hop away from a woman? It was demeaning.

Up and over the stones he jumped, spreading his wings and flapping over the rushing water. He quietly clacked his beak the entire time. If he could have grumbled, he would have. Ridiculous. Absolutely ridiculous that he was lowering himself so far. All for a little witch who wouldn't get out of his head.

He reached the other side of the stream and changed back to himself in a burst of feathers. Running a hand over the nubs, he spun toward the stream.

A small part of him wanted to catch her coming out of the water. He wasn't proud of it, but a man had to take his chances when they appeared.

She was up to her neck in the water, arms protectively crossed over her chest as if he were a horrible creature that just crawled out of the muck. Obviously, she knew he was there before he'd turned. Which meant she'd been watching him as he made his way across the stream.

He refused to entertain the thought she might have seen him hopping across the stones like a fool. "Have you completed the portal yet?"

"Does it look like I've completed the portal?"

"Considering I don't know what the spell entails, I couldn't answer that question knowledgeably."

Her long hesitation suggested she was holding her tongue. Since he was used to her scathing retorts, he lifted a brow. "Nothing to say?" he asked. "Cat got your tongue?"

"Hey!" Lorcan shouted from the other side of the stream.

The witch shifted from foot to foot. "I'm standing in ice water, faerie. And you're preventing me from leaving the stream, so I'm freezing my legs off. Turn around."

"I have no intention of doing that."

"Turn around or I will curse you again. This time with something a little worse than a binding curse."

Bran wanted to laugh, but he also didn't want to tempt her. The witch knew how to open a portal to the Otherworld. What else did she know?

He turned and listened intently. Water trickled from her body, striking the pool with electric pings that made him envision precisely what she looked like. She was a mythical creature all on her own. Long, dark hair dripping pearls into the swirling eddies of the stream.

Then he heard her cursing and grinned. She had to be freezing, he knew how cold that water was. And dressing in little more than a thin white shift, she wouldn't warm up any time soon.

Served her right for swimming when she should have been working on the portal. He could proposition to her that his body was twice as warm as her clothes...but those were dangerous thoughts.

"What else do you need?" he asked. "There must be a reason you've been lazing in the stream, other than natural laziness."

"Witch spells cannot be cast with a wave of our hand like a

faerie, Unseelie. Work and preparation are required. And an attention to detail that far surpasses what you might be used to."

"Excuse me?"

"You can turn around now."

He spun on his heel, words burning at the end of his tongue. He wanted to tear into her for the suggestion he wasn't capable of preparing for his own magic. But she stood at the edge of the stream looking...*adorable.*

She wore his clothing, baggy and far too big. The black tunic and tan pants didn't suit her complexion in the slightest, and she looked like the ragged witch she pretended to be. But her hair was braided, the long tail leaving soggy marks on his shirt. Her strong stance and twitching fingers clearly said she was pleased with herself.

The witch rolled up her sleeves and gave him a shrug. "Something to say, Unseelie?"

Bran shook his head. "Not a thing, witch."

She seemed surprised, her arms immediately crossing, her weight shifting from side to side. That surprise was a win, proof he had finally bested her.

At least that's what he told himself, but knew it was a lie.

He cleared his throat and marched toward her with his hands clasped behind his back. "About this portal."

"What do you want to know?"

"How soon can you complete it?"

"I need to build it first, and I need Lorcan to bring back a sacrifice."

Bran nodded. He'd heard of black magic that required blood. A few witches in his day exclusively used such ingredients in their spells, and even a few faeries utilized the old ways.

He circled her slowly. "From my understanding then, we're only waiting on Lorcan to bring something back. A bird, perhaps?"

"A bird would suffice."

"Why is that, precisely?"

She huffed out a breath. "First of all, I don't appreciate the tone. I know what I'm doing. Second of all, a bird tends to have the correct amount of blood for a spell, and I have no interest in wasting life for no reason."

"Would a raven be an appropriate size?"

"Are you offering?" She looked him up and down, head tilting. "I'm not sure your shifted form would really be big enough."

The jab stung, but he was learning how to read her. She wasn't trying to be rude; she was trying to distract him.

Bran knew how women distracted men by curling their fingers and shifting back and forth. Their attention wandered up and down his body. They licked their lips or ran fingers through their hair, all a ploy so he didn't see their true thoughts.

She did none of that. Instead, this little witch stopped all her movements and widened her stance with insults prepared to spew from her lips.

There was a spark between them, and he planned on using that to his advantage. He looked her up and down.

"Why are you circling me like a vulture?" she grumbled. "Can you not sit still, or is this another flaw I haven't seen yet?"

"When was the last time you had a lover?"

"A what?" she spluttered, coughed, then crossed her arms

firmly over her chest. "I don't see how that assists us getting into the Otherworld."

"I'm trying to figure you out." He plucked at his shirt on her shoulder. He lingered, stroking the fine muscles of her neck before sliding his hand down her arm.

She shrugged him off. "Stop it."

"Why? Does it make you uncomfortable?"

"Anyone I don't know touching me and circling me like I'm a rare piece of meat would make me uncomfortable." She jerked away from his hand again. "Unseelie, I'm warning you."

"Are your cheeks red, I wonder? Are you blushing, little witch?" He wanted to see the vibrant color spread across whatever face she had. The longer he knew her and the more tantalizing she became, the more he didn't care what her face looked like. A face was just a face, but a woman who challenged him on a daily basis was a rare beauty not to be overlooked.

"One last warning, Unseelie."

"Is that a hint of interest I hear? Why, witch, if you were interested, all you had to do was —"

Her hand struck the center of his chest right over the starburst of her curse. Electricity rocketed from her fingertips and sent him flying through the air. Bran landed hard, the wind rushing from his lungs and black spots dancing across his vision.

Damn, the girl was powerful.

She placed a hand on her hip and tilted her head to the side. "I'm sorry, were you saying something?"

He tried to speak but could only wheeze.

"That's what I thought. You sit right there, Unseelie, and let this woman do all the hard work. Say yes."

"Yes ma'am," he croaked, still heaving air into his lungs.

"Oh, I like the sound of that."

She sashayed away from him, although she had to stop a few times to hitch up his pants. He almost offered the belt in his pack but knew she'd send him right back onto the ground.

This little witch captivated him far more than any faerie ever had. It wasn't her lack of face, or even her "glowing" personality, but the inner strength he sensed inside her. She was made of steel and vinegar and, somehow, he found that wildly appealing.

She called out from the water's edge, "Is the offer of a bird still there?"

"You're too late." He crossed his arms behind his head and relaxed on the ground. "You insulted me. Now you can find your own bird."

Muttered curses magnified by the water reached his ears. Bran grinned and let his eyes drift shut. If she wanted to do all the work, then she could. She'd admit her interest soon anyway. He'd make sure of it.

Aisling finished the final touches in her circle of runes with a flourish that was unnecessary but satisfying. If the Unseelie didn't think she could perform magic as well as one of the Fae, then she would show him what a witch was capable of. And this was by far her best spell.

A circle of runes marked the dirt near the rushing water. It was a dangerous place to set it up but would keep the portal open for as long as possible. Streams negated magic, and that power would protect it from anyone tampering with her spell.

She dusted her hands off on the Unseelie's stolen pants and nodded. "That'll do."

Lorcan stretched his paws on the ground, arching his back with his butt in the air. "It's done?"

"As done as it'll ever be. It won't cut us in half at least."

The Unseelie stirred from his spot in the shade. "Was that ever a worry?"

"It's always a worry with a portal. If they close too early" — she slapped her hands together — "smooshed."

"Are you trying to be unsettling?"

She arched her brow. "Are you unsettled?"

He sat up and ran a hand through his hair. One side was adorably ruffled and sticking up in all directions. The other was darkened by the faint growth of fine, downy feathers.

She wanted to touch them. She curled her fingers into her palm as she told herself she would never do so. Touching him wasn't an option. It didn't matter the mere brush of his fingers had made her knees weak. She couldn't let him know he plagued her thoughts.

Though it was entirely possible he already knew. Her cheeks heated with the memory of his husky voice asking her if she was blushing.

Damned man had no right to make her feel like this. He shouldn't be able to tread where no man had before.

Aisling huffed out an angry breath and turned on her heel. "Lorcan, did you get that grouse?"

91

"I got a pheasant."

"Close enough." She held out her hand. "Give it here."

Instead of jumping to place it in her hand like she expected, he laid it at her feet, wrinkled his nose, and left to sit by the Unseelie. "You're being too bossy."

"I'm trying to concentrate on opening the portal and keeping us all alive."

"You're showing off. And I don't appreciate being treated like a familiar."

She gaped at him, eyes wide. "You *are* a familiar."

"No, I am a witch trapped in a cat's body. That doesn't make me an animal." He flicked his tail. "Open the portal already, would you?"

Aisling angrily sighed and grabbed the pheasant from the ground. "What is with men?"

"Maybe if you were a little nicer, we would be, too!" Lorcan called out.

The Unseelie rolled to his feet. "I'd like to second that."

"I am nice!"

He reached her and ran a hand down her shoulder as he passed. She twitched her arm away.

"No, witch, you aren't." He chuckled. "But I kind of like that about you."

She didn't want to ponder why those words made her stomach clench. He wasn't all that attractive, not with those feathers on his face and that eye that never stopped moving. Sure, he was tall, lithe, pretty in a way that was almost feminine if he didn't look like he might attack her at any moment. But none of that made him *attractive*.

A voice in her head laughed.

Aisling had never been able to lie to herself. There was always some bell in her head that rang loud and clear. The Unseelie was growing on her even though she didn't want him to.

His laughter held the slightest hint of cruelty. He moved as if he were preventing himself from flying into a rage or backing her against the nearest tree. And he stared at her with a gaze so hot she could feel the flames again. Only this time, she didn't mind the heat.

Foolish, distracting thoughts. She shook her head, tightened her grip on the pheasant's neck, and marched toward the rune circle with renewed purpose. She'd build the walls around herself so tall he wouldn't be able to break through. Fraternizing with a faerie never ended well. She needed to guard herself.

Aisling checked the runes one last time and then held out the bird. Thankfully, it was already dead. Lorcan knew how little she enjoyed killing an animal for magic. It was necessary, but always felt wrong.

"Open portal, hear my call. Open swift and smooth, let us not fall."

She opened her hands and let the wound on the bird's neck open. Blood splashed on the runes that began to glow a sickly red.

It wasn't the same spell she'd used months ago. That one required a faerie to assist, and though the red-headed lass hadn't realized it, Aisling knew she had faerie in her. This spell was for humans alone.

The ground fell out of her circle, and a thick substance took its place. It moved like water, but it wasn't. Sticky and viscous, the magic that would transport them was unlike anything she'd ever seen before. The previous portal was blue and shimmered with faerie magic. This was blood red and entirely human.

Aisling chewed her lip and placed her hands on her hips. "There's the portal."

"*That* is the portal?"

She glanced over her shoulder at the Unseelie who stared at her creation dubiously. "Do you have a problem with it?"

"It hardly looks safe."

"Portals aren't safe. If you want safe, go find a faerie-created one. We're sneaking into the Otherworld. It's not that easy."

"I don't need to sneak into my own home, and I don't care who knows I've passed. I can go through a faerie-made portal and not risk my neck."

"But I can't." She hesitated, staring at the portal as if it might bite her.

"What is it?" He stepped so close she could feel the heat of his chest against her back. "Are you frightened of your own spell?"

She swallowed, staring at the red mass of liquid. Memories plagued her of an ancient woman smiling at her with a warning on her lips. "My grandmother always said everything would change if I went to the Otherworld. She warned me against ever stepping foot in these forbidden lands."

"You live with another witch stuck in the form of a cat. You beg for scraps because no one pays you for your services. And the townsfolk tried to burn you alive. Would change really be so bad?"

He had a point.

What did this life give her? She had free reign to perform whatever magic she wanted, but the shackles of human knowledge chained her. They couldn't understand her desire to create, give life, use magic wherever she went without guilt or fear.

The Otherworld was filled with people who used magic. They weren't like her, but no one could see her face. Was it really all that dangerous?

Her grandmother would say yes. She'd never told Aisling what would happen if she went there. She only said time and time again that her life would change forever.

Aisling blew out a breath and nodded. "You're right."

"No reason for hesitation."

"Not at all."

"Just jump right through that portal, and we'll break this binding curse."

"All I have to do is jump."

The Unseelie scratched the ground with a talon. "You aren't jumping."

"Shouldn't you go first?" She looked over her shoulder at him. "I've never been to the Otherworld. Who knows what might be waiting for us?"

"Where did you put the portal?"

She shrugged. "Wherever there was a spot for it. Somewhere in Unseelie, considering that's where you wanted to go."

Aisling watched him swear, grumble, and then turn toward the portal with a livid expression.

"Unseelie isn't a safe place. You can't put us just *anywhere*."

"Well, that's what I did."

"It's a foolish decision, although I suppose I should have expected it to come from a witch who curses people without discretion." He paused at the edge of the portal and pointed at her. "You follow me in the next few heartbeats or we're both dead. Got it?"

"Painfully."

"Good."

He stepped forward and the red liquid laced up his legs. Tendrils pulled down on the fabric folds of his clothing. The last thing she heard was his cry of disgust before he was sucked down into the writhing mass.

Aisling glanced down at Lorcan. "No time to hesitate."

"It has to be better than death, right?"

She wasn't so certain of that. Still, she swung the Unseelie's pack onto her back, held her breath, and jumped through the portal.

CHAPTER 4

THE BLOOD OF A DEAD GOD

Aisling opened her mouth in a silent scream as the portal hurtled her between worlds. The red fluid squeezed, wrapping around her ribs and chest like a snake tightly coiling. She couldn't breathe, think, exist in this pulsating pain.

She tried to call out for Lorcan but couldn't force sound through her throat. He had to be here with her. He had to make it because he was the only thing she had left. Aisling tried to struggle against the cords of magic, but it only made the vise around her chest tighten even further.

And then all pain disappeared as she was spit out onto the ground.

Coughing, she rid her body of the lingering magic that stuck to her. The muck slid back toward the open portal in a sluggish crawl.

It spat a furred body at her that she caught against her chest. Lorcan scratched wildly, hissing and cursing magic for all he was worth.

"Shhh" she soothed. "We survived it Lorcan. Enough."

"Get off me!"

"Stop trying to run. We don't know where we are."

"Let go!"

The Unseelie's raspy voice broke through their argument. "I'd let the cat go if I were you, witch."

"He's going to run off and we'll never find him again, *Unseelie*."

"I can feel every scratch he's opening up on your body, and I don't appreciate the annoyance. Let him go, now." The steel in his voice warned he was about to get angry.

Considering they were in the Otherworld, she had no idea what he could do. Were faeries more powerful here? She was loathe to find out.

She released her grip on Lorcan, who took off through the thicket like something had caught his tail on fire. Glowering, she stared up at the Unseelie even though he couldn't see her glare.

"See?" she snapped. "Now he's gone, and we have to wait for him to find us."

"I think he'll catch up."

"I'm not leaving him here."

"Would you stop talking for a moment, witch, and look around you? You're in the Otherworld for the first time. Enjoy it."

She bristled at his tone, but curiosity got the better of her. Sighing, she glanced around, and the sight of the Otherworld stole her breath away.

Trees with trunks wider than houses grew tall and strong. Their branches were not the tangled mess of twigs she knew, but instead grew in recognizable patterns. Branches formed into outlines of flowers, leaves, and tiny creatures. Leaves burst throughout the patterns, giving the animals furry outlines and the plants a lifelike quality.

Under her hands, the earth was soft and loamy. She dug her fingers into the moss and gasped as it released a puff of sweet pollen into the air.

Everything was so *green*. It stung her eyes until they watered. A spear of light illuminated the forest while golden orbs danced in its light amidst dust and magic. Moss covered the ground, stretched up the trees like a crop of emeralds. Dew drops glittered like pearls strewn across the ground and trees.

"Oh," she whispered in awe.

"What do you think of my home, witch?"

"It's almost impossible to describe."

He knelt in front of her, blocking her view of the exquisite forest. Air whooshed from her lungs as she looked upon him in a new light. Everything about the Unseelie fit in this wild place. Tinged with the colors of growing things, his unusual hair fluttered in the slight breeze. Spiraled branches outlined his head like the horns of a god.

Above all else, he held himself with a confidence that surpassed anything she had seen before. He held himself like a lord of man, like a champion, like… Her mouth gaped open.

Like a king.

"Who are you?" she quietly asked.

"I am known by many names. But here, they call me Prince of the Unseelie Court, the Lord of Darkness, Heir to the Kingdoms of Night."

Her fingertips went numb. "You're…you're a royal?"

"If you want to call it that." He reached out as if he wanted to touch her cheek, his hand hovering between them. "My brothers are first in line. It's unlikely I'll ever be king."

King? King of the Unseelie court? She couldn't comprehend what he was telling her.

"So you mean to tell me I cast a binding curse on not just any Tuatha de Danann, which is bad enough, but on an heir to the Unseelie throne?"

"You are correct."

Aisling smacked his hand out of the air and shrieked, "Why didn't you tell me?"

She was a dead woman walking then, because the Unseelie wouldn't take it well that she'd essentially killed their son. Why had she come here? Grandmother was right, and everything was going to change because she wasn't going to be breathing by tomorrow morning.

"Why would I have told you?" Laughter lightened his voice.

"Are you kidding me?" She shoved his shoulders with both hands. He barely moved, so she did it again, grunting as she struck him. "You've killed me, you ridiculous man! I cursed an *Unseelie prince.*"

"I told you it surprised me." He obliged and let her shove him onto his rump. "No one has ever dared to curse me before."

"With good reason! They'd have the entire Unseelie court hunting them down." She pulled at her hair. "Oh gods, I'm going to have to go into hiding. I never should have let you talk me into coming here. Death would be better than what the Unseelie will do to me."

"No one is going to hunt you down."

"I cursed a *royal.* Of course, they're going to hunt me down! An eye for an eye, a heart for a heart."

"They're not going to seek retribution." He stood, wiping dirt off his backside.

She had to hide. She had to run, although she didn't know where to go in these cursed lands. The portal wasn't an option. As soon as she stepped through, their binding curse would be severed, and they both would die.

Was that better? Aisling didn't know. Living was the ideal solution, but was it living if the Unseelie Fae were pulling her apart bit by bit?

"Witch."

"Stop talking, I'm trying to figure out how to keep myself alive."

"Witch!" He stepped in front of her and pulled her hands from her hair. "Stop it. I'm not going to let anyone hurt you."

She froze, staring up at him. "Why would you say that?"

"You're going to help me break the curse, aren't you? That's enough to make amends."

"That's not the Unseelie way."

He arched a brow, the raven eye fixated on her. She realized it was staring directly into her gaze. "What do you know of the Unseelie way?"

"Enough to know that it goes against your rules."

"We have no rules, love. That's why we're Unseelie." The Unseelie gave her a grin that set a fire burning deep in her belly, turned on his heel, and walked away.

She was stunned. He wasn't going to let anyone hurt her? He was going against everything he was, everything his people were, just to make a point? She knew faeries liked to play with humans, but what was the point of this?

"Are you whistling?" she called after him.

"Do keep up, witch. We're in the Otherworld after all."

He had a point.

She sighed and glanced back at the portal, her last moment to decide if she wanted to make a break for it or decide he wasn't lying to her.

Aisling shrugged and started after him. Faeries couldn't lie, and if he was twisting his words, then he was fantastic at it. This was a rare opportunity, and she planned to fight tooth and nail to make certain it didn't end with her head separated from her body.

The brush cracked and shook and then a furry, black body burst out of the brambles and raced through the forest after the Unseelie. Lorcan bounded across emerald green moss, launched himself off the side of a trunk, gracefully arched in the air before he landed on the pads of his feet.

"Aisling, you're too slow," he shouted.

"Are you happy to be here?"

"Of course. It's the Otherworld, you foolish girl!"

Even her "not" familiar liked this place more than the human world. Shouldering the weight of the Unseelie's pack, she shook her head and started after them, taking her time.

Thankfully, there was still human food left. It wouldn't sustain her for a long time, but she wasn't going to touch anything in the Otherworld until she was certain she could return to the human realm. The legends all said a person who ate of faerie food or drank faerie wine would be stuck here forever.

It wouldn't be the worst place to be stuck. She reached out and touched a tree, marveling at the silver bark. Even the plants were a hundred times more elegant than those she had grown up with. Leaves fell in slow motion, tree trunks looked like molten silver, and roots poked through the ground, curled in spiral patterns.

How was it possible for a place to be so beautiful and yet so dangerous?

She followed the Unseelie for an entire cycle of the sun. She counted their steps at times, but lost track of the numbers as soon as something magical crossed their path.

They passed through a part of the forest darkened by a canopy so thick no light broke through the trees. She hopped over a log and gasped when a creature raised a horned head. Its legs were that of a goat, its face sloped with a flattened nose. Twin ram horns grew out of its skull and circular tattoos swirled over its cheeks.

The faerie bowed its head, sagely nodding in her direction. She saw its overly large eyes widen when it realized it couldn't see her face.

They burst from the darkness and followed a river snaking through the forest. The trees were larger here, the size of a castle in width, but short and stout. Their branches were twisted into pathways where faeries walked across the twined wood. The faeries captivated her with their odd forms, their beautiful faces, and the grace with which they moved.

The Unseelie reached into his pack and pulled out a cloak. He wrapped it around her shoulders with a curt nod. "Best not to attract attention."

Aisling pulled the hood of the cloak low over her face. The last thing she needed was for someone to question why they couldn't see her face. There wasn't a very good answer.

A woman toiled in her garden, gently fanning her lettuce

with giant butterfly wings. A man walked past them with pointed ears and mushrooms growing from his shoulders. Over and over again, new and impossible features filled her senses until she was near to bursting.

Aisling reached forward and tugged the Unseelie's sleeves. "Are they all like this?"

"All?" He glanced over his shoulder with an unreadable expression. "This is the Unseelie court, witch. Only the ugly and deformed live here."

Her jaw fell open as he walked away from her. Ugly? Deformed?

She raced to catch up to him, feet nimble as she ran over tree roots and fallen stumps. "Ugly? But these creatures are the most beautiful things I've ever seen!"

"Tell that to the Seelie court."

"But I thought—" She paused as a lumbering beast walked past them. "My grandmother always said that Seelie or Unseelie was a choice."

"Sometimes. Other times, a creature doesn't fit in with what the Seelie court deems appropriate." He rolled his eyes, the raven eye continuing to roll when the other stopped. "Half the Unseelie are here because they aren't beautiful enough. The other half degraded when they stopped following the Seelie court's rigorous rules and did what they wanted."

Aisling furrowed her brow and thought about those implications. The Seelie court was rumored to be filled with the most beautiful creatures to ever live. It made sense they would condemn those who did not fit into their idea of beauty. But why? What was the point?

"Unseelie…" she began.

"I'm not explaining it any further, witch. Keep your attention on your feet until we get through this part of the forest."

When she stopped, Lorcan wound through her legs. He looked up at her with dilated eyes. "He's probably right. There's too many people who could overhear what we're talking about."

She shook her head. "I don't like it. He's hiding something."

"Not everyone is trying to pull the wool over your eyes." He flicked his tail. "If you loosened up a bit, you might see that."

"You've told me that a thousand times, and I'm still the same person I was years ago."

"Don't you think that might be the problem?"

Aisling frowned and called after him, "This isn't about me!"

The small faerie hovels fell away behind them, and the sound of the forest filled her ears. Birds didn't chirp here; they *sang*. Their voices lifted up like a choir. She found her steps skipping to mimic the song.

Why hadn't she come to the Otherworld before when she'd opened the portal for the redheaded woman? It was marvelous and far more than she had ever expected from a place rumored to be cursed.

The sun dipped below the horizon, pink and vibrant red filtering through the canopy. Each tree shifted from summer to autumn. A few leaves fell around her, and Aisling gasped as branches coiled in on themselves.

"What is happening?" she asked.

"It's night," the Unseelie replied. "They're going to sleep."

"They sleep?"

"Everything is more alive in the Otherworld than it is in the human realm. Trees are just as aware as you or I."

Aisling reached out and slid her hand along the bark of a particularly large tree. "Thank you for not squashing me with a root."

A shimmering fall of leaves rained down on her head. Glowering, she picked leaves out of her hair while the Unseelie burst into laughter.

"It's not funny," she grumbled.

"Yes, it is. The trees are laughing at you, witch. They don't mean any harm."

Laughing? The branches were shivering, but she had thought they were annoyed, not laughing. She backed away from the tree slowly, then raced after Lorcan and the Unseelie. The sound of their chuckles filled the air and gave her an easy trail to track.

She found them setting up camp for the night in a valley between roots thicker than people. Hand over feet, she clambered down into the hollow and sat down hard on her rump.

"Fire?" she asked.

"In a forest of trees?" Bran chuckled.

"Good point." Unnerved, she patted the nearest root. "I wasn't thinking. Not particularly friendly to suggest burning your castoffs, is it?"

A sudden burst of light flared in the center of the hollow. Flinching back, she backed against a root. Blue flames crackled bright as a bonfire and nearly as tall.

"I thought you said no fire?" she cried out.

"Faerie fire is different. It doesn't burn." Flames danced in his eyes that sparkled with humor.

"You enjoy unsettling me, Unseelie."

"A little too much." He leaned back against a root nearby, crossed his legs at the ankles, and wiggled to wedge himself farther into the ground. "Are you hungry?"

"I'm not eating faerie food if that's what you're offering."

He waved a hand in the air, a perfect apple forming in his palm. "Shame. Faerie food is far superior than human food."

"Of course, it is. Just like faeries are superior to humans, is that it?"

He took a large bite of the apple, juice dribbling down his chin. "I don't give your intelligence enough credit. You're catching on quick, witch."

"Don't make me curse you again."

"I'd like to see you try while we're here."

It was the second time he'd suggested he was stronger in the Otherworld. Aisling toyed with a loose thread on his stolen shirt and licked her lips. "Is faerie magic stronger here?"

"In a way." He stared up at the sky, lost in his own thoughts. "The Tuatha de Danann made this place as a haven for the Fae. We're more powerful because this is a safe place for us. Happy, content people perform magic far better than those who are distracted by ill thoughts."

Her expression fell. Of course, magic was stronger in people whose souls were centered. Spells required concentration, and natural magic like the faeries performed required more than just knowledge. It was a powerful and beautiful thing when practiced correctly.

Aisling had never managed such magic.

The Unseelie studied her, flames dancing in his eyes again. "Have you ever tried faerie magic?"

"Many times."

"Never succeeded, I'm assuming."

"Why would you assume that?" She stuffed his pack in the roots behind her head, stealing the only cushion they had.

"Because you looked like I kicked a puppy in front of you when I said it."

"I don't even like puppies. I prefer cats." Aisling punched the pack.

"Why are you always so abrasive?"

She frowned, chewing her lip and letting the heat of the fire warm her back. "It's just my winning personality."

"No, don't try to deflect it. I'm genuinely curious, witch. Just what has made you push people away like you do?"

She didn't want to tell him. Not because she didn't like to talk about it; the past was in the past. It had shaped her strangely, but she was dealing with it. She didn't want to tell him because her history felt like a weakness, and he would look down on her.

Aisling punched the pack one more time for good measure. "History. Lorcan raised me. He found me in the woods when I was little, a screaming child left to die. It's just been him and me for a long time."

"Lorcan raised you?" He looked at the cat. "Really? A cat?"

The subject of interest yawned, bright white teeth flashing in the light of faerie fire. "I wasn't a cat then, nitwit."

"So Lorcan shifted...when?"

Aisling spun around and wiggled into the tree roots. "The

first time a pack of wolves, the sorry villagers, attacked me. Lorcan stepped in front of an arrow and shifted to stay alive."

The Unseelie rubbed his chest. He said nothing, but she knew what he was thinking. They were both marked by her in some fashion. His starburst matched Lorcan's. Each was a sign she harmed those who stayed around her. Too bad she refused to take responsibility for either of their choices. Lorcan didn't have to save her, and the Unseelie didn't have to stay to watch her burn. They were both responsible for their own mistakes.

"So you've been alone your entire life," the Unseelie murmured.

"Hey!" Lorcan grunted from his side of the fire. "I was there."

"As a cat."

"Still a person."

"But not someone who could bandage her scraped knees, provide her food, help her fix a shelter should the winds blow."

Aisling snorted. "Even when he was a person, Lorcan made me do all that."

"It was character building."

"You were lazy as a human," she corrected. "A cat was a well-chosen form."

"It's not a choice." Lorcan rolled onto his back, all four feet in the air and bottom turned toward the fire. "Witches turn into cats. We have nine lives."

Aisling touched her fingers to the eyes on her palms. Witches may have nine lives, but she did not. When she was young and the eyes were new, she had tried to skin them from her hands. The knife cut into her flesh too easily for her to hesitate. Lorcan had found her bleeding out on the floor with the eyes still burned into the meaty, exposed muscles.

She'd caught a fever and lay in bed for months while fighting the infection. She even died a few times, only to come back after Lorcan shocked her with a bolt of magic. No catlike form had saved her.

At first, she thought it was because she didn't understand the magic. But then Lorcan had explained to her she wasn't really a witch, and her entire world had shifted.

The Unseelie coughed, looking pointedly at her fingers, tracing the outline of the eyes in the air with his hands. "And those?"

She held her hands out, palms exposed to the fire. "These are my chains."

"Excuse me?"

Lorcan twitched his tail and dramatically sighed. "The visible evidence of her curse."

"Those are what make your face invisible to me?" The Unseelie stood and then quickly moved across the small hollow to kneel in front of her. He didn't touch her hands but tilted his head from side to side as he inspected them. "I don't recognize this kind of magic."

"That's because it's entirely original magic." She was ridiculously proud to wear proof of it, although she despised the curse. "The eyes channel my power through the spell that hides my face. The blackened tips are the shackles that prevent it from being broken."

"All spells can be broken."

"Which is precisely why my grandmother brought me all those faerie spell books. I've spent my entire life searching for a way to break this curse. From the first moment I saw a faerie, I knew I wanted to see and be seen by your kind for the rest of my life."

He looked at her with something important in his eyes. Some unspoken promise she knew would make the wall around her heart crack.

Aisling cleared her throat. "It's a shame I didn't know you back then. I might not have wasted so much time."

"Ah, there's the reaction I expected," he muttered. He reached forward, his hand hovering so close to her cheek she could feel his warmth. "Does the spell prevent anyone from touching your face?"

Aisling didn't know. A faerie had never expressed interest in touching her, let alone something so intimate.

She resisted the urge to gnaw on her lip, glad to know he couldn't see her facial expressions. He would notice how uncomfortable she was, but also how intrigued. Aisling was rarely the recipient of kindness, affection, or any kind of regard.

The mere thought of someone touching her face made her heart race. It was overwhelming, perhaps a little too much with the fire warm against her toes and the light casting the hollow in an icy glow.

"What about you?" she asked, ignoring his question.

"People can touch my face."

"No, I mean your life. You know how I grew up, and I blame my personality entirely on that. Now, it's your turn."

He blew out a breath and dropped his hand. Aisling mourned the loss of opportunity, but also relaxed. Her anxiety disappeared when the subject shifted to the strange man who wanted to touch her.

"I am the youngest son of the Unseelie king and queen. As

such, I am the least important child they have. I was allowed to do whatever I wished and had the ideal Unseelie childhood."

"Is that so?" she mused. "Seems to me if you were so happy with your life, you would have stayed in your castle rather than spending your time kidnapping a witch."

"I didn't kidnap you. You *cursed* me."

"You still brought me here."

"Because I want to break the curse! Do you think I brought you here for another reason?" He snorted. "You give yourself too much credit."

"I'm right. That's why you're getting so upset, isn't it? You weren't happy here."

She leaned forward, peering into his eyes for any hint of emotion. The raven eye rotated back and forth, refusing to meet her gaze. A thought formed in Aisling's mind, and she gasped.

"Your eye..." she began.

"I don't talk about it."

"It can see me, can't it?"

He stared at her, his jaw open and both eyes wide. "It's still my eye. I would have mentioned it if I could see you."

"I'm not talking to you. I'm talking to that" —she pointed to his eye— "because it *can* see me. I didn't realize it until now, but it reacts. It won't meet my gaze, and you've been able to discern my emotions too easily. In some way, you can actually see me."

He hesitated then admitted, "In a sense. The other eye is better at predicting than seeing through curses. I still can't see your face. It's more I can see a semblance of something. Emotion, thought, what makes you *you* rather than just reading an expression."

112

"Have you always been able to do that?"

"Since I was a child. It was the imperfection my parents were most proud of, considering I turned out a little too normal for their liking."

For the first time, she didn't want to insult him. Aisling knew what it was like to be different and the pain it could cause. But in her eyes, he was plenty strange and entirely abnormal.

She tried to lighten the mood by snorting. "What would be their perfect child then? A small furry creature that races through the halls of the castle while setting things on fire with its feet?"

"That is an amusing image, but no. My family is…" He ran a hand over the feathered side of his head and sighed. "Strange is perhaps the best way to say it. Intimidating, frightening to humans…I've even heard them described as nightmares."

She furrowed her brows. "Why is that something to be proud of? Or to aspire to?"

"The Unseelie pride themselves on the absence of beauty. Where the Seelie prefer to adhere to strict rules, we enjoy living our lives as we wish. With both choices comes the temptations of cruelty, pride, and self-righteousness. Neither court has shaken the chains of the old ways from their shoulders." He leaned away from her but sat himself in a furrow much closer to her. "Although the courts are constantly shifting. Change might happen now."

She stared into the flames with this new knowledge dancing in her mind. She'd never known the courts were quite so volatile. The legends made them seem pristine, led by faeries who had learned the art of politics long ago.

From what he said, they weren't quite like that. He

condemned faeries for their flaws and actions. What would he say if she told him more about her own people? About the small skirmishes, the battles, the wars?

Considering his opinion of humans, he probably knew all the stories already.

She shrugged her shoulders. "Politics. I've never been able to understand them."

"You and me both."

Aisling turned onto her side, away from the fire and the confusing faerie who made her senses come alive. She didn't want to give him layers. He was an annoyance, nothing more, nothing less.

He thought of her as a witch, as a creature that was a means to an end. The binding curse was why he was sticking around, and she didn't have any reason to believe otherwise.

She tucked a hand underneath her head and closed her eyes. There was more to the faerie than she wanted to admit, and that made her thoroughly uncomfortable.

They walked for another three days before the Unseelie held up his hand and stopped them. Aisling watched his face with rapt attention as he cleared his throat.

"Not much farther now. We should leave the pack here. We'll return for it later."

"Why?" she asked. But she still removed it without

hesitation.

"I haven't been entirely truthful with you, witch. This is a very dangerous place, and I cannot promise either of us will make it out alive."

Something in her cheered. Aisling could feel he was hiding something, and the sensation of being right was one worthy of celebrating. Somehow, it felt wrong to rub it in his face since he tried so hard to be secretive.

So, she pondered the words and shrugged. "If one of us dies, so does the other. It means we'll be all the more careful in taking care of ourselves. Sounds like a good deal to me."

His gaze cut toward her, fierce and piercing. "You aren't afraid of dying?"

"I've never been afraid of death. We're old friends, he and I." Aisling placed the pack underneath a pile of leaves at the base of a silver tree. "Shall we?"

"Witch—"

"Save it for when we return." She gave him a smile she hoped wasn't as shaky as she felt.

"You are the strangest person I've ever met," he said. He opened his mouth as more words hung at the edge of his tongue, then shook his head and changed the subject. "We walk through a portal in the trunk of a tree. This god is sacred, unnamed, and ancient. He should be alone and unarmed."

"I thought you said he was dead."

The Unseelie licked his lips. "In a sense."

Aisling groaned and stomped forward. "Blasted faeries and their twisting of the truth. If you'd just *told* me, I might have been able to help."

"I couldn't tell you the entire truth of it."

"Couldn't, wouldn't, or shouldn't?" she tossed the words over her shoulder. "All of it's the same. You endanger this entire mission by not telling me the whole of it."

"Even if I had told you, you wouldn't be prepared for what we're about to face."

"You underestimate me."

Blasted man and his ridiculous ideals. He should have told her everything there was to know about this entire ordeal. The binding curse affected her too, no matter that he felt it was a curse on him alone.

She didn't want to be tied to someone else. She wanted to be free, as she was used to. Untethered, Aisling could travel wherever she wished, disappear into the world whenever she chose. And now?

Now she was stuck with a foolish man who hid the truth so she wasn't frightened.

She slapped a branch out of her way. Trees groaned around her, tentatively tucking their branches closer to their bodies.

The path merged into a rolling hill with a single tree on the highest peak. She stalked toward it, all while grumbling about men and their flaws. Neither the Unseelie nor Lorcan stood in her way.

Perhaps the men were more intelligent than she gave them credit for. She likely would have chewed on them if they dared to step in front of her.

Aisling found herself lost in her thoughts until she paused in front of the tree. It wavered around the edges as though it wasn't really there. Narrowing her eyes, she stepped closer. "Well," she muttered, "that's a bad omen."

She heard the soft steps of padded feet, followed by the

faerie's careless steps. They stopped just behind her and stared up at the tree as well.

Lorcan audibly swallowed. "Is that what I think it is?"

Aisling nodded. "Looks like."

The Unseelie stepped forward, his hand hovering over her shoulder as if he wanted to touch her. "What is it?"

"A hanging tree."

For a moment, she saw hundreds of bodies swaying in the breeze. Tied at their necks, they all stared at her with hollowed expressions. They screamed she wasn't one of them, that she would never be accepted within their coven, that she was little more than an unwanted mistake.

Aisling shivered. "Trees like this only form when dark deeds are performed over and over again. They're a rift, in a sense. They appear in every dimension in the same place."

They were a sign of bad tidings for any who walked by their dark branches. Wind whistled through them, rattling dead limbs as the lingering magic reached out for her. The tree desired more death, for that was what nourished its roots and helped it grow.

"We don't have witches here," the Unseelie said.

She gulped. "It doesn't matter. Dark magic like this always finds someone to hang."

With fear settling on her shoulders like a well-worn cloak, she rounded the thick trunk. A shimmering curtain of darkness split the trunk open on the other side. It looked like a woman parting her skirts for a lover, but Aisling knew better.

Smooth wood framed the portal, the bark split open by water-worn pieces that drifted into ash where the portal touched it. Dark webs of power blanketed the beyond from view.

"Just walk through it?" she asked.

"That should do."

"Lorcan? Stay here."

The cat spluttered. "How dare you! I might be of assistance. You have no idea what a cat can do that humans are incapable of—"

"Lorcan," Aisling interrupted. "I know you don't want to go. Stay here and patch either of us up if we make it back."

Her constant companion was anything other than brave. He had never lived a life of danger, never wanted to even though he practiced magic. Quiet happiness and a warm fire was the only thing he'd ever asked for. She wouldn't drag him into the Unseelie's half-brained plan because of her mistakes.

"Fine," he grumbled. "But be careful. I'm partial to your head."

The Unseelie's attention whipped toward the cat. "You can see her?"

"It stands to reason that he'd be able to," she replied with a quiet cough. "He's not Fae."

His brows drew down severely, and he jabbed the air in front of her with a curved finger. "When we return, we're talking about this curse of yours in more detail."

"No, we aren't."

"Don't argue with me, witch. We're stuck together until this binding curse is broken. Your curse is just as bad."

"It isn't." She snorted. "I'll tell you mine if you tell me yours." She stared pointedly at his raven eye until he gave in and looked away. The golden gaze did not stray from hers, however, and she met its intensity with her own. "To our death then?" she quipped.

"Don't *say* it like that."

Rolling her eyes, Aisling stalked toward the portal, shook off the tingling feelings in her fingers, and stepped through.

She had expected a tunnel or a gateway, but she hadn't expected to find herself in a cave so large she couldn't see the top. Bats whispered through the air, and small creatures skittered away from her feet.

Her lungs filled with ancient air. Only a few had breathed it before her, but she knew what they smelled like. Every person who walked these steps had left a perfume in their absence. Sandalwood, lavender, and the faintest scent of moss.

Her eyes adjusted to the dark and drank in the thick fog rolling through the sudden silence. She'd only experienced such stillness once in her life. Aisling had wandered deep into the belly of a crypt. Thirty feet of earth piled above her, and the silence was thicker than water. The same as before, all she could hear now was her own heartbeat.

For a witch who practiced black magic, Aisling hated the dark.

The portal tightened behind her, its drum-like surface emitting a faint thrum as the Unseelie stepped through. The raven eye wildly rotated to take in every detail in the dim lighting.

He froze for a moment, then lurched forward. His hand met her shoulder and forced her to her knees behind a boulder. The gentle touch on her shoulder burned.

Heat spread from her toes to her cheeks. He was *touching* her, and although he'd done it before, this time was voluntary, in an effort to keep her safe.

He swore, the colorful language breaking through her thoughts. Aisling curled her lip to the side. "Those aren't ones I've heard before."

"That's because they aren't in your language. Would you take this seriously?"

"I am."

She wasn't. How was she supposed to take anything seriously when he was so animated, his hand still pressed against her shoulder, and they were risking their lives? Taking it seriously only meant she would have to acknowledge the fear that traced cold fingertips down the back of her neck. She didn't want to feel that.

"Look." He reached out blindly, his fingers finding her chin even though he couldn't see her face. She forced herself to freeze and allowed him to turn her head toward the center of the cave. "How did you not see them?"

"See who?" She peered through the darkness and mist, then shrugged. "I don't see anything."

He arched a brow. "Try again, witch."

Huffing out a breath, she squinted her eyes. Her grandmother's voice whispered in her ear, *"Look harder, Aisling. You can see through the veil like I can. You have to want it, child. Desire to see through what the faeries hide."*

The mist swirled, parted, and revealed what had gotten the Unseelie so riled up.

Ten men stood at attention in the center of the cave, although she wasn't certain she could call them men. They wore fabric draped around their hips, so golden it looked like liquid metal sliding down their bodies to the ground. Swords as tall as her were held loosely in their cupped hands, the pommels pressing against their bare chests.

Each of their faces was hidden by a golden mask. She could see the details from where her and the Unseelie crouched. Birds flew across the metal of one, another was covered in cobwebs that obscured an underwater scene. The masks seemed to depict elements, although she did not know of so many and couldn't guess what some of them were.

"Oh!" she gasped. "Well that's different."

As one, the golden men turned their faces toward the sound. Aisling's eyes widened and she ducked behind the rock.

The Unseelie met her gaze with a panicked one of his own. "That wasn't very bright," he scolded.

"Well, I never claimed to be. What do we do? I thought you said the god would be alone?"

"I thought he was!"

"He's not. Figure something else out, Unseelie."

He grunted. "Stop rushing me."

"I'm rushing you. They looked *right* at me. They know we're here." Aisling flinched at the sound of fabric sliding across the floor. "And now they're coming to see us, apparently."

"Shut up, witch."

"I'm thinking out loud."

"You're muttering and distracting me." He crouched, plunging his fingers into the dirt. "Gods save me from meddlesome women who don't have the ability to stay quiet. This was supposed to be a quick mission. Stealth was the key."

"Well, if you had told me, we could have gone through with that plan."

"Shut *up*, witch."

"If you say that one more time, I'm going to cut off your ear."

He glanced up and arched a brow. "That's your best threat?"

"You try living without an ear. And you can bet you'll remember me every time you look in a mirror. Hurry up, would you?"

The Unseelie lifted handfuls of dirt with a flourish, dark earth trickling to the ground. "Ah-hah!"

She pursed her lips. "You're going to throw dirt at them? We're a little old for that, don't you think?"

The red blush of color on his cheeks was thoroughly satisfying. It didn't matter that magical guards were bearing down on them. She'd managed to annoy him past the point of fear, and that had been her plan all along.

"Perfect," Aisling said. She spontaneously reached up and patted his cheek. "Good luck, I'll go get that blood."

"What? Witch, don't you move."

"It's cute how you think I can't take care of myself." She always had. From scraps with the village children to feeding herself at the early age of five, Aisling had always taken care of herself. If that meant stealing the blood from a god, then that was what she would do.

She darted around him and pressed the eyes of her palms together. Magic charged between them, heating her hands and spreading from her face down her body like a curtain drawn closed. Heavy magic pressed onto the top of her head, uncomfortable but not yet painful.

She'd have to see just how good the guards were at seeing through magic. Stepping around the stone, she took a deep breath and waved a hand.

They did not respond.

So they were some semblance of Fae, she mused. They couldn't see her face, which might be why they had moved closer in the first place. She was an oddity, and even more out of place than anyone else. But they also wouldn't be able to see her if the curse that hid her face spread over her entire body.

"Witch?" the Unseelie hissed. "I don't know what you did, but get the blood quick."

Quick wasn't going to be easy. Only half the guards had wandered toward the rock where the Unseelie still hid. The others were at attention with thick mist swirling behind them. She tried to peer through the strange, murky darkness to no avail.

Somewhere in that darkness, a god lay in wait.

"Hey!" the Unseelie shouted behind her.

The terrifying masks turned as one, all ten slowly converging on him. She turned just in time to see a wide smile break across the Unseelie's face.

"That's it, you louts. Move a little faster, would you? I'll be dead and rotten before you reach me." The guard nearest to him swung his sword. The Unseelie leapt back, the blade cutting through the air mere inches from his stomach. "Not bad, but you'll have to do better than that."

He flung dirt that burst into a swarm of beetles made of bright green leaves, obscuring him from sight. There must have been seeds in the earth, or one seed he managed to spread.

She pressed a hand to her chest and suppressed a sigh from escaping her lips. It was ridiculous to be so affected by a man who knew how to use magic. But as a beetle danced through

123

the air in front of her, one who wandered from the side of its brethren, she noted it even had leaf veins on its wings.

Now is not the time, she reminded herself.

It didn't matter he had created life with magic, with details so powerful they made her heart rattle the cage of her ribs, she had a job to do.

Blood of a dead god. Break the binding curse. Go home.

The thought wasn't as exciting as it originally was. She bit her lip and plunged through the thick fog.

Why wouldn't she want to break the binding curse? Her life was forfeit to whatever he wanted. If he wanted to throw his body into a pit of vipers, she would feel every bite before they each drew their last breath.

A trail of pain traveled from shoulder to shoulder. The thin line burned for a moment before dulling to an ache, which suggested he hadn't backed away quick enough. She wanted to shout for him to be a little more careful but didn't want to bring the guards to her side.

"Damned Unseelie," she whispered. Thankfully, the pain wasn't terrible enough to be fatal.

She beat back the fog, but it stuck to her. Tendrils hooked around her arms, trying to hold her in place. Aisling gritted her teeth and bared them in a grimace. "You will not take me. Let go."

They didn't listen. Instead, they coiled tighter until they were bands around her wrists and ankles. The fog quickly became a darker presence with a life of its own. She could almost see tall, lithe figures in the gray mist. They stood at a distance, never coming close enough for her to confirm they were there.

But she could feel them. Their magic was a living, breathing thing in the thick swirls of mist.

Another sharp sting bloomed on her shoulder, this time bisecting the previous slice. She didn't have much time left. The Unseelie was losing, or at least allowing himself to get cut, and if there were poison on those blades, then both of them were as good as lost.

"Enough," she growled.

Aisling lifted her hands with her palms bared to the figures. She felt the tattooed eyes blink, their magic coming alive and focusing their attention on whatever stood in her way. Magic built at her fingertips.

"Fire burn, blister, and sear. Make it so that they feel fear."

She couldn't see flames in her palms, but she could feel the heat waves wafting into the air. She released the balls of energy with a gasp. This magic didn't feel like hers, and yet it was as much a part of her as air.

Magic sliced through the fog and left a trail for her to follow. The thick swirls of white parted cleanly, as if she had cut through them with a knife.

A faint whine echoed throughout the cave, and then sudden silence. The guards had paused in their onslaught. She heard the Unseelie give a sudden shout of glee, and then a heavy thud echoed as something hit the ground.

"Get moving, witch!" he shouted. "I can't keep their attention for much longer!"

She didn't want to tell him that was because of her. He'd yell at her again, and she had too much on her mind to win an argument with him.

And she refused to lose even a single argument to the

insufferable man.

Sprinting forward, she thanked the gods the Unseelie had let her keep his clothes. Her skirt would have prevented her from running like this. She flew through the cave, arms pumping and feet pounding the ground.

The fabric sound of the golden guards marching forward paused. Aisling nearly lost her balance when the screeching sound of metal filled the caves. Their masks scraped as they tracked the sound of her movement, desperately needing oil but laden with dust and grime. Were they looking at her? The Unseelie gave another shout, and a metallic clang echoed through the cave.

"There," she muttered.

In the center of the cave, a small table rose out of earth and stone. Pillars surrounded it. They were anchored to the ceiling, crystalline structures pulsing with a darkened light that looked more magic than stone.

Perhaps that was how they held a god. How else would anyone capture a creature like that?

She slid to a halt behind the altar and crouched behind it. Out of breath, she took a moment to organize her thoughts. Blood of a god. She had nothing to put it in. "Bollocks," she muttered. Of all the things to think of, they couldn't have considered that?

Aisling glanced around for something that could hold liquid. A rock would do, anything really, but the ground was barren.

She grimaced. There were only a few ways to hold blood. In her palms, but considering the guards, that was a bad idea, or… She swallowed and licked her lips. The less desirable choice was the only option.

Swiping a hand over her mouth, she hoped the Unseelie's spell didn't require untainted blood.

Aisling peered over the altar. A body was laid out on top, made of stone, and so detailed it could only have been created by magic. She knew enough about curses to see the man for what he was.

He had not been a handsome god in life. Scars covered his face, his chest, even his legs. She could see every bit of him. They'd not taken the time to carve clothing onto the dead god. His brow was strong, his ears a little too large, and his mouth far too wide. But his chest was well formed, his hands strong, and she thought he had a kind look about him.

In her experience, the kindest-looking people could be the most dangerous.

She blew out a breath when she realized the next obstacle. He was a god made of stone. How was she supposed to cut his flesh?

There were a few spells she could use. One would destroy the entire stone structure, the other just him. Somehow, neither seem the right way to solve this.

She leaned over him with a pressed hand flat beside his head. "What are your secrets?" she whispered. "What am I supposed to do?"

A bright burst of heat speared her shoulder, an echo of pain slicing through the binding curse and causing her to cry out. This was no flesh wound. This was a magic blade sinking into his shoulder and pinning him to the ground. It was just above his heart. Not mortal, but a grave wound that could turn deadly in mere moments.

Heat blossomed on her shoulder and blood saturated her shirt.

"Bad enough it shows up on me, too," she gasped. "Unseelie, you should have been more careful."

Dizzy with pain, she pressed a hand to her shoulder and then to the chest of the dead god to steady herself. Blood would assist her magic, although she was so disoriented she couldn't find the words.

Air wheezed between the lips of the dead god. Her jaw dropped open, and she stared in shock as the stone around his mouth cracked. Fissures broke through the fine marble like cracks in clay. They traveled up his face, centering around his eyelids which opened to reveal a gaze filled with black.

She swallowed. "Welcome to the land of the living."

A small dimple appeared in the corner of his cheek, sending flakes of stone crumbling onto the altar. "That is the first time someone has greeted me thusly."

His voice was the sound of a mountain caving in on itself. It made her ears ache, and she heard an answering cry far away. Wincing, she pressed one hand to her ear.

"There's a first time for everything. Even for a god, I imagine."

He chuckled, the sound somehow worse than just his voice. "I am not usually amused when I am awakened."

"You haven't woken up with a pretty woman sitting on your lap in a long time then." Even through the pain, she managed to bat her lashes and hoped he wouldn't hear the sarcasm in her voice.

"You've got an impressive tongue for a creature so young."

"Flattery will get you everywhere, dead god."

"But not everywhere with you, changeling."

His words struck her in the chest with more force than the sword that had slid through the Unseelie's body. She gasped, flinching back as her gaze locked with his. She couldn't think, couldn't speak. All she could hear were the words echoing in her mind.

Changeling.

Stone shattered, and his arm lifted, his cold fingertips gently touching the side of her face. "Did you think you could remain hidden forever? That no one would ever see the woman beneath the facade?"

"How is this possible?"

"Magic cannot hide your face from a god." His thumb stroked just underneath her eye. "Your grandmother warned you that your life would change if you came here, and it will. Hiding your face won't save you."

"It's the only way to stay safe."

"In the human world, I would agree. But you are no longer in the human world. Here, you are far safer than you have ever been. You aren't a changeling here. You're just a faerie."

"Shhh." She pressed a bloodied finger to his lips. "Don't say it too loud. No one knows who I am, *what* I am. And I would like to keep it that way."

Swords cracked against each other, the echoing battle looming in the distance.

He licked away the blood and more stone fell away. She grimaced. Blood magic was dangerous, and giving such a precious gift to a creature like this was asking to be cursed.

Not that she could be cursed any worse than she already was. Binding curses signed away a person's life. This dead god couldn't hurt her more than she'd already hurt herself.

"What do you wish from me, changeling?" he asked.

"Why do you think I want anything?"

"The guards will not let me pass. Every few centuries someone is wily enough to break in, and every few millennia, someone is intelligent enough to figure out how to wake me. Each and every one has their reasons, but always because they want something."

She lifted a shoulder. "If you're all knowing, then you should know why I'm here."

"Ah, yes, the binding curse."

"I need to remove it."

He lifted a brow, cracking the stone on his forehead. "I fail to see how I can help."

"The Unseelie with me, the man now fighting the guards, knows a spell which can break the binding curse. It requires the blood of a dead god."

Her heart skipped a beat at his expression. It was a pitying look, and she expected him to say that the Unseelie was wrong. That the spell wouldn't do anything other than waste their time.

"In a sense, he is correct," he murmured.

Relief made her sag against his chest. The dull throb in her shoulder was more manageable now. Perhaps the Unseelie had time to cast a healing spell. Perhaps he was winning again, or he had left her in this cursed place alone.

The god shook his head. "But I do not believe that is why he is here, changeling girl. You forget you are dealing with faeries, and faeries are master manipulators. He wants something else, not just the binding curse to be unraveled."

"That's his business, not mine."

"Like you're here because you're finally taking steps towards your family?"

Her gaze narrowed. "You know nothing of my family."

"No, but I can look into your heart and know why you are here. Don't judge the Unseelie for twisting his words when you are doing the same."

Aisling wanted to shout at him. She wanted to scream he wasn't right, that he judged without reason or sense.

But he was right. She was using him just as he was using her. It wasn't fair that his deception stung so fiercely.

"I need your blood," she whispered, "and I'm afraid I can't wait much longer."

He searched her gaze for something Aisling couldn't comprehend. She waited, allowing him a moment, until he finally nodded. "There is a knife above my head. Take it and drive it through my heart."

"What? I can't do that. I just need blood. I don't need to *kill* you—"

"Changeling." He placed his hand over hers, their fingers laced together over his heart. "I am already dead. They plunged that dagger through my heart a hundred times so long ago the earth doesn't remember my name. Let my blood run out and take it for yourself. It is a gift."

The Unseelie shouted from beyond the mist, and she felt another spike of pain trail down the column of her back. She'd have a welt there, but he would bare a scar.

"I'm sorry," she whispered.

Lifting his hand, she pressed a kiss against his fingers in the only way she knew how to show respect. He was not a named god, but he was one she would forever remember.

Her fingers wrapped around the hilt of the stone blade, and he sighed in resignation. "Your admiration is a gift I had not thought to receive. I wish you well on your journey, changeling child."

Aisling wasted no time. She lifted the blade over her head and brought it down in the center of his chest. His breath wheezed out, slow and steady as though planned. His eyes and mouth closed, and the stone smoothed over his features once more.

"Goodbye," she said in quiet farewell.

Blood pooled around the knife. Carefully, she pulled the blade free from the stone sheath and watched as the wound healed. It filled up with stone, pushing out a small bit of blood that solidified in the center. A red gem, glimmering so brightly it seemed to have its own life, sat in the center of his chest.

Relief made her knees weak. She wasn't going to have to carry the blood in her mouth. Thank the gods for small gifts.

Aisling plucked the stone from its resting place and tucked it into the pocket of her stolen pants. Sharp edges dug into her thigh.

"Don't take any more blood," she grumbled. "I've already given you enough."

She heard the faintest chuckle in response, as if the dead god could still hear her.

She turned and bolted through the mist. It parted for her this time, perhaps reacting to the magic of its master held safely against her body. Mustering a spell felt like a stretch, so she wasted no time for the mist to change its mind.

Aisling burst through the other side of the fog and came to a stumbling halt. The Unseelie was alive, she would have felt his death, but she hadn't expected the carnage splattered across the cave floor and walls.

Only two guards remained alive, both pinned to the back wall of the cave with their own swords trapping them. The other eight were strewn about in bits and pieces. She noticed an arm near her foot and nudged it with a toe.

The Unseelie stood in the middle, covered in blood, chest heaving and eyes narrowed. He held one of the golden swords in his hand, stolen from a fallen guard. She'd heard stories of this happening before. The bloodlust faeries felt when in battle and their rage that tore through storm and stone.

Aisling cleared her throat. "Got it."

"What took you so long?" he growled deep in his throat.

"Oh, I'm sorry, was I supposed to rush cutting into a dead god's corpse?"

"When I'm battling all ten of his guards, yes, you're supposed to rush, you fool woman."

She ground her teeth together and gave him a curt nod. "The next time I'll make sure not to serve him tea and biscuits while you're murdering his guards. Are you quite finished arguing with me, or are you going to insist we stay here until you think you're right?"

"Get through the portal before I add you to the pile."

She smiled sweetly and cocked her hip. "Oh, Unseelie, I didn't know you were such a romantic. Dying with me all because you have such a *fat head*."

"Shut up, witch," he grumbled as he made his way toward the portal.

"You owe me an ear now."

In one swift, fluid movement, he leaned down and

133

snatched a piece of gristle from the floor. He tossed it over his shoulder for her to catch.

She snagged the object from the air and opened her palm to reveal an ear.

Aisling burst into laughter and let it fall back to the floor. "I *knew* you were a romantic!"

CHAPTER 5
DREAMS OF BLOOD

Aisling stumbled through the portal, magic clinging to her legs and trying to drag her back into the carnage left in the cave. Shaking off the sticky tendrils, she placed her hand on the hanging tree for balance.

Her head was swimming. Her eyes refused to focus on anything other than the ground, and her shoulder ached like mad. How did warriors do this? They went to battle day in, day out, for weeks on end. No wonder so many of them died.

The Unseelie began to pace away from her, but stumbled when pain blasted through their bodies. He reached out a hand that did not catch the tree and fell onto his side. The heavy thump echoed through Aisling, a mere pang when she knew it knocked the breath from his lungs.

"Stubborn man," she muttered under her breath. "I can help, you know."

"Yes, you could have. While I was fighting off those cursed things, you were taking your sweet time figuring out a puzzle."

"Would you stop arguing for a second and let me look at you?"

He rolled onto his hands and knees, glaring up at her from the ground. "Why are you so arrogant?"

Laughter burst out of her chest. "Oh, that's rich, coming from *you*."

"I'm fine."

"I can feel that you are not, in fact, fine. You're driving me crazy with your pain, so let me help."

"I don't need help from you."

"Just a few seconds ago you were saying I could have helped. Get your story straight. And while you wrack your brain for the next insult, lean against the tree so I can tend to your wounds."

She shoved her hands under his armpits, ignoring the pained groan and answering jolt in her shoulder, and dragged him to the tree.

"For a small woman, you're surprisingly strong," he ground out.

"A lifetime of hard work will do that to you. Lean back."

She managed to get him wedged against the tree, hating to leave him there for even a second. Bad magic pulsed inside the bark. She pressed a hand against the trunk, waiting to feel the cold sting of darkness.

When she didn't, she pulled it away and nodded. "I think it's contained inside the tree, at least for now."

The Unseelie listed to the side and pressed a hand against the ground for balance. "Are you a healer?"

"No, I'm not a healer."

"Then why should I let you heal me? I can do it."

"Are you really in any condition to be using magic?" She gave him a severe once over, plucking at the sodden fabric soaked with his blood. "Looks to me like you should just shut your mouth. But if you must open it and speak, 'thank you' is acceptable."

He snapped his mouth shut and glared at her. But at least he stopped talking.

Aisling brushed aside the long tail of his hair and peeled back the shredded fabric of his shirt. The open wound was seeping. Sluggish red rivers trailed down his chest and arms.

Muttering under her breath, she focused on her own pain to identify any other wounds. Finally, she leaned back and gestured with her hands. "Off with the shirt."

He arched a brow. "If you wanted to see me naked, then all you had to do was ask, witch."

"I thought I said not to talk?"

"I'm not very good at that." He gingerly reached for the hem of his shirt and lifted it over his head.

She might have enjoyed the smooth planes of muscle if she wasn't breathless with her own pain. Aisling stilled her ragged breathing and reached out with shaking hands to help him remove the torn fabric. The sooner this was over with, the better they both would feel.

She hoped.

"All right," she managed to breathe, "that's over with. Now, it's just getting the blood to stop."

"Shouldn't it be cleaning the wounds?"

"Blood first, clean later."

"I'm pretty sure that's backwards, witch."

Impulsively she bit out, "Aisling."

The Unseelie stilled. He didn't even breathe as he stared up into her face, both eyes searching for hers even though he would never see them. "What did you say?"

His eyes burned. Aisling swallowed and touched a hand to her chest. "My name is Aisling."

"That's a foolish thing to tell a faerie."

"You kept me alive in there. I think you've earned the name." She mockingly shrugged. "Besides, if you hurt me, you hurt yourself."

"Not forever. We're going to break the binding curse."

He seemed almost panicked by her admission. Why would he be so sorry on her behalf? It was his choice to use her name or not.

Aisling shook her head and slapped a hand to his wound. The sharp jab of pain was worth it when he hissed out a breath. "Stop dwelling on it, Unseelie. It doesn't mean anything."

She picked a long strand of thread out of his shoulder wound and brushed her fingers over the bloodied flesh. It wasn't going to be clean any time soon, but faeries were supposed to heal fast. Theoretically, her plan should work fine.

His hand covered hers, warm and strong. "Bran. My name is Bran."

Aisling's lips curved into a brilliant smile he wouldn't see, but she hoped he might be able to feel. The name filtered through her mind like the first ray of sun after a storm. *Bran.* A strong name that fit him like a glove.

"They named you after a raven?" she said with a quiet chuckle. "A little obvious, don't you think?"

"You didn't guess it?"

"I wasn't trying to."

He huffed and leaned back against the tree. "Don't think much of it, witch. It doesn't mean anything."

She smirked. A name might not mean something now, but it did mean something in the end. And if he finally trusted her, then perhaps he would explain what their fool's errand really was.

"This isn't going to be pleasant," she began, "but it's going to help."

"That doesn't sound promising."

"It's not."

She grabbed a handful of mud at the base of the tree and mashed it into the open wound on his shoulder. The earth was fairly clean. No people had passed by, and the only thing she was concerned about was animals. The mud would dry and close up the wound until they could find a quiet place to rest.

He hissed out a breath. "What are you doing?"

"Hush, you said I could treat your wounds."

"Not like an animal!"

"If it works for animals, then it'll work for you. Hush."

It would at least give them time. Lorcan would know what to do, but he didn't know they were back. Where was the damn cat anyway? The witch had spent much of his human life healing others. That was why he'd wanted to use magic in the first place.

"Turn," she instructed. "Let me get your back."

Grunting, Bran pushed himself from the roots and knelt at her feet.

He was so tall his head reached her chest. His eyes drifted shut, pain and exhaustion swelling over the two of them in a crushing wave. She listed to the side but forced herself to remain standing and cross behind him.

Her hand on his unharmed shoulder balanced her. Even

wounded and in pain, he was warm. She flexed her fingers, feeling the cords of muscle bunch against her palm.

The long lines of his back captivated her gaze. Defined muscles bulged, dipping into the hollow of his waist, creating hollows in the small of his back. He had dimples there. Even corded with muscle, he had small indents begging to be touched.

She swallowed hard, and the eyes on her palms blinked open.

His muscles flexed as she drew her hand from the nape of his neck and followed the sword slash down his torso. It was a shallow cut, but she could hardly focus on that. All she saw was the swath of pale skin slowly bumping with gooseflesh as she stroked a gentle hand over him.

"All done," she whispered. "That will stop the bleeding long enough for Lorcan to clean the wounds."

"Why were you so free with his name?" he asked, voice hoarse. "You weren't free with your own, so obviously you know what I can do with a name."

"It's not his name." At his sharp glance, she shrugged. "He's a secretive one. Lorcan is what I called him as a child, and it stuck."

"Then it's as good as a name."

"Not for magic." Aisling patted his shoulder and stepped back on shaking legs. "We need to get away from this tree."

"Where is your companion?"

"Damned if I know. The cat does what he wants."

A branch above their head shook wildly. She glanced up to see a furry body slowly standing, stretching his paws and arching his back before leaping down to land at her feet. Lorcan yawned again, tiny fangs blinking in the light.

"Were you looking for me?" he asked.

Insulted, Aisling gestured at the blood on both herself and the Unseelie. "What do you think, cat?"

"No need to get snippy," Lorcan grumbled. "I was waiting for the two of you for hours. I thought I'd take a nap."

"You're always napping."

He didn't respond. Instead, he climbed up the long column of the Unseelie's legs. His large feet punched each wound on the way up, and she swore a grin spread across Lorcan's face at the answering grunts.

"Down," he advised. "All the way down or it won't heal right."

Bran cast her an incredulous glance before he laid out on the dirt. "What are you going to do?"

"Heal you. Isn't that what you want?"

"Never been healed like this before."

Lorcan settled himself on the center of Bran's chest. He lifted a paw, licked it slowly, and sneezed.

Aisling covered her mouth, holding in a giggle as Bran glared at her again. "Is this how he heals? I'll admit, it doesn't seem very useful."

"I don't think he's started yet."

"Oh, that's fine then." Bran's fingers curled in the dirt as he stared up at the sky. "I'll just lay here, bleeding out."

When Lorcan slapped the paw directly over the faerie's wound, they both hissed at each other. "Healing is an art, Unseelie. I'm not going to rush it, and you aren't going to rush me. Otherwise, I'll grow another arm from this wound and we'll see how much you like that."

141

"I'm sure the other Unseelies would love it," Bran gritted out.

"Oh, I know how much you all enjoy your freaks. I'll make sure your new limb is as uncomfortable to look at as possible."

"You wouldn't dare."

Aisling clapped her hands. "Idiots! Just heal him Lorcan, please. And Unseelie, keep your mouth shut while he does it. I'm tired of feeling your pain when I didn't earn these wounds."

"You most certainly earned those—" Bran's voice was muffled by a cat paw stuck squarely over his mouth.

"Why are you two always like this?" Lorcan asked. "It's like you couldn't get along if the world was ending."

"He's sweet on me, and I just can't lower myself to be interested in a faerie." Aisling mock-flicked her hair over her shoulder and spun away on her heel. "Get it done, Lorcan. I'm going back to the campfire. You two can join me when you're done pissing in the corners."

She kept her shoulders squared and head high as she descended the trail, when in reality she wanted to fall apart. She was exhausted, her shoulder was on fire, her back ached, and she wanted nothing more than to sleep for a hundred years.

They couldn't know it, of course. The binding curse would transfer her exhaustion to the Unseelie, but he could easily mistake it for his own. They'd had a trying day.

Her ankles twisted in the muck and mire. It sucked at her legs, trying to hold her firmly in place for whatever creature that would wander upon her. The last thing she needed was some bog faerie finding her stuck in the mud. The Unseelie court was rumored to eat weaklings.

"You won't find me very tasty," she muttered, pulling her

legs out one by one. "I'm too tough and far too bitter."

That was the worst part about this journey. Aisling didn't like the self-revelations she was having. Her life had been simple. She'd been rude, caustic, downright mean to drive people away so she wouldn't have to remember what it felt like to be left alone in the dark.

But that damned Unseelie was wiggling his way through her defenses, and she could already see the writing on the wall. She *liked* him. As a travel companion, partner, and a person.

The sparkle in his eye when one side of his mouth lifted in mirth made her gut clench. The whispered promise of mischief whenever they spoke made her knees tremble. And most of all, the way his fists clenched when they argued made her want to grab onto him and never let go.

He didn't know who she was, *what* she was. There could never be anything between them when secrets filled the space with fire and brimstone.

"Never going to happen," she muttered and shook her head. "It's too risky."

It couldn't go anywhere. She was a woman with more than one curse. All her pieces and parts had scattered to the wind until she hardly knew who she was. How was she supposed to bring another person into her life?

She was getting ahead of herself. He might not even be interested in her.

A blast of healing energy slammed into her shoulder, forcing her onto her knees at the edge of the muck. Blowing out a breath, she stared at the bubbles popping in front of her.

"Damnit, Lorcan," she grumbled. "There's no need to be so

forceful about it."

The Unseelie was probably annoying him so much he felt the need to heal by force. Damned cat always let emotions get the better of him, which was why his spells hurt like hell. Even the ones that weren't supposed to hurt at all.

Aisling forced herself to stand and made it back to where they'd left their pack. She crumpled into a ball in the roots, eyes wanting to drift shut but mind racing. She was so tired, yet not a single part of her mind was ready to sleep.

She floated in a daze until they caught up to her. Bran looked about as tired as she felt, and he quickly joined her in the roots and fell asleep immediately. She'd marvel at how easily his tall frame folded later. Instead, she glared at Lorcan with red rimmed eyes. "Was that necessary?"

"Very." He flopped over her legs dramatically. "He's insufferable."

"That's what I've been saying."

"Yes, but now it's affecting me, and I don't appreciate it."

Aisling rolled her eyes and skated her hand over his coarse fur. He wasn't like the other cats she'd pet. Lorcan's fur pricked at her fingers, short spikes of fur digging into her palms.

He rolled so she could scratch his belly. "What happened in there anyway?"

"Hm?"

"In the hanging tree. What happened? Did you get the dead god's blood?"

"Yes," she whispered, "I did."

He twisted to look up at her. "Why do you sound like that?"

She stared into the darkness, her tongue thick and slow in

her mouth. "He knew."

"Who knew? Knew what?" Lorcan dug his claws into her leg. "Aisling, talk to me. You're scaring me. What happened?"

"The god. He knew every secret. He saw right through the magic hiding my face, and he knew exactly what I am." She glanced down at him, lifting a hand to ghost over her pointed ears hidden by the curse her grandmother had laid. "He gave up his life again, willingly, without complaint because he knew I was a changeling."

"Not all faeries hate changelings."

"Changelings are a reminder that faeries aren't perfect," she replied. "And they will never like that reminder. Besides, it's still not safe for me here. If there is one who can see through the curse, then how many others can? Wasn't that the entire point of this affliction? To hide me from those who would cause me harm?"

"Stop it, Aisling. No one knows why your grandmother did what she did. No one knows who you are, even if they know *what* you are. There are too many layers in this secret for anyone to unravel without help."

She breathed out a low sigh, anxiety settling in her stomach. "You're right. No one could know."

"No one will know. Ever."

Lorcan curled into a ball at her side, and his breathing slowly evened out. She waited until she knew he was deeply asleep before she let her head thump back against the tree trunk.

Aisling envied him. He lied so easily, without thought to what he was saying or why it wasn't true. They both knew she

145

would never be able to keep this secret. The faeries were smart folk. They'd see right through her twisted words because she hadn't ever had to work her tongue around a lie.

How was she going to walk among these people even for a short time and not blurt out who she was?

Aisling curled around Lorcan and rested her head on the root. She would have to figure out something, and soon. Bran was too intelligent a man to not piece together the truth. He would figure it out, and then everything would come crashing down around her ears.

Lorcan snorted in his sleep and wrapped an arm over hers, his paw resting on her open hand and his whiskers tickling her cheek. At least she was safe. For now.

Mist swirled around her ankles, stroking her cheeks and playing with her hair. It was alive and wanted nothing more than for her to awaken.

Aisling lifted up onto her elbows, staring in shock at the strange magic stroking her calves. She recognized the touch and the way it floated through the air without a care in the world.

"Grandmother?" she whispered.

A part of her recognized this was a dream. Everything was too foggy, pale, and not quite lifelike.

Aisling rose from her nest in the roots. She peeled out of her body like the skin of a snake. Without color or solid shape, she was a reflection of herself but without fear or worry.

She spared a glance back at the two men sleeping by the tree.

They wouldn't know she was gone. They could get their rest, and she could regret this in the morning. But family called, and she wasn't one to deny her grandmother anything.

Aisling slipped into the mist. It would guide her where her soul needed to travel, easily transferring her between realms if necessary. Her grandmother used magic like she breathed, never questioning how her magic was possible and using it as much as possible.

She followed the shimmering mass of mist to a cave carved into the side of a mountain cliff. She hadn't remembered there being mountains in this part of the Unseelie lands. Perhaps she had missed it.

She stared up at the great monoliths and doubted herself. This wasn't in the Unseelie-controlled lands. This might not even be Ireland anymore.

A tiny hand tucked into hers, rough palm abrading hers.

Aisling startled and looked down at the tiny horned creature holding her hand. There was a puff of sparse hair on top of its head, large eyes blinking up at her with blue irises filling the space from side to side. It grinned and sharp, filed teeth filled its mouth near to bursting.

"Hobgoblin," she grumbled. "What are you doing here?"

"Escorting you to the mistress."

"I didn't agree to be touched."

"Wouldn't want you to run," he replied. His voice was the quiet scratch of nails on flint, hard and painful to hear.

"I wasn't planning on it."

"One can't be too careful."

She wanted to punch him in his little frog-like mouth. The hobgoblin had no right to drag her into the cave like she was someone's expected pet. This was her grandmother! She knew how to enter like a lady and not piss off the woman who cursed her.

Water dripped from the ceiling of the cave, splashing against her shoulders in icy droplets. This was an old place, an ancient place that radiated pain and heartache.

Was this where her grandmother spent her days?

"Not far now," the hobgoblin giggled. "You'll soon see, little changeling."

"Don't call me that."

"Why not? It's what you are."

Aisling leaned back just enough to eye him. He was about the right height to kick across the room. She might even be able to hook a toe underneath him and send him flying through the cave into the wall.

"Granddaughter"—a familiar voice stretched toward her from the darkness—"be kind."

Feeling chastised even though she was an adult, Aisling shook off the hobgoblin's hold and started toward the sound of her grandmother's voice. "Oh, come now, that's not how you raised me."

"I raised you to be human."

"They are not kind."

Her legs still ached with the burn of a bonfire set by men and women too afraid of magic to consider it to be good. Her back remembered the beatings, the thrown stones, the sticks tossed that left bruises decorating her body like a patchwork quilt.

No, humans were not kind. They did not know how to be generous to those they deemed different.

"Come here, child. It has been too long."

Light bloomed in the darkness like a rose unfurling its petals. Aisling stepped through its silver light into a small cavern lit by magic and fire.

Her grandmother was crouched next to the golden flames, her speckled skin like that of a sparrow's egg. She glanced up, mismatched brown and blue eyes glowing with their own power. Her dark hair was pulled away from her face, which only served to highlight the severe angles and aggressive snarl curling her lips to the side.

"Come sit by my fire, granddaughter."

She could not say no to Badb, the war crow. The Tuatha de Danann could turn her inside out, upside down, and right-side out if she wished to. She was sister to Morrigan, creator of fear on the battlefield, the woman who feasted upon warrior's souls.

Aisling sat when she was told to.

The warmth from the fire sank deep into her soul. Badb offered a stone cup filled with herbs that smelled of earth and healing. Aisling drank deeply, cupping the handcrafted vessel carefully with her pale hands. "Thank you, grandmother. It is a great honor to be brought here."

149

"Is it?" Badb's lips twisted in a sneer. "We both know you don't believe that."

"I couldn't lie about it either."

"Don't take me for a fool. Changelings can lie through their teeth once humans teach them the darkness in their souls. Your soul was darkened the moment I left you in the arms of that witch."

Lorcan had been a terrible father figure, but then he'd been a child then, too. Aisling bristled on his behalf. "He did his best."

"And his best was to turn you into one of *them*. The witch knew what I thought of his kind."

"He also knew you left me in the arms of a stranger rather than keep me where I belonged." It wasn't the first time she'd spat the words at Badb. "He did what he had to for our survival."

"Have you survived? In a sense, I imagine. You're still alive. Your heart is still beating." She leaned forward and rapped a long-nailed finger against Aisling's chest hard enough to hurt. "But what's in there is no more Fae than your cat. You have to learn everything all over again."

"I'm trying," Aisling whispered. Pain shot through her body, and not from her grandmother's harsh thump. She knew she wasn't a faerie, never had been, never would be accepted in their arms as one of them. What she didn't know was why she'd been left to die in the forest all those years ago.

Changelings were unwanted faeries. Old creatures who wanted to die causing mischief with their last breath. Ugly children their parents were ashamed of. And though Aisling hadn't seen herself in the mirror since she was a little girl, she knew she was neither.

Her childhood self had been passably pretty, if not a little awkward. Her legs were like that of a newborn foal and her eyes as large as the moon. Perhaps she asked too many questions, her curious mind devouring information like she was starved. Or maybe it was as simple as her family not wanting her.

"How are they?" Aisling asked quietly.

Badb knew of whom she spoke. Aisling always asked about her family, the people who left her behind with little care to even check in on her. It didn't matter they didn't care.

She would care enough for all of them.

"Surviving," Badb grunted. "Your mother is slowly sinking into her own madness. Your father is tearing out his hair at the loss of your sister. Your brother is still fighting everyone he can find and enjoying it a little too much."

"Nothing has changed then."

"Faeries don't change. And that is the most important lesson I could ever teach you."

When the fire flared, Aisling's eyes were drawn to the light. She saw figures dancing in the flames. Men and women, bodies lithe, twisting in a macabre dance around a woman in the center. Her head tilted back, she screamed in pain or anger, Aisling couldn't tell.

"Why did you bring me here?" she quietly asked.

"I didn't."

Aisling's gaze cut across the fire and tangled with Badb's. The patchwork woman shook her head.

"What?" Aisling asked. "Who would have brought me here, if not for you?"

"There are other people interested in you, granddaughter. I told you never to come here."

"My life changing isn't a bad thing. Sometimes it's what we need to fly."

"Or to fall." Badb slowly stood and stretched her arms over her head. The fabric of her simple dress lifted, revealing powerful thighs thick with corded muscles.

"I don't intend to fall, grandmother."

"You've never intended anything in your life. You have drifted endlessly in your own world and are now unprepared for what *this* world will throw at you. I wanted to spare you this fate, but it appears you have chosen it for yourself."

"At least it is a fate I have chosen." Aisling twisted her fingers in her lap, refusing to give her grandmother the satisfaction of seeing her nerves. Tuatha de Danann were unpredictable creatures, and it mattered little that Aisling was her descendant. There were always others.

"Little changeling, there is nothing sweet about a fate you have chosen for yourself. Fate is cruel either way." Badb lifted a long-fingered hand and pointed back to the entrance of the cave. "Someone is waiting to see you."

"Then why did the hobgoblin bring me in here?"

"I wanted to give you a chance to change your mind. I see now you are set on this path, no matter what the end might be."

"Have you seen the end?" Aisling asked. "Is that why you're here?"

"Even I cannot see the future. But you are walking in the footsteps of many before you. I'll protect you when I can, my favored grandchild." She tucked a speckled hand under

Aisling's jaw, smoothing her thumb along the stubborn set of her chin. "I wish you the best of luck."

Aisling worried she might need it. The entire world felt as if it were holding its breath, but she didn't know why. What had her choice changed about her life? How could entering the Otherworld so thoroughly alter her destiny?

She stood, turned from her grandmother, and walked back the way she came.

There was light at the end of the tunnel, dull and weak. Even moonlight was sluggish in this place between places. The rough stone abraded her palm as she used the walls for guidance. The hobgoblin did not appear again. No hand held hers to lead her through the darkness safely.

It was how she'd lived her entire life. And though a small pang of self-pity echoed in the empty chambers of her soul, she also admitted she preferred it this way.

Being alone was safe. No one was going to stab her in the back, throw her to the wolves, tear her limb from limb when they finally left the changeling girl whose family hadn't wanted her.

Her heart was safe, locked away from the rest of the world. She wanted to keep it that way.

Stones skittered at her feet as she brushed her feet over the exit to the cave and stepped into the waning moonlight. Her soul would disappear back to her body once sunlight hit her form. She didn't know how she was so certain of it, but it was like all her magic. The knowledge hid in the deep well of her mind, surfacing only when she needed it most.

She should probably thank Badb for all the faerie spell

books she'd stolen over the years. Aisling had absorbed the spells as if they were things she could consume. They stayed with her, although a few spells floated just out of reach.

A chunk of stone ledge moved beside her. She flicked her gaze toward it and then flinched back. Not a stone, a person, a... *thing*.

It shook its shoulders, unfurling to a height that made her stretch her neck to see its entire bulk. Gray fabric covered its shoulders, falling in haphazard pieces that were threadbare and moth-eaten. Like her, she couldn't see its face at all.

Gasping, she covered her mouth. Antlers stretched up into the sky from its head. They were shedding even though it wasn't spring, bloody strings of fur hanging from the tines. It shook its head, huffing out a breath and snorting at her.

"Who are you?" she whispered.

This was what waited for her? This creature was something out of a nightmare, not faerie but something else entirely. When it stepped toward her, she mirrored its action backward.

"What do you want from me?"

It lifted a clawed hand to its face and pressed a finger where its lips should have been. Mushrooms grew on its shoulders, the poisonous redcaps turned toward her, shifting listlessly with a life of their own.

The creature pointed at her, and a drop of blood fell from its horns onto its finger. She heard a croak behind her and scratching footsteps that were familiar.

A raven hopped next to her, staring up at her with a golden eye.

"One for sorrow," the horned creature rasped.

Another raven joined the other. It flapped its wings, buffeting her legs with wind so powerful they made her stumble.

"Two for mirth."

She saw another land on top of the tree above her, joined by another so dark its feather's glistened.

"Three for a funeral and four for a birth."

Aisling knew this rhyme. The children used to sing it when they saw magpies or ravens in the sky. They counted the numbers of birds in search of an omen. Little did they know, omens only fell from the lips of fell beasts such as this.

"Five for heaven, six for hell." The creature paused and pointed back toward the cave. "Seven for the Raven King and the toll of a bell."

She shivered. There was a message here, a dark message either warning her or sending her in a dangerous direction. She simply didn't know what he wanted her to understand.

"Is this a warning or advice?"

The creature did not respond. It remained still as stone, staring down at her until she could feel the touch of eyes she could not see.

Pushing such a creature was unlikely to end well for her. And yet, she didn't understand its words. The Raven King? Who was the Raven King?

Hesitantly, she nodded. "Thank you."

It sank back into its strange position, on its knees with palms placed upon its thighs. It stared up at the sky, and together they waited for the sun.

Aisling tilted her head back to listen to the ravens crying

out their unhappiness at the disappearing moon. This strange dream had only given her more questions rather than answers. Somehow, she had a feeling the Unseelie might be able to answer them.

She blinked her eyes open as soft, golden rays gently touched her cheeks. Light filtered through the leaves and dotted the ground like will-o'-the-wisps. Smiling, she sat up and stretched her arms over her head.

Though her dreams were strange and uncomfortable, they weren't unwelcome. Badb hadn't spoken to her in years. The illusive faerie was more likely to be screaming over a battlefield than reassuring her granddaughter. Aisling was pleased to know she hadn't been forgotten.

The other creature, however, was less welcome. She didn't know what it was. Some forgotten beast in the Otherworld? A figment of her own imagination as a representation of the faeries themselves?

And what was its message?

The nursery rhyme played in her head again. There was meaning there, something she was supposed to understand and yet couldn't.

Soft fur brushed her leg as Lorcan stretched his paws out. "Morning," he yowled. "Did you sleep well?"

"Not as well as you. You didn't even move last night, did

you?"

"There's nothing more comfortable than dirt." He rolled over onto his back and wiggled. "It's just so warm."

"You should be checking on your patient."

"My who?"

Aisling gave him a severe look. The cat hissed but got up. His tail lashed through the air, a banner as he waltzed toward the Unseelie who hadn't moved all night either.

Lorcan punched his paws up Bran's body, each thump making Aisling wince. The cat sidhe was an impressive beast and weighed almost as much as a dog. He'd leave bruises if he kept that up.

"Why isn't he waking?" she asked.

"Part of the spell. He needed to sleep for as long as possible. His body had to catch up with the healing energy of his mind."

"I don't understand a word of what you just said."

"That's because you were never interested in healing magic. All you wanted to learn was ways to hurt people and protect yourself." Lorcan rolled his eyes. "Feral little thing. And they call me the animal."

He leaned down and hissed in Bran's face, glinting teeth bared and yellow eyes glowing with magic.

It was a slow waking. Aisling watched his fingers twitch first, then his hand curled in the dirt, and finally his eyes drifted open. His brows furrowed in confusion as he stared into Lorcan's eyes.

The cat sidhe opened his mouth in a mockery of a smile. "Good morning, sleeping beauty."

Bran flinched back, scrambling into the roots and sitting up so quickly he dislodged Lorcan from his lap. Growling,

Aisling's companion slunk toward the fire and laid on his side.

"Never do that again, cat," Bran angrily spat.

"You're welcome."

"For what?" His shout echoed in the small glen.

"For saving you, for healing you, for deigning to wake you up when we could have left you lying in those roots asleep for the rest of your life. At least then we'd still be in the Otherworld, Aisling would be immortal, and the story would end perfectly. But instead we woke you up." Lorcan blinked. "Although I have no idea *why*."

Before the Unseelie decided to tear apart her only friend, Aisling stood up and stretched again. "Boys, enough. We've a long journey ahead of us, and arguing isn't helpful."

"It makes me feel better," Lorcan whined. "He's so easy to get riled up."

"Your job is to heal him, not to make him feel worse."

"But what about what I want?"

She eyed him, wondering just how quick he would jump if she lunged at him. "What you want isn't important. You didn't have to come along on this ridiculous journey to break a binding curse I put on the both of us."

He heaved a dramatic sigh. "There's only so many chances to enter the Otherworld. I suppose I can survive."

"Better."

It was like he was her child, like it always had been even when she was little. The man had no sense of self-preservation or responsibility. Shaking her head, she turned toward Bran and took a deep, calming breath.

He looked a little better than yesterday. Color had returned to his pale skin, staining his cheeks red and turning his lips dark once more. Her gaze lingered on his full bottom lip until she realized what she was doing. Her cheeks burned even though he wouldn't know she was staring.

"How do you feel?" she asked, mortified her voice had turned husky.

"Like a tree sat on my chest all night." He glared at Lorcan one last time and then tried to meet her gaze. "But better than before."

It shouldn't warm her to hear that. She shouldn't care at all that he felt better. Aisling tried desperately to fumble the lock around her heart closed, but she could already feel herself slipping. He wasn't right for her, wouldn't ever return her attentions, and yet she couldn't take her eyes off him.

And he could never see her. Not with the curse hanging over her head.

Aisling pulled her hair over her shoulder and knelt at his side. "May I?"

The raven eye whirled, but he nodded. "I think it's completely healed."

"I'll be the judge of that."

He shifted forward, reaching behind his head and pulling off his shirt. The movement was filled with natural grace. He didn't hesitate in the slightest, not embarrassed by his form or body.

Aisling hadn't planned to ogle him like a little girl seeing her first crush in the river, but she swallowed hard and glanced down all the same.

She'd seen his chest, touched the broad expanse of muscle, but he'd been injured, and she'd felt his pain. Now, her mind was clear from the lingering effects of magic.

Smooth skin filled her vision. Not a single mark marred him, no scars, no bruises, nothing but hills and valleys between muscles created by the finest artist.

His shoulders were broad and tapered to a thin waist. His chest was effortlessly flat, and muscles flexed on his stomach as he leaned back against the tree. Twin bands arched over his hips and disappeared underneath the waistband of his pants, an arrow for her eyes to follow.

She swallowed again. "How is your shoulder?"

"You aren't looking at my shoulder."

The amusement in his voice stung. She flicked her gaze to him, fuming at his knowing grin. He couldn't even see her face but, somehow, he knew.

Her pride refused to allow him to keep that satisfied smirk. "Don't flatter yourself. I'm more interested in making sure you aren't going to hurt me anymore."

"Some pain can be fun."

"Is that why you're Unseelie?" She reached out and skimmed her fingers over the wound surface, which was now the only red mark on the warm expanse of skin. "You like pain a little too much?"

"I'm Unseelie because I think rules are made to be broken."

Her nostrils flared as the scent of pomegranate and wine skimmed her face. His breath feathered across her skin like the most delicate of touches, heat fanning across her skin as if she stood in front of a fire. When had he moved so close?

He touched her shoulder, trailing his fingers over the rough fabric of his shirt up to the line of her neck. "It's strange," he murmured, "the spell starts where I can see your pulse racing."

"My pulse isn't racing."

"You could have fooled me, witch." The nickname sounded different now. He shaped the word with his tongue, lovingly stroking the letters until the harsh sound softened into a caress.

Aisling licked her lips. "Fooled you how?"

"Does the curse only hide your face?" he asked, the question hauntingly familiar. "Or can I touch you?"

"I'd rather you didn't."

"Why not?"

"It's been a long time since anyone has touched me," she breathed.

"Then let me be your first."

She was frozen, in fear or in anticipation she couldn't tell. Aisling held her breath as his long fingers slid up her neck. From wherever he touched, heat spread, like tendrils of light splintering throughout her body.

His thumb traced the line of her jaw. He had calluses on the pads of his fingers, the rough texture catching on her soft skin. It wasn't a working man's hand. His palms were as smooth as hers.

"You play music," she gasped as his fingers smoothed over her chin.

"Sometimes."

"You have calluses on your fingertips." She only recognized them because a fiddler had once stopped and asked her for a salve to smooth his own. He played for royalty, he had said, and calluses were a sign of a working man.

"Sh." He hushed her and pressed his fingers to her lips. She held her breath as he stroked the soft outline, lingering in the

161

dip of her cupid's bow.

Bran smiled, his eyes drifting closed as he concentrated. "I thought you would have thin lips."

"Why?"

"Shrews usually do." He traced her frown, chuckling. He lifted his other hand and gently smoothed both hands over her cheeks. "You have a heart-shaped face."

She didn't respond. He would gather too much information if she admitted she didn't actually know what her face looked like. It had been too many years since the curse hid her reflection.

His fingertips ghosted over her brow, feathering over her long lashes, and then tracing the thin line of her nose.

She stared at his expression, watching his own brows draw down. "Witch, I do believe you are a beautiful woman."

"What would make you say that?"

"I know perfection when I touch it."

Aisling didn't know what to say or how to feel about that. She licked her lips, the tip of her tongue touching his thumb where he'd started tracing her bottom lip again. They both froze. His eyes flew open and impossibly locked on hers.

Lurching back, she stumbled away so quickly she almost ended up in the fire. She cleared her throat and shook her head. "There's no such thing as perfection, Unseelie."

"Bran."

"*Unseelie.*" She needed the distance between them right now. He wasn't some young man she met on her travels. He was a dark Fae, the kind that could rip her limb from limb and feel no guilt about it.

She was wasting her time on something that could never

be.

Lorcan flicked his tail away from the fire and glared. "Are you quite done? Give him the blood and get it over with."

"The blood?" Aisling shook her head. "Oh, the blood."

She reached into her pocket and pulled out the ruby-like droplet. It was as beautiful as it was strange, pulsing against her palm with a heartbeat of its own. Her chest clenched.

The drop of blood didn't want her to give it away. It wanted to stay tucked against her thigh, safe and sound.

Bran huffed out an angry breath, his eyes widening. "You still have it on you?"

"What else was I supposed to do with it? It's the blood of a *god*, Bran."

He yanked his shirt back on and scrambled to the pack. Fumbling with the leather bag, he finally got it open and held it out to her with shaking hands. "Put it in here, quickly."

"Why?" She looked down and realized her fingers had unconsciously closed over the small stone. "What's wrong with it?"

"Even the blood of a god can compel people to do what he wishes. He's there for a reason, Aisling. Now, give it here."

The shackles of her name twisted around her throat. She narrowed her eyes and waited as long as she could before holding out her hand. Even a chosen name had power over her, but he didn't know she was a changeling. He *couldn't* know that her name was a weapon if he wished to control her.

Her hand shook, her breath sawed from her lungs, but she still turned her hand over and dropped the bead into the outstretched bag.

"Good job," Bran sarcastically said. "Was that hard for

163

you?"

She didn't give him the response he wanted. Instead, she said nothing as he tied the bag shut and slid it back into the pack she carried. Whatever magic swirled in that creature's blood was dangerous, dark, and far too powerful. She was afraid to consider what it might have done if she had held onto it for a few moments longer.

Rubbing her chest, she turned toward the fire and started kicking dirt onto it. "What's next?" she asked.

"Preferably we'll return to my home, clean up a little, I'll take you out to a nice balcony somewhere so we can look at the stars. It's a pretty castle. Did I tell you I live in a castle?"

A smile spread across her features. "Are you trying to distract me?"

"Is it working?"

"Not at all, Unseelie. There are still two parts of your spell, and I'm very much interested in breaking this binding curse."

A wall of heat pressed against her from shoulder to knee. He had stepped so close she could smell the sweet wine of his breath. "Are you so sure about that?"

Aisling pinched her arm so hard she drew blood. The Unseelie gasped and flinched, lifting his arm and swatting at it as if a bug had bitten him. She pointed to the small wound and cocked her head to the side. "I'm certain."

"Women," Bran grumbled. "Too dramatic for their own good."

"Just get on with it. What else must we endure?"

He waved a hand, and the fire disappeared. Lorcan rolled to his feet, stretching his paws and flexing his toes.

"The remaining pieces aren't as easy as the God's blood."

"That was easy?" she interrupted.

"We're close enough to the next, although I'd rather do it last. We need a vessel made of heart, waters from Swan Lake, and then the spell will need to be performed in my home."

Aisling placed a hand on her hip and arched a brow he couldn't see. "The castle you mean?"

"Yes. The *castle*."

"The vessel made of heart could be anything. What kind of spell *is* this? There's rules to magic, particular steps that have to be followed or it'll all unravel at your feet."

"It's more of a prophecy than a spell."

She curled her hands into fists. "So what you're saying is we're wandering around the Otherworld chasing the tail of something that *might not even work?*"

He swallowed. "That's about the gist of it."

Energy crackled at her fingertips, anger dancing in her clenched fists and begging to be released. "You dragged me here, risked my life, and you're telling me it's all for nothing?"

"Well, not nothing. This might actually work."

A bolt snuck out of her hand and struck the ground near him. Bran jumped, leaping away from the magic while his own rippled down his body. Feathers unfurled across his arm then settled back onto his skin.

"You said this would work," she growled. "You said this was the only way to break the binding curse."

"It's the only way I know."

"It isn't a spell! It's a whim, a muse, something that doesn't exist, and you're risking both our necks for what? A childhood fantasy?"

His jaw jutted forward, the stubborn set somehow familiar.

"This is a real way to break the binding curse. I know this for a fact. I've just never seen it practiced."

"Why not?"

"Because no one has ever been able to successfully do it."

She took a calming breath, which did little more than aggravate her further. "Bran, please tell me we're not on a wild goose chase."

"We're not."

"Please tell me you know what you're doing and we aren't going to end this journey still stuck together."

"Would that be such a bad thing?"

Lips pressed into a narrow line, she pinched herself again. He yelped and slapped a hand against his hip.

"Yes, it would be a bad thing. Need I remind you that we're stuck together until all of this goes away? That what I feel, you feel?" She pointed at him. "If you can't break this curse and dragged me through the Otherworld for no reason, I'm going to make your life hell."

"I was already counting on that, witch. Are you ready to go?"

"Where are we going?"

He winked. "There's only one vessel made of heart in the Otherworld, and that's locked inside the Duchess of Dusk."

"Who?"

"You'll see." He reached into their pack and tossed her an apple. "Last one, witch. Sooner or later you're going to have to eat our food."

"I'd rather starve."

CHAPTER 6

THE PALACE OF TWILIGHT

"Do you even know where we're going?"

"Yes, witch."

"Are you sure? Because we've been beating through these bushes for hours and I'm certain I've seen that tree before."

Bran glanced up at the tree and ground his teeth. He'd seen it too, a few times now. She was less observant than he'd given her credit for if this was the first time she realized they'd passed by it. But he had a feeling she'd been holding her tongue. Lorcan had slunk into the forest, grumbling under his breath that he would find his own way about an hour ago.

He *did* know where they were going; he just didn't know how to get there. The Duchess of Dusk was one of the most elusive Unseelie faeries. She also hated Bran with a passion.

It wasn't his fault he'd been born into royalty. Some things were outside of his control, and if she wanted to hate him for that, so be it. He agreed with her. He wasn't capable of being a king and never wanted a throne. If it was his choice, he'd give it to her and run.

Shame, it wasn't his choice. She'd make a good queen.

He stopped abruptly, taking time to enjoy the warm weight of her body as she collided with him. "Why don't we stop for a second, eh, witch?"

"Would you stop calling me that?"

"Once you stop calling me Unseelie."

When her tiny fists curled, a spike of satisfaction lanced through his chest.

Bran liked to make people uncomfortable. He enjoyed teasing them, frustrating them, really any reaction to make their head spin. Even royals found him unbearable to be around, but that was part of the game. People acted who they really were when they were frustrated.

He enjoyed bothering her far more than anyone else. Perhaps it was because he couldn't see her face. Instead, he got to watch her entire body screw up in anger as she tried to hold herself together.

And she always tried to be so good about hiding her anger. She'd politely respond while hissing the words through her teeth. It was adorable.

The only thing that could make it better was the sight of her face. He had a feeling her cheeks flamed bright red when she was angry. Too much fire ran in her veins for it not to show.

His fingertips burned at the memory of touching her. Her skin was soft as the finest velvet, but her spine was rigid as steel.

He knew a beauty when he touched one. He'd painted the picture of her in his mind's eye. The high cheekbones, delicately arched brows, thin nose and full lips. Each piece of her face fit into an image of stunning beauty, but he found himself focusing on details he would never know. The color of her eyes, the spread of her blushes, the shape of her smile.

Every piece of her was a thinly veiled visage. She wore her wit and sarcasm like a badge of pride when they were really a shield against the world.

He knew because he did the same thing.

Aisling stumbled over a branch and cursed. "Explain this Duchess again?"

"The Duchess of Dusk is the name she's given herself. She's not Unseelie royalty by a long shot, but has appointed herself the unofficial champion of all whom the court will not recognize." He lifted a branch for her to duck under. "As you can imagine, she's not a fan of me or my family."

"I wonder why."

"Well personally, I'm too handsome. She finds my looks to be rather intimidating. Don't you?"

She didn't reply. His gaze caught on her fingers tapping against her side, and he grinned. She might not want to give him the satisfying taste of her lie, but she was definitely affected.

"How many Unseelie have you seen in your life?" he asked.

"You. A hobgoblin. A couple horned beasts. All the creatures we walked by."

"Then you haven't really been immersed in the Unseelie court before now. You've seen the lesser Fae, but you've never seen Unseelie royalty."

"I lived in the human world, Bran. What do you expect?"

"You asked me to prepare you next time. I'm trying to do that." He reached forward and plucked a leaf from her hair, lifting it to the light and twirling it between his fingers. "Or do you want to walk in blind again? We can do that instead."

She snorted. "I was the one complaining about it. Of course, I want to know everything I can know. That's why I asked."

He thought she might have muttered something else under her breath. It sounded suspiciously close to "numbskull," but he let it slide.

"The Duchess of Dusk is the perfect example of what an Unseelie Fae should look like."

"You aren't?" She turned on her heel to face him. A wave of heat rushed from the tip of his toes to the top of his head, and he knew she had given him a scorching once over. "You don't look like the glowing representation of beauty such as the Seelie Fae."

"That's the nicest thing you've ever said to me, witch."

"Don't let it go to your head."

Aisling slowed, reached out a hand, and leaned against a tree. She was tired, but didn't want to tell him. So he feigned a yawn and settled onto a fallen log. She wouldn't take kindly to him pointing out any weakness so he nonchalantly made himself comfortable, leaning back against a trunk and propping his foot up on the worn bark.

"Here's the deal, witch. The Duchess and her kingdom aren't entirely complete." He lifted a hand when she opened her mouth. "I'm not finished. Don't interrupt me. It's rude. Everyone who calls the Palace of Twilight their home is missing pieces of themselves. The land she took over was home to cannibals, now to all those who aren't considered fully formed."

"Are they still cannibals?" she asked.

"Some. It's unlikely they'll try to attack us though, if that's what you're worried about."

"Unlikely or they won't?"

He arched a brow. "We're in the Otherworld, witch. Nothing is certain here."

The disgust radiating through her shoulders made him grin. It was too easy to get her riled, and he adored the way she obviously tried not to stomp her feet and scream at him. He almost preferred it when she shouted.

He kind of liked it.

Aisling blew out a breath. "Spare me the riddles. How dangerous is this place?"

"Extremely."

"Guards?"

"She has an entire army at her beck and call."

"Do we have weapons?"

"We won't need them." He flashed her a grin. "We're going to let them capture us."

"Excuse me?"

"It's rather simple, witch. The Duchess of Dusk hates me. She has been searching for a way to remove my head for a very long time. Now that she has the opportunity, she's going to take it. All we have to do is find the entrance to her kingdom and she'll deliver us to her doorstep."

The witch was so still he thought she might have been staring with a dumbfounded expression. He liked to think he'd stumped her.

"Are you crazy?" she cried out. "I like my head attached to my neck! If she wants to kill you so bad, what's going to stop her from doing it on sight?"

"She likes a show. She hates a missed opportunity to prove

171

to her people how powerful she is."

"That doesn't mean she won't kill you."

"Oh, she'll try." He grinned at her frustrated huff.

"Bran. Please tell me you have more of a plan than we did with the dead god."

"I don't like plans. I find they're constricting."

She threw her hands into the air and stomped in the other direction. Branches snapped under her feet, and she slapped at the trees. They started yanking their branches out of her way, which only made her grumble about plants refusing her an outlet to complain.

How often did she lose her composure like this? Certainly more than anyone he'd ever seen before, but he was trying hard to annoy her.

"Where are you going?" he called out. "We have to be captured together."

"I'm going to spend the rest of my life enjoying my head attached to my neck!" she yelled. "You get captured, deal with the Duchess, and surprise me when we die."

A snort escaped before he could catch it. "We're in the midst of the Unseelie forest, witch. Aren't you the slightest bit afraid?"

She spun on her heel, dark hair flying about in a curtain resembling the night drawing across the sky. "I am the most frightening thing in this forest, Unseelie. They should be afraid of *me*."

Good god, he could love this woman.

He sank down on the fallen log, eyes wide and heart thumping against his ribs. A few nights ago, he might have laughed in her face. He might have argued that *he* was the most terrifying thing in this forest. But the tiny witch was damned strong, an untapped well of magic that rivaled his own, and a mystery about her so thick he couldn't see through it. She might not be stronger than he was, but she most certainly was a sight to behold.

She blew out a curse, spun on her heel, and marched through the forest with her head held high. Damned if she didn't look like a queen.

Bran lurched to his feet, long limbs awkwardly catching on themselves until he found his balance.

"Hold on there," he shouted. "I didn't grant you leave!"

"Did I need to ask for that? I'm not part of your kingdom, Unseelie."

"Bran, damn it. My name is Bran."

"I have an exceedingly capable memory. I know what you're called."

"Then call me it."

"I'll call you by name only when you deserve it," she growled.

"Then you call me Unseelie when you're angry?"

"What gave you that idea?"

He snapped his fingers as he finally caught up to her. "Considering I can't see your face, I thought it might be an endearment."

She growled again. The noise somehow both adorable and slightly intimidating. "What would ever give you the idea it was an endearment?"

"Oh, maybe how you linger on the tones, as if you're already thinking about me reclining on the forest floor, entirely nude and at your mercy."

"I have never had that thought!"

She answered too quickly, and he knew what that meant. She had thought about it. She'd thought about him in more ways than that.

The grin that spread across his face was probably uncalled for. But it was reassuring to know she didn't think of him as just another faerie. Hell, she'd even let him touch her face.

That had to mean something, right?

Aisling was pulling ahead of him again, slipping past branches that snapped down behind her in his way. He pushed at one and tried to be gentle about it, but even the trees were trying to slow him down.

"Hold on," he called out. "Aisling, you're getting too far ahead of me."

"Keep up then."

"Fighting someone in this forest isn't worth it. Just wait for me."

"Not planning on it."

"Damn it, woman, this is my home. Would you listen to me?" His voice escalated, perhaps a little too loud for her liking because the next branch he passed under revealed she was standing with her hands on her hips, waiting for him.

As soon as he entered the small clearing, she advanced on him like a woman walking to war. He didn't know what she was doing, couldn't see her expression to even guess, but knew the stubborn set of her shoulders and the clenched fists well enough.

He stepped backward, hesitating briefly when his heel caught on a root of a tree.

She lifted a hand and pointed at him. "I was raised a witch,

Unseelie. I am calm only because I will myself to be."

"Dangerous," he murmured. "Obviously, you are dangerous."

"You would do well to remember it."

Because he could not help himself, he reached out and feathered a touch down the long column of her neck. "When we get to the castle, I will tie a black silk ribbon around your neck so all know you are mine."

"Why would you say that now? When I'm threatening you?" Her voice was breathless, whispering promises best said when a shadow crossed over the moon.

Bran stepped closer until he could inhale her unique scent of smoke and moss, earth, and the space between shadows. "You were made to wear black velvet with spiderwebs in your hair, while onyx stones dance upon your fingers. You are a midnight woman, made from the ashes of witches burned, wielding magic born from their screams."

The words slipped from his tongue with the red-wine dark taste of prophecy. Magic heated his blood, and blunt feathers fanned down from his head, covering his arm with a fine dusting of obsidian. They disappeared as quickly as they came, until all that remained were his black claws tracing her throat.

She was so beautiful, regardless of her face, the color of her eyes, the fullness of her lips. No, none of that was important. Bran could see her soul through his raven eye, and it was as dark as his.

"Bran," she whispered.

And he was lost.

He touched her chin, tilted her head up. His lungs strained for air, his muscles clenched in anticipation, and his thoughts short-circuited until all he could do was follow his instincts.

Bran leaned down, touched his lips to hers, and the foundation of his world cracked open.

She tasted of woodsmoke and dangerous dreams. Soft and yielding, she pressed her hands against his chest and fisted his shirt. A soft sound vibrated her throat. A sound of need, desire, and a longing so desperate it shattered his heart.

He drew her close, stroking a hand down her ribs while cupping her head with the other. The dark tangles of her hair caught on his fingers, but he didn't care.

In that moment, he felt every inch of his immortal soul. A thousand and one kisses had led him to the velvet touch of her lips, the stinging bite of her teeth, and the century old taste of magic dipped in moonlight.

She destroyed him with each murmured encouragement, every squeeze of her fingers and nip of her teeth.

Bran broke away only when they were both breathless but pressed his forehead against hers because he couldn't bear the distance. Catching his breath, his rubbed his nose against hers. "Witch, if I'd known you kissed like that I would have insisted upon it much sooner."

"You're a man of many talents," she replied. "I assumed correctly that you were practiced in this art."

"I wouldn't say practiced."

"You've done it before."

"You haven't?" He pulled away to stare incredulously down at her. "You lie."

She shook her head, and he desperately wished to see her face. "No. A witch has little opportunities for such whimsy."

"Whimsy?"

"They tried to burn me, Bran. Do you really think any of them wanted to kiss me beforehand?"

He hadn't thought. "They can see what you look like. Surely one of them had some sense?"

Aisling stepped back from him, crossing her arms over her chest and turning her face to the side. He didn't like that. He knew what that meant. She was pulling away.

"No, no you don't get to do that." He leapt forward, forcing her to look at him. "I didn't say anything wrong. That's a compliment."

"I don't want to talk about it."

"Sometimes it's better to talk about things. Look at me, Aisling."

"I am looking at you."

He heard the heartbreak in her voice, understood it was because he couldn't tell, but the raven eye imbedded in his skull said otherwise.

"Look me in the eyes, Aisling." When she didn't move, he swore. "I didn't take you for a coward."

"I'm not."

"Then why won't you look at me?"

She lifted her head, but he could tell it was to look over his shoulder. He sighed and shook his head.

The woman had more walls around herself than most. She didn't want him to know her, to really see who she was, and that was the saddest part of their story. People might sing of them in ages to come.

They'd tell the tale of how an Unseelie prince pursued an impossible woman across the entirety of the Otherworld. And how her heart was locked up so tight that no key could ever open it.

"Aisling," he began.

"Six," she whispered.

"What?"

"Six for hell. You said the Duchess lives in your version of the Underworld?" She pointed over his shoulder. "I think that's where we're supposed to go."

He turned to follow the direction of her finger, gaping at the large mountain that had appeared in front of them. It was unusual for mountains to appear anywhere in the Otherworld, let alone one so large. In the very center, a cave opened its mouth like that of a great beast of old.

"Where did you hear that rhyme?" he asked.

"In a dream."

"Who was in the dream?"

She shook her head. "Let's get going. I don't want to waste any more time trying to find this Duchess."

"Aisling." He reached out and grabbed her arm. "There are many creatures in these woods, some of which are not friendly. Who told you that rhyme?"

"I don't know." She shook her head, and her words trembled. "Someone who frightened me, but who I believe we can trust."

"How does it go?"

She repeated the child's tale word for word until the last line.

"Seven for the Raven King and the toll of a bell."

He rocked back a step, each word striking his chest like a physical blow. She reached as if to grab him, only hesitating when he flinched away from her touch.

"What did he look like?" he rasped. "Tell me now, please."

"As if he were made of stone and something more. Great antlers rose from his head, and gristle fell from them as he shed the velvet." She shivered. "I have never heard of such a beast."

"Neither have I." And he felt immense relief in knowing she had met an Otherworld creature, not the Raven King himself.

There was still time. His plan could still work.

"Perhaps we shall trust this creature," he said and cleared his throat. "The cave, you said?"

"I'm willing to try if you are."

"Lead the way, witch."

"Aisling," she corrected. "Have you seen Lorcan?"

"He makes his own way."

"I'm not leaving without him."

"You say that every time, and yet we always move forward. The witch knows how to find us. Uncanny if you ask me."

Her hands fisted. "I didn't ask, and I won't leave without him."

The brush rustled behind them, and a furry body burst free with a yowl of disapproval. "You were leaving without me!"

Aisling shook her head and reached out her arms. "We weren't! I wouldn't."

He leapt into her arms, glaring at Bran as Aisling stroked her hands over his head. "He would."

"I would," Bran agreed. "In a heartbeat."

"Bran," Aisling chastised.

"What?"

"If the two of you can't stop arguing, I'm only taking one

of you."

"Well, it better damn well be me then, considering those cannibals will eat you alive without me."

"Sounds like they're going to eat me either way."

He stared at her hips as she sashayed away from him, flicking the curtain of her tangled dark hair as she went.

Damned, stubborn woman. She feared nothing, and that would get her in trouble. The Otherworld deserved a healthy amount of respect and fear. If she didn't know how to give it that, then the land would take it.

Shaking his head, he started after them.

The cave was much larger than he originally thought. The maw opened up high above his head where bones hung from tangled roots. Carved runes decorated the walls, and magic gave the air an electric quality, lifting the hair on his arms.

Wind whistled through the cavern, bringing with it the whispered prayers of a thousand men and women. Their voices were funneled toward the heavens, repenting dark deeds while hoping the gods and goddesses might be listening.

"What is that sound?" Aisling asked.

"The pleas of the Underfolk," he responded. "They ask for forgiveness from the Tuatha de Danann so they might return to the Otherworld."

"Have any ever returned?"

"No. Only the condemned are sent to Underhill, and they will remain part of the host forevermore."

He watched her pause at the mouth of the cave and wondered what she was thinking. Underhill was a dark part of faerie history. The Sluagh were notoriously dangerous creatures, stealing souls that cried out for help. Devouring humans added to their own power. They reveled in their own ugliness and hid in the darkest parts of nightmares.

Was she afraid?

"I have met the Sluagh before," she finally murmured. "They were not a kind folk."

"Kindness has never been shown to them. They do not know what such an emotion is."

"That's sad."

"The Unseelie pity them. Their bodies are emaciated, not only from lack of food, but from lack of love. We see them as a reflection of all that is neglected inside ourselves."

She shifted her balance and ran her fingers over Lorcan's fur. "And the Seelie?"

"They fear them as humans do."

Her shoulders squared, and his brave little witch marched into the cave with no further hesitation. What he would give to dive into her mind, to understand her thoughts and reasoning.

What kind of creature was she that she pitied creatures who lacked love? The Sluagh were the worst sort of beasts, and yet she connected with them. She stalked toward them with intent riding her posture like the weight of a crown.

Magic danced down his side, tasting him like the lick of a large animal. He grimaced but plunged into the darkness without hesitation.

"Why do I feel like someone is watching us?" Aisling asked.

"Because they are."

He could feel her. The Duchess. Her magic was one he was too familiar with, but it didn't concern him. Not as much as the secondary magic laced through hers that tasted like opium and dark deeds.

The Duke.

"Damn it," he growled. "This is going to be harder than I thought."

"Why?"

"The Duchess is married now, and the man she's taken as consort isn't the kind of creature we want to tangle with."

"Worse than a dead god?"

"Far worse."

A stone pinged to their right, dropping into the darkness, and echoing when it struck water. They were no longer alone.

Aisling tucked herself closer to him. Not in fear, his feral little witch didn't know what that emotion felt like. Instead, he felt the electric burn of her magic building inside her body.

"Why should I be afraid of him?"

He brushed aside a cobweb and lifted it above her head. "The Duke spent his early life researching dark magic, and then one of the Fir Bolg gave him the ultimate spell book. The Necronomicon."

The answering gulp suggested she knew what he meant.

"Learning magic like that at such a young age twists a person. He figured out quick enough that power wasn't just born, but it could be taken. In the Palace of Twilight, the ultimate honor is to give a piece of yourself to the Duke."

"A piece of themselves?"

Bran grunted. "The last time I saw him he was wearing six sets of arms."

"Doesn't leave a lot of room for much else, I imagine."

"Nothing makes you uncomfortable, does it?" When he lifted a hand, blue faerie light bloomed upon his palm and gently floated into the air.

"No. But when you're raised a witch, and know just how much is truly out there, it's hard to be frightened by something like this."

"You aren't afraid for your soul?"

"I'm not sure I even have one."

She laid the words at his feet like an offering, then slipped past him and continued walking through the cave.

The ball of his magic followed her like a loyal puppy, and he couldn't help but feel as if he were doing the same. She was something else, this witch of his. No fear, no virtue, no sense of right or wrong. Aisling simply *was*, and she was not ashamed of that.

She ducked underneath a stalactite and murmured, "You understand that we're being followed?"

"I do."

"Do you plan on doing anything about it?"

"I don't." He caught up with her and arched a dark brow. "Are you uncomfortable with that?"

"I like to know who is following me."

"That's easy. It's one of the Duchess's personal guard, although I hadn't expected such a welcome. Truly, she must be very worried about what I'm here to do."

Lorcan shifted, draped over Aisling's shoulder like a strange mink wrap. "They'll want an explanation for who Aisling is."

"Yes, you're probably right," Bran agreed. He tapped a finger to his chin, feigned as if he was thinking about it, then snapped his fingers loudly. "I know! We'll say you're my servant."

"Servant?" Aisling's voice echoed. "Absolutely not."

"It's the only believable thing."

"How about apprentice? Lady wife? Anything other than servant."

"Slave?"

She let out an exasperated sigh. "No."

"Servant it is. I'm glad you came around to seeing my way."

"I didn't!" She tossed her hands in the air. "No one would believe I'm your servant. I'm far too obstinate, and we argue at every opportunity."

"Shame. I hope you're a better actor than you are a liar."

"What—"

She didn't have time to finish her next argument because he stepped ahead of her and loudly shouted, "Duchess! I have returned with my faithful servant. We seek an audience with your esteemed self, husband and, if you insist, your court, although I'd rather they watch from a safe distance."

"What are you doing?" Aisling hissed.

"Getting us captured." He looked over his shoulder and grinned. "I did tell you that was my plan."

She dropped Lorcan to the ground. "Hide, come for us when you can."

As the cat dashed away, dark figures lunged from the shadows where they had hidden. Apparently, all he needed to do was request they slink out of their hiding places. It was everything he could do not to roll his eyes.

Bran held his arms causally at his sides. He knew better than to tempt those who were in the Duchess's personal guard.

The guards were too similar to the Duchess. For them, pain

was a pleasure, darkness was light, and screams were music.

"Don't touch me!" Aisling growled as shadows grabbed at her.

"Let them, servant. They won't harm you without an audience."

"Servant?" she growled, lurching forward to stand by his side. "I'm going to kill you for this."

"Don't make promises you can't keep."

"I'll make your life hell, at the very least."

"I cannot wait to see what you come up with."

And surprisingly, he couldn't. This little witch intrigued him with every choice she made and every threat she tossed into the air. She made every nerve ending in his body stand on end. It wasn't that he was frightened of what she might do.

On the contrary, he was looking forward to it.

She growled as a creature pushed her. It was covered in warts, only stood to Bran's waist, and had a mouth full of pointed teeth.

"Goblin," he acknowledged.

It sniffed at her and pushed Aisling forward again.

Bran felt a calloused hand touch his back and knew immediately who it was.

"Daragh," he grumbled. "I thought you would have died by now."

"Hard to kill an immortal." The voice was the grit of the earth, the shattering of bone against rock, and the echo of a dying groan.

It grated on Bran's ears. He'd forgotten how much he hated the bodyguard's voice.

"It's a shame. I think you'd be welcome into the Sluagh."

185

"I will not join their ranks," Daragh replied. He shoved the center of Bran's back, although Bran refused to shift. "Move, Unseelie."

"Is that not what you are?"

He turned, another blue faerie light bright in his hand. It cast the cavern in stark relief, revealing the scarred man standing next to him. Daragh had never been a pretty man. His entire body was pockmarked, horrifically scarred, and he limped from an old wound. Silver hair was pulled back from his ugly face in a swinging ponytail, slicked back by its own oil.

Bran arched a brow. "You still have one arm?"

Daragh lifted the stump in acknowledgement.

"Shame," Bran murmured. "I thought he might have given it back when he was done with it."

"The Duke is never done with our memories."

"What memories does an arm hold, I wonder?" He let himself be shoved forward, talking the entire way. "Perhaps how to hold a sword? What the best angle is to wank yourself off—"

Daragh smacked him in the back of the head. "Shut up."

"My servant threatens to cut my ear off when I tell her that."

The creature's hand fisted in Bran's hair, yanking his head back so Daragh could hiss in his ear, "I'm going to take yours if you don't keep your mouth shut."

He shoved Bran's head forward. Dark hair fell in front of Bran's vision, and it took all his concentration to stay his hand. He could kill them all in one fell swoop. But he didn't dare. Not until he was close enough to the Duchess to take her heart.

They exited the cavern and walked into Underhill. It was

as beautiful and decrepit as he remembered.

Bran hurried forward to walk by Aisling's side as they strode down the carved stone steps in the center of the mountain that descended into the valley below.

Each stately home was carved out of rock, decorated with bones, and looked as though no one had lived in them for centuries. Cobwebs covered their path, and the entire chasm was eerily silent. Not a single person spoke, no laughter echoed from children, not even an animal dared to make a sound when the Duchess of Dusk was waiting for her prey.

"Cannibals?" Aisling whispered under her breath.

He noted she was twisting her fingers together. As carefully as possible, he reached out and tucked her hand into his. "Cannibals."

"Are they going to eat us?"

"I won't let them."

"That's not reassuring."

He flashed a brief grin. "Have I let anything bad happen to you yet? Trust me a little, witch. I'll get us that heart and out of this mess without any problem."

They paraded toward the palace, their personal guard growing as they reached the tall doors. Each beast was stranger than the last. She couldn't make out individual features, only a wave of warts, callouses, and scarred skin. The stained glass windows must have once been an impressive sight, but now, the glass panels were cracked and broken, littering the ground with rainbow shards.

The gates shrieked as a tree-like guard placed his shoulder against it and shoved hard. Bran noted this man was missing both of his arms.

A great honor, he was certain, although he couldn't understand how it was. The Duke's followers were oddly religious in the way they admired the man. If he wanted a new body piece, the faeries would scramble to be the first in line.

The last time Bran had seen such a ceremony, they were euphoric. Losing a limb became a drug, giving a piece of themselves to their leader was the highest enlightenment, and they laid their bodies prostrate in front of him in thanks.

Throughout the entire ordeal, the Duchess had looked on with a pleased gaze. She fed off chaos and had married the perfect man to create such mayhem.

Cracked cobblestone marked the path to the palace where a small group of people waited for them. More guards, some missing limbs, others eyes, but all covered in the history of battle.

Bran glanced over his shoulder. "Have you started decorative scarring since I've been gone?"

Daragh shoved him forward again, grasped his arms, and twisted them roughly behind him.

Bran flicked his head, flipping a curtain of dark hair over his shoulder so his raven eye could stare over at Aisling. She was still handling it well, although she looked sick to her stomach. Likely because the faerie next to her had laid the stump of his upper arm on her shoulder to keep her in place.

"Hey," he murmured, "witch."

She glanced over at him.

"Still good?"

"Last time you were here?" she asked. "Why were you here at all?"

"Foolishly got captured by the duchess."

"Why did she capture you?"

"She liked the look of me. Said I would easily fit into her ranks, even though she thought I was a little too pretty."

He hated the memory, and walking up the cobblestone steps towards the palace with guards all around him was like stepping into his past. This was a path he'd journeyed the last time he tried to snoop in the Dusk Court, and he despised it as much as the last time. The duchess was too twisted even for his liking.

"Why do you have to do everything the hard way?" Aisling grumbled. "I'm not sure I can curse the lot of them."

"Cursing them wouldn't be any good. They like pain."

Aisling set her shoulders, when she squeezed her fists in preparation for a fight, Bran felt an answering thump in his chest. She shook herself and replied, "They haven't felt my kind of pain before."

Every inch of him wanted to know what her choice of pain was. His muscles tensed, his mind blanked, and Bran vividly saw himself killing the entire personal guard just to see what she would look like with blood streaked through her hair.

"Eyes forward," Daragh growled.

Bran gritted his teeth and told himself that attacking the pathetic excuse for a faerie wasn't going to end well. The duchess was already angry with him. He didn't need to make it worse by delivering her guard's head to her front doorstep. But, oh, how he wished he could.

The palace of Twilight was a crumbling ruin. Once a beautiful building, age and mistreatment had seen it fall from its former glory. Moss covered the floor, trees grew through the walls, and holes dotted the ceiling. Spears of light illuminated the strange gathering of Underfolk nobility.

They were all missing pieces of themselves. Some of them limbs, others eyes, a few even half their bodies. They lay prostrate upon the ground before a throne made of gilded leaves.

The duchess sat upon emerald green cushions, her hands resting on armrests carved in the shape of two great cats, their mouths forever frozen wide open. She was a delicate little creature. Small hands, small body, and a face that always looked slightly childish. There was a hole in the center of her chest where a glass heart glowed a bright green.

Before them was one of the deadliest women in all the faerie courts, and she looked like a child.

"Unseelie prince." Her voice rang out, sweet like the first drop of honey in the fall. "It has been a long time since you graced our court with your presence."

"I had little choice, Duchess of Dusk."

"That is not what my little birdies say."

He almost swore. He'd forgotten about the pathetic little creatures she called "birds." Their wings were leathery like bats, but they were still a form of bird. She'd twisted them with dark magic, and now they spied for her.

"Is that so?" he asked. "What did they tell you?"

"Many things. But first that you enter my kingdom with a woman on your arm. I thought you weren't interested in a bride."

Aisling snorted behind him.

He held his breath as the duchess cocked her head to the side and narrowed her gaze on the witch behind him. "Something to say?"

"I wouldn't marry him if my life depended on it."

He squeezed his eyes shut. Why couldn't she ever manage to stay silent? The woman had challenged a faerie with those words, and now he didn't know what the duchess would insist upon.

Bran needed to get close enough to steal the heart from her chest. He had to rip it from her tiny form, and then they could run. He would do whatever it took, even if that meant marrying the little witch to entertain the duchess.

But, he didn't want to marry her like that.

The thought disturbed him. He didn't want to marry at all. That wasn't the steps his life would take him. He was going to break his curse, then galivant off into the world without a care for anyone but himself.

He was Unseelie. That was their way.

And yet... his gaze cast toward her. Aisling stared defiantly at the duchess, no fear or indecision softening her straightened spine. She was a powerful woman in her own right, and he stood between two pillars of feminine wiles.

Bran couldn't decide if he was the luckiest man in the Otherworld, or the most cursed.

The duchess chuckled. "I wouldn't marry him for all the gold in the world, either. In that, you and I see eye to eye."

"Good."

"But you are wrong."

Aisling flinched. "Excuse me?"

"You are interested in him. A woman in love moves differently than those who are unattached. Your eyes remain fogged with the promise of a future. Your heart beats in a rhythm that is unnatural as it tries to match his. And your hips sway as you try to capture his attention."

Bran lifted a brow and turned to stare at her.

"I do not," Aisling replied caustically. "I don't appreciate you trying to ascertain what I'm thinking when you have no idea who I am."

"I'm not reading your mind. I'm reading your body, and that is a very different thing."

"You're reading nothing, because you're wrong."

The duchess tapped her fingernails on the tops of the giant cats' heads. "Interesting. You don't want him to know."

"What I do want to know is why you think you can read me so easily?"

"Because you're a woman walking into this room with not one, not two, but three curses." The duchess held up each finger as she spoke. "A woman with that many nooses around her neck knows when something good has landed at their feet. They also have a great sense of self-preservation. You are going to hold onto him in the hopes that you won't drown. But if you think that will work, then you are very foolish indeed."

Bran's ears were ringing. The words felt as though they were pointed at him, but she was saying them to Aisling. What third curse was this witch bearing? What further secrets was she hiding?

Aisling's chin turned toward him, and he felt the vivid burn of her gaze, though he had never seen it.

He cleared his throat. "Don't look at me. I don't know what nonsense she's spewing either. She obviously doesn't understand that the relationship between master and servant is sacred. I would never lower myself to her station."

The duchess barked out a laugh. "I had forgotten how

entertaining you are, my dear Unseelie prince."

The doors behind them burst open, slammed against the wall, and sharp cracking footsteps echoed to the broken ceiling.

"Not as entertaining as I."

The Duke of Dusk strode into his home with a confidence few could afford. Black boots with silver buckles glinted in the light, dark breeches tucked into their brim. His tunic might have once been an elaborate jacket, red leather stitched carefully to black wool, but now was moth-bitten and ragged. It lay over his thighs and chest perhaps a little too tight, but emphasized his natural strength.

Perhaps strangest of all was that the duke wore a metal mask. Bolts held it against his skull, the skin red and raw at the edges. The last time Bran had seen him, the duke was a whole man. He remembered striking features and eyes that saw straight into his soul.

"Duke," Bran said, nodding in the other man's direction.

"Unseelie. Here to steal my wife?"

"Hardly. That is your own doing, and I will not save you from it."

At least the duke found Bran entertaining. His laughter rang through the court and eased the tension that thickened the air.

"Wife," he said. He strode to the throne, bent down, and pressed a kiss against the duchess's cheek. "What mongrels have you brought to our court?"

"Only the Unseelie."

Aisling snorted again. "I'm no Unseelie."

"Are you not?" The duchess leaned around the duke and pointed at Aisling. "A woman without a face, without a people, without a reason. Just what are you?"

"A woman far from her home who needs your help so that I might return to it."

"Why should I help you?"

"You may be Duchess of the Underfolk, but I am certain you are still Fae. Mine is a story very few know, but you will now be part of it."

The duchess lifted a hand for her husband to take, then slowly stood from her throne. She barely reached the duke's chest, and yet somehow still looked as though she were the stronger one. When he placed a hand on her shoulder, the heart glowed brighter.

Bran hoped she wasn't about to throw them out. Or worse, ask for their head. Aisling played a dangerous game, although it was one he had planned to play himself.

The Fae always liked a good story. They enjoyed telling them over and over again until the words twisted themselves into something new. Hers was a strange tale.

He stepped forward. "I will offer my story. It is how an Unseelie prince became bound by a mere witch."

"That's not an interesting story. It has happened a thousand times, and I know each tale in its original tongue." The duchess waved a hand, and the couple began to walk away.

Bran was stunned. How could she say no that easily? That had been the plan. How else was he to capture her attention? Had she just dismissed them?

"Wait." Aisling's voice rang true and strong.

The Duchess paused but did not look back.

"I offer my story."

"What part?"

"The whole of it. My story, word for word, in exchange for allowing us to remain in your palace for a few nights more and for your secrecy regarding my tale."

"What good is it to know a story no one else can hear?" the duchess scoffed.

"Because then you will be the only person in the world other than myself who knows it."

And just like that, Bran knew Aisling had caught the duchess in a web. Faeries loved a good story, that much was true. But holding something infinitely important and being the only person to know it?

That was an addiction none of them would ever shake.

The duchess turned slightly, the dark fabric of her dress gathering around her legs in a pretty swirl. "You have my attention, witch. I accept your offer." She pointed at Bran. "And yours. We'll start with you, Unseelie prince. Come with us."

Ominous.

Bran stepped forward, sliding the back of his hand across Aisling's in a way he hoped was reassuring. The duchess had promised safety, and her word was law in this palace.

He hoped Aisling wouldn't do anything foolish, but that was like wishing the tide still.

CHAPTER 7

THE DUCHESS OF DUSK

Bran followed the duke and duchess to their personal chambers. The winding hallways and weak, filtered light were exactly the same as he remembered. It was strange how little the Palace of Twilight changed, even after all these years.

The first time she'd dragged him here, he was a young man with a chip on his shoulder. He was still young to the Fae, but Bran liked to think he'd grown up since then.

Now, he traversed the halls with new eyes. Carvings decorated the ancient stone, each magnificent creation a sign of someone who cared enough to leave their mark on this place. Though the duchess and her people were twisted, they loved each other fiercely.

The duke pressed his hand against the duchess's waist, guiding her every step of the way. He wore love on his being the same way as the duchess had described Aisling. The duke never took his eyes off his wife.

"Your mask?" Bran asked as he followed them. "That's new."

"It is."

"The last time I saw you, you were sporting six sets of arms."

"I grew tired of having so many limbs. Everyone expected me to do six times the amount of work."

"Sound reasoning."

The duke snorted. "I wasn't fond of it."

They paused in front of a red door, handprints decorating the edges where hundreds of small goblins had held it open for the duke and duchess. Bran hesitated, allowing them to enter their domain first. He wouldn't put it past them to hide an assassin, just to see the expression on Bran's face.

Inside, a small fire crackled in a gilded hearth. Worn, plush furniture awaited them in a room filled with golden ornaments and red wallpaper. It was a room fit for royalty, and as such was surprising to Bran to see in the duchess's home. She liked the aesthetic of dying things.

"This is a strange room to find in your home," he observed. "I thought you despised bright colors."

The duchess gestured for him to take a seat. "We all change, Unseelie. Even you."

She had him there. He couldn't say her castle had changed without admitting he was a different man than the one who'd wandered these halls all those years ago. A shame, because he dearly loved to criticize the Duchess of Dusk.

Shaking his head, he sank onto the loveseat and extended his arm along the back. "A story for a safe night was the deal I believe?"

They sat down across from him, the duke's hand never far from hers. The duchess smiled and asked, "Tea?"

"I don't trust you not the poison it."

"Silly. I'm not going to poison you before the story." She reached forward and hooked a finger through the handle of a teapot on the small table before them. "I'll poison you afterwards."

"Then by all means, pour away."

While she played house, the duke watched him through the slanted eyes of his mask. Bran recognized the look. He was being measured, tried, and slowly stripped of all his shields. He pitied the man who forgot how talented Bran was at hiding his emotions and inner secrets.

The duchess held out a small teacup, the porcelain cracked but still holding the steaming tea. He took it with a frown.

"Are you in the habit of trying to make your house guests comfortable now?" he asked.

"Only those I want something from." She passed a cup to her husband. "Or perhaps the ones who want something from me."

"I want nothing from you. We were merely passing through when your personal guard accosted us. You really should be kinder to travelers," he said sarcastically.

She leveled him with an unimpressed look. "We all know why you're here Bran."

He hoped she didn't, or this was going to be harder than he thought. Keeping his face still as a midnight pool, he dipped a finger into the steaming water and muttered a quiet spell. When it darkened to a deep black, proving the tea wouldn't harm him, he took a sip.

"Enlighten me then, duchess. I'm afraid you have me at a disadvantage." He kept his tone purposefully calm and collected.

"You want my heart."

Bran choked, spitting tea back into the cup. "Excuse me?"

"Not everyone is as foolish as you seem to think." She smiled. "I'm not going to make it easy for you to steal my heart."

He didn't have to dance around words anymore. She knew he wouldn't lie, nor would he try to convince her of anything other than the truth. Bran licked his lips and stilled his bouncing knee.

Finally, he cleared his throat and said, "I would be disappointed if you made it easy for me."

"Good. Now that all that madness is cleared up..." She leaned forward and set her teacup back on the table with a clack. "Who is this woman you've brought into my kingdom, and why can't I see her face?"

"I don't know the answer to either of those questions," he replied honestly. "She's a secretive little thing. I was traveling by a small human town and paused to watch them burn a witch. Somehow, she saw me through my glamour and flung a binding curse at me hard enough to scar."

He rubbed a hand over his chest, although the mark no longer ached. The memory didn't make him angry now. It filled his lungs with fire of an entirely different kind.

The duchess chuckled. "She cursed *you*?"

"And threatened to do more than that."

"This creature is intimidating indeed. Cursing a faerie prince is a death sentence for most."

"She didn't know I was a prince."

"But she saw through your glamour?" The duchess tapped a finger against her chin. "Stranger and stranger. I've never

199

heard of a witch who could do that."

"Neither have I." And it still bothered him. Lorcan had alluded she wasn't human, but she couldn't possibly be a faerie. He'd know. She couldn't be that good of a liar.

The duke caught his wife's gaze, humming under his breath. "We have met something like that before, although it was a strange meeting and I couldn't guess what the creature was."

"Oh really? Do share."

"He was human, but more. A cousin of mine met him as a child, saw how talented the boy was in sculpting and art, and brought him back to the Otherworld. They tried to teach him magic, but he had no talent for it. In the end, they cut off his hands and replaced them with a faerie's so that he might create the work they so desired."

It was an unsettling thought, although Bran had heard of such things before. "How long did he remain in the Otherworld?"

"Long enough to cause quite the dramatics within the family he'd stayed with. Foolish mortals should never fall in love with faeries."

"You think she's human then? Otherworld touched, so perhaps a little more than human, but was born in the human realm?"

"What else could she be?" The duke set his teacup down. "She's not faerie. I think we all can agree upon that."

Bran certainly did. Aisling was an enigma, but she wasn't an accomplished liar. Everything about her screamed human, from her toes to the top of her cursed head. He wanted her to be faerie. A strange part of him desired nothing more than to know she would exist as long as he.

But dreams were meant to be broken.

The duchess shook her head. "No, I don't believe she's Otherworld touched. I think she's an oddity wrapped in shadows. She'll surprise all of us when the truth comes out."

If it were possible for the duke's mask to look surprised, it did. "Wife?"

"There's something familiar about her, don't you think? I spent countless years in the faerie courts before coming here, and she has an air about her that isn't human. It's not the way she speaks or her mannerisms. It's the way she moves."

"I would say she moves as any might," her husband grunted. "There's nothing special about the girl other than a strange curse."

"I will agree most faeries would have removed such a superficial curse a long time ago, not being able to see her face is an annoyance, but there's something I can't quite put my finger on..." The duchess tapped her finger again, as if the gentle movement could rattle her thoughts to the correct order. "I will speak with her. Perhaps then I can understand what is truly going on."

Bran was almost insulted. "What do you think she will tell you that she won't tell me?"

"Unseelie," the duchess said with a chiding tone, "women tell each other things men couldn't even imagine. You're fooling yourself if you think otherwise."

He met the duke's uneasy stare. A silent message passed between the men. They understood the duchess spoke of an unwritten code and the mystery of feminine secrecy.

Clearing his throat, Bran stood. "On that note, I'd like to

retire to my room."

"Yes, I suppose I did promise you that." The duchess tsked. "A shame, I'd love to put you out with the livestock."

"A shame you agreed to my story for safety."

"I intend to collect on that, Unseelie Prince."

"I'd be disappointed if you didn't." He swept into a graceful bow. "Another time, my lady. Travel has fatigued me."

She snorted. "Nothing could fatigue an Unseelie prince, but your twisted words are appreciated. There will be a guard waiting for you beyond the door. He'll take you to one of the noble quarters."

"And the girl?"

"You aren't in any position to be demanding a room for that girl, Unseelie."

Bran held his ground, squaring his shoulders and preparing himself for whatever fight the duchess was going to throw at him. "She will stay in a better room than mine. After all she's been through at the hands of the Fae, she deserves that much."

"The Fae?" the duchess quietly asked. "Or you?"

He gritted his teeth and shook his head. "Don't try to twist my words, Duchess."

"I'm not twisting your words, prince. As you've said, you're the only faerie she's been with these past weeks."

"I already weary of your sharp tongue."

"As I'm sure she is weary of yours." A wicked smile spread across her face. "Don't worry, Unseelie. I'll take care of your little witch. And when I'm done with her, I'll have all the answers I could ever desire."

"She isn't used to our cruelty and doesn't mince her words

like us."

"I know."

The door opened, and an invisible hand pushed him through the crumbling frame out into the waiting grasp of a guard. He growled but allowed himself to be pushed through.

"Oh, Unseelie?" the duchess called out. "I trust you won't be causing any issues for me while you're here. This truce will only last as long as you are amiable."

"I don't plan on stealing your heart tonight, if that's what you're asking."

Her laughter rang in his ears as the guard dragged him away.

"Hopefully this will be a suitable room," the maid said, placing her back against the wooden door and shoving with a grunt. She was a tall, willowy thing with limpid eyes too large for her face. "The duchess went to great trouble to find you the perfect accommodation."

Aisling doubted the woman had gone through any trouble, but she wasn't going to correct the maid. Having a room at all was a blessing. She could have been in the stables.

Blowing out a breath that stirred the hair covering her face, she waited as the maid wiggled her way through the small gap and then squeezed herself past the door that appeared stuck halfway open. Nothing in this castle worked the way it should.

That included doors that didn't open as expected.

The room beyond was remarkable in its own way. Cobwebs hung from the ceiling, small spiders skittering across the gossamer threads. Dust-covered blood-red curtains hung limp around a mound of pillows, likely meant to be a bed. Adjacent to the pillows, a small hearth crackled with flame, and a still pool of water glistened in the farthest corner.

It was a modest room by all accounts, and any who were accustomed to finer living might have noticed the cracks on the floor, the swirling eddies of dust, and the slight green tinge to the water. But Aisling was a creature born in the shadows of both worlds. To her, this room could not be finer.

The maid watched her with a severe gaze. "Well?"

Aisling blinked. "Well what?"

"Is it suitable, or shall I tell the mistress to find you another room?"

This had to be a test. The duchess was too intelligent a woman to give her the finest room available. Aisling was certain this was one of the worst, but she wanted to keep the upper hand.

She affixed a smile on her face the maid couldn't see and clasped her hands to her chest. "It will suit just fine. Shall I beat the pillows?"

The slight jab raced up the maid's back. Aisling smirked at her stiffened posture and waltzed to the bed. She wasn't afraid of a little hard labor, and if they didn't want to clean her room, then that was no skin off her back.

She grabbed the first pillow and smacked it hard. Dust billowed into the air, white and cloud-like, striking her nose with surprising force. She rocked backward, sneezing multiple times until the air cleared.

The maid covered her mouth and giggled.

"Goodness," Aisling gasped. "How long have these pillows been sitting?"

"About half a century, madame."

"That explains it." She placed the pillow down and gently backed away. "We'll leave it there then. And please don't call me madame. I'm anything but."

"You travel with the Unseelie prince. You must be equal in rank to the Duchess?"

"Unlikely. Didn't you hear him say I was his servant?" It was all she could do not to make a face. "I'm no lady."

"Seems odd that the mistress would give you a maid then."

It was, but Aisling wasn't going to encourage the meddling. She nodded in response and gestured behind the maid to the door. "If you don't mind, I'd like to rest. It's been a long journey."

"I'm certain it has." The maid pointed toward the fire. "If you really are a servant, perhaps that's a better place than the pillows."

"You don't say."

The maid left with her pride still intact. Aisling couldn't say the same for herself.

She glanced at the mound of pillows, her body aching for a single moment of weightlessness. How long had it been since she'd slept in a bed?

Shaking her head, she refused to let the thought linger. She'd slept on the ground most of her life. Worrying about a bed wasn't like her.

Aisling eyed the door, wondering just how long it would

take until the faeries tried to spy on her. She couldn't lay down runes on the floor. They were easily found, and the Duchess likely wouldn't appreciate her ruining the floor.

Instead, she grabbed the nearest candle and circled the room.

"By fire, I ward thee. Guard this space from all ill will and all those who wish to harm me."

Aisling repeated the gesture with flicks of stagnant water, with her own breath, and the last remaining apple cores from her pack. It wasn't much, but it was at least a little bit. She felt the golden light of the wards lift over her head and connect at the peak of the ceiling.

Now, she could sleep.

"That Unseelie is making you soft," she grumbled as she dragged a few of the carpets toward the fire. "You've done this before, and you'll do it again. Ridiculous woman. Lingering on thoughts that have no place in your head. Where's your courage?"

"Where is your courage, indeed?"

Aisling stiffened. She recognized the light-as-air voice but hadn't expected it to show up in her own room.

The duchess stood in her doorway. Her eyes were raised, following patterns in the air that Aisling could not see. The slight woman reached forward and tapped, her fingernail pinging on something invisible.

"Not a bad spell," the duchess said. "You're missing a section here, though." She pointed at a small piece of Aisling's spell, then stepped into the room, unhindered and without trouble.

Aisling frowned. "I missed nothing. Those wards are

airtight."

Their magic traced down her spine, strong and without flaw. She had been placing wards since she was a child. There was no possible way those wards had a hole in them.

The duchess's eyes narrowed. "How intriguing. Why wouldn't your magic be flawed? You are, after all, human."

A bell rang in Aisling's ear. The words weren't entirely truth. In fact, they'd been carefully said to pull out a secret. The duchess didn't actually believe them, nor was she insinuating that Aisling was actually human.

Sarcasm was a faerie's greatest weapon.

She spun on her heel and lifted a hand, the eye in the center of her palm blinking. "What do you know?"

"Nothing as of yet," the duchess soothed. "But I intend to understand what you are. Or perhaps *who* you are, if you know it."

"You know I'm not human."

"I suspected it the moment you first walked in."

"That's a shame," Aisling growled. "I thought it was impossible for anyone to see through the curse binding my face from sight."

"Any face is as much a mask as your curse. We wear false expressions, whisper secrets and lies, until our flesh becomes hard like stone. Your curse hides your identity, not your soul."

Aisling blew out a breath and lowered her hand. "I'm not sure I like that anymore than someone not being able to see my face."

"May I?" The duchess gestured toward the fire. "You promised me your story, and I rarely sleep at night."

"Why?"

207

"Nightmares plague even the best of us."

Aisling searched the other woman's gaze for some clue of her plan. Why was the duchess here? Did she really want only a story?

Twisted words were hard for Aisling to follow. She had dealt with young faeries, on the off chance they had wandered by her hut. But they were usually weak and meddled in human affairs as a way to relieve their boredom. Royalty was an entirely different story. The duchess had thousands of years to perfect careful words and veiled truths.

Aisling worried what secrets she would reveal. Her story would be laid bare in front of this powerful being, but more than that, her soul.

She hesitantly stepped toward the fire and sank down with the duchess.

The tiny faerie reached out her hands toward the warmth and rubbed them together, letting out a happy hum. "It's nice, is it not? A fire on a cold night always reminds me of home."

"I've never thought of a palace as a particularly warm place."

"I never think of this as my home," the duchess murmured. "I wasn't always a duchess."

Aisling nodded. "That's right. You're a self-made woman."

"I fought tooth and nail to own all that is mine and will continue to do so until all the breath leaves my lungs."

Gods, Aisling didn't want to see herself in this woman. The duchess was a dangerous creature, living in a crumbling kingdom of forgotten creatures. Her husband tore away bits and pieces of their subjects to attach to himself, and the duchess reigned over the remains.

She fought. She conquered. She devoured. Through all the hardships of life, she rose victorious.

Aisling's stomach clenched. "My story, Duchess. I promised it with the request that you tell no one."

"And I will not. A faerie vow is one not easy to break."

She hadn't ever told anyone her story. Only Badb and her true family knew where she came from, who she was, and what had happened. Now she found the words stuck in her throat when she tried to speak them.

Finally, Aisling coughed and began. "I was born into a high Seelie family, the youngest daughter of Lord Illuma and his lady wife. They knew I was different from the moment I came out of the womb. Of all their golden children, I was the first to be born with hair as dark as night and skin white as snow. They knew my story would not be one to follow in their footsteps.

"It is social suicide to keep a child who erred toward the Unseelie. And try as they might, the more I grew, the more I became Unseelie. My choices never followed the rules. I wanted to run in the wilds, climb trees, tear fabric, and rub dirt on my skin.

"They tried for years to shackle my natural instincts. They beat honor into my back, poured truth down my throat, and carved duty into my arms." Aisling rubbed her biceps, the memories sending gooseflesh dancing across her skin. "Nothing worked."

The duchess shifted on the carpet, a ripple running through her like a wave. "They tried to force you to be Seelie?"

"Yes."

"Then they tried to unravel the fabric of your soul and make it anew." Anger laced her words with red.

"They were trying to save their child."

The duchess shook her head. "They were trying to save themselves."

"Perhaps that is correct, but I have long since stopped judging them. They did what they could for their family."

"What did they do to you?"

The fire crackled, a spark flying out of the hearth and onto the nearest rug. Aisling crushed the coal under her heel. "They left me in the forest and waited for a family to claim me. A young witch did, a man who goes by the name of Lorcan, although it is not his true name. In return, they took his youngest sister who was a sickly creature. She would have died if the faeries didn't take her away.

"They didn't keep the human changeling as a replacement for me. She now resides with a faerie maid who never conceived children. As far as I know, she lives a charmed life and has flourished quite well. She's turning into the perfect example of a lady's maid."

Another coal popped. This time, the duchess lashed out a hand and snatched it from the air. The ember burned bright red in her palm. Aisling watched as the faerie pressed it against the cavity of her chest and the green glass heart absorbed the heat. The glow brightened, sending strings of green light wriggling underneath her skin.

"And the markings on your skin?" the duchess asked.

Aisling held her hands up to the light. The eyes blinked, their gaze kind and quiet. "A gift from my grandmother. My parents are well known Seelie Fae, and though they gave me up, they do not wish me ill. If anyone should know who I am, they could use it against them. My identity must be kept secret from everyone."

"Until you can protect yourself."

"Which I can." She closed her fingers into fists, digging into the eyes. "But the curse remains."

The Duchess leaned back on her hands, staring into fire, lost in thought. "If you could remove this curse, would you?"

"I have spent my entire life trying to find a way to break my chains. But a binding curse is forever." At least she had thought until now. If the Unseelie prince could prove this spell worked, then perhaps she could find a way to break the curse on herself as well.

"What if breaking the curse would do more harm than good?" the Duchess asked. "You don't know what it holds at bay."

"All it does is hide my face." She held out her hands. "The eyes channel my magic. The black tips conceal my face. It's a rather simple spell woven into dark magic."

"May I?"

At Aisling's nod, the duchess took her hands and pulled them forward. She stared into the eyes, and Aisling felt their magic tangling together.

The duchess's magic was like white lightning. Cold and ancient, it threaded through her veins like the kiss of night on an icy lake. She saw a field of snow in her mind's eye. Cloudless skies that spread over a lake so vast it seemed to have no end. Crystal-clear ice covered its surface, and a pair of dark eyes stared from beneath the cold plains, blinking in the moonlight.

The duchess's magic was seemingly unending.

Aisling swallowed, and her hands shook. The cold seeped underneath her fingernails, pricking her skin and pulling at her own magic. It tasted her in one cold lick before the duchess released her.

"You've been searching for a long time," the duchess quietly said. "But you haven't been searching in the right places."

"What?"

"It's not a binding curse. You have been chained by a protection spell, not a binding curse. That magic was created entirely out of love. A binding curse cannot be born from such an emotion."

Tears burned Aisling's eyes. "A protection spell?"

She had wasted so much time. There were many counter-spells for such a creation, regardless of whether it was an original piece of magic.

The duchess lifted a hand, flourishing a quick movement that revealed a small piece of paper in her hand.

"All your questions can be answered with just this bit of magic." She held it back when Aisling tried to snatch it from her hand. "But you must be certain, little changeling. Undoing the magic that wraps around you will release everything it holds at bay. If you want to remove your curse, you must be certain."

"Anything," she whispered. "I would do anything to see my own face, to be *seen* for the first time in so many years."

"Then take the paper and seek your own fate."

Her heart beat loud in her ears, but Aisling reached forward and took the spell. It was a simple one, and of course one she hadn't considered. She hadn't thought such an intricate curse could be undone with such a simple spell.

Hope fluttered to life in her chest. Anyone could look in her eyes and see who she was, what she felt, all the things that everyone else took for granted. She could finally be a *person*.

"Thank you," she gasped. "Thank you, Duchess."

"Do not thank me, child. Undoing a curse is not always a blessing."

The duchess stood. Her skirts whirled in a graceful arc as she glided away from Aisling who could not stand even if she wanted to. Her knees shook, her soul quaked, and she looked up at the duchess with sudden appreciation for the strange creature.

"Oh" — the duchess paused at the door — "I shall host a ball to introduce you to my people. I find it's much easier to know someone when they are expected to act properly. You'll never forget the welcome our people give you. I'll send a few faeries to prepare you."

Before Aisling could say a word, the Duchess vanished.

She held the piece of paper in her hand as if it were made of the finest glass. She didn't want it to crumble between her fingers. If this was some cruel jest, she might tear the entire palace apart.

Aisling breathed a relieved sigh when she saw letters still darkening the page. The duchess hadn't lied. There really was a spell that could free her.

The sound of scrabbling at the window filled the room. She glanced over to see Lorcan pulled himself up the side of the palace, huffing and puffing on the windowsill before he dramatically flopped to the floor. "Are you going to do it?'

"You were listening?"

"Well I was going to come into the room, but since you insisted I hide, I assumed I shouldn't."

She cast a severe glance his way. "Lorcan."

And yet...

She caught her reflection in the mirror. The smooth surface of her face and the vague blur where her features should be. She was tired of being a suggestion of a woman, a specter caught in a prison of flesh and bone.

Aisling fingered the edges of the parchment and carried it toward the stagnant pool in the corner. She shrugged the tattered fabric from her shoulders and left Bran's clothing in a heap at the edge of the pool.

She took a deep breath, touched the water with her toe, and then slowly walked forward. The pool was deep enough to cover her shoulders. The burn of salt tingled upon her lips, the tangy taste bursting upon her tongue.

Holding the paper against her chest, she watched as the dark ink bled into the water.

"In the names of my ancestors, my gods, and myself, I call upon thee, spirits of water. Come forth, cleanse me of all magics, and restore my soul to balance. By our wills combined, so mote it be."

Tiny ripples formed in the water from each of her exhalations. The ink swirled, growing thicker and darker as magic seeped out of her hands into the pool. It was dragged from her skin each second.

Tiny hands stroked her sides, the water spirits easing the protection spell from her skin moment by moment. Created by nothing more than water, they were incredible specimens and infinitely kind. Their bodies melded with the water, entirely invisible but easy to feel.

They existed on magic, and she was providing them a feast.

A small hand shoved her forward. Tiny tugs and pulls

encouraged her farther and farther into the pool until she finally dunked her head underneath the water.

Dark hair floated around her in great swaths of darkness. Ink spread until she could taste the bitterness on her tongue. She felt the spirits of water pulling at the tattered threads of her curse and wondered just how much it was going to hurt.

Finally, the last bit of the curse unraveled, leaving her palms like veins pulled from her skin. She opened her mouth and inhaled the stagnant salt water.

Aisling shot up to the surface, grasped the edge of the pool and coughed up a lungful of water and ink. It wouldn't end. Her eyes widened, she clawed at the stone as more and more black sludge poured from her lips.

She whimpered but endured as her body rid itself of the lingering effects of the curse.

The dark spell sank into the stones. Charred spots marked where she had purged the darkness that had sunk into her lungs and deep within her bones. And though it was terrifying, it was also freeing.

Shaking, she flipped her hands over. The eye tattoos remained on her hands, but they were no longer pulsing with power. The eyes didn't blink, but the tips of her fingers were now as pale as her skin with tiny half-moons on her nails.

Tears pooled in her eyes. She let out a tiny sob and lowered her forehead to the ragged stone.

"Aisling?" Lorcan quietly asked.

"Yes?"

"Are you done?"

She nodded against the rocks. "I think so."

"Good, because that was disgusting." She heard him hop

down to the floor. He padded over to her, nails clicking with each step. "You know how vomiting makes me uncomfortable."

"And god forbid I make you uncomfortable." Her head felt as though it wasn't attached to her body anymore. It was so heavy and difficult to lift, but she managed just enough to give him a stare. "Excuse me while I try to be a normal person."

"Yes, well, if you could do it without all the…" He lifted a paw to his mouth and retched. "Never mind, I don't want to think about it. It'll make me sick."

"Lorcan. How have you practiced witchcraft your entire life and managed to retain a weak stomach?"

"Well, I didn't do *that*."

"Just get out of my way or I'll get you wet." She hefted herself out of the pool, flinging water in all directions.

He grumbled and raced to the other side of the room. "You know I don't like getting damp!"

"Just shut up, would you?"

"I would like food. I've been tracking you for a very long time, and I require sustenance."

"I'll get you food in a second."

"I would prefer it now."

Aisling stared up at the ceiling and muttered chants that would hopefully calm her down. When they didn't work, she gave up and glared at him. "Can I look at myself for the first time in over twenty years first? Or would you like me to wait on you before seeing how much my life has changed?"

"Before." He nodded. "I am very hungry."

"I should throw you out the window, you useless excuse

for a man."

She turned away from him and made her way toward the dressing table in the corner. The mirror was cracked and tarnished with age, but it would be enough for her to see what magic had hidden from her.

A shard, smaller than her hand, remained free from smudges, and she had to stoop to pick it up. She closed her eyes, fearful of what she might see. Was she pretty? Was she a hideous creature? Worse, would she even recognize herself?

Steeling herself, she leaned down and stared into her own eyes.

The woman in the mirror gazed back at her, a creature unlike any she'd seen before. She had thought, perhaps, she would have aged like her family. Aisling knew her sister was more beautiful than glimmering gossamer webs. She saw some of her family in the mirror, but she also saw herself.

Dark curls framed a heart-shaped face, which was pleasant enough. Slashes of dark brows arched delicately over equally shadowed eyes. A finely sloped nose met wine-stained lips over a slightly stubborn chin.

Yet, there were storms boiling in her eyes. Faint lines feathered from her eyes, lines of hardship, strife, and exhaustion that marked her skin for all eternity. A small scar slashed through her left eyebrow from when the children had thrown rocks at her. Her lips were set in a severe line, the expression of a woman marching into battle. She wondered how often she wore the angry look.

Pattering feet stepped toward her and then paused. "What do you think?"

"She isn't what I expected."

"You mean *you* aren't what you expected."

"Yes." Aisling lifted a hand and touched her cheek, double-checking the woman she saw was actually herself. "I hadn't expected to look so..."

Lorcan jumped up and put his paw atop her hand. "You have always been beautiful, Aisling, no matter what your face looks like."

She touched a finger to her lip once more and blew out a breath. "Let's sleep."

"Are you all right?"

She silently shook her head and sank down next to the fire.

Her face. It was her face after all this time, and she didn't know how to feel about it. She was beautiful; certainly that was the truth. But she hadn't expected to look so much like her family.

Aisling had only seen them once in person since they gave her up, and from afar. They'd traveled with the Wild Hunt, racing through the countryside looking for people like *her*. But they would never come after her.

She had her father's stubborn brow. She looked at herself the same way he had when he steered the hunt away from her small cabin. Her mother's bee-stung lips, her brother's strong jaw, her sister's stunning gaze, all of them combined to a face she recognized painfully. She looked exactly like her sister.

Lorcan curled up at her side. He glanced up a few times before heaving a sigh and placing his paw on her hand again. "Go to sleep, little witch. It is done."

So it was.

Trying to hide her shivers, she laid down on the rug with Lorcan tucked under her chin and told herself not to be afraid. She'd made this choice knowing she couldn't come back from it.

She was still a wild thing, a woman with the heart of a she-wolf and a face that could tear down cities. Now, everyone knew that as well.

CHAPTER 8

BONE DANCE

The maid twisted Aisling's hair, wrapping it around a hot rod that she kept dipping into the fire. She winced at the tug and bit her lip to keep herself silent. Arguing with them had already proven fruitless. It didn't matter her hair was already curly. They insisted it curled the wrong way.

How was that even possible?

A small whimper escaped her lips at a particularly vicious tug. They refused to let her even move from her seat.

Aisling had walked on pins and needles earlier that morning. She worried they might see her face, the maids. How would they react? Would they think her beautiful? Would they know her family? Worse, would they throw her out because she clearly came from a Seelie bloodline?

But the women who walked into her room would never know that her curse was broken, for they had no eyes.

Their skin was dark as midnight, eyeless faces smooth as porcelain. Golden filigree decorated their faces like masks, accentuating the missing features that didn't seem to hinder them in the slightest. They moved through the room with a grace that rivaled dancers.

They didn't appear to be servants, at least not that she could tell. Their clothing was made of the finest silk. It slithered across their bodies, quietly hushing as they shifted and moved. Small circlets were woven through their braided hair. Even their fingers were dipped in gold.

"Who are you?" Aisling asked for the hundredth time.

"We are the favored few."

"I'm assuming you mean the Duchess of Dusk approves of you?"

The faerie sagely nodded.

"Well that doesn't clear up anything, now does it?" Aisling muttered. "Ouch!"

Another woman entered, the perfect twin for the one currently tugging on Aisling's hair hard enough to yank it from her skull.

In the newcomer's arms was a swath of black fabric draped over her arm. "Your outfit for this evening's ball, my lady."

"Not a lady."

The faerie cocked her head and held out the dress regardless. Aisling didn't want to touch it. It looked as though it were made out of far too fine a material for her, and she'd spent her whole life running from such things.

And yet, there it was. So close to touch, and she knew it would feel as smooth as it looked. Silk like that could only be made in faerie realms.

She blew out a breath and stood up. They helped her into the dress, pouring it over her body like a stream of water until it settled around her form like a second skin. The skirt flared just slightly over her hips, pooling at her feet. Her entire body was covered other than a dangerous dip between her breasts that stopped just above her belly button.

From afar, the dress had looked plain. But up close, she could see the dark embroidered threads across her shoulders and down to her waist that depicted the Wild Hunt. Tiny obsidian stones tangled with the embroidery, making her glimmer as she moved. But not with light. She shone with darkness.

"One last piece," the faerie woman murmured and reached forward with a silver necklace. It was an impressively wrought piece. A tangled vine with sharp thorns created to encircle a slender neck.

Aisling gasped as the cold metal touched her throat. Thorns rested gently against her pulse, and each time she swallowed, she felt the threatening press. It was terrifying, and yet all her senses awoke in a wave of heat.

She pressed her fingers against her collarbone. "All night?"

"Yes, mistress, you must wear that for the remainder of the night." The faerie sprayed perfume onto her exposed chest.

"Why?"

A rough voice answered her, "The Duchess wants to ensure we do exactly as she wants."

"Bran," Aisling replied. A blush spread from her chest to her cheeks, and she spun away from him.

He couldn't see her face. Not yet. She wasn't prepared. There were so many things she wanted to say, to explain.

Why hadn't she told him before? Because a piece of her soul wanted him to always see her as the strange witch who had cursed him. She didn't want to be a Seelie faerie, a contender for his thoughts and emotions. She was content with nothing, no one; she was a shadow in the night that never remained in memories.

Until him.

Her breath caught in her throat as the faeries dipped into curtsies beside her.

"Out," he grunted. Their hurried footsteps nearly made her smile until she heard him walk forward as well. "Ridiculous fanfare for nothing. I don't know what she thinks she's getting out of a ball. We have work to do."

"She doesn't know we're here for her heart," Aisling whispered, frozen in the center of the room.

"Oh, she knows. She made it very clear that she was up for the challenge."

"Then perhaps she feels safe with so many of her followers nearby."

"Maybe," Bran replied. "Or she's just cocky. I'm betting on her thinking we're weak. And we are anything but."

She knew he meant it as a compliment, but she couldn't breathe through the tightness in her throat. Aisling didn't feel very strong right now. She wanted to crumple to the ground, press her hands against her chest, and beg her heart to remain still.

"Aisling?" he asked quietly. "Is something wrong?"

Everything was wrong, and she couldn't tell him because she wasn't brave enough to turn around. She wanted him to see her face, but every fiber of her being refused to turn.

"I-I-" she stuttered, then cleared her throat. "Everything will be fine."

"It will." He stepped into the room, his voice deepening. "She gave you a fine dress to wear tonight. Are you afraid to move in it?"

"No."

He drew even closer until she could feel the heat of him against her back. He drew in a deep breath. "You smell like orchids."

"I thought that might be the scent. Do you like it?"

"I prefer your natural scent." He moved her hair to the side, baring her throat to his gaze and the metal wrapped around her pale neck. "That's better. Now I know it's you."

A ragged sigh expelled from her lips.

She could almost feel his frown. "Aisling, what is it?"

"There's nothing wrong, just… changed." Her heart raced, but she turned and slowly faced him. She had to take a deep breath to look up. Her gaze met his, the endless well of the ocean meeting a starry night sky.

Bran blew out a breath. The sound filled her heart with a certain sense of longing she'd never felt before. His expression softened, and he slowly lifted a hand to touch the roundness of her cheek.

Fingertips, so gentle they were like a feather, brushed along the lines of her face. He stroked the fine edge of her jaw, the fullness of her bottom lip, the featherlight eyelashes which fluttered closed.

And in that moment, Aisling felt for the first time what it might be like to be cherished. He touched her as though she were something fragile. Like the individual strands of a feather that might part and forever ruin if he was too brutal.

"Bran," she whispered. She would tell him everything— who she was, where she came from, explain the feelings bubbling in her chest that she couldn't control.

"I'm sorry," he replied.

She searched his dark gaze. "Why are you sorry?"

He wasn't smiling anymore. There was no tenderness in his eyes, nor awe in the lines of his face. He looked at her as if he was disappointed. No, she realized. Horrified.

"This is the Duchess's doing, isn't it?" he asked, but did not wait for her reply. "Know that she gave you this face to harm me. To distract me. I will not let it, but it cuts to the bone that she would try to use you like this."

Aisling's words stuck in her throat. "Whose face do I wear?"

She could guess the answer, but she wanted to hear him say it. She still looked like her family, enough he would have recognized where she came from and who she was related to. She just hadn't thought he'd known her sister like that. Those damning words would remain with her for the rest of her life, but she wanted to *hear him say it*.

"That of a woman I once loved. Both myself and another tried to win her heart, and I was certain she would choose me. But she was promised to a prince, although there was a time when she might have been mine. In the end, she chose the Seelie prince as everyone wanted her to." He pressed a hand against his chest. "It wounded me for years. Centuries."

"I'm sorry."

"It wasn't your fault, little witch." He tucked a finger under her chin and tilted her face to the light. "A remarkable likeness, although I can appreciate the small differences she tried to implement. The Duchess is a cruel woman indeed."

Aisling swallowed, her heart taking flight through her mouth and whispering words she never intended to speak.

"Could you ever love her again?"

"The woman whose face you wear?" He shook his head. "No. Never again. I have changed, and I know there are many layers to beauty, but that of the flesh is the lowest of them all."

His hand slid from her chin, and Aisling felt her heart shatter.

"I don't think the ball should take too long. Rest when we return. I'm working on a plan. It won't be pretty. I underestimated the Duchess, but it will suffice. Have you seen anything that could be useful?"

She swallowed hard and managed to shake her head. "No."

"All right." He ran a hand through his hair and sighed. "Keep your eyes open. Maybe one of the maids will know something we don't. Are you ready to go?"

"Not quite." She pressed her hands against her stomach, holding the butterflies at bay. "If you'll give me just a moment, I need to adjust the corset underneath the dress."

His cheeks flamed bright red. "Ah, well... Yes. I imagine you don't need help?"

"No."

"Then I'll just..." He gestured at the door and raced out.

She blew out a breath and spun toward the window. Darkness met her gaze, as it always did in this place, but this time it felt more ominous than before.

What was she going to do?

Lorcan crawled out from under the pillows, his ears flat against his skull. "Aisling, don't."

"He thinks I look like *her*," she whispered. "Like my sister."

"She wouldn't want him to. Her choice led her down the

wrong path, but that doesn't mean she would step back in time if she could."

"Does it matter?" She lifted her watery eyes. "He doesn't want to see this face. It reminds him of pain and heartbreak."

"He doesn't know it's *your* face."

"He doesn't know a lot of things." She smoothed a hand down her stomach, forcing her eyes to dry no matter how much she wanted to release the sobs. "And now he cannot know."

"You're being foolish, Aisling. You have to talk to him."

"Soon. Soon I will tell him everything, but let me avoid it tonight." With her spine straightened and her shoulders squared, a mask of calm fell over her newfound face. "Perhaps you should make yourself scarce again, Lorcan."

"Don't do anything you'll regret." Sadness darkened his eyes. "Being with him for a moment isn't worth a lifetime of heartbreak."

Aisling didn't know if she agreed. "He's going to leave once he knows the truth."

"You can't know that for certain."

But she did. He wouldn't want to remain with a woman who had a direct tie to the princess who broke his heart. He wasn't the first. Aisling's sister was known to be a heartbreaker. She'd enjoyed that in her youth.

Bran couldn't look at her without his face twisting in anguish. It was as horrid as a kiss of death.

Lorcan shuffled. "You have to go the ball. The Duchess made it sound as though it wasn't an option to say no."

"I will avoid him as much as possible."

"Do you think he'll let you?"

No, she didn't. Bran was insistent when he wanted

something, and right now he wanted her to figure out the way these faeries ticked. He'd want her eyes on everything, trying to find some chink in the Duchess's armor.

Aisling's eyes fluttered closed. She had a job to do. And she would complete that job whether he approved of her face or not.

"That's my girl," Lorcan said with a warm purr. "You have always been a strong woman, and no man's disapproval of your looks is going to change that."

She turned on her heel. Her fingers flexed as she passed the small dressing table. She desperately desired a mask, something, anything to hide the visage she now wore. Still, she pressed her palm against the door and slid through the wedged opening.

He stood waiting for her on the other side, a dark shadow lurking in the center of the hallway like some great beast about to attack her. Aisling had never been afraid of the dark, and now she understood why. All the best things stood at the very edge of her vision, hidden from the light.

"Are you ready?" he quietly asked.

"I am now."

He reached forward, an almost liquid movement until a spear of light shone from the window upon the fine, embroidered sleeve.

Aisling drank him in as if he were salvation and she the damned. Brocade poured over his shoulders in a high-necked jacket. Black silk fell from his shoulders in an open shirt, leaving his chest bared. She wanted to press herself against the warm skin and count each raised muscle, feel each ragged breath.

She laid her palm on his offered arm and felt the broidered

edges pull at her calloused touch.

"The Duchess has something planned," he murmured, glancing away from her face. "I can feel it."

"Maybe she simply wants to enjoy her last few nights alive."

"Unlikely."

He wouldn't look at her. Aisling bit her lip and stilled her expression, reminding herself that people could *see* her now. She couldn't hide behind a curse where no one could see her mocking faces. They could see her just as well as humans now.

Their footsteps echoed as they walked down the empty hallways. Stone crumbled beneath their heels, and enchanted roots pulled back into the ancient walls. Every inch of this place screamed that it was not a home for humans.

She wasn't human. Aisling needed to accept her faerie roots, and yet she couldn't. Every inch of her rebelled that this was more her home than the small hut where her humble beginnings had taken shape.

Every fiber of her being longed for that place. She wanted to see all four walls of the building within easy reach, her beloved spell books lining a small shelf, a fire crackling nearby, and Lorcan weighing down her feet. It was a simple life, but she now knew that the simple lives were the best.

Bran shifted his arm, letting hers drop and laying his hand on her shoulder. "Not long," he murmured. "We'll discover their secrets, and then we'll leave."

She glanced up and caught his gaze. Something softened there, a small spark she had seen before. And then it was gone in the wake of disappointment.

He looked away from her, and every broken shard of her heart screamed.

"Just a little while then," she confirmed. "Then we'll return to my room and plan our next move."

"You go left, and I'll go right?"

They paused before double doors painted with the heroics of Nuada.

Aisling nodded in agreement, pushed her hand against the door, and plunged into the waiting crowd. She tried not to think about the troubled look he gave her.

He couldn't know.

Silvery moonlight filtered through the shards of stained glass windows. It cast the grand hall in gray shadows. Surely, the entirety of the Duchesses court must have been there. Pressed shoulder to shoulder with each other, hundreds of bodies milled around the large, shattered columns.

A man nodded his head as he gently moved aside. A mantle of bones decorated his shoulders, tiny skulls hanging on strings, laughing as he moved.

She stepped over a fallen pillar, the stone bone white and glowing in the light. Her skirts puffed around her. The fabric moved with a mind of its own. Every time she touched it, waves of fabric rippled down her sides.

"There you are!" a bubbling voice called out. "Witch! Come and entertain us."

The duchess was ever demanding, but if Bran wanted to know if there were secrets, she really should go directly to the source. Aisling turned and plastered a smile on her new face. "I am pleased to do so, but my magic is no different than yours."

"Witches have long been able to tap into magic that is

different than the Fae." The duchess lifted a delicate hand and gestured Aisling to her side.

She looked particularly lovely tonight. A pale green dress hugged her curves so tightly that Aisling could make out the indent of her navel. The glowing heart pulsed through the velvet fabric.

Simplicity seemed to be the duchess's style, which perhaps explained Aisling's own dress. She dipped into a curtsey. "It would be my pleasure to showcase any witch talent you desire. I've been trained since I was very young."

"Yes, yes. We all know the changeling child who took her own fate in her hands."

Aisling glanced up sharply.

"Easy, little one. Your beloved has no idea."

"He's not my beloved."

"If he isn't yet, he will be." The duchess lifted a delicate brow. "I know the look of a woman in love. I stare at such a face in the mirror every day. I would have to be a fool not to recognize it in another of my kind."

Aisling gritted her teeth and changed the subject. "What would you have me do?"

"Read the leaves."

"What?"

The duchess pointed behind them at a dainty table set upon the backs of three men missing their eyes. "We've had our tea while waiting for you and that raven-headed fellow. Now we would like very much to know our fate."

"You want me to read tea leaves?" Aisling tried to keep her jaw from dropping. "That's peddler magic. It's nothing interesting."

"And yet, we would like to be entertained."

She couldn't refuse the woman who also threatened their safety. Ducking her head, she stepped up to the table and reached for the first cup that called her name.

Fine porcelain burned her fingertips. It was lovely, although the very edge was chipped. She turned it round and round in her hand until she felt the lingering spark where the person's hands had held the cup.

"Whose is this?" she asked.

"Mine." The voice was lovely, quiet like a song, and yet powerful like the heralding of a storm. Aisling looked up quickly to find herself lost in the gaze of a strange woman. Her skin was blue as the morning sky and her head was covered with dark snakes. One lifted its head and hissed at her.

"What kind of tea was it?"

"Nothing special," the snake-haired woman replied.

Aisling nodded and tilted her head while looking at the remaining leaves. There was a trick to it, although she didn't really need to look at them. The sparkle of magic lingered even where the leaves had shifted.

"I see a bear in your past," she began, "an untrustworthy person who dogs your steps. I see a bull in the current time, an omen of misfortune and an insult from your enemies. It is a warning you should heed."

The blue-skinned woman leaned forward. "And my future?"

Aisling's lip twitched. "An arrow, surrounded by storm clouds."

"What does that mean?"

Anger vibrated through Aisling's hand, and the cup

whined as she closed her fist around it. She met the duchess's smug gaze. "It's a bad omen, and it points directly to you."

The duchess at least attempted to look surprised. She pressed a hand against her chest and feigned shock. "Whatever could that mean? Surely you pointed the cup wrong, my little witch. The arrow couldn't point at *me*."

"It points directly at you, Duchess. And I do not appreciate being used for sport."

"Well then, I suppose my entertainment is finished."

The duchess snapped her fingers, and the blue-skinned woman tried to run. She spun on her heel, hitting the chest of a one-armed guard who appeared behind her. Aisling didn't even hear a squeak as the large man wrapped his arm around her head and twisted violently. The thud of a body hitting the ground was hidden by the symphony of a hundred voices rising in laughter.

She turned towards the Duchess, forcing herself to remain unphased. "Was that necessary?"

"I don't like liars." The duchess poured another cup of tea. "Shall I read your leaves?"

"I thought you said witches had magic the Fae don't?"

"They do. But reading tea leaves is really quite easy, don't you think?"

Aisling took the offered cup with a small shake of her head. "What are the chances you've poisoned this?"

"If I wanted to kill you, I wouldn't do so in the middle of my ballroom."

Aisling looked at the guard dragging away the blue woman's body. "Is that so?"

"Killing someone in such a simple way is an insult. You're

a worthier conquest." The duchess raised her own teacup and clinked the chipped edge against Aisling's.

"I couldn't agree more." Aisling lifted the cup to her lips and arched a brow.

The tea tasted faintly of fruit, but mostly of rot. Overwhelmingly sweet, it burned the roof of her mouth and sent tendrils of ache through her teeth. They anchored in her skull like the thorns of the vine wrapped around her neck.

She didn't detect any poison, and for that she was grateful. Aisling hated the bitterness of nightshade on her tongue.

When the duchess didn't seem interested in speaking, Aisling followed the other woman's gaze.

Bran made his way through the crowd, quietly speaking with all who would lend him an ear. He paused near a man made entirely of bark and grinned. Aisling felt it deep in her gut.

What kind of man could find joy in a place like this? The tree-like man lifted a gnarled hand and placed it on Bran's shoulder, and he didn't even flinch. These were more his people than any other creature they had seen thus far. He was completely at home with the strange, macabre, and even grotesque.

Perhaps that was why she felt him deep inside her soul. He saw the beauty in broken things, but never tried to put them back together. Broken wasn't useless.

The duchess chuckled. "He's beautiful, isn't he?"

"Whatever are you talking about?" Aisling sipped at her tea.

"You know who I'm talking about, child. It's perfectly acceptable to admire things like him, but only from afar."

"And why is that?"

"Men like him weren't made to be touched by women with scars on their hands. He's one of the black-eyed beauties, creatures hiding within pools of decay. You've seen the celestial bodies hidden in the depths of his gaze. A woman is easily lost while stargazing."

Aisling lost her breath. Her chest caught in a heave, holding the air as if the pain in her ribs might overpower the pain in her heart.

Pity radiated from the faerie next to her who reached out and placed a hand atop hers. "Tell me more about yourself, little witch. We shall watch this dark man as he tries to ply my subjects for a way to kill me. As payment for not killing him now, I shall hear more of your story."

Aisling pulled her hand away and pressed the teacup to her lips. "All my life I have been afraid of fire."

"A strange thing to be sure. Witch magic is elemental at best."

"I used to wake up drenched in sweat, thinking that flames were licking at my legs in the middle of the night. I saw people in the shadows holding tinder and flint with wicked grins on their faces. Every night, I walked through the forest and wondered when someone was going to finally find me.

"They tell little girls to be wary of the woods. They say it is filled with creatures dark, powerful, and cursed. What they don't tell little girls is that monsters live on street corners, in warm houses, and that they carry rosy-red candles to banish all that darkness that is supposed to frighten the children.

"Humans fear the dark because it is filled with things they cannot understand." Aisling shook her head. "I have never felt fear while languishing in the darkness. But I've felt fear with a blazing fire burning all around me until even my shadow fled the light."

The duchess hummed. "So it is true—they still burn witches."

"They prefer to hang us." She thought of the hanging tree, the hundreds of souls crying out that she would never be one of them because she already belonged to the Fae. "But a fire will always suffice."

"Then why him?" The duchess nodded at Bran. "Why the Unseelie prince who has never cared for a thing in the world?"

"He saved me from the fire."

"Please. Spare me the theatrics. That is not why you are interested in him at all. Anyone could have saved you from burning. Even that damned familiar who's wandering my halls, shouting at my guards as if he owns the place."

Aisling gently set her cup onto the table and rearranged her legs so she wouldn't kick one of the kneeling men in the face. They held the table up silently and without complaint. Their sightless faces reminded her far too much of herself.

Why was she so interested in Bran? Because of his foolish nature, how he never failed to argue with her, his bravery, his desire to do good, his hatred for anything that was structured. It was all there and more.

"It was the fire," she said with a shaking voice. "Not the physical one which tried to claim my life, but the fear of fire itself. Somehow, he wiped away the remaining pieces of me that desired the light. He understood my fear and welcomed me into the darkness without judgement. He desires the rot and the ruin. The moth-eaten fabric of our being is one and the same."

And it made her heart hurt to think of it. He had already admitted he couldn't look at her face, and she couldn't curse herself again. Aisling refused to become less of a person for him. She couldn't imagine him ever letting go of ancient heartbreak, so where did that leave them?

In a place between places. A world between worlds. They hovered at a standstill, and neither of them knew how to fix it.

He glanced up, as if he felt her gaze upon him. She saw the instant flash of heat, the darkening edges of his eyes, and the flare of the feathers on his skull. Then it all faded away, a mask of disinterest in its place.

"Do you think he's not interested in you because you have a face?" the duchess asked.

"I think you know why he's no longer interested in me, and that is something you hid on purpose."

"Even I don't know the history of every faerie that walks my halls."

Aisling glared.

"Perhaps I knew there was history between him and another, but I didn't know you would look so much like her. It is a striking resemblance."

"You know my sister?"

"I know your entirely family, Illumina. That is your given name, isn't it?"

Power flared in her hip bones, spreading down her legs, and cementing her to the ground. The use of her true name burned.

"That name has not been uttered since I was a child," Aisling growled. "It is not one I consider to be my own."

"Yet it still holds a little bit of power." The duchess reached for her cup, swirled it three times, and turned it upside down. The dregs of tea leaked onto the saucer, stretching like tentacles.

Aisling didn't want to remember the dreaded name. It wasn't attached to her anymore, other than the fleeting memory of a pale woman who had once stroked her hair during a nightmare. "Illumina," the woman had whispered, pressing lips against her forehead. "It was just a nightmare, sweet."

But Aisling had known even as a child it wasn't a nightmare. Her desires and thoughts weren't normal. She wanted desperately to be something more than just a pretty daughter of the Seelie Fae. Her sister played in golden fields filled with pretty blue flowers and never stared at the darkened forest beyond.

Her family had named her Illumina, the daughter of light. And her entire life she had dreamed of beasts in the forest howling her name. But she didn't fear the monsters.

She wanted to *become* one.

"I've never seen leaves like this," the duchess murmured. She reached in a single delicate finger and touched it to the bottom of the cup. "Not a one out of place, and each resting in the quadrant of your future."

"Is that so?" She tried to stop her voice from shaking.

"I see a war crow," the duchess continued, "returning from battle, blood dripping from its wings. I see nightshade, bitter and poisonous, wrapped around a heart. I see a crown, a blood-drenched land, and feathers falling from the sky like rain."

Aisling's quiet gasp seemed to echo as all sound fell away from them.

The duchess looked up and met her gaze, fear glowing in

the depths of her emerald eyes. "Perhaps you shall be the one to kill me after all."

"Where is your husband?"

"He prefers to remain away from such revelries."

"Then you are in grave danger," Aisling whispered. "I don't want to kill you."

"Because you see something of yourself in me?"

"No," a choked sob burst from her lips, "because I see myself becoming you."

They stared at each other. Two dark women with souls stained from the blood of innocents. Magic sang in their bones, lamenting the deaths but celebrating the power that came with such a loss. They both had suffered at the careless hands of those who had tried to strip them of their power, and both had shown their enemies what happened when they tried to burn a woman who carried fire in her breast.

She feared losing the piece of herself that made her warm to others. Aisling had always been withdrawn, but she *felt* deeply. Every stone, every cut, every threat—they stung her soul. But she could see a time when such things would no longer bother her.

And this cold woman in front of her was the outcome.

The duchess reached forward and skated a tea-stained finger over the back of Aisling's hand. "You are here for my entertainment, little girl. Don't forget that."

Hidden meaning slipped underneath the words.

If I die, it will be an adventure.

Aisling nodded, then dashed the tears from her cheeks. "Then by all means, how might I entertain you tonight?"

There was a healthy amount of respect in the duchess's

eyes as she rose from her seat. Aisling realized she'd been seated on another of the kneeling men. His back immediately curved, as if he had been stuck in the same position for so long his muscles spasmed.

The duchess lifted her hands over her head and clapped loudly. "My family! We have a rare treat to entertain us. The Unseelie Prince and his witchling have graced our court with their presence. I call upon them to dance!"

"Dance?" Aisling choked out. "I don't dance."

"You'll learn."

Hands pressed her forward, shoving her through the crowd past all manner of Unseelie creatures. They were missing eyes, ears, arms, lips. Each grotesque face gnashed at her, jeering and pushing her forward until she was turned around in the center of the ballroom.

She slammed against another person, shoulder blades pressed against his heat, and immediately knew who it was. She heaved a sigh while telling herself to ready herself. He'd look at her again as if she was something horrible. And she would have to endure.

He turned, his breath fluttered against the nape of her neck, and Aisling forgot how to breathe. It was so easy to remain detached when she had held herself away from him. But now she felt naked, bared entirely to him, and she didn't know how to act.

"Aisling," he muttered, "they're expecting us to dance."

"I didn't agree to be the show of the night."

"It's not the worst thing we've done together." She could feel his eyes on her. They drifted across her shoulders, dipping down to the curve of her waist. "Shall we?"

She swallowed. "I don't want to make you uncomfortable with my new face."

"You couldn't make me uncomfortable if you tried," he replied with a chuckle.

"Is that a challenge, Unseelie?"

"It always is between us."

The words filled her with a sense of purpose, an understanding of their predicament. He wasn't holding his discomfort over her head like a trophy he'd somehow won. They would march forward through his past.

She let out a shuddering breath as his fingers danced over her shoulder. Each digit carefully whispered down her arm. Two of his fingers slid under the soft skin where her heart beat furiously, then he lifted her arm delicately into the air.

A musician ran his bow across a violin's strings. The thrumming call echoed in a single note, vibrating through her soul. An answering call rang out on the other side of the room.

Bran gently stepped forward, heat blanketing her shoulders. She tried to focus, to breathe, but everything faded away as his other arm reached in front of her. His hand spread wide over the rounded curve of her waist, then sliding forward until his palm was flat against her stomach.

When he tugged her backward, every muscle in her body tensed. Fire spread from his palm, but she wasn't afraid. Instead, the heat spread through her body until she felt as though she could fly.

His voice whispered in her ear, "Are you ready?"

She tilted her chin just enough to catch a glimpse of dark feathers. "Unseelie, I do believe you are trying to seduce me."

"Witch," he growled, "what would you do if I was?"

They spun into movement, gliding across the floor with her back pressed against his chest. He controlled her body and soul with every tiny nudge and pressure. She knew exactly what he wanted her to do, how he wanted her to move, and she yearned for him. It didn't matter that she didn't know how to dance. *He did.*

Control was not easy for her to give up. He damned her to yield, and every time she stiffened, his body compensated. Slight shifts, a pressure at her hips, small indications of what he wanted her to do, and she didn't even need to see his face.

Unseelie flashed by, their faces twisting into one macabre vision of monster and Fae, melded together into one impossible being.

As the violinists lifted their song into a crescendo and beasts beat drums, he released his hold on her hip and spun her in circles. She saw only flashes of starlight until he brought her back around and caught her firmly against his chest.

Aisling focused on the bruise of his lips, parting into a smile that seared her to the bone. His arms slid under hers, and her quaking knees didn't matter since he held her up. He spun them in circles, around and around the ballroom. Moonbeams danced across her shoulders, dripped down the open part of her dress, pooled in the center of her being, and filled her with feminine light.

He didn't recoil from her face. The more he stared, the less his gaze ached with disappointment.

"What are you staring at?" he asked.

"You."

"Why?"

The ache in her chest spread until she could hardly breathe.

She wanted to tell him he haunted her thoughts and dreams. She was terrified of his rejection and hadn't realized that until this moment. Their travels had turned her into a different woman, and she didn't know herself anymore.

Instead, she lifted a shoulder and stepped closer. "You're the only thing to look at."

He arched a brow, and the raven eye stared her down. "Not the answer I was expecting."

"And what were you expecting, Unseelie prince?"

The violins wound down, and a final beat of the drums hung in the air. Bran slid his hand up, cupped her head, and gently dipped her backward until all she could see was the dark feathered side of his face surrounded by shards of broken stained glass.

"Even with all your darkness, you are too good for me," he whispered.

"I will never believe that," she replied.

"Why not?"

"Because you have a crooked smile that is both cruel and kind. You are Unseelie, yet your hands speak of softness and a desire to do good. You have stardust in your eyes, and I find you utterly brilliant."

"Careful, witch," he warned, "I might think you enjoy my company."

"I do." The words tumbled from her mouth without warning. She hadn't meant to admit it, but there it was, out in the open, ragged and shivering in the cold air of the ballroom.

His eyes widened, shock running through him in a shiver that carried into her. His arm tightened around her waist, his bicep flexed to pull her forehead to his. Breath fluttered over her lips that was more powerful than a kiss.

"What are you doing to me?" he whispered, the words slipping down her throat and burrowing into her heart.

The duchess's voice cut through their revelries. Her slow claps echoed through the ballroom. "Bravo! Such a wonderful performance, it shall entertain us for centuries."

Bran slowly straightened, keeping his grip steady and reassuring. "It is our pleasure to oblige, Duchess."

"I'm sure it is." The grin on her face twisted into something feral. "Run along now, little children. I don't think you want to be here for the hunt."

Aisling watched the blood drain from Bran's face. He turned and wrapped an arm around her waist, hurrying her through the ballroom as quickly as he could without running.

"Bran?" she asked. "What is the hunt?"

"The duchess's twisted version of an evening out. The duke will not come to such a party, but he always expects pieces to be delivered back to him."

"Pieces?" She twisted in his arms to see the first splatter of blood whipped across the Duchess's face.

Aisling had never seen such joy in the pain of others. The first scream didn't start until they reached the door. Then it was a symphony of voices raised to the rafters of the ballroom, all crying out for help.

They ran down the halls as if the Wild Hunt pursued them. Aisling's breath turned ragged, her shoulders ached from running and, bound by a corset, her ribs protested the movement. The thorns dug into her neck. Each breath sank the metal deeper into her throat.

Finally, they reached the door to her room. Bran set his

shoulder against it mid-run, banging the worn wood against the door, whipping her through it with a well-placed hand.

She careened past him. Her gasp echoed in the room, but neither of them reacted to her startled sound. There would be time for that, but not just now. She pressed her hand against her mouth to silence her loud breaths, and he remained with his ear against the door, listening for any who might have followed them from the cursed ballroom.

He let out a half chuckle. "Well, that's something you don't see at every ball."

"I wouldn't know," she said, laughing softly and staring down at the floor. "You missed your opportunity to try and convince me all Unseelie balls end with a sacrifice."

"Why would I do that?"

There was something different about his voice, a smooth quality that was like velvet sliding across her skin. Aisling shivered.

Don't look up, she told herself. *He doesn't know how to handle the emotions that come with this new face. He thinks you were given the face of your sister to torment him. Don't look up.*

But she looked.

He was leaning against the door, arms crossed over his broad chest and ankles linked. A lock of his hair fell like a waterfall and obscured part of his face. His feathers were nearly grown in on the side of his head, lying flat, reflecting blue in the dim light of fire and moonlight.

He stared at the ground for a few moments before glancing up at her with a hooded gaze. When he bit his lip, she was certain death would strike her down where she stood.

She reminded herself that he saw her sister. That he had

246

loved her sister. But it was a look she recognized, only amplified by thousands.

"Witch," he murmured, "tell me you don't want this."

She shook her head. What else could she say? She was a woman who knew what she wanted. She desired the man in front of her so much she could barely breathe.

Bran pushed himself away from the door and strode toward her with slow, purposeful steps. "Tell me that I'm good enough for you."

"I can't."

Was that her voice? That breathless, wondrous tone had never escaped before.

He circled her, a great black raven, surveying the battlefield and choosing the fallen warrior upon which he would feast.

"Tell me you're frightened of me."

"I'm not."

He paused in front of her, then slowly reached out to touch her exposed collarbone with the back of his knuckles. "Last chance, little witch. I won't stop after this."

Could he hear her heartbeat? It thundered in her chest, an insistent sound clamoring for his attention. "I am not afraid of you, and I do not want this to stop." She swallowed her nerves and met his heated stare. "But if you think I couldn't prevent you from touching me after this moment, you do not know me as well as you think."

His knuckles dragged down her front. Gentle and ever so slow, they scraped between her breasts and then paused at the delicate skin between her ribs. "You are in the presence of an Unseelie prince." He leaned forward until his breath fanned across her neck. "You have no idea what I'm capable of."

247

The air disappeared from her lungs. Unbidden, she remained frozen in the center of the room. He circled her again, slow, stalking steps in time with her heartbeat.

"Close your eyes, little witch," he breathed in the shell of her ear. "Feel. Don't see."

For the first time in her life, Aisling closed her eyes and gave all control up to another person. She was not afraid, but elated. She trusted him.

His hands skimmed over her shoulders, stroking muscle and delicate bone. He lifted the weight of her hair off her one shoulder and placed it in a silken slide across the other. He dragged claws down the nape of her neck, following the bumps of bones through the fabric of her dress.

Leaning forward, his calm voice echoed in her ear, "Do you know what I thought when I first saw you?"

"Now *that* is a foolish girl?"

"No." Amusement warmed his tone. "I thought, there is a woman with a raging storm inside her. The fire won't burn her. It wouldn't dare insult a goddess."

When he popped the first catch of her dress, she rocked forward with a gasp.

"Steady," he soothed, then released another catch. "I thought, they don't know how strong she is."

Another button, then another, each releasing with a sudden snap. Down he went until his knuckles pressed firm between the dimples of her hips.

"I thought, they don't know how powerful she is."

The button parted, fabric gaping open, and the tips of his fingers stroked the small of her back.

"They thought they could burn you." A slow hiss feathered

across her ribs. "They didn't remember something born in a bonfire would only thrive inside its heat."

It was too much. The brush of his fingers, the appreciative sounds he made, the words he was saying.

"Bran—"

"Sh," he hushed. "I have all night with you, little witch. And I intend to use every hour."

"I have to tell you something first."

"In the morning. We'll tell each other everything in the morning."

Did he have more secrets? Were they both lying to each other in their own way?

She shook her head. "Just…know that I understand. That this face is not the one you wanted to see, and if I could change it, I would."

He reached in front of her, slid a hand over her jaw, and tilted her face to stare back at him.

"You captivated me without a face, Aisling. What makes you think this one would deter me?"

She breathed out a ragged sigh that quickly turned into a gasp when he untied the laces of her corset. She was still fully clothed, and yet she felt him everywhere.

Her ribs expanded with much needed air. Every eyelet released more string and bared more of her skin to his gaze. It took time, enough time that her fervor cooled and she was able to think straight again.

At least until he pressed a kiss against her shoulder and hummed out a breath. "I've always hated these things."

"I prefer wearing a man's shirt."

"I'll see you in nothing more than mine tonight."

"Silk?" She leaned her head against his shoulder, letting it loll to the side so she could inhale the scent of poppy and wine. "Unseelie, I think you're spoiling me."

She couldn't think as his hands slipped beneath the corset and curved over her belly. He parted the stiff fabric and let it drop to the ground with a muffled thud. There was still her sleeved slip and undergarments between them, but she felt every inch of his touch.

"Allow me," he begged.

"Please."

With a slow, languishing slide, he pulled his hands from her torso and snuck them into the gaping back of the slip. Inch by inch, he dragged the fabric down her arms. Carefully, he tugged her hands free then lifted one to press against his cheek.

Feathers tickled her fingertips.

He turned her palm and pressed a kiss to the center, only to released her to smooth his hands down her hips and nudge her dress to the floor.

She stood naked as the day she was born, cold air brushing over her hip and belly. The wall of heat behind her disappeared as he rounded her. His eyes took in every detail, every curve, and every valley.

Aisling refused to be self-conscious. She knew her body. Understood that it was desirable, the same reason why she'd hidden it for so long. Yet the blatant admiration in his gaze still heated her.

He stepped forward, pausing only when she lifted a hand.

"I am bare while you are fully clothed."

He arched a brow, waiting until she continued.

"Remove your clothing, Unseelie." The order was firm, far

more confident than she felt.

"Let me worship you first, my goddess." He swept into a mock bow. "Then I shall bare all you desire to see."

A censuring retort fizzled on her tongue as he lunged forward and took her mouth in a searing kiss. He pried her lips open with teeth and tongue, devouring her breath and pouring himself into her until she had no idea which way was up.

He backed her toward the bed, step by step, enchanting her with the strength of his body, the heat of his attentions, and the desire he stoked within her.

At the slightest of shoves, she fell back onto the pillows. Dust plumed around them and was banished with a wave of his hand. Magic sizzled from the top of her head to her toes.

She wanted to ask what spell he used, but he was on her again. His teeth worried her bottom lip, pulling and plucking until she was certain it was swollen, yet she couldn't bring herself to care. He was an enchantment, and she the thoroughly cursed.

He stroked down her thigh, tucking a hand under her knee and drawing it up so that he could seat himself between her legs. He rocked against her, then pulled back to gasp in air.

The cords of his neck stood out as he fought against himself. He growled, "I have single-handedly ended battles, worn blood like armor, made kings tremble at the mention of my name, and no one has brought me to my knees until you."

She slid the palm of her calloused, tattooed hand under the gaping fabric his shirt, feeling the finely sculpted muscles of his chest. She lingered on the hollow where neck met shoulder, stroking the artery pulsing against her fingers, then cupped the back of his head and pulled him back down to her.

They paused, lips barely touching, breath mingling in a heated mist.

"The stories always say the cruelest of all creatures are wrapped in sin and pleasure," she breathed. "And you are the most dangerous enemy I have ever battled."

"Do you think I'm going to destroy you?"

"Yes," she moaned. "Yes, I think you will."

And then there were no words.

She closed her eyes and focused on the ragged sound of his breathing and the sensation of his knuckles, the callouses on the backs from fist fights.

Her eyes snapped open to devour the sight of him. He arched back, whipping his jacket and shirt off in one swift movement. Lethal, he was barely contained energy vibrating in a body that pulsed with power.

Shadows danced across a lean but strong body. Moonlight smoothed the planes of his chest and the ripples of his stomach into carved alabaster. The fire behind him gilded the edges of his form and sent copper strands dancing through his hair.

He was beautiful. A man with wings of a raven, the strength of a lion, and the eyes of a god.

His ribs expanded, muscles rippling with tension as he stared back at her. He traced the outline of her body with his gaze, and she felt it as sure as a touch.

Bran reached out, nothing else moving but his hand, and gently stroked her shoulder, the curve of her waist, the outline of her hip. He blew out a breath and shook his head.

Aisling didn't ask what he was thinking; she knew. He stretched forward, stripping himself of any lingering fabric, and pressed skin to skin. She gasped when he ran his fingers over her from top to bottom, again and again.

He pressed his lips to the hollow at her collarbone. Dragged teeth and tongue over the peaks of her breasts, followed the line of her body to the dip of her belly button. He nipped her hipbone, licked the back of her knee.

Over and over again, he discovered new mysteries she hadn't even known her body had hidden. He branded himself to her until all she could think, feel, *know*…

Was him.

Her world began and ended with this strange, impossible man. It didn't matter that when he leaned forward, pressing himself inside her, a flare of pain startled her.

Feathers pressed hard against her cheek, surely leaving marks behind. As he drew back, rocking onto his heels and dragging her up into his lap, she wondered if he had given her wings.

She inhaled his exhale, drugging herself on his scent and taste. He delicately brushed his fingers across her back, playing the raised bones like a harp. He strung magic through her until she was certainly as divine as he thought her to be.

She threw her head back, and he pressed his lips against her throat.

"With me now," he whispered, his voice rasp. "Together, as we should have been from the start."

Every fiber of her being gathered up into one great bunch and then splintered apart. She shattered into stardust. He pulled her against his chest as if he were gathering up each individual piece. He shuddered, silent and satiated as she.

Aisling was lost in the nebula he had created. She slumped against him, curled against his heartbeat as he pressed a kiss to the top of her head.

Her heart fluttered like a wounded bird. She was suddenly not herself, but a piece of him as well. He existed somewhere in the bottom of her ribs, a warm and tender reminder that, for at least one night of her life, she was a treasure.

"Stay," she whispered to his chest, "just for one night."

He dragged her down to the pillows and cushioned her head against his heart. "Sleep, little witch. I'll keep the nightmares at bay."

And so she fell into a deep, dreamless sleep.

CHAPTER 9

DEATH OF THE DUCHESS

Aisling stretched, feeling sore in muscles she'd never known existed. She had no idea what time it was since the sun never reached this forgotten place, but she knew she was comfortable and warm. She hugged a pillow to her chest with a sigh.

When was the last time she had slept on anything resembling a bed? And certainly never something as cloudlike as this.

Muffling a sleepy snort, she rolled onto her side and opened her eyes.

They widened in shock. He was still here. Bran, the raven-haired warrior who had dismantled her person last night was still spread across her bed like some kind of Fae god.

Aisling blinked. Even in sleep, he somehow was dangerous to look at. Dark lashes fanned across his cheeks, leaving bruised smudges against his pale skin. One hand lay open next to his jaw, the other flung across his smooth chest.

She'd never seen a man with a smooth chest. Human men were beast-like in their build, dark, swarthy, tanned by the sun and dusted with hair to protect them from the elements. But this Unseelie had no need to be protected. He would beat back anything that tried to harm him with little more than a look.

Aisling made a face. She couldn't afford to lose herself like this. He was a man, and they were all the same.

Weren't they?

The pressure in her chest grew unbearable. She was always a loner. She didn't need anyone in her life, and no one had ever wanted to be involved in her witchcraft. This man had forced himself through her walls, shattered the cage around her heart, and now she was... falling.

Falling so hard and so fast that it stole her breath. She pressed a hand against her chest, but that didn't help.

Gulping in air, she carefully swung her legs over the edge of the mound of pillows and crawled toward her clothing. Not the dress, that would be too obvious. Instead, she found the clothing she'd arrived in.

Dirt stained the fabric and grime covered the hem, but it was familiar. She pressed the fabric to her face and inhaled the scent of hard work, long hours, and endless days. She hadn't washed it, and the scent of the journey, of her journey, was still on it. To some, it would have been a vulgar smell. But to her, it was home.

She slid the ragged clothing on, quietly moving about the room so she wouldn't disturb the sleeping faerie in her bed.

"Things I never thought would exist," she muttered. And top of that list was an Unseelie prince, splayed out across silken pillows, without a stitch of clothing.

Goodness, that would be seared into her brain for the rest of her life.

She didn't mind the strangely thin leg which ended in a bird foot. She didn't mind the feathers decorating his face and head. He was just Bran, the most handsome man she'd ever laid eyes on.

Aisling allowed herself one more pleased sigh before she slipped out the door.

The hallways were empty. Her footsteps echoed and bounced off the cold stone. It suddenly felt like a tomb, and gooseflesh popped up over her arms. Strange, she hadn't felt uncomfortable in the Palace of Twilight until now.

Rubbing her hands up and down her grimy sleeves, she darted through the halls and peeked through doors until she found the way out of the palace.

Even the guards were sleeping, she noticed with amusement. They leaned against the walls with their helmets drawn low over their faces. Perhaps the "hunt" was more exhausting than Aisling had imagined.

She liked to think the duchess wasn't quite so indiscriminate in her killings. Surely her court knew who was going to be the sacrifice for the night. But considering the exhaustion lining the faces of the Fae, she might be wrong.

A small wooden door gave under her hand, the rotting wood sticking to her fingers and moss curling toward the heat of her palm. She gave it a friendly pat and slipped out the side of the palace to step into an immaculate garden.

Thus far, the Palace of Twilight had offered very little beauty. There was a stunning quality to the age and grace of the rotting castle, but not beauty.

Perhaps all the beauty was funneled to this garden. Bright flowers burst into bloom all around her. Their glimmering petals held tiny drops of dew perfectly suspended. Hundreds of blossoms carpeted the ground and filled air with pollen. In the distance where two swans treaded water in a large pond, trees hung heavy with pink petals.

It was serenity captured in a single moment.

Aisling let out a breath and stepped onto the thin gravel path. It meandered through the plants, trailing like a long snake through the foliage. She followed it without question, noting the poisonous plants that decorated the edges.

Wolfsbane, monkshood, belladonna, all beautiful plants but dangerously poisonous. What else had she expected in the duchess's garden? The faerie was as deadly as a viper. It stood to reason that her garden would reflect the same.

Feet crunching on the stone, she rounded a corner and stopped dead in her tracks. In the center of the garden, a small gazebo had been built out of twisted black metal. Jagged edges clawed at the sky and pointed out as if it were protecting the inhabitants from all else.

Within the strange cage sat the duchess and her duke. Her long black gown trickled onto the emerald grass, undulating at the ends like a strange beast she'd wrapped around herself. A dramatic plunging neckline revealed the glowing green heart that pulsed inside the cavity of her chest.

In contrast, her husband was dressed in simple clothes. He wore a simple shirt, laces untied at his neck, breeches, and unlaced boots. The duke did not seem to be interested in appearances, other than the ever-present mask covering his face.

A small table was set up in front of them, a chess board on the table and ready to play. None of the pieces had been moved, and Aisling thought it unlikely they were playing together. They sat on the same side of the table.

The duchess glanced up and grinned. "Ah, our little witchling! I thought we might see you this morning."

She was trapped. Aisling wanted to bolt from the garden and race back into Bran's comforting arms, but she knew better. Refusing a faerie their toy was the same as a death wish.

She sighed and walked toward them. "Did you now, Duchess? I'm afraid I didn't even know I would find this place."

"They always do." The duchess gestured at a chair opposite them. "Do you play?"

"Not if I can help it."

A spark glittered behind the duke's mask. "Then you have played before?"

"Yes, but rarely." She sat on the plush chair and plucked at the strings of her sleeves.

Was this an intelligent decision? Likely not. Faeries were too secretive in their ways, and she didn't want a simple chess game to turn into a game of wits. Narrowing her gaze, Aisling pinned the duke with a stare. "We play for nothing more than amusement. There are no bets on this game."

"That's entirely boring, little witch," he replied.

"I have nothing to give, and I suspect you have nothing you would like to lose. This game is for entertainment and educational purposes, that is all."

He leaned back and stretched an arm behind his wife. His fingers played in the strands of the duchess's hair before he nodded. "This one is brighter than we gave her credit for, love."

"She is unusual, isn't she?" The duchess patted his hand. "Play her for fun, darling. Perhaps then you shall be able to

259

defeat the huntsman."

"He doesn't know how to play at all. Every win he claims is by luck."

She leaned forward and moved a pawn two spaces ahead. The game was on, and she didn't know what else to do other than to sit quietly in her dirty clothes.

The duchess's eyes were a physical touch. She was weighing Aisling, the way she looked, the way she acted, the movements she made. Aisling felt like a bug under a microscope.

"I thought my maids had destroyed those rags," the duchess finally said. "A shame that they still exist."

"They're my clothes, ma'am."

"And why is that you put them back on? You've been gifted the finest gown the faerie court can make, and you choose" — she waved up and down — "that."

"They are comfortable."

"You mean *you* are more comfortable hiding behind rags. Is that it?"

Aisling bit her lip. The duke moved a pawn forward on the other side of the board. Not a particularly good choice, but enough that Aisling could form a plan. "You see right through me, Duchess."

"It's foolish for you to hide. You are a powerful creature in your own right. Your outward appearance should match that power."

"I disagree," Aisling murmured, shifting a chess piece forward. "I think the most powerful creatures are those who don't appear to be. The smallest spider is the most poisonous. Such is the way of the wild."

The duke snorted. "The drab spider is no less deadly than the flashing bejeweled fish. Poison is poison, ladies, no matter the form."

He plucked one of her knights off the board and leaned onto the table. She recognized the look in his eyes. He thought he had her, but Aisling was never one so easily trapped.

She nudged a piece to cover her queen and arched a brow. "Would you not agree that poison is most effective when it is a surprise?"

"No." The duke shook his head. "What you're describing is personal satisfaction. There is a certain enjoyment in knowing the person has no idea you are the one killing them, or that they were going to be killed that day, but poison is effective no matter what form it is dispensed."

She carelessly moved a pawn forward, frowning down at the board.

The duchess smoothed a hand down her skirts. "Little witch, have you given more thought to our conversation?"

"Which conversation is that? We've had plenty." The surliness in her voice was perhaps a little daring, but Aisling refused to show weakness with these faeries.

"You removed your curse."

The blunt words made Aisling flinch back. She curled in on herself, feeling suddenly weak and vulnerable. Her curse had always been her sanctuary, and it was still uncomfortable to remember people could see her face.

"You already knew that."

"I did, but there was another thing I said long ago. You are a thrice-cursed woman, and I wonder if you have discovered the third."

"I have only been cursed twice."

The duchess lashed out a hand, quick as a snake, and wrapped her thin hand around Aisling's forearm. She saw vividly the gnarled skin underneath the duchess's glamour. She was a creature made of roots and bark, earthen and coarse. Then the glamour slid back into place, and a beautiful woman stared back at her.

With surprising strength, the duchess flipped Aisling's hands over to reveal the eye tattoos still in the center of her palms. "You relieved yourself of one curse and freed the next, little witch. Now, the question is what this mysterious curse is."

Aisling hissed out a breath. "What twisted magic do you speak of? I was only cursed *twice*."

The heart thudded, the low sound echoing in the garden. Each thump drew Aisling closer and closer to the Duchess. Her lungs seized, but she couldn't struggle against the duchess's magic.

"Show me your secrets," the duchess murmured. "All that was promised to me, little witch. Show me the stories written in blood magic upon your skin."

Power crackled in the air, surrounding them, building and lashing out at their skin until it finally burst with a blinding green light. Aisling closed her eyes and threw her free arm over her face, but it was too late.

She experienced the memory all over again. The blistering pain of magic searing into her hands, the ache, the agony, the raw edges of flesh that could never be cut from her skin. Over and over again, she saw the memories until it suddenly was all clear.

Badb turned her tiny hands over, stroking her fingers over

the eyes, but she wasn't creating the tattoos. No.

She was tracing them.

The eyes had been on her hands long before the addition of the black tips. Aisling's eyes snapped open, and the green light burned into her eyes, but it didn't matter. The foundation of her world had shifted.

Badb hadn't been cursing her; she had put the tips on her fingers to lock away a curse which had already existed in the palm of her hands.

She yanked her arm away from the duchess, chest rising and falling with panicked breaths. Why hadn't she remembered it that way? The memory had always been in her head with Badb placing all the tattoos on her. Who had meddled with her mind?

"Ah," the duchess mused, "so that's who you are."

"You know nothing of who I am."

"Tell yourself whatever lies you need to feel better, little witch. But I see you as none have seen you before." She leaned against her husband's shoulder and sighed happily. "Do you remember him, my love? Before he was sent to Underhill, locked away with a key sunken at the bottom of an impossibly deep lake?"

"Who?" Aisling asked, her stomach twisting in knots.

The duke leaned back and tucked his wife against his side. "Ah, of course it would be him. He was magnificent in his day. And now? Ruling an empire of rot. A shame, really. He might have been something great if they had given him the chance."

"Such a shame," the duchess replied. "He was highly entertaining but also so incredibly powerful. I suppose it makes sense why they chose him, and even more why he chose her.

Odd they would send her away to be a changeling, though. Can you imagine? The audacity of her family."

Aisling slapped her hand down on the table, chess pieces rocking with the force of her anger. "Tell me!"

An odd spark glinted in the duchess's eye. "Why the Raven King, of course. Or did you not know you were chosen to be his consort?"

She felt all the blood drain from her face. "Consort?"

"Every king must have his queen," the duke replied. He leaned forward and knocked down her queen with a single move. "When the queen falls, so does the king. Checkmate."

She couldn't breathe. Her chest tightened, and she couldn't see straight. It wasn't possible. She couldn't possibly have been chosen to be the consort of the Raven King. She'd never even *seen* him...

But that was a lie. She'd seen him her entire life, from childhood stories, to saving her friends, to the ravens above her hut, even guiding her here. The Raven King was the hero of every story she told.

And now, she knew she was meant to be his bride.

Aisling choked on a gasp. "It cannot be."

"Why? Because you are in love with the Unseelie Prince?" The duchess laughed. "Stories don't always end up the way we want them to, do they?"

"I won't be a consort to anyone I haven't met."

"Oh, I'm sure you'll meet him soon. After all, you removed the curse keeping you hidden from him. All he has to do is find you now, and I'm certain he wants you by his side. He's infinitely more powerful with you in his kingdom."

"Kingdom?" Aisling stared at them. "What kingdom?"

"Underhill! Goodness girl, do you not know any of the legends? He rules the Wild Hunt when it's not released upon the earth. The creatures who steal human souls." The duchess leaned forward dramatically. "The Sluagh."

Aisling swore a wind had risen at the word, sliding across her arms and raising goosebumps in its wake. Though she knew they wouldn't steal her soul, she had lived her entire life in fear of them. Evoking their name was as good as screaming into the shadows for them to come and take her.

"I am no one's consort," she whispered. "I make my own path."

"Not with those marks you don't." The duchess clapped her hands, grinning. "Oh, this is so much fun! I had no idea we had two royals in our midst. Now it's going to be so much easier. Don't you think, darling?"

"Easier?" Aisling gulped and flicked her gaze between the two. "What do you mean easier?"

"I'm sorry for this, my dear. I really am. You have been a pleasure, and if you were anyone else, I'd like to keep you as a pet."

Aisling wasn't going to stay and listen to whatever else the Duchess had to say. She stood quickly, upended the table into their laps, and whirled into a run. Thank the gods she'd had the intelligence to change into pants or she wouldn't have been able to race back toward the palace.

She needed to collect Bran and Lorcan. Then they all needed to flee this dastardly place. There wasn't enough hidden magic in the world to convince her to stay here.

A clawed hand caught the fabric of her shirt and shoved her forward. With a shout, Aisling fell onto her knees. She kicked out with her leg, catching a rib that cracked loudly.

The duchess dug her nails into Aisling's sides. Each dig made her flinch, long furrows opening in her skin as the faerie forced her to turn onto her back.

For such a small woman, the duchess was surprisingly strong. She held Aisling underneath her with ease, hardly panting with the difficulty of suppressing her movements. A wild grin spread across the faerie's face. "My sweet, you are always entertaining."

Aisling spat in her face. "Go to hell."

She managed to wiggle an arm free and desperately clawed the duchess's heart, which was so close.

The faerie leaned back a fraction, just out of her reach. "No, I know why you want that my dear, but you aren't going to have it. Killing the Raven King's consort will likely anger him, but that is part of the fun. I'm much more interested in killing the Unseelie Prince, and when I explain why you had to die, I'm sure he'll understand."

"Why do you hate him so much?"

"I don't hate him." Claws raked down her sides. "I want to *be* him."

Anger heated Aisling's blood. She snarled and twisted harder, trying her best to reach the heart inside the duchess's chest. "He is infinitely more powerful than you."

"Oh, sweet little girl. Do you think I have to go through you to get to him?" The duchess shook her head and tsked. "No. All I have to do is poison you. And you did say you preferred poison as a surprise, didn't you?"

When the nails dug deeper into her side, Aisling realized she couldn't quite feel the pain in the same way. Instead, all she felt was a growing cold sensation spreading through her sides and sinking deep into her bones from the sticky coating on the duchess's nails.

"What did you do?" she whispered.

As her body fell into a quiet stillness, the duchess leaned forward and pressed her lips against Aisling's ear. "Tell me, little witch. What flavor now coats your tongue?"

Lips thick, her teeth wanted to chatter but muscles refused to move. Aisling managed to furiously bite out, "Bitter."

"That's right. The bitterness of nightshade is so distinct. Those of us who are poisonous creatures wrapped in silk and satin know the taste well. But those who are little more than drab spiders would use something more painful, like belladonna. Sweet, innocent, little witch. You're going to die slowly, and I will enjoy watching every second."

The duchess slowly lifted herself from Aisling's body, and she couldn't do anything to stop her. Her arms were heavy, laden with the weight of the world. Her legs stilled, toes losing all feeling. Every sense dulled until the power inside her gave one last gasping flare.

The glamour fell away from the secret garden hidden in the heart of the Palace of Twilight. The gazebo disappeared. Twisted metal became gnarled branches, blackened silver turning to dusky bark.

Aisling stared up into the rattling branches of the hanging tree and realized she hadn't traveled that far after all. Witches always died under the branches of this tree.

An enraged roar echoed from within the crumbling palace. The Unseelie prince screamed his anger, more animal than man. But he was too late.

She tried to whisper his name, but her lips couldn't move. She twisted a finger in the dirt. It was the only movement she could manage when all she wanted to do was stop him from risking his life.

Her eyes found the duchess, staring up at the windows of her palace with madness in her gaze. "And so the hunt begins," she breathed. "The beast calls for its mate, a howl of rage and mourning. He feels you dying. Every small bit of life leeching out of you is also pulled from him."

Glass shattered, and she felt the answering ache in her shoulders and the top of her head. He'd burst free from a window.

A dark shadow crossed in front of the moon. A blanket of ravens made from his magic, his grief. Aisling allowed a single tear to leak from her eye as a dark feather floated from the sky and landed atop her cheek.

Wind buffeted them, as powerful as a storm, electric and so near she could feel him. The ravens swarmed then coalesced into a man kneeling on the small path. Slowly, he tilted his head up and leveled the duchess with a gaze raw and filled with rage. "What did you do?" he growled.

"Only what you would have done if you were in my position."

A ripple of feathers flared from his head and spread down his back. The darkness swallowed his form. It covered his body in magic and a nightmarish abyss with not a single of light in its heart.

"You are not allowed to touch *her*."

"And you are bound." The duchess gave him a pitying smile. "You can feel the weight of the nightshade, Unseelie prince. Let yourself fall into its comforting embrace. Stop fighting so hard as you have your entire life."

"You haven't bested me yet."

Aisling sucked in a breath, a small whimper escaping her lips when he launched himself toward the duchess. He was a blur of dark feathers and the wide expanse of the night sky. And he didn't get anywhere near the duchess.

Appearing out of thin air, the duke locked his arms around Bran. They grappled, twisting like two great snakes. Bran's teeth flashed in the moonlight. Pointed fangs sharpened to deadly tips that sunk into the duke's forearms.

She heard the creaking of ribs, felt the flare of pain, as the duke squeezed down on Bran's torso. An agonizing groan filled the courtyard, and then Bran managed to wiggle an arm free. He reached behind him, sank his fingers beneath the duke's mask, and pulled it so hard the bolts ripped out of the duke's face.

Both Aisling and Bran sucked in air as he was dropped. He rolled, crouching with one hand pressed against the ground and a wary eye on the duke who now covered his face with his hand.

"My mask," he huffed, "my mask. Give me my mask."

"No." Bran snatched it from the ground and snapped it in half.

"*What have you done?*" the duke roared.

The scream blistered Aisling's ears. Blood leaked from the canals, dripping down into her hair. She tried to scream, but the nightshade had paralyzed her.

Bran stumbled to his feet, and the duke turned toward her, revealing the nightmarish face he had hidden from the world.

She remembered Bran saying the duke liked to steal bits and pieces of people. She hadn't realized he could steal *eyes*.

Every inch of his face was covered with multi-colored eyes. They blinked at random intervals, but each stared into her gaze with equal parts horror and resignation. Though he tried to cover his hideous appearance by lifting his hands, she could see he knew what was coming for him. *Who* was coming for him.

Bran burst into an unkindness of ravens and attacked the duke's eyes. Each carefully cultivated globe was punctured by beaks that glinted in the light. No pity was shown for the man who had stolen so much from so many.

Feathers flew in the air, but the duke did not try to stop him. He fell to his knees before Aisling and held his hands out in supplication. She felt the anguish, the agony, the pain that had been buried so deep in his soul he did not recognize himself.

Strength flowed from Bran, allowing her to reach out a hand and touch the duke's bloodied palm.

"Thank you," he sighed. "I am free."

Aisling turned her gaze from the cursed man. The duchess pressed her hands against her lips, and a shriek echoed from her chest. The heart fractured, a thin line cracking from top to bottom.

"My love," she whimpered, reaching out a hand as if she might touch the duke. "What have you done to my love?"

"Only what you would have done if you were in my position." Bran lunged forward, clumsy but still on his feet. The duchess didn't notice him because she was too busy staring at the duke. Still, she locked her hand around Bran's wrist as he reached for her.

Aisling watched his face twist as both their arms began to shake.

"No," the duchess whispered. "It wasn't supposed to happen like this."

"You handed me your heart the moment you laid a finger on her."

Bran plunged his hand into her chest, grasped the green glass heart, and pulled it free.

A soft sigh eased between the duchess's lips. Her face smoothed into a soft, pleased expression, and she fell to her knees in a graceful movement. Weak and dying, she slumped to the side.

Aisling wheezed out a sound. She wasn't certain Bran would even hear it. But then he was there, kneeling over her with black feathers floating around them like prayers. Phantom wings of darkness stretched from his shoulder blades and hid galaxies within them.

"Aisling?" he asked, smoothing her hair away from her forehead. "Can you hear me?"

A shuddering breath was her only answer. She couldn't tell him that she'd drank nightshade since she was little, that the poison would only paralyze her, not kill her.

Instead, the darkness swallowed her whole. Yet even as she lost all sight of the world, she still saw stars behind her eyelids.

CHAPTER 10

FLIGHT TO THE ISLES

Bran pulled her limp body up and pressed his forehead to hers. The cold chill spread through his body. Bitterness filled his mouth, a filthy taste of poison and the ache of guilt.

He hadn't even noticed her leave the bedroom. Sleep had finally claimed him, a deep, dreamless state that made his waking languid and calm. When was the last time he'd slept like that? It had been years, centuries perhaps.

It made little sense that a witch would be the first to finally ease him into that welcoming darkness, yet she rarely made sense.

He'd felt bereft the moment he woke up. Some piece of him knew she wasn't on the other side of the pillow mound, but he had still reached for her. He wanted to feel warm, pliant skin. He wanted to see a smile on her stolen face, even if it wasn't hers.

Instead, he'd been welcomed by cold air and pillows lacking even the slightest indentation from her body.

A crazed part of his mind wondered if he'd made her up in his head. Such a woman couldn't possibly be real. But memory caught up with him, and the witch became solidified in his mind again.

It was then that a lance of pain speared through his body. He'd lurched onto his feet only to fall against the wall with an aching gasp. Leave it to Aisling to get herself in trouble while he was asleep. No other woman would dare wander around the Palace of Twilight without someone at their side. But his witch? She looked danger in the eye and laughed at its arrogance.

He'd thrown on the same clothes he'd worn the night before and then flung himself out the window. The rest was a blur. Pain, fighting, battle, the thrill of a still beating heart cold and crystalline against his palm.

And now they both were still and quiet. His heartbeat slowed, and adrenaline dissipated until he felt the cold silence of her soul.

"Nightshade won't be the thing that kills us," he told her.

Pattering feet echoed in the garden. Bran drew her closer to his chest, a feral snarl escaping from his lips as his gaze searched for the next opponent. He'd defeated the Duke and Duchess of Dusk. Let the others come. He would tear them limb from limb.

Lorcan careened around a corner and skidded to a stop in front of them. "What happened?"

"Nightshade."

"Is she dead?"

"Not yet."

Lorcan hissed. A line of fur raised on his back. "I should have remained closer."

"I said *yet*," Bran growled. "I know those who might save her."

"And you? Will you even be able to get her there?"

He looked down at her, limp in his arms and so painfully cold. His heart turned over in his chest, a ridiculous emotion considering he was certain he could save her. But she wasn't meant to look so weak. She was supposed to be spitting fire at him and shouting, not so still and quiet he could barely see her chest move.

"Put her into a sleep," he quietly requested. "A sleep like death."

"I don't know a spell like that."

"Don't lie to me, witch. It's not a curse. She'll wake up from it. The poison will slow, and I will have more time to get her help."

"Where are you taking her?" Lorcan leaned forward and sniffed her dangling hand. The raised fur along his back smoothed. "I won't risk her life on more faerie magic, Unseelie."

"I will bring her to the only safe place in the Otherworld for a woman such as her." He gently lifted her hand and tucked it against her chest. "Scáthach and her maidens are the only ones who can stop the effects of cursed nightshade. They will heal her."

"You want to bring her to the Fortress of Shadows? Are you mad?"

"Do you think they will turn her away?" Ferocity laced his words. "They will take her in, they will heal her, and they will admire her spirit. She will stay alive until then."

"It is a long journey."

"Not if we open another portal." Bran shifted her in his arms, looping her legs over his before shakily rising to his feet.

"Cast the spell, Lorcan."

"You don't know how to open a portal."

"Cast the spell."

"Even *I* don't know the spell she uses to open up a portal. You're going to get all of us killed!"

Feathers rippled across his face and down his arms. "Cat sidhe, I swear to my ancestors if you don't ensorcel this woman immediately, I will be picking your bones from my teeth come morning."

"You wouldn't dare."

But the cat must have seen something in Bran's furious gaze because he muttered something under his breath and began to etch runes into the ground. Every now and then he would glance up, note the shaking of Bran's arms and legs, and hiss out a long breath before continuing.

Bran recognized the spell. It was a simple one, rudimentary really, but it would do the trick. Sleep spells were quiet things, like the state they induced.

Lorcan stood on his back tiptoes to reach Aisling and gestured with a paw for Bran to lean down. He stooped. The cat leaned forward and nearly touched his muzzle to Aisling's lips. A slow exhale was all he needed to cast the spell. Silvery light sparkled around his whiskers, sinking into Aisling's nose and lips.

The spell worked instantly. The cold slowly drained out of Bran. His muscles filled with strength, his shoulders straightened, and he let out a slow groan of appreciation. "Not bad, cat. Maybe next time I'll ask you to create the portal."

"I don't know *how*, and neither do you!"

Bran gave him a wink. "When you grow up in the Dark

Castle, you learn a trick or two about magic. The most important is that if you watch a person cast a spell, you can do it for yourself."

"Not possible. I've watched her cast that spell numerous times."

"Then perhaps you should apply yourself a little more, cat."

He strode through the garden, away from the cursed tree. He could feel the dark magic pulsing in his mind. It made shivers dance over his flesh.

A hanging tree. Why hadn't he ever seen one before her? Bran was known for his ability to see through glamour, and yet such a vessel of dark power had always eluded him. It was almost an insult that he could only see it now that she was in his life.

Lorcan trailed after him, huffing out breath after breath until he finally grumbled, "You can't actually make the portal just by watching her, can you?"

"Of course, I can."

He set Aisling gently on the moss, brushing a strand of hair away from her face. He should have been there. The Duchess would never have been able to get her claws into such beloved flesh if Bran hadn't been lazing about in bed.

Innate laziness had never bothered him until this moment. Unseelie valued leisure and detested any mandated work, and yet...

He should have been there.

The scratches along his ribs pulled, but nothing compared to the deep gouges in her sides. He'd have to figure out how to stop the bleeding, but he wasn't much of a healer. His sister was better at all healing spells.

One of his sisters. He couldn't remember which one.

Kneeling on the ground, he began to trace runes into the earth. He'd committed each to memory the moment he first looked at them. They weren't unusual runes, but strange in their combination. No one would have thought to mix languages. Some of these were ancient Tuatha de Danann, and others were ancient Celtic.

Faerie and Human. Melded together to create something unique and unusual. Like a changeling herself.

Shaking his head, he leaned back and nodded. "That's it."

"You aren't using my blood, Unseelie," Lorcan grumbled from his post near Aisling's head. "And I'm not leaving to find you a bird."

"It doesn't need as much blood as she thinks." He sank a nail into the fleshy pad of his thumb. Spreading three drops around the circle, he blew out a breath of air, spat, then flicked his fingers to send faerie fire into the ring.

The ground rippled and caved in. It looked nearly identical to hers, although there was the faintest hint of shadow, his own magic intertwined with this strange spell she had discovered.

"Let's go," Bran grumbled. He turned and reached for Aisling, only to find his hand stinging from a clawed mark.

"Hang on," Lorcan scolded. "I want to know exactly what your plan is. Why should Scáthach help us at all? She doesn't know me, she certainly doesn't know Aisling, and it was my understanding those maidens weren't overly fond of the Unseelie Court."

"She won't be the person we're begging for help."

"Then who?"

Bran blew out a frustrated breath. "She's bleeding out.'

"She's not bleeding that fast. Answer the question, faerie."

"An old friend."

"An old lover, you mean?" If cats could raise their eyebrow, Lorcan did so. "I'm not foolish. Just what favor are you calling in? There are other ways."

"It's not a favor when you help a friend. And the person who'll help us is just that, cat. A *friend*." He stressed the word as much as physically possible.

"Lovers are always a little bit more than friends, but not quite more at the same time. Be careful wherever you take us. I don't want to pick up the pieces you leave behind."

The cat was overly protective of Aisling. He understood the sentiment. Lorcan had been her only family for nearly her entire life. It was an admirable quality, but not appropriate when he could see blood pooling around her body.

He didn't respond to the insane accusations. Instead, he reached forward and scooped her back into his arms where she belonged.

The thought made him hesitate.

Where she belonged? Was he thinking like that now? They'd only shared one night of passion. It was a little early to be pledging his honor to her. And yet...

No. He shook his head to clear his mind. Now wasn't the time.

"Are you coming?" he called out.

A hiss was his answer, but Lorcan streaked forward and dove into the portal without hesitation. The cat was brave to a fault, Bran would give him that.

Shaking his head, he adjusted Aisling in his grip. "I'll hold onto you through the whole thing," he murmured. "I won't let go, no matter how the storm rages."

He pressed his lips to her forehead and let his eyes drift shut. The doors to the palace had opened. Enraged roars and shrieks of anguish filled the courtyard as the Duchess's people saw the body of their esteemed mother lying on the floor without her heart. It wouldn't be long before they turned upon him.

Bran stepped forward into the portal and let the thick magic swirl to his thighs. His hands closed tight around her.

Lips tight to her skull, he smiled sarcastically. "Little witch, you had no idea how close you were to a perfect spell. You just had to tilt the arc slightly, and you could have traveled wherever you wanted in the Otherworld. Now, I'll take you to the human realm just to fix you."

Magic closed over their heads and pulled at their form. Unlike the first time, this magic was gentle. It plucked at the strands of their hair, a faint whine emanating from the red glow as it brushed against the wounds on their sides.

Sometimes magic was alive. It breathed in the essence of the person who created it and became something else. Bran loved creating spells for this reason. Every now and then, he felt as though he had created life.

The portal deposited them on a rocky shore. He knelt on the smoothed stones, waves lapping at his knees. Seagulls cried out overhead, and the calm of the isle's shores eased his soul. Bran glanced up and saw the rolling emerald mountains rising up from the ocean like they'd been perfectly placed by a giant.

His soul loosened its knots of fear. This was home. Even far from the courts, the scent of peat, heather, and fresh rain would always remind him of where he came from.

This land felt right. Holding Aisling in his arms felt right. For the first time in his long life, Bran understood what it meant to belong. It wasn't a physical place. It wasn't the acceptance of others. Home and love started from within.

"Bran?"

"Elva?"

She stood where sand met moss, wearing pliant, leather armor and a frown. A breeze stirred the spun gold of her hair. Braids tunneled through the bright mane like fjords furrowing through the earth. Her skin was rosy and impossibly gold rather than tanned.

Eyes the color of aquamarine met his with a surprising sternness. This wasn't the woman he remembered, or at least not the simpering violet she had been long ago.

He noted the swords at her back, the solid stance, and hand resting on her hip as if ready for whatever he might try. His lips twisted in a smirk, regardless of his body's shaking. The spell would only work for so long. He needed them to help Aisling soon, otherwise he, too, would fall into a deep sleep.

"Are you going to attack me?" he asked. "Or are you going to help?"

"What are you doing here, Unseelie?"

"Unseelie, is it? You know me better than that, Elva." He purposefully used her name. It was a reminder they had been childhood friends. She owed him more than she ever would admit after all she'd put him through. Their past was complicated, and something neither of them liked to think about.

Something sparked in her eyes, and he knew she

understood the dangerous tone of his voice. He wouldn't stand for her pushing him to the side. Regardless of her station in life, they had once been friends.

Seelie or Unseelie, he would not take no for an answer.

"Scáthach will not be pleased with such an intrusion. Men are not welcome here."

"And I arrived with full understanding of that. It's not for myself that I seek sanctuary." He shifted Aisling in his arms, the long waterfall of her dark hair nearly touching the ground. "I ask that you and the maidens take my...take her. Heal her."

Elva softened her stance, her hand falling to her side finally. "Give her here. Who is she?"

He didn't want to let someone else take her. He wanted to stay by her side through the healing, help her through the bitterness of nightshade. Yet he knew the foolish thoughts for what they were.

His own legs weak, Bran stepped forward to transfer Aisling into Elva's arms.

The golden faerie stopped him with a lifted hand. "You're shaking."

"A binding curse will do that to you."

"What did you do?"

Now there was the chiding tone he recognized. Grinning, he lifted Aisling higher and raised a brow. "Do you want to help or not?"

Elva cursed. "Always getting yourself in trouble, Bran. What have you brought me, a witch?"

"A changeling, I believe." He hesitated then plunged ahead. "I have to warn you, the Duchess of Dusk spelled her to wear your face. It was a cruel jest, and I don't want you to take it the—"

Elva lunged forward, her hands desperately smoothing the hair away from Aisling's face.

He had never seen such a panicked expression on her face before. She wasn't just afraid; she was terrified the woman he held in his arms might be dead. All color drained from her face as she stared down into Aisling's still form.

"It's removable," he gruffly said. "Heal her first, and then we can talk to her about removing the spell."

"Bran, you idiot," Elva breathed. "Give her to me."

"It's just a spell, Elva." He couldn't understand the hundred emotions flickering through Elva's eyes, or the way she lifted Aisling from his arms with infinite care.

"It's not just a *spell*," she spat, her eyes burning with anger and something deeper he couldn't understand. "I don't remember you as a blind fool. She's not wearing my face, Bran. She's my *sister*."

The foundation of the earth shifted. So stunned he was at the revelation, Bran didn't know which way was up, and his vision blurred.

And, *of course*, Aisling was her sister. How had he not seen it before?

The truth had been in front of him all this time. In the way Aisling gestured with her hands when she spoke, the way she tilted her head when she was angry at him, the jumping of her leg when she was impatient. Elva's mannerisms were written all over Aisling like a brand.

Of course, they were sisters. He should have known it from the first moment he set eyes upon the beautiful woman strapped to a tree. The women of their line were always bound by one thing or another, Elva by her beauty, Aisling by her magic. And he was drawn to them like a moth to a flame.

"Bran?" Elva said, pulling him out of his silence. "You cannot stay here."

"I stay where she is."

"This isle is not home to men."

"And yet we have called this place home before. Where she goes, I go."

Her lips twisted into a snarl, and she looked him up and down. "If this is some half-hearted attempt to win me back, I'll have you know—"

"Stop." Bran lifted a hand, then slowly curled it into a fist. "Now is not the time. We'll have that conversation later. It's been a long time coming. But right now all I am concerned about is her wellbeing. Take her wherever you need to, but know that I will follow close behind."

Elva's gaze narrowed and then skated away from the raven eye that was on Aisling's form. "You've changed, Bran. I'm not sure yet whether for the better or the worse."

"We'll find out sometime."

He wasn't going to argue with her. He *had* changed. Aisling was an influence that was hard to refute. She had a way of making people see the world the way she saw it. More than that, her gentle touches and unabashed bravery had worn away at the sharp edges of his anger.

Seelie Fae saw him as an animal. Unseelie Fae saw him as a pretty meld of human and animal without any bite. Aisling saw him as a man, and she was the first person to take a step toward acknowledging he had a soul.

"She's bleeding," he quietly said. "We should get her

283

help."

"Can you stay upright if you follow me?"

Probably not, but he squared his shoulders and nodded.

They made their way across the rocky shore, picking their way over seaweed-laden stone and algae-filled crevices. He nearly slipped a few times but caught himself at the last second. When they reached the top of a small rise, the sea fell away. Emerald green grass spread out before them like a blanket laid out for a god.

A fortress jutted from the earth in the distance. Made out of black stone, it had earned its name. The Fortress of Shadows was the home to the most powerful women in all the Otherworld. Kings had begged for their support, then for their training, but only one had ever managed to convince these women to bend a knee.

Even then, it hadn't ended well for him.

Letting out a breath, he followed close on Elva's heels as she made her way up the meandering dirt path and entered the home of the great Lady Scáthach.

Bran vividly remembered the stories told of her. How she had taken down an army by herself. How she had risen from the ground a grown woman, her arms powerful, her sword sharp, and her soul that of a woman crying out for revenge.

She was feared throughout the Otherworld, not because she was evil, but because she was vengeance personified.

Dark walls jutted out of the earth and towered above them. Elva walked past with little reaction to the archer's who pointed drawn bows at them.

Women peered out of their tents laid out across the fortress grounds. Each and every one of them was training to be just as deadly as Scáthach. Many would succeed and go out into the world to take over their own kingdom, to kill those who wronged them, to train husbands and sons in the true art of war.

Compared to them, he felt small. Bran was no little man. He was tall and broad, although lean in a way his siblings were not. But these women were powerful in every sense of the word. Muscles bulged in their necks and biceps flexed as they crossed their arms and stared him down.

Armor clinked as the breeze shifted their chainmail. Even in their home, they were prepared for battle.

A chicken rushed past, strangely silent as it fled some hidden force. It didn't bode well. Bran gritted his teeth and hoped that Aisling's strange familiar had made himself scarce. The last thing he needed was a black cat to cross his path.

The doors banged open, and Scáthach herself strode from the fortress and made her way toward them. She was a giant of a woman with red hair like a bloom of fire, terrifying in her height and power in her every movement. Muscles flexed, armor creaked, but above all else, it was the storm hidden in her gaze that made Bran's feathers raise on his arm.

"Be at peace, Unseelie," she called out. "I have not the energy to deal with you yet. Bring me the girl."

Elva raced toward the mistress and deposited her sister into the outstretched arms. "She is badly wounded."

"Cursed?"

"In many ways," Bran called out. "A spell to keep her asleep. It slows the poison."

"Not entirely useless then." Scáthach pressed her ear to Aisling's lips and then straightened. "She'll live."

The warrior woman turned on her heel and strode toward the fortress. Bran moved to follow her, only to halt when Elva's hand slapped hard against his chest.

"No man enters the Fortress of Shadows."

"Does this not count?"

"You know you are within the surrounding walls. Stop trying to mince words, Bran, and keep your feet anchored to the ground."

Heavy doors closed behind Scáthach. The reverberating thrum echoed in his head, but all he could feel was the distance between himself and the strange witch who had wiggled her way into his heart.

Elva's gaze burned. "You aren't yourself," she mused. "Come with me. I'll get you something to eat, and perhaps we can slow the effects from the binding curse."

"I thought you told me to stay put." He wouldn't mind, even though it surprised him, but a part of him wanted to stare at the doors until they opened again.

Could Scáthach actually save her? Or had he brought them both to their doom?

Elva shoved him forward. "Come on then. Stop staring like a love-sick puppy. You know I always hated it when you did that."

"I'm not staring at you."

"No, you're staring at my baby sister, and that's even worse."

She had a point. He couldn't imagine what was running through her head. With all the history between them...

Bran cursed. Not one memory had crossed his mind since coming here. Really since meeting Aisling. How could he have forgotten the deep river of broken engagements, childhood dreams, and promises whispered in the dead of night?

Fool. He was such a fool.

Ducking his head, he followed her through the crowds of women standing and eyeing him as if he were candy. A few times Elva knocked one back with her shoulder, others she grinned at as she led him to her tent.

When Elva pointed to a small carpeted area in front of her home, he sat without question. He drummed his fingers on his knees. His gaze flicked toward the fortress every few heartbeats. It wasn't that he didn't trust Scáthach — she was a warrior woman capable of much more than he knew — but worry gnawed in his belly regardless.

"She will heal," Elva said. She pulled the sword from her back and set it on the ground gently. "It was not a mortal wound."

"I'll feel better once she isn't leaching the life from me." He rubbed the starburst mark underneath his shirt.

"We have a while to wait. Tell me what happened, Bran. Every bit of it."

He took his time explaining what had happened. There was history between them. Elva had been his first love, his first heartbreak, and everything in between. She deserved to know every detail and then some.

To her credit, she listened intently through the entire tale while sharpening her blade, only setting it aside when he spoke of the dead god and the Duchess. Sometimes she interrupted with questions, but mostly she let him talk.

Every word lifted a weight off his shoulders he hadn't realized was there. She'd always been good at this. Elva's talent was that she made people feel like they were important. She listened, she understood, and she healed without a word.

It was both her blessing and her curse.

As he spoke of the nightshade running through Aisling's veins and his flight through the window, he felt a rush of energy and power pouring back through him. A long sigh of relief escaped his lips.

Elva nodded. "And so it is done."

The fiery trails down his sides disappeared. "How is she doing it?"

"Scáthach is a mystery to all of us."

"Even to those who live with her?"

Her gaze slid to the side. "She says every warrior must also be a healer. To understand what can cause the most pain, we must also know what does not."

"How intriguing," he murmured, his eyes finding the fortress again.

Was Aisling scared? It made sense she would be. She was good at pretending that nothing affected her, but he'd seen the flashes of fear in her gaze. She would awake to a stranger bending over her, perhaps even touching her, and he wasn't there to ease her worry.

"Sit down, Bran."

He hadn't realized he'd risen.

Slowly, he settled back down onto the carpet and let out a breath. "What you must think of me."

"There are many things I think of you, Unseelie prince. But I'm uncertain you could ever guess them."

He ran a hand over the feathers on his skull. "Perhaps not. But I know how I was back then. I made life difficult for you when you didn't choose me."

"I was a pawn in my life. My parents wanted a daughter who was royalty. They didn't care who I chose."

"They didn't."

He remembered those days well. He was supposed to have a Seelie bride. His mother wanted someone who understood their ways so she could pry secrets from their lips. He had desired Elva but hadn't been able to throw her into his mother's web. In the end, he chose to be selfish and take her for himself, regardless of his mother's plans.

So, he'd wooed her. He poured so much energy and affection into her that he had surprised himself. Before Elva, Bran hadn't known whether or not he could be the soft, kind person he had been with her.

And then the Seelie king had arrived.

He rode a golden steed, not a single strand of pure white hair out of place. Bran had seen him and known immediately that he had lost. Elva wouldn't choose a man who was half beast. She would choose the paragon of the Fae.

When she left him empty-handed, he had felt his heart shatter into a million pieces. It had taken years to build himself back up, and even then he had shards of self-doubt that still dug between his ribs.

He looked at her now and saw a person. There was a woman under all that golden beauty. A woman who had been through much and regretted her decision of husband a thousand times over.

His expression softened. "How are you?"

A pretty blush spread across her cheeks, and the smallest of smiles made her lips twitch. "After you helped the Seelie king take back his throne from my husband, I left the castle for good. He banished Fionn to the human realm. I do not know where he is or what he does and I am glad of it. I'm learning how to be myself again. It is taking more time than I expected."

"We all discover that, some point or another in our life." Bran stared down at his hands and wondered when they had become these people. He had forgotten how to be confident. She had forgotten how to be a person. And yet they both waited at the door of a fortress for a woman neither knew.

"Did you know of her?" he asked. "Your sister?"

"Illumina left us very early in her life, but not as most changelings do."

He lifted a hand. "Illumina?"

"It is her name." Elva's eyes narrowed. "She never told you her name?"

"She said her name was Aisling."

"That is the name she chose for herself, but not by birthright. Her name is Illumina. She is my youngest sister and the last of our family line. Our parents kept her for as long as they could, but it was clear she would never be one of the Seelie Fae. They could not stand such a slight upon the family name."

"So they got rid of her."

"It was late in her life to do so. We had to call upon…less than savory familial contacts to take her to the human realm. I remember it being very painful for her."

Bran ground his teeth, jaw creaking as he held himself still. "Such practices were outlawed a long time ago."

"Yes, they were. And yet, we still did it."

"Who helped you?"

"My grandmother." Elva glanced up, her eyes burning

with the same rage he felt coursing through his veins. "Badb."

The great Tuatha de Danann, perhaps the most mysterious of them all, was Aisling's grandmother? He should have known. Only the speckled goddess of war could create a spell so profoundly confusing and infinitely simplistic as that which bound his witch.

Before he could ask another question, Scáthach's deep voice interrupted them. "She will live, but she must stay in your tent until she wakes."

The tall woman strode toward them with Aisling limp in her arms. He rushed forward, only to have Elva overtake him. She held her sister carefully, propping Aisling's head against her shoulder. "It will be my pleasure to watch over her until she wakes."

"She may stay as long as it takes," Scáthach said, "but he must go."

Bran shook his head and suppressed a growl. "Where she goes, so do I."

"Then you will both leave when she wakes. My charity extends only to women. I have housed a man on this isle before, although perhaps not the same as you, Unseelie. I know well the bitter betrayal of man."

He wouldn't question it. All knew the story of Cú Chulainn, who had come to Scáthach for training, then had lain with her twin sister and begot a child. There was bad blood between Scáthach and her sister after that, but her nephew was beloved. She sent him to fight with his father as he desired above all else. But Cú Chulainn slayed his son by mistake. The aching wound of guilt never left Scáthach alone, even in her dreams. Now she remained on her isle and trained women to fight, renouncing all men.

Elva shot him a dark look. Perhaps she didn't want them leaving, but he had not forgotten their purpose. He was so close to freedom that he could taste it. Even Aisling's wound would not stop him now.

She would do the same if it were her curse. He was certain of it.

He followed Elva into her tent, nearly stepping on her heels in his haste. The sour taste in his mouth and the rolling of his belly would ease if he could just *see* her. Or perhaps feel her. He had the strangest desire to hold his hand above her mouth to feel her breath on his palm.

That wasn't normal, was it? He didn't know what was happening to him. He'd never cared about another person before, not like this. He hardly recognized the emotions when he'd thought his entire life that he had already been in love. And now, he couldn't focus until he knew she was all right.

He didn't like it.

The tent flap quietly shushed behind them. Light filtered through the small holes in the fabric, creating a pattern of stars all around them. Leave it to Elva to make a tent in rural Scotland beautiful.

He rushed to the small cot where Elva had laid Aisling down. Hovering behind her, he reminded himself that Elva was family. She had a right to see her sister, to make certain she was alive and well.

Elva huffed out a breath. "If you're going to lurk behind me, just see her already. You're driving me insane with all that nervous energy."

Bran barely waited for her to shift before he crouched

beside Aisling. He hovered his hand above her lips, waiting for the faint puff of breath. When he felt a brush of air against his fingertips, all the tension eased from his shoulders.

When he was a younger man, he would have been embarrassed to come apart in front of Elva. He had wanted her to see him as nothing more than a man. Someone who was strong, capable, and impossible to shake. Now, he barely noticed she was in the room as he let his forehead drop to rest on top of Aisling's sternum.

He felt her heartbeat against his forehead, felt her chest rise and fall, and all was right in the world.

"You scared me," he whispered. "I know you're fine, I could feel you were going to be fine, but I still couldn't shake the dread."

Slight movement shuffled behind him. "You weren't like this. This isn't how I remember you."

Bran tilted his head to the side so he could see Elva. Discomfort marred her usually beautiful expression. He should sit up, but Aisling's heartbeat calmed him. Instead, he left his head on her chest and spoke to her sister in quiet tones. "I wasn't. I was a different man back then, even after you left me. Selfish. Unkind."

"What changed?" She swallowed. "And don't give me that bullshit answer that *she* was the one who changed you. We all know that love doesn't do that."

"I'm not sure you're right about that. But no, it wasn't her." He shook his head. "It was you. You changed me because I knew what it meant to lose someone. To piece myself back together in a way I was comfortable with. It was the first time in my life I had to decide who I wanted to be, and not what other people wanted."

"Losing someone will do that? Force you to become a better person?"

"I didn't lose you, Elva. I never had you to begin with."

Bran refused to feel guilty when his past lover spun on her heel and ducked out of the tent. If she wanted to run from their past, he wouldn't try to stop her. Hell, he'd been running from it for as long as he could remember.

Thankfully, he no longer had to run.

Aisling shifted under his head. He felt the world tilt sideways when one of her hands lifted and settled on top of his head.

"Bran?"

"You're awake." He lifted his head, sliding her hand down to his cheek and holding it there.

She was groggy, and her eyes didn't focus the way they should, but it was good enough. She was awake, alive, and he felt an immense amount of pleasure to know she was still by his side.

"Where are we?" she asked. "I don't remember this place."

"What's the last thing you remember?"

"The Duke..." She shook her head. "I don't think he wanted to be what he was."

"No. Some people try to change the fabric of their being so the person they love will return their affections."

"Is the Duchess even capable of love?"

"Was she?" He shifted her hand until he could press a chaste kiss against her fingers. "That's a question neither of us can answer. How are you feeling?"

"Groggy," she whispered. "Like someone hit me over the

head with a tree branch. What happened?"

"The Duchess poisoned you."

He watched her eyes clear slightly. "Nightshade."

"Likely, it was always a personal favorite of hers. I brought you here when we couldn't wake you."

"We?" She struggled to sit up, but he pressed a hand against her shoulder to keep her lying still. "Where is Lorcan? He should be here. He would know how to heal me."

"He said nightshade was beyond him."

"It's not beyond him," she said with a snort. "He's healed countless people who suffered from poisoning. It's how he learned how to be a witch. Nightshade is no less challenging than belladonna."

Bran cursed. "That lying little— He's the reason we came here."

"How did we *get* here?"

"I—" He cleared his throat and leaned back. "I might have opened a portal."

"You can open portals now?"

"Well…yes?"

Even weak with exhaustion, she gave him a look that chilled him. "Could you always, or is this a recently discovered talent?"

He swallowed. "Recent."

"Bran, you can't go around stealing spells from people! What if you had seen the rune at the wrong angle? What if—"

He let her continue to scold him, but stopped listening. A grin spread across his face. He never thought he would be so happy to have someone berate him for being foolish, but here he was. It meant the world that she could yell at him because it meant she was alive and well. She was still breathing, and was all that mattered.

Finally, he refused to take the beating anymore. He leaned down and covered her soft lips with his own, pressing his grin against her still-moving mouth.

"Aisling, stop talking."

"And another thing!"

He mock groaned, framed her face with his hands, and willed her to silence with every lingering kiss. He relearned the textures of her mouth, the velvet softness of her lips, the delicate shape of her teeth and slight hesitation of her tongue. He lingered, rediscovering the pieces of her he should have savored far longer than one single night.

Finally he pulled back and inhaled her soft sigh.

"You foolish man, you could have gotten us both killed."

"It wouldn't be the first time I put us both in danger."

"Hush." She reached up and ghosted a fingertip over his brow, gently setting his feathers back in order.

He licked his lips. "I brought you to the Fortress of Shadows. It was the only place where I knew they could heal you. I apologize if this is the last place you want to be. I didn't know who your family was, and I —"

She pressed her hand against his mouth. "I woke up a little earlier than I let on. I heard what you were saying to Elva. All of it, really."

If she had cracked the earth open under his feet, she wouldn't have surprised him more. His jaw fell open, but he didn't know what to say. How could he explain he had loved her sister? Should he? That was hardly a conversation anyone ever wanted to have with someone who had become important to them.

She nudged his jaw closed. "It's okay, Bran. We all have a past, and I fully intended on telling you mine before this. I never expected the Duchess to try to kill me, or my sister to have a history with you, or to realize I could have met you a long time ago if my parents hadn't given me away."

He hadn't thought of it like that, but it made him infinitely angrier to realize he could have met her from the first moment he stepped foot onto Seelie lands. He would have known her face as a child, watched plump cheeks with rosy peaks change into the graceful planes he now adored.

"I wish we had more time." He touched a hand to hers. The raven eye shifted and locked upon her gaze. "We have had little chance to get to know one another."

"I think I know you fairly well, Unseelie."

"Do you, witch?" He leaned down and pressed his forehead against hers. "I suppose you know me more than anyone."

She yawned, her jaw cracking with the sheer force of her exhaustion. "I thought they healed me."

"You're awake, aren't you?"

"Barely."

He pressed a kiss to her cheek and stood up. "I'll see if I can buy us one more night."

"We aren't staying?"

"I can't." Bran hesitated in front of the door, wondering just how much he should tell her. "Men are not welcome here."

Would she push? Would she try to wiggle her way further into his life until he revealed every secret he kept?

"Oh. Well, that's foolish." Her words shaped around

another yawn. "It's too bad, but we're a pair for the time being. Where you go, I go."

And damned if he didn't love her in that moment. She didn't question him. She didn't wonder why they had to leave so quickly when she was injured. Aisling was a strange and unusual woman. It was a shame he was going to lose her.

He ducked out of the tent and smoothed a hand down his belly. It would all be over soon. He would take her to the Unseelie Castle. They would remove the binding curse, and then they could figure out what they were going to do. If his mother didn't try to eat her, or worse.

The shattered pieces of her trust would be difficult to put back together, but he had centuries to win her back. Now that he knew she was a faerie, he could make his plans more concrete. He wouldn't have to watch her die. He wouldn't have to see her slowly age. No, they would gracefully age together over the span of immortality.

"Please don't ask me." Elva's voice cut through his revelries. She sat on a log across the fire, forearms braced on her knees. "There is much I can take, but you and my sister spending the night in my tent while I am out in the cold is not one of them."

"What? What do you think we're going to be doing in that tent?"

"Please. I know what men and women do in private." She rolled her eyes. "I was the Seelie king's consort for centuries, Bran. Give me a little more credit than that."

"I will ask you for the same then." A row of feathers spread down to his fingers, only disappearing when he flexed them. "I don't know what that king did to you, but Aisling and I have traveled a very long way. She's injured, tired, and still unwell. I ask for nothing more than time to rest our heads before we travel. That *is it.*"

It sickened him to the core that she thought he might try anything other than to rest with Aisling in his arms. There was too much to do, too much to think about, and she was still injured. For all that he was Unseelie, he was still a gentleman.

Elva stared at him, and he was certain it was confusion in her eyes. "I'll see what I can do."

"Scáthach didn't seem all that interested in letting me remain a moment longer."

"She won't know. Just stay quiet tonight, and I'll make sure no one bothers you."

He turned to duck back into the tent, but hesitated. Casting a brief glance over his shoulder, he branded the image of her into his mind.

Elva had tied her hair back in a braid. The mass of golden locks coiled, twisted, and turned, glimmering in the firelight. She was so flawless it almost hurt to look at her. Perhaps that, more than her kindness, was her curse.

"Thank you," he said. "I want to take care of her, you know."

"I can see that."

"And it bothers you?"

She looked up, ghosts swimming in the aquamarine pools of her eyes. "I don't know who you are anymore."

"People can change, Elva. Strange as it seems."

He brushed the tent flap aside and plunged back into the darkness where past memories didn't make his heart ache. There was nothing he could do for the stunning faerie woman.

She had made her choices, and lying in them sometimes stung.

"Bran?"

Aisling's quiet voice soothed his tired mind. He could do nothing for Elva. There wasn't time, and she wouldn't accept any help from him. There was perhaps another who could open her heart to love and kindness, and maybe Bran could help her find him.

For now, Aisling's sister would remain a fragile, broken image of what she might have been if she hadn't wasted so much time with someone destructive. If he remembered the Seelie king, and he certainly did, there was more to Elva's story than she was telling anyone.

He stepped toward the small cot and let his shoulders finally droop. "We can stay the night."

"And then?"

"Then we go to the next place. It is the last, and hopefully our binding curse will be broken at that point." He rubbed his chest, which suddenly ached.

"Bran, where are we going?"

Gods, what would she do when she found out? He didn't want to put her back into a dangerous situation, but they were so close. *So* close to finally breaking this curse and being themselves once again.

He sat next to the cot with his back against the rungs. It was too small to contain the two of them, and though he desperately wanted to hold her in his arms, he also wanted to make sure she slept. Of the two of them, she needed it more.

"We're going to the Unseelie Castle. Unfortunately, I cannot keep you away from my family much longer."

"I'm not afraid of them."

"They're all half animal. Beastly creatures who are more magic than man or woman. Surely, you've heard tales of my parents?"

Aisling shifted, and her fingers played with the long tendrils of his dark hair. "I have heard the stories of the Unseelie king and queen, half spider and half Fae. I have heard every story told to scare children in the middle of the night. But I am not frightened."

"You should be."

"Are they going to hurt me?"

He'd kill them if they tried to lay a finger on her. Family be damned, he didn't like them that much anyways. "I won't let them."

"Will they curse me?"

"Never."

"Will they somehow break us apart so that I will never see you again?"

Bran turned slightly and narrowed his eyes. "Would you want that?"

A piece of him broke off at the mere thought. She wasn't just a conquest he had found, but the first person he considered a friend. She didn't look at him as though he was some kind of faerie abomination, and he liked that. Bran liked being a person in someone's eyes. How could he ever survive losing such a feeling?

Aisling smoothed his ruffled feathers with a soft smile. "No. I think I like you enough to keep you around for a while yet."

He arched a brow. "A while?"

"A woman has to keep a man wondering where things are

going. I won't make things easy for you."

With a snort, he turned back around and closed his eyes. "You've never been very good at that. I don't think *easy* is in your vocabulary."

"And why should it be? I prefer to travel the brambled path."

"You're more likely to have sticks stuck in your hair at the end of that journey."

"But it will be infinitely more interesting."

Gods, he could love this woman so easily. Bran reached behind him, picked her hand back up, and placed it on his head again. "Don't stop."

"You like this?"

"Hm."

She stroked her fingers through his hair without flinching when she touched the feathers. In this hour between dusk and midnight, Bran felt like a simple man. Nothing more than flesh and bone. Feathers didn't matter because they didn't matter to her.

For once, he felt nearly whole as he fell asleep with her hand resting on his shoulder and his head laid against her side.

CHAPTER 11
THE LAST JOURNEY

Aisling crested the small hill, her feet sinking in spongy emerald moss that sprang back into place the moment she lifted her weight. It was as if she had never stepped up this hill at all. No footprints marked her journey.

For a moment, she lost track of herself. She frequently found herself lingering upon memories of facelessness, of being someone who wasn't real. Her greatest fear was that the curse would return tenfold, and she would be punished for attempting to remove it.

To lose everything that had made her into a real person would strip away every happiness she had found.

Shaking herself from the dark thoughts, she picked her way around granite stones. Her sister waited at the top of the munro that looked out over the sea.

Her sister. Aisling had never thought to say those words again.

She'd always known she had a family. Badb had made certain she was aware of that. They had left her, given her up, didn't deserve to have any space in her mind. But she'd still thought of them.

Who wouldn't? Family was some mythical support system that would never harm you. She couldn't remember anything of them in the beginning. Not even the slightest memory of her mother kissing her forehead or her father ruffling her hair.

Those memories had come back as she aged. Little by little, the spell Badb had woven unraveled in her mind. She remembered them all too well now. She saw their cold expressions as they made her leave them forever.

Elva appeared at the top of the rise. Her hair whipped around her, loose and tangled by the breeze. Legs spread in a confident stance, hands clasped behind her back, she was the picture of a warrior at attention.

What had happened to the bubbling child she remembered? Aisling had looked up to her, she remembered that much. She didn't recognize the woman before her and couldn't reconcile that spoiled child with this stoic future.

She should thank her for the borrowed clothing. Simple brown skirt, a tight bodice, nothing fanciful, but clothes that would suffice in meeting Unseelie royalty.

"We're leaving," Aisling said as she reached her sister. "Thank you for the boat. It will be easier than creating a portal."

"You could stay, you know." The breeze lifted a strand of golden hair and smoothed it across Elva's cheeks. "It's not a bad life here."

"And do what? Learn how to fight?"

"It's not a bad thing to know."

Aisling shook her head. "I've taken care of myself for years now, Elva. I don't have any reason to remain here."

"We could be a family again. If you'd let us."

When she turned to look at her sister, Aisling saw there were tears in Elva's eyes. How strange for the seemingly unshakeable woman to express such emotion.

"A family?" Aisling tried to soften the words as much as possible. "That option was taken from us a long time ago."

"We can have it again. I never wanted to let you go. I cried for days after they sent you away, threw every tantrum I could, but they wouldn't bring you back."

"That doesn't change anything, Elva."

"It should!" Her shout was stifled by the wind, ripped away from her and dulled by the elements. "I lost you, and then I lost him, and then I lost everything because I thought I wanted a throne. I look at you two and I see...something. I don't know what it is. I don't know how to feel that way, and I think you might be able to teach me."

"That's too much to lay at my feet." Aisling reached out and took her sister's hands. "No one can teach you that but yourself. You'll learn again, I'm certain of that. But in the meantime, stop trying to rush the healing. You don't have a cut that can be patched with a bandage. It will take a long time."

"It has been a lifetime."

"And it could be yet another lifetime, but you will endure. It is what we do."

Elva reached out and touched a finger to Aisling's jaw. She followed the sharp line to her chin where she tapped the end. "You aren't the creature I thought you would grow up to be."

"I became who I wanted. Know that I do not regret losing my family. It made me the witch I am. I would not trade that for the world."

Aisling saw recognition flare in Elva's gaze. Not

necessarily for the words, but something else that burned deep in her soul. Perhaps she had heard similar words before.

They turned together and stared out to sea. It was a clear day, a good omen for the journey she, Lorcan, and Bran would make. Still, it was strange to say goodbye to family she had just found once again.

The first moment she could, Aisling had cast a spell to watch her Seelie family. Her father had recognized it immediately and cast a counterspell. Her mother had disappeared from view too quickly for her to watch. But Elva had allowed her to watch for hours on end.

Aisling had been captivated by the way Elva would brush her hair, the tiny sheets of gold that she would press to her face and make her skin glimmer. It had been like watching a princess every morning.

Until she disappeared forever, and Aisling hadn't been able to see her until now.

She wished she could have more time. This was a woman she would like to know. Her past, her future, her story, all of it was infinitely precious. Aisling felt as though it was being ripped from her hands.

"To love someone who cannot love themselves is a great and terrible burden," Elva quietly said.

Aisling looked out over the crashing waves. "Or it is a rare opportunity to show them that no matter what darkness lies heavy in their mind, someone else can always find their light?"

"You really believe that?"

"I have to." She waited a moment, then turned her back on the sea. "I'd like to see you again when all is said and done."

"You shouldn't trust him."

"Who?"

"Bran. He's not who you think he is, and you aren't telling him the whole truth." Elva reached out and plucked a white down feather from Aisling's shoulder. "You need to tell him everything before you finish this journey."

"What, about the Raven King?"

She wasn't afraid of the truth. Aisling had spent her entire life under one curse or another. This was just another mountain in her path, and she would climb it.

"You're the consort to a very powerful creature. The Raven King isn't even a faerie anymore. He's something else, something darker, and you cannot run from him."

"So you say. I've been running my whole life from every person I've ever met."

"Illumina, he deserves to know."

"I gave up that name a long time ago." Aisling swallowed hard, tucking her shaking hands into her skirts. "And what he doesn't know won't hurt him."

"If you're afraid of hurting him, then are you really loving him?"

"Love?" She shook her head. "Neither of us are capable of that. Besides, he'll find out eventually. Maybe that will be our next adventure. Break the binding curse, then break the consort curse."

"It's not possible. It's not just a curse — it's a vow. Magic has no control over what you were born to be."

Once again, Aisling shook her head. She refused to believe any of the words Elva was saying. There was always a way out. There was always a possibility to release herself from the chains of her past. She just had to find them.

"I hope to see you again, sister," Aisling choked out.

"I'll ask you one more time. Please stay."

Her heart was breaking. This was her first family member who would even speak to her. Elva had admitted to missing her, to not wanting her to leave, and every fiber of Aisling's being said to stay. To see what would happen if she entertained the idea of *family*.

But she couldn't. Not yet.

She shook her head, but didn't trust her voice not to waver with emotion.

Elva sighed. "It's a shame. I don't want to see you walk the same path I did."

"Why?" Aisling managed.

"Because I've hardly recovered from it."

"Then I shall have to be stronger than you."

Keeping her head high, Aisling walked away from her sister and back down the Munro. She told herself not to cry. There was no reason to cry.

Elva's life might not have been the one she wanted, but that did not mean Aisling would repeat Elva's mistakes. She couldn't explain what she felt for Bran. It wasn't love, or infatuation, or even the rose-glow beginnings of either. She felt in him a kindred spirit, someone else who had been afraid their entire life of what others thought of them.

Every second with him was refreshing. He knew how to speak, how to act, how to *be* the kind of person who set her at ease. She could be a witch, and he would never build a pyre upon which to burn her thoughts, desires, and dreams.

That was the difference between what Elva knew and what Aisling had experienced. Through all the lies and deceit, she would make sure that Bran remained in her life.

The grass rustled beside her, parting to reveal a black fluffy body with hair tufted in all directions.

"Lorcan!" she cried out. Aisling stooped and opened her arms for him, only breathing easy when he launched himself at her.

With his furry body clasped to her chest, she felt invincible.

"I was so worried about you," she muttered into his neck. "Where were you?"

"They don't like men here."

"I'm not sure that extends to cats." She laughed, hooked her hands under his armpits, and lifted him away from her. The grumpy expression on his face made her laugh even harder. "Where have you been?"

"Trying to stay away from these women! They knew who I was immediately." His fur bristled. "I tried to tell them I was nothing more than a cat, but that apparently wasn't the right thing to say."

"My guess is saying nothing would have worked best."

"Probably. But they wanted to know where I came from, and I refuse to be thought of as a ship cat. They eat rats, you know."

"Your tastes are far more refined." She stood with him in her arms, letting him drape himself over her shoulders like he had when she was a child. "What gave you away? The talking or your size?"

"Are you suggesting I'm gaining weight?"

"You're heavier than I remember."

His paw stretched, flexing until the claws glistened in the afternoon sun. "Careful, witch. I'm right next to your throat."

"You wouldn't dare."

As they bantered back and forth down the hill, she felt her heart lift. Perhaps her old family wasn't in her life, but was that really the end of the world? She had created a new family for herself. Two men who loved her, who had taken care of her, even risked their lives to make certain she was happy. So few could say that.

Family wasn't flesh and blood; it was the people who set her soul at ease and filled her lungs with air.

Lorcan pressed his cold, wet nose against her cheek and asked, "We're really going with him?"

"Where else would we go?"

"Anywhere. We're in our world for now, even though it is the Isle of Skye. We could take the boat, flee across the ocean and find a portal, find the rest of your family. Make our *own* family. The possibilities are endless."

"I'll still be cursed."

"You smell different." Worry tainted his voice with bitter tones. "Not like yourself."

"I traded one curse for another."

"Breakable?"

She shrugged a shoulder, jostling him. "Doesn't seem likely, but I won't just give up. The Raven King's consort seems like a title for a lady, not for a witch."

"Well, if you can't get out of it, he's got another thing coming for him." Lorcan paused, then leaned back enough to pat her with a paw. "Don't worry. I don't think Bran is the type to give up either."

"No, I don't think he is."

They stepped off mossy green grass and onto the sandy

shore at the base of the mountain. The air was cleaner here. Crisp, it burned her lungs every time she inhaled. Aisling savored the pain as she made her way toward the small boat where Bran stood staring at the waves.

He was a dark smudge against the sun reflecting on the water. His form wavered, shimmering in the light, but always remaining the same. Never once had he hidden himself behind a glamour. He was as he looked. Beast and man melded into one mysterious figure who had stepped out of the shadows like an ancient god.

He turned toward her, light silhouetting his body, and stretched out a hand. "Are you ready?"

She placed her hand in his and let him guide her into the small boat. Lorcan disappeared underneath the benches, while sand and stones crunched under Bran's feet as he shoved them into the waters.

Aisling shaded her eyes and stared up the mountain to see her sister's small form still as a statue. Elva lifted a hand in goodbye. A small piece of her soul would stay on the isle within a broken sister whose heart had been shattered too many times.

Someday, she would return. Someday, she would build the relationship they should have had.

Aisling just wished that day could be today.

Bran hopped into the boat, set his hands onto the oars, and propelled them away from the island.

"You all right?" he asked.

"I'm not sure yet."

Bran nodded at the isle slowly becoming smaller. "Family is odd, isn't it? No matter how different we are, we want to love them."

"Speaking from experience?"

"Too much," he replied with a chuckle. "My family is the strangest of them all. You'll meet them soon enough."

"I never knew what my family was really like. I watched them with spells sometimes, but I can't say I actually *know* them." She paused, then corrected herself. "Not that I remember really. There's pieces and parts of memories, a past that seems like it came from a different person."

"I wish mine came from a different person," he said with a snort.

Aisling twisted her fingers in her lap. There was so much between them. And instead of saying anything, they let the space fill with the quiet gurgle of oars dipping beneath waves.

Finally, she blew out a breath. "Bran, I haven't been entirely honest with you."

"I know," he interrupted. A black feather drifted away from his head, hitting the water and dissolving into seafoam. "We both have secrets, Aisling. Just...let them be as they are until we've finished this. We'll pick up the pieces then, come clean, say whatever it is we have to say."

"Let them remain until the curse is broken?"

"Just a little while longer." The sad smile on his face mirrored her own. "There's so much I want to tell you."

"Then we will stay as we are for now."

"And start over when this is finished."

"Start over?" She arched a brow. "It's a little late for that."

"Well, as much as we can. I intend to revisit part of this journey."

She propped an elbow on the edge of the boat, placed her chin on her fist, and cocked her head to the side. "What might that be, Unseelie?"

The bright flash of his grin nearly blinded her. For a moment, Aisling let herself believe this could work. They would break the binding curse and ride off into the sunset, searching for a way to break her own curse. It was possible because they would make it possible.

The waves splashed by them. The sun touched them with warm rays that didn't ache or turn vividly hot. Gulls cried out overhead and then circled back toward the isle when they realized no fish would be caught.

Every stolen moment was perfection, and she savored every second knowing it would all be ripped away.

Water pinged the wooden planks of the boat. The sound was strange, unusual considering the waves were still placid. Aisling straightened and looked around them in suspicion. "Bran?"

"Finally heard it?"

She tried to stare him down as if she were brave but tightened her fingers on the edges of the boat. "I thought we were going to row back to Ireland and find a portal there."

"That would take us the better part of a month in a boat this small." His raven eye wriggled in its socket. "There are faster ways to get home."

"Which are?"

Bran released an oar and pointed over her shoulder. "Standing stones."

"We're in the middle of the ocean."

"They pop up everywhere, you know. Portals are portals, regardless of where they form."

"And what does a standing stone portal look like when it's

created beneath the waves?" She already knew what he was going to say. The spray of saltwater flecked her face, and when she licked her lips, she could taste the sea.

"A bit like a whirlpool."

"Have you gone mad? We're in a rickety boat the size of a child's toy. A whirlpool will tear us apart!"

"Weren't you the one who said almost dying is an adventure?"

"I've never said that Bran." She whipped around and glared at him. "You're going to get me killed."

"Oh, don't you worry, witch." He flashed her a smile, pulled the oars up into the boat, and held out his hands. "When have I not saved you from almost certain death?"

Aisling rolled her eyes and took his hands. "One of these times, you're not going to be able to save me."

"Never."

"You just steered us into a whirlpool, didn't you?"

"Absolutely."

"I think I might hate you."

He gave her a wink. "You're a faerie, remember? You can't lie anymore."

Cat claws dug into her calves, and she held onto Bran as the boat tipped backward, then slid down into the belly of the whirlpool.

Water crashed around them, great eddies of powerful liquid spinning so quickly it looked like clear glass. Aisling could see the ocean beyond, dark waters and spears of light sinking through the ocean into the murky abyss. She caught a glimpse of a dark shadow as they plummeted toward the seafloor.

Her hair tangled in front of her face. She hooked her heels underneath the bench but never once felt worried. Bran held her hands, secure and firm. She felt the gentle push of magic on her shoulders holding Lorcan and herself down.

He muttered a spell, dark hair whipping around his face, feathers ruffling.

Just as she was about to ask how much longer, the boat struck solid stone. She felt the wood shatter underneath her, the blinding pain of her legs cracking, flesh rending, muscle tearing. Aisling saw a bright flash of white magic but didn't have time to cry out in pain.

A gentle burble of waves lapped at the boat's hull. Aisling let out the breath she had been holding with a gasp and opened her eyes wide.

They were floating on a calm, dark sea, their boat intact as if nothing had happened. Stars dotted the night sky above them, reflecting in the glassy water as if they sat inside a galaxy. Thousands of tiny pinpricks of light surrounded them.

Bran's gaze met hers. She saw the galaxies inside his eyes and felt them expand in her chest.

"What was that?"

"Standing stone traveling."

"You didn't warn me."

He lifted a shoulder. "I couldn't describe it right anyways. Best to just experience it."

She shuddered, then released his hands. "I'm never doing that again."

"You might not have a choice."

"I'm *never* doing that again, Bran," she firmly replied.

Aisling leaned down to peer underneath the bench for

Lorcan. Her hair fell in a waterfall to the bottom of the boat. His claws were still latched onto her calves, but shadows covered everything other than his outstretched paws.

"You can let go now," she said.

"Not after that. Tell that Unseelie when I get off this boat, I'm going to claw his eyes out."

Aisling chuckled. "You are not."

"I am, and more. Cats eat birds."

Bran snorted. "I'd like to see you try. Some birds are too tough to chew on."

"I'll survive it," Lorcan growled.

"Boys," Aisling interrupted with a burst of laughter, "are you quite done?"

"Not yet. I still want to claw at him. I get to at least scratch him with one paw."

"No, Lorcan."

"One scratch."

"No!" She shook her head and leaned back up. Her head swam at the quick movement, spinning the stars all around Bran until he blended into the darkness between them.

She'd never thought a man beautiful before him. They were sturdy creatures with broad shoulders capable of lifting much weight. But he was more than that. Bran was artwork embodied. Graceful lines, arches that rivaled the greatest architecture of her time, a face that would make a sculptor weep. He was two sides of a coin. Smooth, handsome skin on one side, rough, ragged beast on the other.

"Have you stared your fill?" he asked.

"I don't know if I ever will."

"Look behind you, Aisling. Your first sight of the Dark

Castle is one to remember for the rest of your life."

She took a deep breath and turned to see the home of the Unseelie.

Jagged spires rose into the air with points sharper than that of a blade. High peaks rose as far as her eye could see, both mountain and castle tangled together, all at the edge of an ocean that churned to rise up the steep cliffs. Slashes of red and orange light marked windows glowing from candles and magic.

A flock of dark shapes circled the castle. Not birds, for they were too large to be normal birds, but winged beasts, half faerie, half animal. The wind carried the sound of laughter, but not joyful, and screams, but not agonized. Both echoed, tainted with pleasure in pain.

Aisling should have been afraid. Her heart should have caught at the sight of such shadowed darkness, but she couldn't force herself to feel that way. Instead, all she recognized within herself was a strange sense of curiosity and foreboding.

"The Dark Castle," she repeated. "Home of the Unseelie court."

"Only royalty."

"Your home." She glanced over her shoulder in time to see his grimace. "Or…where you grew up."

"That's a little more accurate."

He picked up the oars and steered them toward a small alcove she hadn't noticed before. Stairs rose out of the ocean, lit by small, hovering orbs casting yellow light onto the sea. She'd never been afraid of water. Aisling had always been able to swim. But this blackened mire made her nervous.

"Remember I said we need the waters from Swan Lake?"

"Yes," she whispered. The boat bumped against the stairs.

"It's hidden deep underneath the castle. We'll go in through the library. We'll have to avoid my sisters and hope they haven't changed the spell. Otherwise, we're walking into a labyrinth."

"Easy enough?"

He shook his head and hopped onto the slippery stones with a confidence she envied. "It won't be. Listen to me, Aisling. None of my family is normal, but my sisters most of all. They can't see you, but they can hear you. So stay quiet. Not a word until we get out of the library from here on out. You understand?"

"You're frightening me, Bran."

"Impossible." He held out a hand for her to take and gave her a wavering smile she didn't believe. "You're much too strong to ever feel fear."

"Flattery will get you everywhere." She placed her hand in his and let him pull her from the boat in one smooth movement.

He kept his hand under her arm for a moment to steady her, heat sinking into her bones until he left her standing alone on the slippery rocks. Bran knelt next to the boat. He asked, "Are you coming Lorcan?"

A faint hiss emanated from under the bench.

"I'll take that as a no. We'll see you sometime soon then?"

Another hiss was the response.

Aisling hid her grin behind a hand. "He'll catch up. He always does. It takes him a little while to muster the bravery, but once he does, he's unstoppable."

"You don't say?" Bran grumbled and stood. "It's not safe for any of us to be alone here."

"I don't worry about Lorcan. For all that he might be a little

318

smaller than most, he's a dangerous man when he wants to be."

They grinned at each other before he swept an arm out in a flourishing movement. "My lady. Please ascend the staircase."

"For me?" She pressed a hand to her chest. "I didn't know you were such a gentleman."

"Quietly now, Aisling. We can't afford anyone discovering we're here."

She patted his arm as she walked by. "You're learning. For once, you actually told me that I need to be quiet."

Bran grinned, then ran a finger across his lips.

She'd keep her mouth shut if that's what it took to get them through this safely. He was getting a little better at keeping her informed. She knew that noise would alert his sisters, although she didn't know why that was a bad thing.

One would think a family reunion would only help them. He could waltz into the grand hall, or whatever it was the Unseelie called it, ask for a small vial of liquid, and then the curse would break.

Seemed easy enough.

She couldn't figure out if he was making this difficult because he had to, or if it was because Unseelie Fae loved to see chaos unravel. There would always be a part of him that wanted to create as much mischief as possible.

Aisling carefully watched her steps on the slippery stairs and decided she didn't mind the mischief overly much. It certainly made life interesting.

As they reached the top of the stairwell, Bran tapped a finger on her shoulder. She paused and let him step ahead of her. When he slid his hands over the slick stone wall, runes glowed crimson under his touch.

Blood magic. She'd never seen such an ancient spell before. They were created in a time of war or hardship and were rarely removed. Most people would hastily leave a place tainted by magic like this.

Bran hissed out a breath and wiped a bloody palm on his pants. With the price paid, the stone wall faded out of existence, allowing them to step into a cave system deep inside the Unseelie castle.

Liquid dripped from the ceiling, pinging quiet sounds that covered the echo of their footsteps. Faint white mist glowed at the floor, but even the dim light wasn't enough to cast a shadow. They relied on their hands pressed against the walls to guide them.

Aisling stepped where Bran did, every turn opened up to more tunnels, the options unlimited. The air felt charged with electricity, magic pulsing in her veins and making the tips of her fingers burn.

Bran held up a finger and pressed it against his lips.

She wasn't *making* any noise. Pursing her lips, she gestured in a silent way to declare that she was following the rules.

He glared and pointed at her, then exaggerated a deep inhalation and exhale.

Was he saying she was breathing too loud?

Aisling wanted to reach out and smack him. She knew how to be quiet, and if her breath was a little louder than he wanted it to be, then he would need to knock her over the head to quiet her down. She glowered at him as he raced forward on silent feet and pressed himself against the wall.

Bran didn't look at her. Instead, he simply lifted a hand and gestured for her to move forward.

Aisling glanced around the cave. There was no glimmer of magic in the air suggesting a spell hid someone from their view. They were in a cave system of tunnels, and no one was here.

She sighed and walked toward him. And though her footsteps were quiet, they weren't nearly as silent as his had been.

His expression darkened. He waited for her to get close before he grabbed her arm, shoved her against the wall, and blanketed her body with his. Leaning down, he pressed his lips against her ear.

"What did I say about being quiet?" he hissed.

"There's no one here."

"It's the Unseelie castle. You can't know that for certain."

"I can see there is no one standing there staring at us. We're in a tunnel system, Bran. Of all places to worry about someone being hidden, I can see down both ends, and there is no one else but us."

"We have to be quiet."

She huffed out a breath and growled in his ear, "It's one thing to be careful when we need to be, but you just look foolish."

Her words were like the slash of a sword through the heat between them. He stepped back a few times, storm clouds thundering in his gaze.

Aisling knew she had a way of throwing him off. She watched with amusement as he crossed his arms, then untangled himself and stuck his hands on his hips, then shook his head with frustration and tossed his hands in the air. "They changed the spell. I'm walking blind here. All the halls are different."

"If you can't figure it out, then let me walk normally when *there is no one here.*"

"Fine," he whispered. "Go your own way. See how that works out for you."

"I will."

"I said that was fine."

"You have no idea what I'm capable of, Unseelie. You've already told me where the waters are. I don't need you."

He lunged forward and stuck a finger in her face. "You need me to break the binding curse."

"I don't."

"I have the other ingredients."

He had her there. She would need the rest of the spell to complete it, and he wasn't likely to hand it over to her.

Aisling huffed out a frustrated breath. "Fine. Then we meet back here."

"You foolish woman!" He ran a hand over his feathers, clearly struggling. He couldn't protect her if he was going to shout at her the whole time. Finally, he pointed at her again. "You keep yourself out of trouble and come right back here when you find anything. Otherwise, I'm coming for you and the entire Unseelie army couldn't stop me."

She reached forward and patted his cheek. "I love how cocky you are."

They both froze with her hand pressed against him. Good gods, had she admitted to loving him? No. She'd admitting to loving a part of his personality. It meant nothing. He had to understand that.

His gaze heated, and all the stars in his eyes burst to life. They whispered promises of long nights, velvet sheets, and a man who blended in with the night sky.

Aisling snatched her hand away and stepped back. "We don't have time for this."

"We will soon."

"Just find the water and then find me."

"I'll say the same to you, witch."

He cast a lingering glance over his shoulder, then disappeared down the tunnel. He walked carefully, quietly, and so slowly it made her roll her eyes.

Aisling turned the other way and traced their steps back to a previous fork. She picked a tunnel that felt like it might be the right way. It disappeared down into darkness, mist swirling over the stones sluggishly. Wall sconces slowly flickered to life as she passed, casting the tunnel in a sickly red glow. Her shadow danced over the walls, then blinked out of existence as if she'd never had one.

She ran a hand over her arms. This was her choice. She wanted to wander about on her own without his ridiculous precautions. Her own fault she was alone in the most dangerous place in the known world.

She put her back to the wall as the tunnel split again. Leaning around the edge, she peered both ways before choosing to stick to the left. If Bran was right and this place really was a labyrinth, then she knew how to get through it.

Somehow, she doubted he was right. The area she had stepped into was still just a tunnel system. The walls were chewed away, perhaps by some large beast that had created these in an attempt to make its way through the mountainside.

She shivered again. What kind of beast could create tunnel systems like this?

A quiet echo of sound skittered down the tunnel. It sounded like a moan, of a creature or person in agonizing pain.

"Wonderful," she muttered. "Just what I need to make this even more interesting."

Aisling was careful the farther down the tunnel she went. The moaning grew louder and louder until she pressed a hand to her ear. It made her eyes cross. She blinked them quickly, rubbed at one with a hand, then stared wide-eyed at the wall in front of her that seemed to waver for a moment.

She touched her finger to the slick wall beside her and flicked a droplet of water at the magicked wall. "By earth and water, dispel all glamour and see it true."

The spell held.

Her anger spiked, shattering the strange sound spell that held her in its grasp. "Dispel all glamour," she repeated, "and see it *true*."

The wall shook, then the spell dissolved. Wind swept through immediately. It tangled around her legs, shook the fabric of her borrowed skirts, and threaded through her hair until it flooded back down the tunnel.

A gaping hole in the side of the tunnel revealed a picturesque view of starlight reflected on a calm sea. The darkness was beautiful, intimidating, and so painfully dangerous that it made her eyes sting.

The water far away stirred. A great beast rose from beneath the waves, its scaled side glistening in the moonlight as one large arch lifted out of the water and then slowly disappeared again.

They had traveled across those waters without a care in the world. She hadn't even considered looking down at the waves, she'd been so caught up in staring at her own Unseelie.

What kind of beasts had stared back at them?

Aisling shivered again, brushed her hands over her arms, and turned. She took a right instead of a left, meandering through the labyrinth.

It felt as though she had been traveling for hours. Her feet started to ache, her back threatened to seize, and her heart thumped hard in her chest. The tunnels never seemed to end.

Every single one was exactly the same as the next. Water dripped down the walls. Ragged pieces stuck out from the wall of everything she saw. It always ended with two choices, and she always took the right.

If she had to turn around, Aisling was careful to retrace her steps. They hadn't brought anything with them to mark their passage. She took to tracing runes in the algae on the walls. No one would notice the scratched marks as anything other than a strange way for algae to grow. But she knew what her own marks meant.

Just when she thought she might lose her mind, her foot knocked against something on the floor. That was different.

She cocked her head to the side and stared down at the open book. Its pages fluttered, colorful paintings flipping so quickly she couldn't quite make out what they were. Aisling stooped, picked it up, and turned it over to see the gilded cover.

"A History of the Unseelie Court," she whispered. "Interesting."

Tucking the book under her arm, Aisling continued in the same direction. A few more books appeared in the distance, each more intriguing than the last.

Soon, she was holding the complete series of the Unseelie

Court—a surprisingly large, multi-volume series that consisted of fourteen gold-leafed books. When her arms could hold no more, she put them in a stack against the wall. Regret chilled her. It seemed a shame to leave them where the elements would eventually destroy them.

Books were sacred. They took a long time to bind, even longer to write, and each handwritten word was a marvel. She found it strange that the Unseelie faeries tossed them on the floor with little care for them.

Aisling had seen more books in her life than most humans. But then again, she wasn't after all.

Light flickered to life at the end of the tunnel. It moved in a circle before zipping back into the air.

She froze.

It appeared again, farther away this time and without even the slightest bit of sound. Was it someone carrying a light? Or was it some kind of Unseelie creature luring her deeper into the depths?

"You are not afraid," she told herself.

Her palms grew slick with sweat, but she forced herself to move. She had to keep going, had to find the waters, had to break the binding curse. All of this and more.

More books appeared in the hallway, scattered like dying creatures that fluttered their wings as she passed by. She stepped through them carefully. Now she understood Bran's hesitation. A tunnel system deep underneath the earth filled with books wasn't precisely normal.

The tunnel mouth opened up into a room. Aisling pressed her back against the corner and peered around the edge, then gaped at what she saw.

They had made a labyrinth of the shelves. Walls made out of books and hammered wood stretched so high above her head that they were eventually obscured by mist. Thousands upon thousands of books haphazardly thrown onto shelves filled her vision until she was overwhelmed. They spilled out onto the floor, pages open, water-stained, and torn.

There was no care shown for the books, but what did it matter when their number rivaled that of the heavens? She pressed a hand against her chest and stepped forward into the Unseelie library.

She was but a speck, a small figure standing next to monoliths created of the written word. Aisling meandered through them and let her fingers dance along the spines.

The stone floor was smooth. Many feet had walked the same steps as she, each taking their time to find the perfect volume that would answer their question or fill their mind with worlds untold.

Her foot stepped on a swath of pages that covered the floor, ripped from a book and littered across the floor like fallen leaves.

Sudden silence made her freeze. Aisling hadn't been aware of the natural sound of the room. Dripping water, the rush of bat wings, the faint whine of wind, it all stopped the moment she made a sound loud enough to echo.

A high-pitched screech came from directly above Aisling. She tried to still even her breathing until she didn't make a sound at all.

Something crawled above her. The shelves creaked with some weight that toppled a few books to the ground. She didn't dare look up, but quickly found she wouldn't need to.

Whatever had heard her, was coming down.

Fabric rustled above her, and a body dropped down to land two steps before Aisling.

The creature was covered in white fabric that floated around it as if it were in water. Strands of white hair fluttered in the air as it moved. Its head jerked back and forth, pointed ears twitching as it listened for yet another movement.

Aisling slowly reached up and covered her mouth. Its eyes were gone, just gaping holes in its pale, white face.

She realized it was female. Its body was vaguely feminine, but Aisling was loathe to consider it anything other than a creature. Stick-like arms arched out from its sides, fingers twitching.

Strands of glistening web were anchored to the creature's back. She nearly cried out when she saw the rusted metal hooked through its skin. Dried blood scabbed at the edges of the wound, but it did not seem to bother the creature.

It twitched again, shifting and shuddering until it reached up and tugged on the webbing. The gossamer strands pulled, and the creature was yanked back toward the ceiling.

Aisling slowly dropped her shaking hand.

What was that? One of Bran's sisters? Surely not. It didn't look like him at all, but he had said…

She took another step forward, forgetting the paper strewn about the floor. The crunch echoed, and an answering scream made her shake in fear.

A body flew out of the shadows, catching her around the waist and pulling her back. The creature returned, blades in its hands and mouth gaping wide in a silent scream. It landed on the ground and crouched. Its head tilted to the side, waiting for the next sound that certainly would come.

The hand pressed against her mouth was familiar. Taloned nails held her cheeks, a broad chest quaking as he held his breath along with her.

Bran's sister let out a low, vibrating croak. It filled the air with a scent of magic that burned her nostrils and filled her lungs with the painful need to cough. Her chest rocked forward. His hands clenched on her ribs and around her mouth. They stayed silent until the creature tucked her twin blades back beneath the folds of her skirt and tugged on the webbing again.

She lifted into the air, and Aisling let out the breath she had been holding in a slow wheeze.

Lips touched her ear, so close that the hair in front of her face didn't even stir. "That was one of my sisters."

Aisling nodded in response. She couldn't quite bring herself to make any sound just yet.

"Silently, avoid the papers. They drop them from the ceiling so they can hear people walk."

She'd figured that. The papers were each hand painted, words scrolling along the sides in such beautiful script that it made her eyes water. How could anyone toss aside such incredible pieces of artwork?

Bran reached back and held out a hand for her to take. A river of pages stretched out in front of them so wide she would never be able to step over them. Furrowing her brow, she took his hand without hesitation. She didn't know what he was going to do, but she knew he would do it well.

He curled his fingers around her hand, slipped his other at her elbow, and then tossed her across the papers like she weighed little more than a feather. Aisling ground her teeth together for silence. Ridiculous man!

She stayed on her feet, only by luck more than skill. He leapt over the strewn-about paper and landed in a crouch beside her.

The grin he sent her way made her want to smack him. He had no way of knowing she wouldn't have screamed!

He winked.

Aisling's nostrils flared in anger and if her eyes could have set him on fire, she would have. Come to think of it, she knew a spell that would work wonderfully if only he would stay still long enough for her to make sure she didn't hit the books…

"Come on," he whispered.

Something rustled above them at the sound. She didn't want to meet any more of his sisters, so she skittered forward, slipped a hand into his, and allowed him to drag her through the molding library.

They raced between the monolithic stacks of books, pausing only when one of his sisters dropped down from the ceiling. Sometimes it was because they made noise accidently, other times his sisters simply lowered themselves to find yet another book.

Aisling watched their movements carefully every time she had to freeze. They weren't protecting the books. It didn't seem like they cared if they were harmed, so what were they doing?

At one point, Bran pressed her into the shelves and shielded her body with his. Arms braced on either side of her, he stared down into her eyes and didn't move until his sister was pulled back up to the misty ceiling above.

"They record everything that happens in the Unseelie world," he murmured, so quietly she almost didn't hear him.

Aisling arched a brow, silently asking why.

"My mother likes to know everything that happens in the Unseelie court. Nothing gets by her."

A little overprotective if anyone cared about Aisling's opinion, but who was she to judge the choices of a queen? She'd never been one. Who knows what she would do if she was given a court to watch over.

Likely something as crazy. Aisling would want to know each and every one of them, try to remember their names and families. She wouldn't want anyone she was responsible for to feel as she had while growing up.

They were foolish thoughts. Bran would never be king anyways. He had too many siblings ahead of him in line for the throne. He'd said so himself...

She froze for a moment, her fingers curling into a fist and her stomach clenching. What in the world was she thinking? She wasn't going to marry Bran. She certainly wouldn't be his queen if he ever —

Aisling stopped herself again. There were dangerous paths down that road, and she refused to allow herself to wander them.

He slipped past a stack of books taller than him, their pages leaking onto the floor in a waterfall of bright colors and stained ink. She watched for a moment, waiting for him to peak his head back around as he waited for her.

This time, just his hand appeared, gesturing her forward.

Snapping his fingers at Aisling was only going to get her to walk slower. Her brows furrowed before she meandered toward him, slowing when he gestured faster with his hand.

They weren't making any sound. His sisters weren't

screeching, and she didn't hear the strange hushing sound as they slid down their webbings. They were fine. Why was he trying to rush her?

She made her way to stand next to him, rounding the corner to reveal a great darkness spread out before them. And so the library ended, and the throne room began.

It was a massive room filled with smoke and fog. The center was strangely lit with an eerie blue glow. Magic coiled around the giant thrones, one larger than the other. They could easily have fit ten humans standing side by side. She'd never seen anything like it.

Bats flew around it in a swarm, their high pitched cries reaching her ears like the chiming of bells. This was not a safe place.

She glanced up at Bran and realized he hadn't intended to bring them here. His jaw had dropped, his eyes were wide, but most of all it was the first time she had ever seen his hands shaking.

Aisling reached out and took his hand, squeezing it firmly in hers.

He looked down at her, starlit eyes glowing with an emotion she couldn't place.

"What's the matter?" she asked.

"This is where my mother lives."

Rustling began above them, somehow similar and yet infinitely different than the sound his sisters had created. Her spine stiffened. Aisling made the mistake of looking up, and her blood chilled in fear.

The ceiling was made of webs. Great swaths of sticky residue, stretching as far as the eyes could see. It was beautiful in a sense. Glimmering silver with blue refractions that bounced off the shinier pieces, reflecting light back onto the floor until it look as though it were underwater.

The webbing stretched in places where a bulbous form had once rested. Her stomach churned in realization. Bran had said his family weren't normal. She hadn't realized just how distorted their figures would be.

A gap in the webbing draped over the throne. Strands of web hung in great loops, carelessly left in snarled hanks.

Aisling gaped at the overly large shadow that walked among the webs. A long spider leg reached out of the darkness, gently tapping the throne before it slid down into the seat. Another leg followed, again and again until all eight limbs were gracefully poised on the throne.

Spindly hairs rose in spikes along the arachnid's appendages. Light gleamed from their points, reflecting off the smooth plates that covered its legs. The swollen belly lowered into view, spinneret flexing as the Queen of the Unseelie Court descended into view.

Vomit rose in Aisling's mouth, and she turned away so the queen wouldn't see her gag. No creature should look like that.

The queen was a combination of woman and spider. Where the eyes should be on a normal arachnid, a human torso grew. She was obscenely muscular, almost masculine in each ridge that rippled along her stomach and stretched across her shoulders.

She settled on the throne. A few of her legs extended forward, perhaps in an attempt to be comfortable on a seat designed for creatures with only two limbs. She placed her arms gracefully against the rests at either side, shook her dark hair forward until it covered her chest, then flicked a finger toward them.

"So, the wayward boy returns."

"Mother," Bran gritted through clenched teeth.

"I always knew you would come home. The question was simply when."

"It wasn't by choice."

"Of course, it wasn't. It never is with you." Again, she flicked her fingers. "Come, my son. Let me look at you."

He pushed Aisling back as he stepped forward. She sank into the shadows, praying that the Unseelie queen hadn't seen her. The last thing they needed was more trouble. And that spider woman seated on the throne was one of the few people who could cause it.

She watched Bran ascend the steps to the throne and kneel in front of his mother.

"As pretty as ever, I see," the queen said, distaste twisting her words into an insult rather than compliment.

"It's not something I can change, mother."

"Your brother did. Your sisters did. But you were always my stubborn child, running off everywhere you could. If I didn't know better, I would say you were Seelie."

She reached forward and tousled his hair. Aisling winced at the sound of cracked feathers now floating to the floor. The queen shoved Bran's head back, nearly toppling him down the steps. "It's a shame. You could have been something great. What have you returned for this time?"

Bran placed his hands on his thighs. "Waters from Swan Lake."

"Why?"

"I have never asked for anything from you before, mother."

"I want to know why." One of her legs rose and scraped the ground with an ear-piercing sound. "What has suddenly made my son return to the dark castle?"

Aisling knew this wouldn't be easy for him. Admitting to his mother he had been cursed, by what he had thought was a human no less, wasn't going to go over well. Especially if he was the least favored child, which she could already see was the truth.

"I was cursed," he growled. "I need to break the curse."

His mother reared back in surprise. It wasn't the reaction Aisling had expected, and it startled her so much she nearly came out of the shadows to help him.

The queen's whisper echoed in the throne room. "Why would you want to do that?"

"It is my right to decide whether or not I want to remain cursed."

"But removing it—"

Bran interrupted her. "This is what I want, mother. Regardless of you or father's opinions, I am doing this."

Were they talking about the same thing? Aisling's brows furrowed as she tried to make sense of the conversation. It was almost as if they were talking about something he hadn't told her about...

She had a feeling she should have insisted they know each other's secrets before coming here.

The queen's gaze suddenly lifted, slicing through the shadows and meeting Aisling's with an intensity that made a cold shiver dance down her spine.

"Who is lurking in the shadows?" the queen murmured.

"What gift have you brought me, my son?"

"She is not a gift for you."

"It is customary to bring your queen a sacrifice."

"You are my mother," he carefully replied. "Always my mother first, and my queen second. If you kill her, then you also kill me."

The queen glanced at him sharply before the meaning of his words dawned on her. "This? This little bug is the one who cursed you?"

"Mother," Bran warned.

"Come forward, shadow, let me see you."

She felt like an insect caught in a web. Clearing her throat, Aisling stepped forward until the strange blue glow caught upon the fabric of her skirts and danced in the dark locks of her hair.

"Ah," the queen said. "So you have fallen in love with yet another creature of light."

"I am not Seelie, your majesty," Aisling replied.

"You are not of my court."

"I was a changeling. Left by my parents to die in the woods, replacing an unwanted babe in hopes that humans would take me in."

The queen lifted a strong brow. "And did they?"

"No."

"Typical. Humans always think they want something until they finally get it. They love the chase more than they like ownership." She tsked. "You're little more than a scrap."

"I look less intimidating than I am."

The queen tossed her head back and let out an echoing laugh. "My, my, you've got a little bite to you. Curious thing.

And you managed to curse my son? I wonder whether that says you are a powerful witch or he is weaker than I thought."

"Your son is a powerful faerie," Aisling growled. "I have never been afraid of another living being until him."

"High commendation for such a feisty little creature." One of her legs dragged along the floor. "What makes you think he's so powerful?"

"I've seen what he can do."

"Which is?"

Aisling huffed out a frustrated breath. "He's killed, he's cast curses, hexes, spells, you name it. There are many things your son is capable of."

"It's almost as if you're complimenting him."

Bran met her gaze, still kneeling on the floor. A slow grin spread across his face. "No, mother. She wouldn't ever compliment me."

"If she sings your praises any farther, I might wonder why you are last in line."

"You don't know her," he replied. "She's far too fearsome to ever compliment someone who didn't deserve it."

Aisling's cheeks burned, her heart thumped painfully against her ribs, and her skin came alive. She would sing his praises until the moon and the sun met on the horizon. He deserved every word she could create because no one had ever said them to him before.

The queen's eyes flicked between them. "And the binding curse?"

The tips of Bran's pointed ears turned red.

She wouldn't let him take the fall for this. Aisling squared her shoulders, lifted her chin, and firmly replied, "It was mine."

"Is that so? And where did you learn how to cast such a spell?"

"From my grandmother."

"Who is?" The queen impatiently tapped her long nails against the arm of the throne. "I weary of these games, little girl. You will tell me the answers I want to know."

"Badb," Aisling spat. "My grandmother is Badb, the war crow."

She had the satisfaction of seeing the queen's eyes widen in shock before she let out a snort of laughter. "Of course, she is. The meddling witch could never leave well enough alone when it came to my family. Ridiculous, speckled thing. She's still alive I take it?"

"Alive and very well."

"Just to spite me, I'm sure." The queen glanced down at her son and made a disgusted noise. "Get off your knees. You look pathetic."

Bran slowly rose, unfurling his great height while feathers rippled down his neck and disappeared underneath the collar of his shirt.

"Mother—"

"Don't interrupt me. You know I don't like that kind of behavior."

"And you know I'm no longer a lap dog."

"When were you?" The queen glared at him. "You were always a difficult child. And now you're insisting upon breaking a curse you have no right to break."

"*Enough.*"

Aisling had never heard him speak like that before. The echo of beasts rang in his voice, the growl of an unknown creature stalking its prey in the darkness. For the first time, she understood why there were many who feared him. It wasn't because of his power or his self-control, but because of what he hid from the rest of the world.

His mother lumbered to her feet. The heavy abdomen attached to her form dragged on the floor as she walked, audibly scraping the smooth stone.

"You dare speak to me that way?" she asked, her voice the quiet before the storm.

"You will not speak to *me* like that. Not in front of her, not in front of anyone."

The queen cocked her head to the side. She observed her son as if he had said something that confused her greatly. "It has been too long since you have lived here with us. Perhaps you need a reminder of who your parents are."

Aisling didn't have time to warn him about the leg reaching through the webs for him. She barely noticed the dark shadow, infinitely larger than the queen, until it snaked around Bran's waist and yanked him up into the webbing.

"Bran!" she cried out, racing forward as if she might grab him.

"I think not." The queen stretched out a leg.

Aisling couldn't stop her momentum. The grotesque appendage caught her at the shin, sending her tumbling onto the floor in a heap. Her hair pooled around her, dark strands melding into the floor until she couldn't tell where the castle ended and she began.

She spread her fingers wide. She was here, in the castle, and no matter what the magic in this room tried to tell her, she still existed. The queen would not break her.

The ground shuddered as eight limbs stomped toward her until the queen hovered just out of reach. She could feel the heat emanating from the distended stomach. The faint scratch of bristly hair touched the back of her legs.

"How do you know my son?"

"I cursed him."

"The binding curse? A relatively easy fix, but I sense you have seen him before."

Aisling shook her head. "I'd never seen Bran in my life."

"Bran?" The queen's laughter shook through Aisling, who realized the Unseelie queen had played a card. The queen now knew how close they were. "Curious indeed, you are a surprising little changeling. Strange, really, your kind is rarely interesting."

"I'm not the average changeling."

"I can see that." The queen stepped away. One of her legs trailed along Aisling's, and she had to clamp her jaw shut so she didn't whimper. "Still, it makes you even more interesting."

"I have no desire to be."

"You've been interesting all your life to many different people. First your own, the granddaughter of Badb was sure to get attention. Then by humans because you've always been different, unique, *other*. And now you are interesting to me. I'll let you decide which of those is the most dangerous attention to catch."

"Human," she spat. "The answer will always be humans." She pushed her body into sitting and glanced over her shoulder.

The queen's face twisted in surprise before her slanted eyes narrowed again. "Humans? Dangerous? If that's what you truly believe, then I wonder if you've ever actually seen danger."

Aisling took in a deep breath. "If I asked you whether or not you were going to kill me, what would you say?"

"I haven't decided."

"That's why I rank faeries lower than humans when it comes to danger. You cannot lie to me."

The queen tapped a finger to her chin. "What would a human have said?"

"They would have said no. And it would've been a lie."

"Oh, I like you, little girl. I like you quite a bit." The queen sat back on her haunches and gestured for Aisling to come closer. "Let me see you."

Aisling never thought she would go quietly to her grave. But each step brought her closer and closer to death, wrapped up in a gossamer skin and a sharp grin.

She took a deep breath and paused before the queen. "You wish to read me?"

"I wish to peel back your skin, crack open your skull, and peek inside your head to see how you work." The queen reached out her hand impatiently. "Consider this my gift, as my son seems fond of you. I will only ask to see into your past."

If the queen spoke the truth, then it was a good deal. Aisling placed her hand in the queen's.

Magic tingled where their palms met, the queen's covered in faint, bristly hairs. And for the first time since she broke the curse upon her face, the eyes on her palms opened.

The resulting surge of magic tossed her head back. She opened her own eyes wide, staring up into the ceiling, but she couldn't see anything. Memories flashed before her gaze, too quick to focus upon and too hard to remember. They zipped through her mind at lightning speed until she grew queasy and weak.

Her heart sped up, her lungs worked to bring in enough air to keep her alive, and her mind threatened to shatter. It was too much, too fast, too powerful as the queen's magic sliced through her sanity and dashed it to pieces.

"Oh," the queen murmured and finally released her hand. "So, that's who you are."

Out of breath, Aisling replied, "And who might that be?"

"The little runaway. It seems you and my son have far more in common than you might think."

"Explain."

"Your parents made a deal. One Seelie daughter, beautiful, accomplished, and kind. In exchange, we would grant her a comfortable life. It is a good deal between parents whose children will never take the throne. It was supposed to be you" — the queen pointed at her — "but you disappeared. And then the deal was off. Your sister chose who she wanted, your brother went off to war, and your parents never had another child."

"They broke a deal with you?"

"You were children. Breaking a deal is rather easy when the expected child doesn't turn out to be Seelie after all."

The queen stared at her with a speculating gaze that made Aisling thoroughly uncomfortable. She was only supposed to endure the queen peering through her memories, not her thoughts.

"I am changeling. I am witch. I am many things, and you cannot place the mantle of one upon my shoulders without acknowledging the others."

"A smart woman. You'll do well here." The queen shifted,

bringing a leg up as if she was going to stand, but paused at the last second. "You are the Raven King's consort."

Anxiety spiked in her chest. "I know."

"Then you understand he is not going to let you go easily."

"I've yet to find a man who didn't try to get out of a marriage."

The queen smiled. "There are always ways to test your mettle, witch. But if you wish to break your curse and renounce your future, you may go and speak with him."

Aisling stared at her, stunned. Speak with him? The Raven King? The queen made it sound as if...as if...

"Is the Raven King *here*?" Aisling quietly asked. "In the castle?"

"Directly below our feet, in fact. You're going to cross paths with him regardless." The queen hefted herself to standing and made her way back toward the throne. "If you want the waters of Swan Lake that is."

Her head was spinning. Aisling pressed a hand to her brow and stammered, "Why would you let me get the waters? You clearly did not want Bran to break this curse, although I don't understand why."

"You won't understand everything in your life, little witch. And let me punish my son as I see fit. It makes no difference to me if he wants to break his curse. It's the honor of it all. An Unseelie wears a curse like a badge of pride. It is honorable to struggle through life, even more honorable to kill those who cursed you. Bran has never fully accepted our ways. Not like you."

Aisling wanted to argue, but she almost agreed. Bran didn't fit in with any court. The Unseelie valued freedom and

343

disorder, but Bran wasn't likely to willingly harm someone. He was too busy finding his own way in life to waste time on others. But then he certainly wasn't Seelie with their laws and rules to abide by.

She shrugged. "If it's all the same, he wants to break the curse. I'd like to do that for him."

"What if I told you breaking the curse was a great risk for you?"

"I would still do it," Aisling said. She didn't hesitate to answer. "He's done enough for me."

"So you owe him?"

"Even if I didn't, I would still do this."

The queen nodded and laid a hand on top of her dark throne. "Then I wish you all the luck with the Raven King. Perhaps you might convince him to break the contract. But I think you shall find something else down there."

"Down where?"

The queen lifted a hand and pulled herself up into the webbing.

"Your majesty, where are you speaking of? I don't know the way to the lake."

A quiet chuckle filled the air, and Aisling knew something bad was about to happen. She waited only a heartbeat before a hole opened up in the floor just under her feet, and she plummeted into the darkness.

CHAPTER 12

THE RAVEN KING

She fell for what felt like ages before she struck cold water. Ice and silence covered her head as she plunged into the dark depths.

Aisling hung there for a moment, floating in the oblivion and regaining her senses. Was this Swan Lake? It felt like regular water. No magic slid along her lips and greeted her with frozen fingertips.

Light speared through the frozen lake. No water sprites, no nymphs, not even a kelpie, which she would have expected to see in the Dark Castle. Nothing but silence and shadows cast from ice chunks floating over her head.

She kicked toward the surface. Fabric tangled around her legs. The supple boots on her feet pulled her down. Her lungs burned.

Aisling broke the surface and gasped in air. Shivers traveled down her body as the cold sank deep into her bones. Her lips grew numb, and her fingers filled with painful, icy pricks. But she swam, hoping she would eventually hit some kind of shore.

Her feet touched pebbled stones. She couldn't have hit land already. She could still see water as far as the dim light would let her see. But it was certainly rocks underneath her feet. Solid ground threatened to twist her ankles as she waded her way through the lake and toward a small island in the center of the freezing water.

The air vibrated with the chiming of bells. On and on they rang, quieter than a church bell but higher than the gong. They were the small bells tied to a horse's bridle, the ringing in a servant's quarter, the endless call of a high-pitched chime.

She nudged a large chunk of ice out of her way, fingers burning from the small touch. Her shirt stuck to her chest. She pulled it out, then let it fall back with a sticky slap. She had to get out of these clothes or she would freeze to death. But how?

"How fortuitous. I never thought I would see *you* in my lifetime."

The voice was filled with a thousand midnights, darkness and starlight wrapped so tightly they were bound for all eternity. She saw flashes in her mind's eye. Visions of raven feathers crushed in a muddy boot print that slowly filled with water. Scales sliding upon a carefully laid porcelain floor, muscles flexing as a creature slithered across the opulence.

The crisp scent of fallen leaves filled the air, a hint of magic that added a sickly sweetness that caused her to recoil. Fruit rotted in her visions, and the eyes on her palms twitched.

"Lurking in the shadows?" she called back, swallowing her fear. "Hardly intimidating."

"The shadows are my home, changeling child. It's you who are unintimidating, standing in the light."

A shiver rocked her body forward violently. She splashed

a few steps in the water to gain her footing, then raced to the small incline out of the water.

"Who are you?" she asked.

"I think you know."

"I wouldn't have asked if I knew, faerie." She took a shot in the dark. He had to be Fae, otherwise he was something far more dangerous.

"Good," the voice replied with a deep chuckle. "That's a start."

Aisling curled her hands into fists. "I am here for the waters from Swan Lake."

"Why would you want that?"

"To break a curse."

Wind buffeted her back, pushing her forward again. She whirled too late. Whatever had rushed past was already gone.

"A curse?" the deep voice asked. "What kind of curse?"

"A binding curse."

"Odd thing to want the waters for."

"I was told it was the only way to break a binding curse." She tried to peer through the darkness. There had to be a shift in the shadows, something that would reveal where this creature was. "Were they wrong?"

"You trust me enough to believe my words?"

"I trust no one, but I also know you cannot lie because you are most certainly Fae."

The voice growled directly in her ear, "So are you."

She spun again, lifting her fists to strike him in the jaw, but there was no one behind her. Smoke stirred around her raised hand. Aisling took a steadying breath. "How are you doing that?"

"Doing what?"

"You know."

He chuckled. "You're a forward child, I'll give you that. What do you think I am?"

"If I had a guess, I wouldn't have asked. Tell me what you are, or tell me if this is Swan Lake. Those are the only words I am interested in hearing you speak."

"So rude," he tsked. "You already know what I am."

Out of the darkness above her, a single raven feather floated down to rest upon her raised fist. As dark as obsidian, it gleamed nearly blue in the dim light. It felt like velvet as it touched her knuckles, slid down her hand, and drifted onto the water.

"Raven King," she gasped.

"The one and only. But you already knew that, didn't you?"

A fluttering of wings made her glance up from the feather drifting away. Her breath frosted in the air, the fog obscuring her vision for a moment. The instant it cleared, she saw him.

Ravens poured from the darkness. They shrieked and screamed as magic drew them together, splicing their forms until he was nothing more than a mass of squirming feathers and gnashing beaks. They settled as one and revealed a man larger than life.

He looked like...

"Bran," she gasped.

The Raven King arched a brow, and his lips quirked into a smile. "Close, but not quite."

Aisling could see the differences now, although they were slight. This man was much older than Bran. His nose was more hawk-like, and the feathers spread across his face were much more pronounced. Wrinkles fanned from his eyes and deepened the grooves around his mouth.

He wasn't quite Bran, but he wasn't something else either.

The Raven King floated above the water, stepping toward her without creating even the slightest ripple from his movement. Feathers spread from his shoulders in a quivering cloak that shone emerald and sapphire. He advanced with purpose, a knowing grin on his face.

"You look just like him," she whispered, stepping back until her heels struck water.

"*He* looks like *me*. But the resemblance is uncanny, isn't it?"

The Raven King paused before her, and she stared up into his gaze and noted the differences. His raven eye was red, not yellow. His jaw was a little weaker, his nose a little longer, but he was right. They could have been brothers.

"Family trait?" she asked.

"Not a drop of blood relation."

"Strange."

"Not when you factor in magic." He reached forward and twirled a strand of her wet hair around his finger. Steam rose from the tendril that touched his flesh, then magic pulsed up the strand, drying as it went. "You are not as I imagined you."

"Sorry to disappoint."

"Hardly."

She watched him through narrowed eyes as he circled her. The cape billowed behind him, raven heads stretching for freedom only to be slammed back into the fabric by an invisible hand.

Aisling didn't know what game he was playing, but it

349

wasn't comfortable. His eyes looked her up and down, measuring her worth, finding all the flaws in her features. She felt the gentle nudge of magic and had to force herself not to retaliate with whatever spell she could think of.

"When they chose you as my consort, I wondered what you would look like as you aged. The last time I saw you, you were just a little twig." The Raven King held up his pinky finger. "All limbs and eyes. You were strange looking, but I could see you would become an intriguing woman."

"You have no right to comment on my looks."

"Don't I? I'm your husband."

"Not yet," she growled.

"There is no other for you." He frowned, winged brows drawn down severely. "It's a shame you can't see that, but there will be time."

She had no plans to remain here. The Raven King could follow her to the ends of the earth if he wished, but she would never stop running. He could capture her, but she would escape. He could chain her to a wall, but she would chew off her hands to run from this dark creature.

His laughter filled the air with dark promise. "I can see your thoughts clearly, changeling child. You should know the chase only excites me."

"Good to know," she replied. "I'm glad at least something about me will entertain you. Perhaps you'll keep me longer than your previous consorts."

"There were no others." The heat of him pressed against her back, not quite touching but overwhelming all the same. "Each Raven King only gets one. One life, one kingdom, one bride."

"This must be very frustrating for you."

"Why's that?" He touched her hair again.

"Because you're going to be alone for a very long time."

She spun on her heal with a palm raised, magic glimmering in her hand. The spell was simple, child's play really, but it would work. Electricity barely contained itself before she lifted her palm and let it free.

The white light blasted across the water. Tiny waves marked its path until it struck a wall and fizzled out of existence.

"What?" she gasped.

His voice whispered in her ear again, "It's not that easy to kill a king."

Every fiber of her being hated him. She clenched her fists, muscles locked in place, and ground her teeth together so hard they ached. "I will never stop trying."

"I would be disappointed if you did, my dear."

Cold air replaced him. Aisling whirled, her gaze searching for him in the shadows until she found the warped form. Ravens shifted underneath his skin, one poking out a head from his neck and descending back down into the pale flesh.

He offered a hand for her to take. "You wished for the waters of Swan Lake?"

"Yes." She bit her lip, debating. Taking his hand felt like a promise. If she did anything wrong, she might be stuck here for the rest of her life. She had no intention of remaining here for any longer than absolutely necessary.

"Come now, changeling. Do you really think I would try to trick you now? That would be too easy."

Bravery surged in her veins, so she reached out and took

his hand.

Claws closed around her hand, so long they touched the thin skin of her wrist. "That's much better."

She disagreed. His skin was almost leathery in texture. Feathers bit into her palm, digging into the eye tattoos and sinking into her like the barbs of a rose.

"You know where the waters are?"

"I know more than that. Now, while we're walking, why don't you tell me why you want them?"

"To break a binding curse."

"Yes, you've said that already. Explain it to me."

He pulled her out into the water, but this time she remained above it. Her feet touched the still surface that now reacted like the mirrored finish of polished stone.

"I could tell you the story, but I don't think you would listen."

"Tell it all to me. It's a long enough journey."

And so she did.

Aisling spared nothing from her tale, even the things which she knew would anger him. To his credit, he didn't react. The Raven King nodded solemnly when she spoke of the dangers they had faced. He glanced at her with sad eyes when she spoke of the dead god and his strife. He twitched when she mentioned the death of the Duchess.

But he never stopped her from talking. Not once did he react more than a subtle shift in his demeanor. It would be impressive if she wasn't so set on disliking him.

"You have had an incredible journey," he said when she finished.

"Different than the way I've lived, I suppose. Magic has

352

always been a part of my life. It feels as though I have been preparing to be here, in this moment, for as long as I have drawn breath."

"Here with me?" He lifted a dark brow.

"Not quite."

"Of course not. Presumptuous of me to even consider it. You have been preparing your whole life for…what? Him?"

She knew he meant Bran, and her ears burned in embarrassment. "No. To be in the Unseelie Court. It's where I was always meant to be, isn't it? My parents sent me away because I was one of you."

"I'm not Unseelie, changeling. And neither are you." He raised both their hands up to gesture at the waters around them. "This is Swan Lake, but if you're going to use its waters for a spell, then you must take it from the heart."

He pointed directly down where she could see the center of the lake.

A woman floated deep below them. Her long hair was white as snow, strands hanging in constant suspension. White swan feathers floated in the water around her, slowly spinning in circles. She held a vessel in her hand from which glowing blue water trickled out. Steam rose in twisting coils from the water directly above her, as if it were warm instead of cold.

"Who is she?"

"The heart of the lake." He crouched, taking her with him until they both pressed their palms against the solid surface. "The very first Raven King's consort."

"What happened to her?"

"He was supposed to be eternal, the first and only. But another wished for his wife's hand. They battled for centuries.

The Wild Hunt was lost to the winds, destroying the human world and growing ever more powerful. Cernunnos himself had to step in. He slaughtered both the men and banished her here for all eternity."

"Why was she punished?" Aisling stared down at her, horrified.

"She was too beautiful for any man to cast eyes upon. He feared she would continue to walk the earth, causing war after war until she finally died. But he couldn't kill her, for her beauty turned even his heart."

Aisling spread her fingers on the smooth surface of the lake. The reflection of her face melded with the pale woman's until she couldn't tell the difference between them.

She'd spent her life running from those who wanted to define her because of how she looked or what she could do. This woman had suffered the same fate and paid the ultimate sacrifice.

"You wanted the waters," the Raven King murmured. "Go and take them."

"How?"

He reached into his cloak and pulled out a small glass vial. "All you have to do is jump."

Aisling took it from him and turned it over in her hand before looking up to meet his gaze. "How?"

"That's the easy part."

He released her hand, and she fell into the water with a splash.

Aisling dunked under the surface. Cold water rushed into her mouth, filled her ears, and sent tendrils of ice through her body that stiffened her fingers and legs. Struggling back to the surface, she gasped in a breath of air.

Then she dove under the glassy surface and swam toward the floating woman. A sense of foreboding made her check around her, but the light from the heart of the lake was weak. Anything could be watching her in the depths of the waters.

Rushing now, she reached out and gently touched a hand to the woman's cheek. Downy feathers, so pale they were almost transparent, covered the sides of her face. She looked as though she could be Aisling's sister, and she wondered what that meant. Just how strange was this place? Did she see other people in every face that existed here? Or was there more to this?

The woman opened her eyes.

Aisling flinched back, bubbles escaping from her open mouth before she frantically shut it.

Their eyes met, and she suddenly *knew* this woman. It wasn't a memory. It wasn't even a feeling, but something deep inside her soul recognized this frozen body as her own.

The woman slowly reached out her hand with the small porcelain vessel from where the waters flowed weakly. The light was dim, growing dimmer by the second.

Was it dying? Was it possible for a lake to die?

She stretched forward and took the smallest amount of water that she could from the glimmering blue light. As if sensing another vessel was nearby, it spun toward the small vial in her hand. Funneling it in was easy. The water wanted to go with her, strangely enough.

Aisling carefully put the cap back on the vial. Her eyes lingered on the floating woman's figure. A small part of her worried she would someday become this poor soul, forever damned simply for being a woman.

This was why she had kept herself hidden for so long. It was easier to hide under the guise of dirt and grime than be renowned for beauty.

She kicked her feet and shot toward the surface. Lungs burning, head whirling, she crested the surface with a loud gasp. Dark hair obscured her vision until a warm hand smoothed it back from her face.

The Raven King smiled down at her, his eyes appearing almost sad. "Did you find what you were looking for?"

"I did." She lifted the vial for him to see.

He stared at it with obvious disdain before holding out a hand for her again. "Would you like to come out of the water now?"

"Yes."

Aisling's tone was oddly meek. Something about the sight of the floating woman had affected her. She didn't feel like herself, but a fragile version that could be shattered by a mere touch.

His warm hand closed around her wrist, pulling her out of the water and back onto the glassy surface as if she weighed little more than a feather. He waved a hand in front of her. Warm air blasted, drying her clothes immediately.

"Thank you," she murmured, confused at herself and the entire situation. "How do I get back into the castle?"

"I'm sure the queen will send one of her daughters for you." He paused. "Actually, why don't I bring you up myself?"

"You can do that?"

"I'm not imprisoned," he said with a chuckle. "No one can cage the Raven King. Besides, I haven't seen the Unseelie queen in a very long time."

"I'm not sure you want to."

"She is a rather startling sight, isn't she? Her children are almost worse."

Aisling shuddered at the memory. The Unseelie princesses would haunt her memories for a very long time. "I agree with you."

The Raven King held out a hand for her to take, dark claws curving up like needles. "Shall we?"

She didn't really want to. It was a strange sensation to want to stay in this frozen wasteland with a floating version of herself underneath their feet. But if she went back into the Unseelie castle, there was always the possibility of this all being over.

Bran didn't seem interested in running off as soon as the binding curse was broken, yet there was always a chance he was twisting his words.

She wasn't sure what would happen if he rejected her. He was the first person she had let in…ever.

Taking a deep breath, she reached out and took his hand. "To the castle we go then."

"Hold on tight."

He tugged her close to his chest. Ravens stretched through his form, wings beating against her back and beaks desperately trying to peck at her front. To his credit, the Raven King held her just far enough away that the creatures who made him couldn't harm her.

They lifted into the air with ease. The swarm of wings took them far away from the frozen lake and straight up toward the small hole she had fallen through. Aisling's breath caught in her throat, but she held her body limp. The last thing she needed was to plummet back into the icy waters.

The Raven King soared through the small opening and landed lightly on his feet. He set her down with an exaggerated gesture, snapping out his cape like a great wing and twirling her before letting go.

Aisling spun in a circle before she caught herself, angrily glaring at him and clutching the vial to her chest. "Was that really necessary?"

"A show is always necessary when entertaining the Unseelie Queen."

An answering chuckle echoed from above them. The webbing bowed under the queen's weight as she stepped over them. "Raven King. It's been a very long time."

"Not too long, I hope. I wouldn't want you to forget my pretty face."

"How could I? It's been my personal goal to scratch your eyes out since the day I met you."

The Raven King pressed a hand to his chest, narrowing his eyes at the leg that revealed itself through the gap over the throne. "I'm flattered you've been thinking of me for hundreds of years, my dear queen."

"Precisely the reason why I've wanted to kill you since the day we met." The queen lowered herself from the ceiling and rested on her throne with a sarcastic grin. "What do you want?"

He lifted his arm and pointed at Aisling. "She would like to perform a spell."

"She or my son?"

"Both, it seems. They have the same end to their desires."

The queen rolled her eyes. "Are you going to make a show of this?"

"Would you expect anything less?"

"Do I need to get my son?" The Unseelie queen extended her long nails in front of her, staring at them. "So far, your performance is underwhelming."

"Oh, it's only going to get better, darling. You should bring him down."

"He's with his father."

The Raven King reached out and snagged Aisling's arm, dragging her against his side. "He'll want to see this."

The queen narrowed her gaze on them. Aisling could see thoughts ticking behind her eyelids. She was trying to figure out what the Raven King was planning. The moment she figured it out, her eyes lit with excitement.

"Oh," she exclaimed. "Oh! You intriguing man. How unique." She glanced up at the webs, her gaze softening. "Fine, my darling king, put our son down so I can see what's going to happen."

For a moment, Aisling thought she was talking about the Raven King. But his hold tightened on her, and the web ripped open in the center of the room. Bran was tossed down, though he landed in a crouch.

Flipping his hair back in a wave of movement, he glared at his mother. "Was that necessary?"

"Just keeping you on your toes."

"You go too far, Mother."

"No, I'm not going far enough." She pointed at the Raven King. "I think you'd like to hear what *he* has to say."

Bran's gaze cut toward them. He stiffened immediately, then lunged to his feet and reached out to her. "Aisling, come here. Now."

Before she could answer, the Raven King cut in. "She's going to stay right here with me. I heard a little rumor you were trying to break a curse."

A muscle jumped in Bran's jaw. "You can't stop me from doing that."

"I can try."

"It's my choice."

"No, it's really not." The Raven King chuckled. "You can't change fate, my boy."

Head spinning, Aisling shoved at the Raven King's chest. "Would you all stop talking about something I clearly don't know?"

"Aisling," Bran growled, "stay out of this."

"No! This isn't about the binding curse, is it?"

"We promised we would come clean later. We need to finish this first."

"I'm not sure I want to." She clutched the vial to her chest, the blue light glowing through her fingers.

His eyes pled with her. "Don't change your mind now, of all times. Give me the vial, I'll break the curse, and all will be well."

"What are they talking about Bran?"

The Raven King released her and strode between them, slowly clapping his hands. Mist swirled at his feet, and a raven stretched out of his shoulder, snapping its beak at her. "So it is as I thought. You don't know what he's trying to do."

"Stay out of this, Raven King," Bran spat.

"I don't think I will. You're misleading this beautiful woman, and I would be remiss to allow you to continue." He flipped his cape over one arm with a flourish. "Aisling, my dear. There is no way to break a binding curse."

"Faeries can't lie," she whispered. "This will work."

"The ingredients you have gathered, and I thank you for telling me the story in such detail, are not for a binding curse. You see"—he pointed at Bran—"he is my successor. Each Raven King has someone who will take their place once every thousand years. He has a chance to break the King's curse, of course. An impossible task that can only be performed under great duress. Remarkable really, because no one has managed to do it before you."

Bran lunged forward. Webs shot from the ceiling and pinned him to the floor. He strained to get up. "Aisling, don't listen to him."

She ignored him and lifted the vial in her hand. "Then what is this for?"

"That's the best part, my dear. All the things you've struggled—risked your life—to gather will break the King's curse. A few runes, a circle of magic, a faerie who has no idea what she is doing." He lifted his hands and swayed from side to side as if waltzing. "The blood of a dead god placed inside a still beating heart, and make no mistake, the duchess's heart is still beating. You pour the waters of Swan Lake inside, not to drown it, but to give it life. The cursed man drinks the elixir, and all of a sudden, he is free from a future ruling the Sluagh in Underhill."

"What good does that do to break our binding curse?"

The Raven King tilted his head back and laughed. "Look at him, Aisling. Truly look at him. Why do you think he doesn't look like his parents? All his siblings resemble spiders in some way, or did you think that it was magic? He's not like them for a reason. He's been selfishly leading you all around the country because he had no choice. Time was running out to break the King's curse, and you had to go with him because you were bound to him."

She stared at Bran, really looked at him as though she were trying to climb inside his soul. She saw the raised feathers on the side of his head. The slash of dark down that covered his forehead and narrowed to a point above his nose. The angular features of his face and the bird leg that clawed desperately at the ground, trying to get to her.

She saw him for what he was. The lies, the secrets, the forbidden past that he hadn't trusted her with.

"Bran," she whispered on a near sob. "Why didn't you tell me?"

He shook his head. "I couldn't."

The Raven King rubbed his hands together. "You see, if he breaks the King's curse, then he's back to the spider-like faerie he was before I chose him. It will break the binding curse and the King's curse. Both have been placed on him—Bran, the Raven King's heir, not Bran, the Unseelie prince. A binding curse can only remain attached to the person originally cursed. If he's Bran the Unseelie prince, then the binding curse doesn't exist."

"Then do it," she said. "Why does this matter? The curse is broken either way."

With an embellished whirl, the Raven King dramatically turned toward Bran. "That's where the best part is revealed. Because Bran doesn't know that *you*" —he turned and pointed at her—"are *my* consort."

Silence echoed in the room louder than a scream. She

straightened, determined to remain poised, and then met Bran's horrified gaze.

"No," he muttered. "No, not you."

"Her," the Raven King replied. He circled Aisling, pressed his lips against her ear, and murmured, "Go ahead. Why don't you show them what all those years with humans taught you? *Lie.*"

"No," she whispered, lips twitching in fear.

"Do it."

"*No.*"

"Tell him you aren't what he thinks you are. Tell him a lie."

"I can't."

The Raven King tsked in disappointment and stepped away from her. "I don't know how the magic found her of all people, but I am perfectly happy to keep her. If Bran breaks the spell, Aisling, then you are mine. If he doesn't, then he is damned for all eternity to take my place as the Raven King, but he has you."

She stared into Bran's night-sky eyes and knew what he would pick. She slowly crouched, set the vial on the ground, and rolled it to his clenched fist. "We both know what you want."

"You don't know what it is you're saying. He's the *Raven King*, Aisling. He's dangerous."

"So are you." She smiled, although it was a little shaky. "And so am I. This is my fate, Bran. I know what it is like to be bound by a curse that makes you someone else. I wouldn't want you to live with it for the rest of your life, just because you were afraid I couldn't take care of myself. I've done it before, I will do it again, whether you are the Raven King or not."

She poured her heart out and still she couldn't say those three words that meant more to her than life itself. It wasn't right. It wasn't now, and he didn't need to have any more added guilt to his choice.

Cast the spell. She tried to project her thoughts to him so she wouldn't embarrass them both. *Taste the ambrosia of freedom. Live it for me.*

The Unseelie queen clapped her hands, all eight legs dancing on the floor to the same beat. "That was the most entertainment I have had in centuries! My goodness, the three of you with all these curses floating between you. It's enough to make my head spin."

Aisling glared at her. "This doesn't include you."

"But it does, because that is my son, and I *want him back.*"

The Raven King whirled. "We had a deal."

"You broke that deal the moment you set the Wild Hunt on my daughters and chased them back to this realm."

"They had no right to be in the human realm."

"That is not your choice."

Aisling tilted her head back and screamed, *"Enough!"*

The entire room fell silent again, every person staring at her as though she had lost her mind. And perhaps she had.

She looked at the Unseelie on his knees, still stuck to the floor by his own family, and sadly shook her head. "Do it, Bran. Just get it over with."

"This was never the choice I would have made," he replied. His face twisted in sadness and disappointment. "For either of us."

"I know. But it's the right choice."

She would survive; she always had. Every moment of her

life had been spent alone. She knew what it felt like, and she would handle it when it crashed down upon her once again.

Memories would help her exist wherever the Raven King brought her. Judging him so quickly was likely cruel. Perhaps he would be a good man. That had been her sister's fate, after all. Now Aisling could understand exactly how Elva felt.

"Sweetheart," Bran murmured, "have a little more faith than that."

He lifted his hand and brought it down hard on the small vial. It shattered under his touched, the blue glow dying instantly upon touching the ground.

"What?" she gasped. "Why would you do that?"

Bran looked up, met her gaze, and smiled. "For you."

Aisling had only a second to appreciate the moment before blistering pain shattered through her body. She threw her head back, eyes wide, a silent scream shaking her to the very core.

Her flesh melted, her bones realigned, the crunching sounds of transformation echoed in her ears until that was the only thing she could think of. She lifted an arm and finally managed to scream as feathers poked through her skin, shredding her muscles along the way. Her spine shifted, neck elongating and shoulders dropping.

Finally, she laid flat against the floor in a panting, heaving mess. Something wasn't right. She didn't feel like herself at all.

Aisling lifted her head, feeling the subtle grace in the movement. She shook it and tried to speak. All that came out was a strange croak.

She shook her head again and met Bran's horrified gaze.

"Aisling," he gasped. "I'm so sorry."

The floor was polished near to a mirror. When she looked

365

down at herself, she let out a quiet, disappointed sigh.

A swan stared back at her. White feathers, so pristine they didn't look real, covered her body. A black beak pointed into a lovely line that ended just above *her* eyes.

She tried to flap her wings but didn't know how to control this strange body. She looked up as another sound filled the room. The rushing of ravens.

They left the Raven King in a swarm and dove into Bran's body. He arched back, tearing through the webbing with sudden violence, opening his arms wide to welcome their possession. The cords of his neck stood out in stark relief as he screamed.

When it was complete, they stared at each other. No longer Unseelie and Witch but something far more.

Bran panted through the pain and reached out a hand for her. "Cursed again, Aisling? Don't worry. I'll save you. I promise."

The setting sun turned the waters pink, violet, and indigo. The rainbow colors glimmered all around her like a painting pulled directly from an artist's mind. And she, the tiny swan set in the center to remind everyone there was beauty in the world.

Aisling adjusted her wings gracefully. She lifted one, then the other, stretching them out so she could stare along the gentle curves of the feathers. So pretty, each and every one reflecting sunlight like an opal. It was said that a single feather from her wing would feed a faerie family for centuries.

They had never seen someone like her before. It had been thousands of years since a Raven King had a consort. Even then, those who were alive during that time couldn't remember what she looked like.

Some said she was the most beautiful woman in the world. When she sang, the sky would weep for the haunting sound. When she laughed, the trees dropped leaves so she might play and twirl beneath their branches. And when she cried... They did not speak of when she cried.

A soft downy feather floated from her neck and landed atop the water. It curved up at the edges. The current carried it toward the shore, but it never made it. Aisling violently shredded it with her beak, dipping it underneath the water time and time again until it was ruined.

"That wasn't very nice," a deep voice called across the waters. "We could have used that."

She snapped her head up, glaring at Bran where he stood on the shore.

The Raven King stared back at her. He was himself, but not. The same man, same flesh, same body, and yet something was missing from the man she knew and loved.

He had let his hair grow out as they traveled to Underhill. No longer half shaved, tangled feathers grew through his long hair. He had braided small pieces of it, creating a wild tangle of raven, obsidian strands and Celtic knots.

Unlike his predecessor, Bran did not wear a cloak. He wore black leather armor, each piece crafted to depict the Wild Hunt. It stretched across his body to meet epaulettes crafted from dark feathers and black diamonds.

He held out his hand and called her name. "Aisling, it is time."

And so it was, and so it would be, for all eternity.

She floated toward him slowly. They had all the time in the world and none at the same time.

The shore was a body's length away from her when she stopped and tilted her head to the side. Bran smiled at her, his raven eye locked on her form as if she was the only thing that existed.

"You are beautiful," he quietly said. "Even now. Even like this, you still captivate me."

She ducked her head, shy and incapable of responding.

"Just a few moments now. Can you feel it?"

Every fiber of her being felt the moment. She knew the exact time when the moon would strike the water and the curse on her body would lift. The sun dipped below the horizon and silver light poured over the lake.

Its soothing touch spilled from her head to her toes. Water rushed up her body in a funnel that spun around her as her wings lengthened to arms and fingers, her webbed feet gave way to gently arched feet, and her elongated neck settled back on her shoulders.

Silver moonlight spun the droplets of water to pearls as they fell back to the lake.

Aisling sighed, lifted her arms to her hair, and took a moment to enjoy her body again. She stretched out her hands, staring down at the black tattoos that now spread all over her form. Ogham marks linked both arms, proclaiming her "Raven Consort."

"Come here," he called for her. "We have but a few moments."

She waded through the water and raced to his side.

Bran caught her in his arms with a chuckle, tucking her against his chest until she could hear his heartbeat. He was warm where she was cold, strong where she was weak, and it felt so good to let him take the weight on her shoulders for a little while.

He leaned down and whispered a siren song, "Do you know the reasons I shouldn't kiss you right now?"

"I can't think of a single one."

Bran pressed his mouth to her brow. "No one has ever taught me how to be soft with a woman. I touch you with hands that only know how to give scars."

"Then add to mine, and I will wear them with pride, for I know they were given with the intent to heal, not harm."

He slid his velvet lips down to her cheek, barely touching her. "You are so *good*, a light in my darkness, and I cannot snuff out another candle."

"I know how to survive in the dark."

Again, he moved, lingering on the end of her nose. He lifted a hand and gently scraped the claws across her neck. "You are the sun, burning my wings away. But I will laugh in bitter triumph as I tumble toward my end because I know I got close enough to kiss you."

"You foolish man, I am not the sun, and you are not a winged creature. You are my Unseelie prince, and I am your witch."

"My mother always told me if I saw something I wanted, I should take it."

She surged forward, standing on tip toes until she could feel the heat from his mouth. "This is the first and only time I will agree with your mother."

He spared a moment for a chuckle, then gave in to both their desires. Bran kissed her with the strength of the thousands of stars that stared down on them. She felt each one as they appeared, individual pinpricks of light creating constellations. She felt the colorful galaxies all compressed into one moment as he held her against his heart.

Every moment was precious, every second a stolen gift.

Bran drew back with a quiet sigh. "They're waiting for you."

"I know."

"They like you."

"You say that every time, but I'm not so certain they do. Not yet."

"Soon," he said and pressed another kiss to her lips. "Soon they will see what I do. Give them time."

"Be safe tonight."

He stepped back from her with a wicked grin that didn't meet his eyes. "You know I always try."

"You're not very good at it."

"I'm not very good at a lot of things. I'll try to be better, witch."

"You do that."

He released the power inside of him, bursting into an unkindness of ravens that swarmed away from her. They screamed at the night as the last star flickered to life. She watched them go, knowing at the heart was her cursed king.

A tear slid down her cheek, but quickly dashed away

before anyone might see it. It would not do to be weak here of all places.

She picked up the dress one of their servants had laid at the shore's edge. Black velvet smoothed along her fingertips, cool to the touch. It slid over her body with a sound like rushing water. Trickling down her curves, it appeared almost as a second skin. Twin slits on the sides revealed her long legs.

It dipped low in the front. More tattoos covered her there, swirling patterns and ogham marks that told the story of the Raven King. She was more than just a consort, more than just cursed. She was the living, breathing embodiment of all that was the Raven Kingdom.

Underhill.

Aisling strode from the lake, the long train of her black gown whispering along the ground behind her. She crunched through fallen leaves, because it was always autumn here. The trees tried to push out buds, but they always fell, and they always died orange and yellow in the distance.

The scent of pomegranate filled her senses. She knew why, of course. Bran's magic was stronger now. It almost had a life of its own.

Footsteps padded beside her.

"Lorcan," she breathed. "You have returned with news?"

"Nothing yet. No one has ever heard of the Raven King's consort, let alone a way to break the spell."

"Either spell?"

He shook his dark head, the white starburst on his chest glowing in the moonlight. "Neither."

"At least we're trying," she replied. "That is good enough."

"I won't live forever."

"Do you really think I will ever let you die? My faithful friend..." She paused, stooping to run a hand over his soft fur. "You are immortal for as long as you wish it."

"It scares me that you have that power now."

"It scares me, too."

She stood and squared her shoulders. They were waiting for her.

Through the forest of dead trees, she traveled barefoot on the plain dirt path. All the way to the winding staircase. It crumbled constantly, magic picking up the pieces and putting it back as it did for the entire labyrinth that made up Underhill.

Staircases lifted from the ground. They ended in midair, against the sides of buildings, or sometimes just stopped entirely. The tangled network of paths were known only by those who lived there.

A collective sigh lifted into the air. She could always hear them, though she could rarely see them.

At the foot of the correct stairwell, a Dullahan waited for her. He held his grinning skeletal head in his hands and nodded at her arrival. His coach made of skin stood behind him at the ready. She smiled softly at it and took his offered hand.

"Not today," she said. "I'll have you carry me on another tour soon."

The Dullahan bowed over her fingertips, and she bent to press a kiss to the head in his hands.

The paths were still a mystery to her, but there was always someone willing to guide her. They made certain her steps were true and that the stairs never lead her wrong.

"This way, mistress," a soft voice called. "They are waiting for you."

"Thank you."

The Dearg-Due had been a pretty woman in her day. It was a shame she had been killed. The jagged knife wound on her throat would forever bleed, fueling her need for human blood to survive.

Aisling did not hesitate to reach out and touch a finger to the wound. Blood slicked her fingers, but it slowed at her touch.

"You waste your gift on me," the Dearg-Due whispered. "Please, mistress. There are more that are worthy."

"There are none more worthy than you." She touched a fingertip to the other woman's chin. "I know where to go from here."

"As you wish."

As it would always be for the rest of her life. Aisling smiled and made her way into the castle that was missing bits and pieces. The inside was nearly worse than the outside.

The center of the castle had been eaten away by a network of tunnels beneath it. She picked across the largest hole and made her way to the great hall where the most dangerous of all Underhill's inhabitants waited.

They wouldn't hurt her. They wouldn't dare touch the Raven King's consort.

Double doors opened, silver handles gleaming as someone on the other side turned them. She let out a slow breath as the first of the Sluagh greeted her.

Haggard and thin, the creature before her was half bird, half woman. Its paper-thin skin revealed a sickness embedded deep inside its body. Light flickered within, the remnants of souls they stole to give themselves something upon which to exist.

Leathery wings stretched from her back. Aisling noted new holes the Sluagh tried to hide as she folded them around her body like a cloak. Had Bran taken them on a hunt recently? Or were they attacking each other?

The Sluagh covered as much of her body as she could. They still thought she would find them disgusting, the last bit of their humanity embarrassed by their appearance.

She reached out and brushed a hand over the creature's head, sparse strands of hair digging into her palm. Following the bone of its skull, she gently trailed her fingers over its distorted face and the beak painfully protruding through its nose and mouth.

"Hello, my dear. How are you?"

"I am well, mistress."

"Are they ready?"

"As always."

The great hall was filled with Sluagh. More than she could count, more than she could ever comprehend. A wave of leathery flesh, gnashing beaks, and beady eyes stared at her in anticipation.

Stairs awaited her, and at the top a podium, a gnarled crown sat on a black cushion. Made of twisted roots and solidified vines, it was a terrifying and beautiful thing.

A small group of Sluagh waited for her. They were larger than the others, their bodies stronger and far more powerful.

The first reached for her, claws digging into her wrists. "May our minds work together to better this kingdom."

Aisling lifted their clasped hands and pressed them to her forehead. "May I see your true form and be seen in kind."

She moved to the next who laid a hand over Aisling's heart.

"May your reign be true and guided by your heart."

Aisling smiled. "And by the old ways in a language more ancient than words."

The last Sluagh waited at the top of the stairs. Aisling ascended, the train of her dress carefully adjusted to slide down the crumbling steps like a black waterfall.

This creature was barely alive. It trembled as it stepped forward, falling slightly into Aisling's arms to press their foreheads together.

"As above," it croaked, "so below."

Aisling gently cradled the creature. "As within, so without."

Another of their kind stepped forward to take the crone from her arms. Aisling took a deep breath and reminded herself they did this every night. She was cursed as a swan during the day, and Bran cursed as a raven during the night.

This was their existence. Their punishment.

She reached forward and took the gnarled crown in her hands. Lifting it high in the air for all to see, she then settled it upon her head and felt the thorns draw blood in retribution. She turned on her heel and listened to the screaming cry of the Sluagh.

The ancient crone stepped forward, her voice suddenly strong and ringing true.

"All hail the Raven Queen!"

AFTERWORD

And thus ends the first part of The Faceless Woman.

I hope you enjoyed reading this just as much as I enjoyed writing it. This story was an adventure in every page, and the characters more beloved than any I have written before.

Part 2 will be released in November 2018, entitled *The Raven's Ballad*.

Well met, and blessed be.

ACKNOWLEDGEMENTS

There are a hundred and one people every time to thank while writing a book.

NATASA - I thank you in every book I write, but without your incredible art and talent, these stories wouldn't be anywhere near as amazing as they are. I cannot wait to continue working with you for many years to come!

CORINNE - The glorious editor who took this book and let me know when and where all the stupid parts were (and there were a lot, lemme tell you). Thank you so much for taking so much time AND a rush job to make sure this story is as incredible as it could be. I thank you a million times over.

ELLEN - Proofreader extraordinaire. She call all the stuff I couldn't, and for that, I call her an angel.

SARAH & SONIA - The loveliest friends a girl could ask for, thank you for helping me through the faerie parts of this and for keeping me sane while writing.

EMILY & RENEE - These two listened to every witchy fact I could come up with, and more! Thanks for creating our own little coven. <3

PARENTS - I always thank my parents for their support, and I always will. This story is largely due to them cultivating my love of the arts from day 1.

AND FINALLY - To every reader out there who has a little bit of "witch" in them. If you feel different, strange, unwanted, know that you are precious to me and that I will walk beside you on the shadowed path we call life.

Thank you from the bottom of my heart.

ABOUT THE AUTHOR

Emma Hamm is an author in Midcoast Maine, where she lives on a blueberry field. She's always been a writer, but only recently took the time to publish the Otherworld series, a retelling of classic fairytales set in a fictional Medieval Ireland.

To stay in touch
www.emmahamm.com
authoremmahamm@gmail.com